Bountiful

SARINA BOWEN

This title is published by Tuxbury Publishing LLC.

Cover photograph by Pat Lee. Cover design by Sarah Hansen / Okay Creations.

For Jo Pettibone.
Sharp eyes, warm heart!

part one

july, 2015

one
zara

THE FRIDAY NIGHT that changed my life started out like any other.

It was a summer evening, and the bar was doing a brisk business in local beer and conversation. I had a good playlist cranking over the stereo, which always helped to make the time fly. Vance Joy's "Riptide" had a nice, fast rhythm that made tending bar feel more like a dance than a job.

Even better, there was a hot guy with hair the color of a darkened copper penny watching me from a barstool. I'd seen him around a few times. He and his friends liked the booth in the back corner. Mr. Hot liked Vermont ales, and when his friends were around, they sometimes drank tequila. The top-shelf stuff. And they were good tippers.

Tonight he was alone, though. And I felt a zing of interest every time he came into my line of sight. If I were a believer of that kind of thing, I might say that I felt a ruffle of awareness. Even a premonition.

But I wasn't a believer, and I've never been good at predicting who would matter in my life and who was just passing through. So it was probably more fair to say that those tingles I felt from the hottie were plain old sexual attraction.

It wasn't just me, either. I could feel his eyes on me as I made drinks and counted out change for other customers. His were nice eyes, too. Green, if I wasn't mistaken. I didn't mind the attention. His admiring gaze made me feel more like a pretty girl at a bar and less like an overworked single woman who'd recently been rejected.

I poured drinks. I smiled. I sent orders to the kitchen for my cook. Rinse and repeat. By eight o'clock, the biggest problem I'd faced was a group of drunk college boys who were a little too loud at the corner table.

"Guys? Can I ask you to use your indoor voices? Throwing coasters isn't cool, all right? We have a dartboard in back if you really need to throw things."

"Sorry," the soberest of them said.

On my way back to the bar, I noticed that my redheaded friend had watched the whole encounter with interest. "Everything okay?"

"They are not a problem. See that?" I pointed at the shotgun on the wall behind me.

Green Eyes smiled. And, wow. His smile was something else. It softened up his rugged face and brought out his bone structure. On one side, there was even a hint of a dimple. As if this man were too tough for dimples, so it didn't dare show itself. And his laugh was like a well-aged whiskey—deep and smooth. "I assumed the shotgun was just for show."

I shook my head. "I don't keep it loaded, because that's just asking for trouble. But I could load, aim, and fire in a very short timeframe. So, no. Bessie is not just for show."

"Bessie, huh? That's my sister's name. And she's about as subtle as a shotgun. I didn't know people named guns."

I picked up the rag again and wiped down the bar. "Well, I have four brothers. They like to borrow stuff without asking. I gave my shotgun a girl's name, hoping to discourage them from walking off with it."

"Did it work?"

"No. But eventually I figured out that if my stuff was a girly color like pink or purple, they'd leave it alone. That's how I came to own a pink bike and a pink phone. And I'm not even a fan of pink."

And there was that laugh again—rich and heavy. But it was interrupted by one of the drunker college boys, who approached the bar for three shots of Jack Daniel's.

Business first. I turned my back on Mr. Hot to grab three shot glasses. "Who's driving?" I had to ask as I grabbed the whiskey bottle. I hovered the bottle over the rim of the first glass and studied the kid's flushed face.

"My brother's picking us up in forty minutes," he said as his ears turned red.

"You promise?"

"Oh yeah."

"All right, then." I poured.

"Can I buy you a drink?" the college boy asked suddenly. "That shirt is really pretty."

"Aw, thank you. And that's sweet of you," I said with as much enthusiasm as I could muster. "I can't accept a drink. Company policy. But the offer is lovely."

"You're welcome," the kid mumbled. Then he grabbed his three shots and disappeared as fast as you can say *rejected*.

When I chanced a glance at the copper-haired hottie, he shot me a knowing grin.

And once again that smile did funny things to my insides. Something told me the girls never turned this guy down. Not only was he a looker, he was slick in a way I couldn't really put my finger on. Maybe it was the shiny watch on his wrist—the truly expensive kind the locals never wore. Or maybe it was just the confident glint in his eye.

He was about my age or a couple years older. Thirty, maybe. And I couldn't help but notice that he was in fantastic shape. He had broad, muscular shoulders that strained his cotton polo shirt. And the swell of his biceps made me want to run my hand over his smooth skin to test the strength of the muscle beneath.

I wasn't about to do that. Not that he'd offered. If he *did* offer, though...

Pushing that thought away, I went to the back to grab another keg of Long Trail. I had a bar to run, and no time for fantasies.

The next person to walk into the bar interrupted my lustful thoughts, anyway. He took the middle barstool and ordered a Corona with lime. Actually, he didn't order it. He just said, "Beer me, sis."

Ladies and gentlemen, my twin brother, Benito.

The familiarity of his demand annoyed me just as a reflex. There was nobody on earth I knew as well as Benito. He liked his coffee with the barest splash of milk, which made no sense because you couldn't even taste the difference. He had a scar over his left eyebrow from the time he jumped off the swings at school and landed on his bicycle. And he had another doozy of a scar on the side of his rib cage from the time he was knifed during his first and only tour of duty in Iraq.

Benito was a daredevil. Even though I was only twenty-eight, I already had four gray hairs. And I'm sure at least three were because of him.

"How's your Friday going?" my twin asked me.

"Can't complain. Well—hang on—I guess I can. Uncle Otto is on my case to switch beer distributors, because he's got it in his head that North Corp is ripping him off. But we've been through this before, and they're still the best deal in town."

My brother rolled his eyes. "I'm sure you'll set them straight. You always do."

"Yeah, but it'll take two hours of my life."

"You could always quit. That would show him."

"I think about it *all. The. Time.*"

But we both knew I wouldn't go through with it. In spite of family aggravation, I had a pretty sweet deal right now. Not only did I run this bar with only occasional interference from its owner, but my uncle let me live in the tiny apartment upstairs for free. The place wasn't worth much, but free was a pretty hard price to beat. If I didn't work here, I wouldn't be able to afford my own place and still add to my nest egg. Unless I moved in with either my mom or—wait for it—my overbearing uncles.

No and no.

And anyway, thinking about my crappy prospects wasn't good Friday-night conversation. "What's happening in your life? You don't usually stop here on weekends."

"I have news." He grinned, and I braced myself. News could be good or bad, but you could never tell with Ben. "I finally talked my way into a job at the DEA, Zara. Got the offer this afternoon. I head down for some training in two months' time."

"Oh, *Benny*." It came out sounding more distraught than I meant it to. *But here we go again*. My brothers had bad luck with dangerous jobs. While Benito had only sustained the one knife wound, our older brother Damien nearly got himself killed in Afghanistan.

My brother's face fell. "I think you mean, '*Congratulations* Ben. Nice work nailing down the job that you're under-qualified for, but you worked your ass off to get anyway.'"

As it usually did, my temper flared. Being half of a set of twins meant always wanting to hug him and punch him simultaneously. "I *am* happy about your job offer," I said, my tone making a liar out of me. "But there *are* careers where nobody shoots at you! Now I'm gonna worry that you've run afoul of a Mexican drug cartel. I don't want to wake up to a telegram informing Mom and me that you're dead."

"They don't have telegrams anymore, Z."

"Don't be an asshole," I grumbled.

"If I'm an asshole, why do you care if I'm dead?" Benito asked.

From two barstools away, my redheaded observer chuckled. He didn't even try to pretend he wasn't listening in.

Benito and I just stared at each other for a moment, years of history passing between us. Looking into his dark eyes was like looking in a mirror. I saw struggle there. Small victories and just as many defeats. Our family usually landed on its feet, but nothing ever came easy.

The worst part was knowing that some of Benito's earlier troubles had been my fault. I'd once robbed my brother of happiness. At least once. So I probably owed it to him not to be a dick about the new job. "Just stay safe, okay?" I whispered.

A smile flickered across his lips. "I'm always safe."

That was categorically untrue. He drove his motorcycle like a crazy man, and that was only the most convenient example. But for once in my life I didn't argue the point. "You owe me six bucks for the beer," I said instead.

"Nah," he said, laughing. "You just treated me to a congratulatory beer, that's all."

Because old habits die hard, I gave him a look of burning irritation, and he pulled out his wallet.

When I returned to his spot at the bar ten minutes later, I found a ten-dollar bill, an empty bottle, and no Benito.

And, damn it, I *missed* that asshole. I missed the heck out of him already.

I should have been nicer.

The ginger hottie smiled at me when I went to check on him. "What's so funny?"

"You are."

"Eavesdrop much?"

He didn't even look ashamed. "I have a sister. We fight like crazy, too."

"We don't *always* fight," I said reflexively. *Only about ninety percent of the time.* "But I was right, anyway."

He snickered.

"Seriously. Do *you* have a job where people shoot at you?" I asked, clearing away his empty glass.

"Well..." He looked thoughtful. "Depends what you mean."

"Never mind," I said curtly. "I don't want to know. Another Long Trail? Or do you want to sample something else?"

"Another one." He rested his chin in his hand, and his gaze turned hot. "Thank you."

The way he said it—his words polite, his gaze anything but—sent a lick of heat through my belly. I got him his beer and made a lap around the bar, grabbing empties and taking orders.

The night went downhill from there.

Fifteen minutes after my brother left, his barstool was taken over by my least favorite customer—Jimmy Gage. He was an ex-cop in his late forties, and one of the few people I could say I was afraid of.

He ordered a Bud Light and a burger. I ran the order straight into the kitchen and asked my cook to rush it.

"Why?" Titus asked. "Did I miss an order slip?"

"Nope. Just don't want to tangle with Jimmy Gage."

Titus nodded and threw a patty on the griddle.

To make matters worse, Rita—my waitress—chose that moment to take her third cigarette break of the night. She didn't like Jimmy Gage any more than I did. But that left me shorthanded on a Friday. I found myself watching the door too often, wondering where the heck she'd gone.

And even then, I would have considered the evening salvageable if not for the next customer who walked in. Since I was waiting on Rita to show up again, I'd leveled a searing glare at the door as it finally opened. But, damn it! The open door revealed the *last* person I wanted to see walk into my bar—my former hookup, Griffin Shipley.

Unfortunately, Griff got the grumpy stare I'd been aiming at Rita. So not only did I lock eyes with the man who'd most recently battered my ego, but I gave him a death glare, too. And when he caught a look at the fury rolling off me, his face softened at once into something resembling sympathy.

"Oh, fuck me sideways," I whispered under my breath. I dropped my gaze to the bar top. But it was kind of like shutting the barn door after the horse was out. Too little, too late. My little emotional fireworks show was already over. *Nothing to see here. Move along.*

After that I made myself very busy behind the bar. And it was Griff's cousin who came up to order a pitcher, which meant that we were officially avoiding each other tonight.

Lovely.

Damn you, Griffin Shipley. I wanted to be over him already, but I just wasn't. "It's not you, Zara," he'd said the night he called it off. Because they always say that. "I'm not in a place in my life where I can make time for a relationship."

"But we're not *in* a relationship," I'd pointed out, hating myself for arguing. Our fling had been more of a friends-with-benefits arrangement.

He'd cleared his throat. "I know that. But you're not happy with the way things are. And I don't want to be the kind of guy who strings you along."

That's when I'd stopped arguing. Because he wasn't wrong. I wanted more than a quickie after work. Griff was one of the few single men around here who was going places. And I wanted to be a part of it.

He didn't see it that way.

So here I was on a Friday night, still single and tending bar. Same story. Same town. All I had going for me was a rapidly filling tip jar and the green stare of Mr. Hot over there on the bar stool, watching me work. I felt his gaze like the warmth from a campfire.

I should have stayed away. Instead I got burned.

two
dave

EVEN THOUGH I'D been to hundreds of bars in nearly as many cities, The Mountain Goat was rapidly becoming my favorite spot. And I had big plans for my visit tonight. So I settled in at the bar, taking in the scene.

For much of the year I lived on the road with my teammates. I'd been to chic urban dance clubs as well as quiet country dives. There was literally nothing in a bar that could surprise me anymore. And I hadn't come to The Mountain Goat in Tuxbury, Vermont to be wowed. But there was something about this little roadside place that charmed me.

These past four weeks I'd discovered that Vermont had a way of making everything more genuine. This bar wasn't phoning in its rustic decor. The place had clearly stood here for ages. It had weathered clapboards outside and dark paneling inside. The bar was a long expanse of walnut, polished to a high shine. Every few feet a votive candle burned in a little glass cup. Since Vermont took its craft brewing seriously, the beer list was impressive. I even liked the music.

The best thing about the place, though, wasn't a thing at all. It was the bartender.

Zara. Even her name was exotic. She had wavy black hair down her back, lean limbs and cheekbones that meant business. Hers was a dark-eyed, serious brand of sexy.

She wasn't even my type. Or so I'd thought. She was skinnier than the women I usually picked up. But it worked on her. She had graceful arms and an elegant neck. I spent a long time looking at her neck, and thinking of how it would taste beneath my tongue. And whenever she strode the length of the bar, I imagined her slim legs wrapped around my body.

Watching her was like rediscovering espresso after a month of weak airplane coffee. She'd turned my crank the first time I laid eyes on her. But making my move had taken awhile, because I kept coming in here with my teammates.

Tonight I'd decided I wanted a taste. Badly. So I'd wised up and arrived here alone. It was the best way to get what I wanted.

And I *wanted.*

She and I had been watching each other all evening, even though we'd barely had a conversation. But I was a patient man. When the right moment came, I'd turn on the charm. I was willing to play the professional athlete card, too. Although something told me that swagger wouldn't be the right play for Zara. She might be too forthright to care that I got paid millions to fly around the rink a hundred nights a year.

It wasn't a hardship to bide my time during her shift, drinking excellent beer. In fact, it was downright entertaining early on. First had come a rather amusing spat with her brother. Watching Zara go toe to toe with him had done things to me. When she'd squared her shoulders and lifted her perfect chin, I'd felt my body respond. There was a spark in her eye and a flush on her cheekbones. I wanted her to turn all that fire my way.

But things seemed to go downhill for my girl as the night wore on. The door opened to admit a big, bearded man with a couple of his friends. There was nothing too interesting about him, except for the way Zara's eyes widened when he came through the door. She'd looked away, as if embarrassed by something. Her body language changed after that, her spine lengthening even more. Her face tensed.

I was good at two things in this life: shooting a six-ounce rubber puck into a net, and reading people. The second thing actually made the first one easier. The ability to read the opposing goalie well was what made me such a valuable sniper.

My mind wasn't on hockey, though. It was on Zara. And something about the bearded guy was bothering my favorite bartender. I could sense Zara's disappointment. There was a story there, but I didn't know what it was.

After that, a perky little blonde came in, sat down at the bar, and ordered a salad. I overheard Zara and this cute little stranger discussing the men who'd come in beforehand. "Watch out for that crew," Zara said. "The Shipley boys think they're God's gift."

The perky blonde didn't seem to heed Zara's advice. Not fifteen minutes later she relocated to a seat at the bearded guy's booth.

And then? The whole bar watched as the blonde left with the big bearded guy.

Zara continued to serve the remaining customers with perfect efficiency and grace, but she didn't look as fiery anymore. Instead, her dark eyes were downcast. And for the first time since I'd noticed Zara, her shoulders had an unhappy set to them.

Still, she watched me. I felt her eyes on me, just as mine liked to dart over to check her out.

Customers trickled out one by one as the hour grew late. The kitchen closed and the cook went home. Soon it was down to a table of college kids in the corner, myself at one end of the bar, and another dude at the opposite end.

That other guy was a piece of work. He was older than Zara or myself. The gray in his hair made him in his late forties, if I had to guess. But he was lean and muscular. What made him stand out was his mean eyes.

Zara didn't like him, either. She was very polite, but she avoided eye contact.

The dude didn't appreciate that. The more distance she kept, the worse his leer. His eyes were practically stapled to her chest. "Zara, honey," I heard him say as he fished out his wallet to settle up. "Griff

Shipley ain't the only man in the county. You're feeling lonely, you can come keep me warm anytime."

That's when she locked eyes with me for the first time in an hour. As if to say, *Do you believe this bullshit?*

Grabbing his credit card off the bar, she gave him a tight smile. "If you're cold you can turn up that electric blanket, Jimmy."

He snorted. "Your problem is that you're too uptight. Maybe if you loosened up a little, Griff Shipley wouldn'a split on you."

"Is that so?" She slapped a receipt and a pen down in front of him, and that was that. The fool went home alone not two minutes later.

She let out a sigh of relief when the door closed on him. "Last call," she said to me as she wiped down the bar. "Can I get you anything else?"

"Not unless you'll let me buy you a drink. Seems like you might need to unwind after that last bit of bullshit."

She gave me a wry smile. "You're sweet to ask. But I can't accept. Company policy."

"Uh-huh." I took out my wallet and put a fifty on the bar. "First of all, I'm not *sweet*."

Her eyes widened a little when I said that. Now I had her attention.

"And secondly, company policy *my ass*. It's you who calls the shots in this place. Nobody else but you. I can see why you need a handy excuse, though. If you couldn't pull the 'company policy' out of your pocket sometimes, the men would be buying the sexy bartender drinks left and right all night long, I bet. You'd never get a moment's peace."

A smile stole across her features. "Yeah, sure. I have to keep a stick back here behind the bar just to beat back all the men."

"You don't need that stick, gorgeous, because you give 'em the evil eye and they run off, knowing they're not man enough for you. But every guy who drinks in this bar has the secret, fervent wish that fortune would smile down on him just long enough for him to earn an hour of your undivided attention."

Zara rolled her dark eyes, but a telltale blush splashed her cheekbones. "You know how to lay it on thick."

"No need." I shook my head. "Just telling you how it is. Now I think you should do a shot with me, and we'll toast your unapproachability."

She laughed, and her eyes lit up for the first time tonight. "You are smooth, mister. I'm almost tempted."

"Almost? Damn."

She smiled. "There aren't any taxis out here in the woods, and I've been pouring your beers all night. If you do a shot with me, it won't be safe to drive away from here. And it's quitting time."

"Well. Now that you mention it…" I reached across the bar and laid a hand very gently over her smooth one. Our gazes collided as I stroked my thumb across the back of her hand. "Driving after doing shots with you wouldn't be such a great plan. I'd have to stick around for a couple hours until it wears off."

Zara waited a beat before retrieving her hand from beneath mine. "I see."

"Do you?" I put both elbows on the bar and leaned forward. She was trying to play it cool, but my not-so-subtle message was getting through. I saw the blush beginning to creep across those fine cheekbones. She and I had chemistry, damn it. We'd been eye-fucking each other all night. "Look. I think you had a stressful evening. And I'm really good at stress relief. Like, pro level."

She braced both hands on the bar and smiled at me. "Are you always this forward?"

"Nope." I shook my head. "Some women can't handle the truth. But I've watched you run this place. You're in charge of everything that happens inside these walls, and I'll bet that gets old. I'm thinking you might like to hand over the reins once in a while. Let someone else take charge. Tonight that someone is gonna be me."

Time slowed down as our gazes locked again. Eddie Vedder sang "Black" over the sound system while she and I held a well-matched stare-down.

I won it.

She turned away and grabbed the rag on the bar, wiping invisible spills off the gleaming wood. "Awfully sure of yourself."

"It works for me," I rumbled. "Complaints are few and far between."

The college kids in the corner picked that minute to push back their chairs. They waved to Zara and trailed out the door.

Leaving me as the very last customer in the place.

Turning her back on me, Zara left the bar to see to their table. She pocketed a tip and grabbed four beer bottles with one sweep of her hand. Then she wiped the table down.

I waited.

She returned to the bar and ditched the empties in a bin.

"You grow up around here?" I asked her as she turned her attention to closing out the cash register. I was perfectly capable of bland, nice-guy small talk if it put a woman at ease.

"Look," she said, her eyes on her work. "Let's skip the twenty questions. How about you keep your trap shut for a couple of minutes so I can finish up here. If you're good and quiet, I'll take you upstairs with me."

That shut me up for a second. She'd beat me at my own game. But I wasn't going to complain. "Upstairs, huh? Nice commute."

"It works for me. Especially in a moment like this. If I had to give you directions to somewhere else, I might decide you're not worth the trouble."

"No you wouldn't," I said quietly. "You've been watching me, too."

Her dark eyes lifted briefly to acknowledge the truth in this statement. But she didn't admit it out loud. "Do me a favor," she said instead. "There's a security camera in the corner over the juke box. Walk toward it slowly."

"Sure, gorgeous. I'll do even better." I took my wallet out of my back pocket and fished out my driver's license. Then I walked toward the security camera, looking it in the eye, and held up my license.

Zara was watching me when I turned around again. "Thank you. A girl has to be careful."

"I'll bet." I sat back down on the bar stool.

"I'm Zara," she said in a low voice.

"I know. Learned that the second time I came in here. I'm Dave Beringer."

"Well, Dave." She closed the register drawer. "Don't move off that stool for a minute. I'm going to lock this in the safe, and then we'll go."

"Take your time," I said. "I've got all night long."

Her eyes flared as she turned away.

Not a half-hour later, I knew I'd have her gripping the headboard of her bed as I took her hard from behind. And a minute or two after that I'd make her sob my name.

three
zara

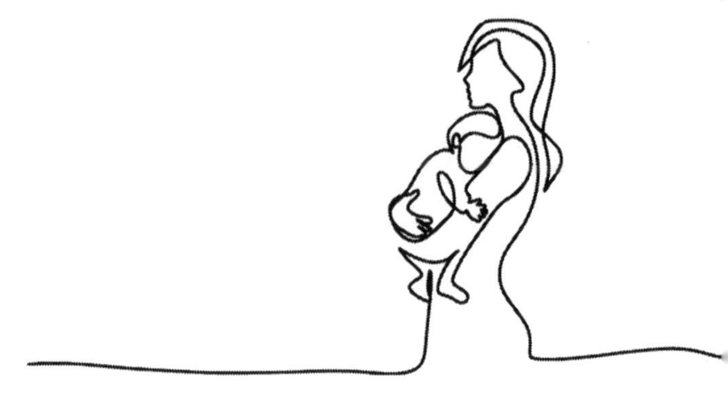

YOU ARE INSANE, I whispered to myself as I dropped the cash bag into the safe and locked it up.

Taking strangers up to my room wasn't something I ever did. Too risky. I didn't even have a credit card receipt with this guy's name on it. Dave always paid cash.

But that wasn't even the biggest problem with this plan. I knew in my gut that Dave wouldn't have gotten that invitation to my bedroom if it weren't for my Griff Shipley heartache. I was going to let my disappointment in one man guide me toward a bit of foolishness with another man.

Smooth, sister. Really smart.

Griff and I had been finished three months ago, and I'd told myself I was over it. But tonight was the first time I'd seen him with someone else. Audrey something-or-other. A cute little blonde, all smiles and curves. My polar opposite.

Of course she was.

If Griff were a different man, I wouldn't be feeling so much rage. But he was a smart guy with a degree in chemistry, a zeal for farming, and a head for business. When he broke off our arrangement, he'd said he was too busy. But what I heard was, *You're not a good fit for a man who's moving up in the world.*

Enter Audrey. When I'd taken the recycling outside, I'd caught them together. Bad timing. Griff had her leaning up against the side of the building, his mouth inches away from her adorable rosebud lips. But it was the expression on his face that had really killed me. It was so…warm. Like something in her eyes fed his *soul.*

The excuse he'd given me played on repeat in my brain: *I'm not in a place in my life where I can make time for a woman.* But he had time for cute little Audrey from out of town. He'd never once looked at me the way he'd looked at her tonight.

I'd felt such anger when I'd seen him so happy. I'd wanted to burn my whole life right to the ground. They were probably having fantastic sex right now while I closed down the bar for the millionth time in a row. Afterward, they would probably plan their wedding.

Tonight made me so damn lonely I wanted to punch something. Since I couldn't do that, I was going to settle for a few hours with Mr. Green Eyes. *Dave.* He wasn't my type at all. Coppery hair and a clean-shaven face? I usually liked 'em scruffier. Dave was wearing casual clothes like everyone else in the bar, but somehow he gave off a rich-guy vibe. Maybe it was the luxury watch on his wrist. Maybe it was the small pack of friends he often turned up with—they dropped fifty and hundred dollar bills for their tabs and never drank cheap beer.

I knew I should send him home alone. But I wasn't going to. I wanted his eyes on me a little longer. And his hands, too. I wanted to feel the way I felt when his eyes traveled over my body.

What did I need from a rich guy from Connecticut or New York? Nothing. Guys like that weren't interested in the bartender except for easy sex. Which I was about to give him. In return I was getting a night of forgetfulness.

He was pretty nice to look at, too.

I took one last glance around the kitchen, making sure nothing was left out of place. I was stalling, I supposed. A one-night stand was nothing new to me—I'd been having them since high school. But taking a risk on a stranger wasn't usually part of the bargain.

Hopefully I'd be able to look myself in the eye in the morning. Because I wouldn't be looking at Hot Ginger. He'd be long gone.

When I reentered the bar area, he was waiting for me, chin in hand. "You okay? You can still kick me out, you know." He gave me a friendly smile. "I'll only take it a little bit personally."

That smile made me remember why I was doing this. Wowzers. I felt a little more alive every time he looked at me. That buzz in my chest wasn't fear, but anticipation. The man had a *seriously* hard body that even a polo shirt couldn't disguise. I hadn't had a good frolic in months.

I was due. And he was waiting.

"Come on," I said crankily. Grumpiness came naturally to me. And I'd be damned if I'd let the man see that I was uncomfortable. "Let's go."

A minute later I had the bar locked up tight for the night. I put my key in the other door, the one leading to my upstairs apartment. After letting myself in, I pocketed the key and flipped the lights on over the narrow little staircase. He followed me, and it was odd having company in this cramped space. The first stair creaked as I stepped on it.

This would be the awkward part. He and I both knew what would eventually happen upstairs. But first we had to get past the small talk. I'd offer him a drink. He'd say something kind about my tiny little apartment. I'd try to figure out who was going to make the first move…

Suddenly, a warm hand reached out to curl around my forearm, stopping my progress up the stairs. Then another hand closed firmly around the length of my hair. It might have been terrifying except that warm lips softly kissed the skin at my neck. Goosebumps broke out all down my back.

"Zara, sweetheart."

"I'm not *sweet*," I said in an almost normal voice, though my heart thudded as his grip tightened on my hair.

He laughed. "Touché. But keep your cute, grumpy ass right here for a second. There's something I need to say."

"Then say it."

A low, growly noise of approval came from somewhere deep in his chest, and I barely managed to contain another shiver of excitement. "You are a feisty one. I like that. I'm going to show you a very good time now," he whispered. "But if there's anything I do you don't like, just say 'time out.'"

"Okay," I rasped, a little scared and a whole lot turned on.

"Say it for me right now. For practice." He kissed me again on the back of the neck, his tongue touching me so tenderly.

"Time out," I breathed.

His hands dropped away and he stepped back. Only cool air kissed my neck now. "That's all you have to do," he whispered. "I'm not having fun unless you're having fun."

"O-kay," I stammered.

A big hand palmed my ass. "Now get up those stairs so I can get you out of these clothes."

Well. Small talk must be off the table, then.

Trotting up the stairs and into my darkened one-room living space, I tiptoed over to a lamp beside the bed and switched it on. Two seconds later, he was right there beside me, giving me a nudge until my back hit the closet door. He cupped the side of my face and bent down to kiss my throat. The sound of his happy groan vibrated in my chest. "Fuck, you're beautiful. Been wanting to taste your skin since the first time I stepped into that damn bar."

I wasn't used to hearing compliments and didn't entirely trust them. But his lips and tongue worshiped my sensitive neck, sending shivers down my body. His breath whispered across my skin as his hot mouth placed yet another kiss on my neck. He gave a gentle suck, and I melted back against the door.

My life choices were starting to seem pretty damned smart. I reached up to cop my first feel of his sculpted pecs, and he chuckled against my skin. "Find something you like? Take my shirt off, beautiful. Do it now."

Eager to obey, I pushed the cotton fabric up his chest, my palms indulging in every bump and ripple while his smirking eyes watched my progress. The humor in his expression made this easier. His mix of bossiness and amusement put me at ease.

Apparently I was taking too long, because he reached up and opened the button at the collar of his polo, then grabbed the back of his shirt and shucked it over his head. And, *wow*. He was built. Even his muscles had muscles.

"You must spend a lot of time in the gym."

"You have no idea. Enough talking, beautiful." Grasping both my hands, he put them on his warm chest. Then he leaned in and kissed my neck again. And *damn*. His eager lips and bossy tongue did wonderful things to my mood.

He didn't kiss my mouth, though. Maybe that was too intimate for a stranger. I hoped he wasn't lying about being single. Because…

I lost my train of thought when one of his hands tugged my jaw aside so he could kiss the other side of my neck, while his other hand tagged my hip. He yanked me roughly against his body and then groaned as we connected.

The needy sound echoed through my body. I gripped his rock-hard biceps and kissed the skin beneath his ear. He smelled like fresh air and eager man.

And he'd been right. This *was* exactly what I needed tonight.

Dave slowed down, teasing me with a single touch of his tongue to my ear. His hand squeezed my ass, slow and dirty. And when I inhaled with surprise, *that's* when he kissed me for real. His mouth slid over mine, his lips confident and firm. I opened to him immediately, and when his tongue met mine, our heartbeats clicked into sync. As if I'd known him for years.

Finally my critical mind fell silent. Everything went quiet, except for the sweet sounds of lips and tongues. Kissing had always been a language I understood. With deep, dark kisses he drew me in further, until I was pancaked against his incredible chest, panting into his mouth. He tasted me again and again, our kisses bottomless.

I've got you now, his body told mine. *You can let go*. His strong arms held me like a scaffold, not a cage. I leaned into all that strength, and he encouraged me with a happy moan from deep inside his chest.

At some point the room spun around. My back hit the surface of the bed. A second later he was straddling my thighs, looking down at me. "You don't need this anymore," he said, tugging my top up to expose my belly. And as I grabbed the fabric and pulled it over my head, he groaned, because I'd been wearing a top with built-in support, and no bra.

Baring my meager bust to someone I didn't know should have felt weird. But his look of eager joy steadied me. He bent over to begin dropping kisses on the swells of my breasts. I let my hands sift through the soft strands of his autumn-colored hair, and I shivered when his lips closed around my nipple and began to suck.

"You like that, don't you?" he muttered.

So much. But I didn't say that out loud. I'd always been a very sexual person—more easily aroused than women were supposed to be. And I'd been teased for it my entire life. *Slutty Zara.*

But nobody would ever have to know about my adventures tonight.

Dave's hands and mouth were everywhere at once, tonguing my nipples and tweaking them, kissing the underside of my jaw. "See?" he grunted. "I know what you like."

No kidding. My hands trailed down his neck to his muscular back. And when he hitched himself a little higher to kiss me again, I moaned as he fit his hips against mine, and I arched to meet him.

Things were escalating fast. I sank into the mattress, submitting to sensation over logic. He tasted of beer and temptation, and those were my two favorite flavors.

Examining his powerful body became my new hobby. His broad shoulders were deliciously freckled. I kissed my way across one of them and bit his neck.

"Naughty girl," he rasped into my ear. "I have other uses for that mouth of yours."

"Do you now?" I challenged, my hands sliding down his chest, my fingers sifting through the fine hairs of his chestnut-colored happy trail.

"Unzip me," he ordered.

With shaking hands, I did. The sound of his zipper opening ratcheted my blood pressure up a notch. It had been far too long since I'd had sex.

"Keep going," he growled.

I shoved the fabric down, and the boxers, too. An ambitious erection sprang free. He was long and rosy-hued and leaking for me. *Whoa*. And he was a redhead everywhere. My mouth watered with anticipation.

A big hand palmed the back of my head. He wrapped his hand with my hair, and tugged me toward his body. The grip was firm and steady. "Suck me, honey."

I did. Immediately and shamelessly. As I took his salty sweetness into my mouth, he was heavy on my tongue.

"Aw, fuck," he said, his voice raw. "Good girl." The praise lit me right up. I gave him a good, hard suck and heard his breath hitch. "Jesus." He put a hand under my chin and stopped me. I looked up with wide eyes to see his pupils blown and his face red. He smiled at me. "Off with those jeans."

I released him. But I didn't move fast enough for his taste. He pushed me down on the bed again and reached for my zipper. I wriggled out of my clothes, kicking off the shoes that were still clinging to my feet.

And then I was naked with a perfect stranger named Dave.

"Fuck," he groaned. "You're stunning."

Or just stunned, maybe. Because, holy hell, his body was not to be believed. There was a naked superhero on my bed. Impressive abs led down to the deep V of muscle between his hips. He had powerful thighs, and when I ran a hand over one of them, the wiry hair on his quads tickled my palm.

Impatient, Dave rolled toward me, interrupting my train of thought with another mind-melting kiss. But now his hands free-ranged over my naked body. One callused thumb gripped my hip and then squeezed, showing me just how strong he was. Instead of scaring me, the treatment made me moan into his mouth.

I liked to be manhandled, and somehow he knew that. Or maybe it was just a lucky guess.

We rolled around, kissing, as I tried to kick the last of his clothing off the edge of the mattress. He grabbed his jeans and drew his wallet out of the back pocket.

"I have fresh condoms," I whispered. "If that one's been in your wallet for too long…"

"Put it in there today." He grinned at me. "I had big plans for you."

Good lord, the ego on this man. "And what if I said no?" I grabbed his chin and held him. We regarded each other for a long moment. He wore a feral expression, but he didn't shake off my grasp, even though we both knew he could.

"Then you would have missed out," he rasped. "Now shut up and let me demonstrate."

Maybe I should have been offended. I'd thrown all my principles to the wind tonight. But none of it mattered as he spread his naked body over mine and kissed me again. He had a bossy tongue and questing hands. His erection was a hot brand against my stomach.

I expected such an overconfident man to move things right along, but that's not what happened. His brand of cocky was the teasing, torturous kind. Thick fingers eased between my legs, sliding over my clit until I was achy and slick. I was close to climaxing. But when I sucked on his tongue, he moaned and sat up.

The crinkle of the condom packet made me sigh with relief. My limbs fell heavily onto the comforter as I waited, anticipating the main course.

So what did that bastard do? He leaned over me and took my nipple between his lips, rolling it until I wanted to scream.

"D-Dave," I tried, my hips writhing on the bed. I reached down his body, seeking my prize.

But he batted my hand away. "No you don't. Not until I say so." He switched to my other tit, his mouth burning my tender skin with its pleasant torture.

Frustrated, I pushed his head off my boob.

He responded by grabbing my hands and pinning them to the

bed. He moved up my body, poised over me, looking down at me from inches away. "Is there a problem here?"

"Seriously?"

"Did you forget the rules? On the stairs, I was very clear about who was in charge tonight."

I blinked.

"Now when I let go of you, I want you to roll over," he demanded, not releasing my hands. "On your hands and knees. Got it?"

My breath came in gasps, but I nodded.

He let go of my hands and I quickly rolled over onto my forearms.

"Up. On all fours."

"You are such a pain in my ass," I panted, just to retain my equilibrium.

That's when the sound of a slap rang out, and my left buttock begin to sting. "*That's* a pain in your ass."

Did he really just *spank* me? Stunned, I turned my head to look at him.

He smirked at me, then cupped a hand around his ear. "I still don't hear you calling a time out. So get over here." He took my hips in two hands and tugged my body backward. I felt myself slide along the cotton fabric, and the loss of control was startling.

His large palm began to rub the skin he'd just spanked. I felt heat and friction and shock wherever he touched. And when he spoke again, his voice was remarkably gentle. "Don't worry, beautiful. You'll get what you need."

I waited, holding myself up on shaking hands. This was already the strangest sexual encounter of my life. Someday when I was old and gray I'd think back to it and wonder, *Did that really happen?*

Behind me, Dave made an achy, needy sound. I trembled as the blunt head of his cock eased between my legs, teasing me. I held my breath and closed my eyes. And then he finally pushed inside, filling me completely. There was a pause, and then he pushed again, adding even more of himself, even as I quivered and threatened to shatter. I bit down on my lip hard enough to draw blood, but the pain wasn't sufficient to stave off my first orgasm. I opened my mouth in a silent cry as waves of pleasure overtook me.

I didn't make a sound, though. There was no need to advertise his power over me.

"Damn." Dave let out a shuddering breath. "Wow." He knew, that bastard. He pressed a kiss against my shoulder. "You sexy thing. Aren't you glad you invited me upstairs?"

"Getting there," I lied. Then I filled my lungs with air, trying to calm down a little. Some men thought it was freaky the way my body responded so quickly. "Do you always talk this much when you're naked?" I asked, just to be a pain.

"No." He chuckled. "You make me crazy." Then he thrust even deeper, rocking me forward. I bit my lip again to keep from moaning. "I don't know why," he panted. "You just do."

He gave another slow pump of his hips, and I couldn't hold back my gasp of pleasure. I let my head fall to the pillow and just took him in. With another chuckle he nudged my ankles even farther apart. I was completely at his mercy.

This was the best I'd felt in months.

"That's right," he whispered in my ear. "Just like that." He gave it to me deep and slow. I pushed my face against my pillowcase and took stock of all the places my body hummed. My overly sensitive nipples were erect and brushing against the sheet. I felt the heavy swing of his balls against my body.

God, it was beautiful. I felt my pleasure building again. All it took was a moment's concentration—I drew my awareness to the press of his cock inside me. I steadied myself against the bed and let it happen. This time, I didn't hide it. I moaned softly as my body tightened around his.

"Fuck yeah," he said, picking up the pace. "So beautiful."

He pumped his hips a few times then slapped my hip and ordered me to roll onto my back. Drunk on pleasure, I did as he asked.

The view improved. He took both my knees in his hands and pushed inside. I looked up at his incredible body as he put it in high gear. Hips pumping, chest flexing. I squeezed his trim hips with my knees to encourage him.

He looked down at me with lust-filled eyes. "One more, gorgeous. Give me one more." With a wicked grin he reached down to finger our connection.

I threw my head back and came for the third time.

Roaring with satisfaction, he followed me over the cliff.

four
dave

HOLY. Shit.

I lay there, limbs heavy, as tired as if I'd just skated a game straight through double overtime. My thoughts were sluggish, liquid things. We'd collapsed side by side on Zara's bed, but I wasn't ready to let her go. In an uncharacteristic maneuver for me, I reached for her and pulled her onto my chest.

She was breathing hard, her head on my arm.

"Does that always happen for you?" I panted. "Or should I be inducted into your personal hall of fame?"

She laughed without bothering to open her eyes. "You want the truth?"

"Yeah. But go ahead and lie a little if it sounds nicer."

She squeezed my arm. "You're hilarious. But the truth is that sex comes easily to me. Literally."

I chuckled. "So you're saying I'm not special?"

She turned her head and gave me a warmer smile than I'd gotten from her yet. "Are you fishing for compliments?"

"No." I gave her a playful pinch on her beautiful ass. "Some people can catch a football. Some people can play the piano. But you can have three orgasms on a Friday night without breathing hard."

"I'm breathing hard."

This girl. She killed me. I'd had a lot of sex with strangers. That was pretty much the only kind I ever had. Sometimes it was good, and sometimes it was really fucking awkward.

But not tonight. Tonight it was *great*. Zara and I just clicked somehow on a higher level. I wasn't done with her yet, either. But first I needed a rest. I wasn't a teenager anymore.

I lay quietly, listening to our pounding hearts. A lovely calm washed over me, courtesy of endorphins, a beautiful girl, and an irresistible summer night. I became aware of a cheeping sound in the breeze coming through Zara's window. It was the summery, lifelike sound of nature, the kind we never had in Brooklyn.

"What kind of birds sing at night?" I croaked, my voice as tired as the rest of me.

Zara gave a little snort of laughter against my skin. "Birds *don't* sing at night. What you're hearing are frogs."

"*Frogs?* Like, the kind that hop through ponds?"

"Is there another kind of frog?"

For some reason this struck me as hilarious. And when I laughed, she did, too.

"City boy, much?" she asked.

"Yeah. Brooklyn. But I grew up…"

Her hand moved so fast that the woman would have made a decent goalie. She covered my mouth with her slim palm. "No personal stuff."

"Why?" I asked after pushing her hand off my lips.

She shook her head. "This is just about sex. Don't wreck it."

Hmm. "Is this about the bearded guy tonight? Your ex?"

She turned her face away. Apparently that was the wrong thing to say. Nobody had ever accused me of being smooth with people's emotions.

"Sorry," I said quickly. "None of my business."

"It really isn't," she agreed.

"More for me, then."

She huffed out a laugh and gave me a friendly smack on the thigh. "Come on. I have to be up early," she said matter-of-factly. "You'd better go."

"Um..." Honest to God, it took my poor little brain a moment to figure out that she was kicking me out of her bed. *WTF?* said my ego. I was a professional athlete and accustomed to delivering all the eviction notices. "Okay. Is this because I brought up your ex?"

"Not hardly. It's just late. I had a fun time."

Well, ouch. Those were words I'd said on more than one occasion when I wanted to hurry out of some woman's bed. It's just that I'd never heard them before, myself.

I sat up. "Lucky for you, we can have a fun time again later in the week. You work every weeknight?"

She turned her head and studied me. Those coal-black eyes were more critical than I was used to seeing from women.

Staring back at Zara was really no hardship, though. She was as pretty as the day is long. And I found myself noticing things about her that I don't usually bother to notice. The length of her neck. The way her tanned skin passed over her regal-looking collar bone. Her nipples were dark against small, perfect breasts.

"I work most nights," she said eventually. "I manage the bar for my uncle."

"Right," I said, having already figured that out. "So I'll come by on Wednesday or Thursday."

"Maybe I won't feel like hanging out after work," she said. But her eyes made a trip down my chest.

"Maybe you will, though," I said cheerfully. This was more fun than I'd had in months. She made me work for it. Nobody ever did that. Not since I was a poor rookie in the minors. And often not even then.

"We'll see," she said. But her gaze was soft and lazy.

I leaned over and kissed her nose. "You're fun to talk to. You know that?"

"Talk, huh?" She gave me a slightly embarrassed smile.

"Yeah. And other stuff, too." I winked, and she actually blushed. A little, anyway.

Then, for the first time in my life, I got out of bed with a woman before I was ready. I put on my clothes while she watched.

"Don't get up," I said. It was a joke because she didn't look like someone who was about to escort me to the door.

"Goodbye, Dave," she said softly.

"See you in a few days," I reminded her, and she just shook her head.

Then I let myself out into the Vermont summer night, where frogs were singing their strange song.

five

zara

DAMN YOU, *Dave Barrier*. Or Carrier? *Whatever your name was, get out of my brain.*

It was Tuesday night, and I was working behind the bar. Like always. But thoughts of his wolfish grin kept invading my mind.

I'd indulged in our tryst because I'd imagined we'd never see each other again. And everything about the encounter had been thrilling and perfect—right up until he'd uttered that nonsense about coming back again.

And now my stupid little heart was *waiting* for him. I kept glancing at the door every time it opened, wondering if he'd walk through it.

God. Damn. It.

Like every girl, one of my life goals was to avoid becoming my mother. And while my mom had many admirable traits, she'd spent decades of her life just like this—waiting for a man to walk through the door. She'd had five kids with my father—a guy who showed up in town when he felt like it and then disappeared for months at a time.

My mother had never given up on him, though. Never asked for a divorce. Never stopped hoping he'd show up and tell us we meant the world to him.

Spoiler alert: he never did.

So every time I found myself watching the door for a man, I wanted to kick myself. I knew from experience that men had very short attention spans when it came to women. When Dave had said, "I'll see you next week," what I'd heard was, "Thanks for the good time."

"Hey, can you make frozen drinks?"

I looked up to see that two women had taken seats at the bar. The one who'd inquired about my skills with the blender was unfamiliar to me. But her companion was not. Jill Sullivan and I had once been close. If by "close" you meant the sort of friends who were always in competition, and who were always trying to undermine the other.

Jill had been the rich, fashionable one. I had been the sexy, adventurous one. I'd craved her clothes and her car and her giant bedroom. She'd craved my confidence and my twin brother.

Neither of us got what we wanted.

"Hi, Jill," I said. We were grownups now, right? Old wounds shouldn't haunt me.

Besides, Jill didn't look so hot. She had red eyes and splotchy skin. Furthermore, (and this wasn't just me being catty) she'd put on quite a few pounds since I'd seen her last. I felt an unexpected tug of sympathy for the girl who had battered my self-esteem during our senior year.

"Hey," she said, then took a deep, steadying breath. If I wasn't mistaken, she'd been recently crying.

"What can I get you ladies?"

"I would kill for a frozen margarita," her friend said.

"That won't be necessary," I said smoothly. "Salt?"

She shook her head.

"And for you?" I laid a coaster in front of Jill.

She sniffed. "What do people drink the night after they walk in on their husband banging the nanny in their bed?"

"Oh, shit," I breathed.

Jill just turned her eyes skyward. "That was even harder to say out loud than I expected it to be."

"I think you should drink whatever sounds good," I say. "Especially if it's something he never liked."

"Two margaritas, then," she said.

"Coming right up." I'd probably be calling these two a cab later. I'd lay money on it.

It was a summer Tuesday, and quiet. So I had time to sneak looks at Jill as I made their drinks. I used to think she was so glamorous, with her straight hair and blond highlights. Now she just looked like a tired housewife. And those highlights looked like they required some serious time spent at the salon.

I wasn't exactly living the high life here behind the bar at The Mountain Goat, but our lives suddenly didn't seem so different after all. Like me, Jill hadn't finished college. After failing to get Benito's attention, she'd married the high school quarterback. He worked at a car dealership in Montpelier. They had a kid. Or two?

Funny how I hadn't kept track. Who knew that jealousies can dry up and fall away, like autumn leaves?

Jill and her friend drank their margaritas and then switched to white wine. I brought them a plate of potato skins on the house, claiming that anyone having a terrible day deserved carbs. But I didn't want them drinking all that alcohol on an empty stomach.

"What have you been up to, Zara?" she asked after thanking me.

"This," I said.

"Fun job," she replied, and I couldn't decide if she was trying to be nice or just patronizing me. Or both. That's how it had always been between us. She'd lend me one of her silk scarves to dress up my poor-girl clothes. But then she'd make sure everyone knew the scarf was hers. The memory sent a flare of ten-year-old anger through me.

And then I took a deep breath and let it go. Holding on to that bullshit? I didn't need that.

"This job has its moments," I said. "But mainly I'm here because it pays the bills." I wouldn't play Jill's reindeer games anymore.

"I guess I'll be needing a job soon," she said, peering into her wine glass. "I'm leaving him."

"Oh, honey," her friend said, rubbing her back. "You can, but don't decide tonight, okay? Just take a breath."

That was good advice, so I backed away. Unfortunately, the bar's door opened to reveal Jimmy Gage, my least favorite ex-cop. And—damn him—he took a seat at the bar just two stools away from Jill and her pal.

All the hair stood up on the back of my neck. Swear to God, I would have rather seen Griff Shipley *and* Blond Audrey instead. Even if they were liplocked and handing out wedding invitations.

Jimmy waved me over. "Coors Light," he grunted.

"Tap or bottle?" I asked quietly, praying he was in a mellow, forgetful mood tonight. Because ten years ago, Jimmy had pulled Jill and I over for speeding on our way to the graduation dance. And Jill had sassed Jimmy and gotten us both into a pile of trouble. There had been big drama. And I'd behaved very, very badly.

In other words, tonight had quickly become a train wreck of historical, emotional baggage that I'd hoped was behind me. And to think that only an hour ago my new obsession with a certain green-eyed stranger had been my only problem.

"Tap beer," Jimmy demanded. "Happy-hour price."

My nerves jangled. Happy hour had been over for an hour already. Forget *please* or *thank you* from this asshole—he wanted half price, too. And I was going to let him get away with it, damn it.

I poured his beer and set it in front of him. He nodded, putting a five on the bar.

After that I was practically tiptoeing around my own bar, just waiting for things to get even worse. And it only took Jimmy a couple of minutes to notice Jill and her friend swilling wine down the bar. "Hey ladies," he said, his cold eyes measuring them. "Buy you a drink?"

Jill sat back, startled. Her gaze collided with mine, and I looked away. "No thank you," she said slowly. "We need to slow down our alcohol consumption, I think."

"Diet Coke?" I prompted, reaching for the soda gun. Jill used to love her Diet Coke, which I'd pretended to despise because I hadn't been able to afford to feed dollars into the cafeteria vending machine.

Jill nodded gratefully.

Jimmy was still watching her, though. "You always were an uptight little bitch," he said. "I heard it's still true."

"Hey!" I gasped, stunned that he'd go for the throat like that.

The asshole gave us a humorless grin and returned to his beer.

And it was right then—at the very moment I'd forgotten all about him—that the door opened on Dave. He sauntered in alone again, passing Jimmy and the two women to take the same barstool he'd occupied only three nights before.

He put his muscular forearms on the bar and studied the beer list. And for no good reason I began to relax. It was almost as if he'd aired out the room with his calm presence. Jill's friend eyed him appreciatively from one bar stool away, but he didn't notice (or pretended not to).

"Evening. What can I get you?" I asked him, as if I'd never seen him before.

He turned his gaze on me, and there was humor in it. "What's tasty around here?"

"Vermont beers," I said firmly. "I recommend Sip of Sunshine from Lawson's Liquids. Bright, hoppy IPA. Beer snobs drive a thousand miles to taste it."

"Is that right?" he asked, his eyes hot on mine. The only thing he seemed to want to order was *me*.

And right now I *so* did not have the time for that. I tapped the bar impatiently. "You need a minute to think about it?"

"Nah. The Lawson's sounds good."

I poured his beer and set it in front of him without a word.

"Thank you, beautiful," he said, his voice gravelly.

Yowza. The things that man made me feel. Even so, I left him alone with his beer. Mopping down the bar, I tried to monitor the tense situation which continued to brew between Jimmy and Jill.

"Sorry to hear about your marital troubles." Jimmy snickered.

"Not sure you know the meaning of the word *sorry*," Jill's friend piped up.

Jill and I flinched at the same time. Fights at The Mountain Goat were rare. Fights between an ex-cop and a soccer mom were rarer still. But it was possible that I was about to witness one.

"You ladies need anything?" I asked, my glance taking in all the free tables in the room. If my marriage were imploding, I'd probably want a little privacy at one of those tables. But what the hell would I know? Nobody had ever asked me to marry him.

And probably nobody ever would.

"Why aren't we still friends?" Jill asked now, her eyes in a drunken squint.

"Oh, honey." I sighed. "Just different paths."

"We had so much fun together back in the day!"

Sometimes we did, and sometimes it was awful. "You'll have fun again," I said with false cheer. "Don't take on the whole world at once, okay? One problem at a time. You can't change your whole life in one night."

"I can change your life in one night." Jimmy chuckled. "Could show you a few things."

"Nothing I haven't seen before," Jill's mouthy friend put in.

My blood pressure went up another point.

"No man strays if you keep him satisfied," Jimmy taunted. "Get on your knees for him sometimes, you know? I bet you didn't."

"Jimmy," I warned, finally too pissed off to be afraid of him. "Keep your nose out of it."

But he only sneered at me. *Shit.* I'd already set my phone out on the bar in preparation for calling the police if things got too heated. Not that it would help diffuse things. Jimmy would hate getting a lecture from the police department that had fired him for graft.

This was already the longest Tuesday shift in history.

Dave waved at me from the other end of the bar. His glass was empty. "Another?" I asked quickly.

His gaze traveled down the bar. "Everything okay?"

"Sure," I ground out. "Beer?"

"Love one, gorgeous."

I met his gaze and got an unexpected jolt. Apparently I wasn't too distracted to remember what it had been like to look up at him as his powerful body—

"Your man spends a lot of time at that car dealership," Jimmy said loudly, pulling me out of my reverie. He was taunting Jill again. "Fondling those new cars instead of your titties. Bad call on his part."

My famous temper flared.

"Shut. It," I demanded, abandoning Dave to move down the bar. "You harass people in my joint, you will never come back in here. Think about that. You'll have to drive to Montpelier for a beer. It's not worth it."

"Don't push me, honey. It's not worth it," he echoed. The asshole looked up at me with a sneer on his face. He was wearing a Ted Nugent T-shirt with an AK-47 on it.

Now I'd had it. "You know what? Wearing an assault rifle on your shirt will not make your dick any bigger." Everyone in the bar laughed, but I wasn't even done. "Now get out of here or I'm calling Officer Brown."

Jimmy went white, and then red. And then everything began to happen at once. Dave got off his bar stool and moved around behind the girls. Jimmy grabbed his beer glass in one fist. Then he swung. Dave let out a shout of warning, and my stomach lurched, but I didn't move. I don't know whether it was fear or foolish defiance that kept me rooted in place. Maybe both.

But for his own reasons—human decency or self-preservation, I'll never know—Jimmy didn't bludgeon me with the pint glass. He threw it instead. It landed with a deafening crash against the wall behind me, taking out several of the liquor bottles lined up there.

And then, even before the scent of leaking brandy and the sound of broken glass began to pierce my frozen senses, he bolted toward the door.

"You want me to catch him?" Dave asked, hands in angry fists at his sides.

"No," I said firmly. He was gone, and I wanted him to stay that way.

For a long beat, no one else said a word. I took in the sight of my stunned customers. "Show's over, guys. Sorry about that."

"Sorry, Zara," Jill and her friend murmured in turn. "We can help with the mess."

"I got it," I said. "Need me to call you a cab?" It was always better to make the offer early. It was a reminder to them of how inconvenient it would be if they did need one an hour from now.

"No," Jill's pal said. "Can you pour us another Coke, though? We need to level out before I drive home."

"Sure thing." I got their sodas and then went in back to find a broom and a dustpan. I kicked off my heels and put on a pair of muck boots I kept for messy jobs.

"Can I help you with that?" Dave asked when I began to sweep the space behind the bar.

"No." That's when I realized I'd never gotten him another drink. "Shit. Can I pour you something before I get too involved here?"

"Another Lawson's. Or I'll wait. It's really okay." I poured the beer, and he tucked his chin in one hand and gave me an appraising glance. "Pretty exciting night in here."

"Ugh, I know. I've been looking for a good excuse to kick him out, anyway."

Dave smiled, and his almost-dimple showed. "Are you sure you don't want a hand? I can't believe that fucker left a mess for you to clean up."

"Just like a man," I teased. "I probably had it coming, though. You can't insult someone's T-shirt *and* his dick and expect no reaction."

Dave winked at me, and I felt it everywhere. "Good thing he didn't pull out his equipment to prove you wrong."

I surveyed the mess on my bar. "That would have required less clean-up, though."

His laugh was a bark. "Want me to hold the dust pan?"

"Nah. This really won't take long. Shame about the good bottle of cognac." I clicked my tongue.

An hour later the mess was long since gone. So were almost all the customers. I'd restocked the bottles Jimmy had broken.

All that remained of the incident was the faint smell of brandy and my shaking hands. I was unnerved. Jill had gotten weepy on her bar stool, and the sounds of her sniffles weren't helping. All while Dave watched me with heated eyes.

Then, finally, Jill and her friend left, leaving me and Dave alone again. And I did something completely out of character. I took two shot glasses off the rack and popped them onto the bar. Then I took the bottle of Jose Cuervo and poured two shots, pushing one of them toward Dave.

He watched me with gleaming eyes. "Rough night?"

"The roughest."

"I can make it better." His voice was a caress against my heated face. "Come here, gorgeous." He patted the bar stool beside him. "Sit with me a minute."

I hesitated for at *least* half a second.

"Zara," he said, his voice as low and rich as I'd ever heard it. "It wasn't an invitation. It was a firm request."

Goosebumps leapt to the surface of my skin. And then I obeyed him, ducking under the bar gate and sliding my bottom onto the bar stool beside him. The room looked unfamiliar from this vantage point. "So this is how the other half lives," I joked.

Dave took his shot and tossed it back. Then he placed mine in front of me.

The lime wedges were in reach, so I grabbed one and squeezed it into my shot. Then I drank it up with as much confidence as I could muster. Dave did strange things to my ego. He made me want to be as sexy as he kept telling me I was.

"Good girl," he purred, taking the shot out of my hand. He gave my bar stool a tug, sliding it toward him with me in tow.

Then he grasped my shoulders in firm hands and kissed me. Hard.

six

dave

One month later

ON AUGUST FIRST, I stepped out of my rental truck at The Mountain Goat for the last time.

But I didn't go inside right away. Instead, I stood there for a couple of minutes, listening to the engine tick, my ass parked against the door. Faint music could be heard from inside the bar, but I turned in the other direction and looked up. The Milky Way arched overhead, a stripe of messy starlight. I knew now that in an hour the moon would outshine it, making it harder to see.

I was thirty years old. But until six weeks ago, the Milky Way had been only a phrase in textbooks and the name of a candy bar. Where I grew up outside of Detroit, there was too much industrial light to see any stars. And where I lived in New York City, it was even worse.

A couple of weeks into my Vermont stay I'd bought a terrific pair of binoculars—had them FedExed to the cabin. First I'd researched telescopes, but it turned out that a decent telescope is four feet tall and doesn't like to be moved around. And since all I *did* was move around, I decided to settle for binoculars. I was just a stupid punk from the wrong side of Detroit, anyway. Not an astronomer. What did I know from telescopes?

The binoculars showed me more of the sky than I'd ever seen

before. Especially the moon—when I focused my lenses, its landscape suddenly looked like a real place. I'd been astonished at how visible the craters were and how near-desolate surfaces came into view through the binoculars' lenses.

Much like the moon, Vermont had also been just a shape on the map for me until a couple of months ago. It had been my teammate's idea to rent a cabin up here for two months, to do some hiking and fishing. He'd played hockey for the University of Vermont, and loved the place.

Since I was a single guy—and the hockey team was my whole life —I'd agreed to come along.

Getting in the car in Brooklyn, all I'd known of Vermont was nice cheese and beer, because both those things showed up on restaurant menus in New York. But I hadn't known about the stars.

Now my vacation was over. Earlier tonight I'd packed up my little room in the rental cabin. After tonight, my new binoculars would collect dust on the windowsill of my apartment, where my teammates would probably pick 'em up and try to spot women changing their clothes through the windows of Brooklyn.

We were just a bunch of overgrown kids, really. Couldn't take us anywhere.

Standing in the parking lot, I took one more look at the Milky Way. I knew I wouldn't see it again for a long time. A week from now I'd be back in the city, living in the weight room and out on the ice, fighting for another chance to make the playoffs. Then the travel would start up, and I'd live out of a suitcase.

I had a great life. I was halfway through the best NHL contract of my career, paid like a superstar. But I'd miss the stillness of the deep woods, so I stood still for one more moment to appreciate it. It was a warm night, but not sticky. I loved that about Vermont. The air smelled sweet, but it was silent. The end of summer had approached, and the frogs and crickets had gone quiet. I took one more deep breath of the nighttime.

Then I went inside the bar.

It was a Wednesday, and as I took a seat on a stool, I noticed the crowd was a little thin.

As usual, Zara took her time coming over to greet me. "Evening," she said eventually, placing a coaster onto the polished wood in front of me. "What can I get you?" The lack of familiarity in this greeting made me bite back a smile. Even though we'd spent a lot of time together these past few weeks, Zara always kept my ego in check.

If this was how she wanted to play it, then so would I. "What do you have on tap?" I asked, as if I didn't already know. I'd spent many summer nights sitting on this very stool, drinking my way through the Vermont craft-beer selection.

She jerked a thumb over her shoulder, indicating the signboard which made it painfully clear to anyone with eyes which beers were on tap.

"Right." *Point for Zara*. "Pour me an Allagash, pretty girl."

And that's when I got my first smile of the evening. It was so quick another man would have missed it. But I have sharp eyes. Ask anyone.

She grabbed a pint glass and pulled my beer while her other hand was busy opening a bottle for someone else. Zara was always crazy busy back there, even on a slow night. She did so many laps around the bar that I swear she'd covered more miles than I did during a championship hockey game. I enjoyed watching her move. She had an economy of motion as she wiped down a table or rang up a check. It turned me on almost as much as the cleavage I could see every time she leaned down to clear a glass off a table. And she had a long, regal neck that begged to be traced with my tongue.

When she set the beer down in front of me, I didn't get my wink. Not even a quick one. But this was our dance, our tentative association. Maybe it wasn't how normal people behaved. But I'd discovered these past couple of weeks that neither Zara nor I had any taste for normal.

I took a sip of my excellent beer and settled in to watch her work the last hour of the night. Zara didn't remind me of any other woman I knew. Or any other bartender, for that matter. She was like a storm front on the move—always two steps ahead of the customers. Those busy hands. Those long, elegant limbs. I admired all the parts of Zara I could see. But her cool demeanor always suggested the important stuff was still hidden from view.

I'd seen it, though. And I didn't mean this in a crude way. I'd seen the expression on her face when she truly let go, and I'd heard the laugh she unfurled when she thought nobody was listening.

But even in my arms she kept a tighter lid on herself than any other woman I'd met. Sometimes when I looked at her, she seemed to be focused somewhere else—as if her soul was tuned in to a back channel that none of us mere mortals could hear.

The Milky Way and Zara. My favorite two exotic things about Vermont.

A Green Day song came over the sound system, and I saw her move her shoulders in time with the beat, not for anyone's benefit but her own. "Last call," she said to no one in particular.

After that, Wednesday's crowd died out in a hurry. I didn't have long to wait. Soon enough she was walking around, stacking the chairs upside down on the tables. Ignoring me. Once I'd tried to help her with this task and gotten snapped at for my trouble.

I finished my beer instead.

Eventually I was the only man left in the bar. Without a glance in my direction, she counted the cash in the register, then disappeared into the back, presumably to lock it in the safe.

I got up off the stool, anticipation humming in my veins. I walked to the door and then slipped outside, where the stars were waiting. Leaning against the clapboards, I tipped my head back until I saw Jupiter in the sky, where it had just risen. And then I heard an owl hoot. A real owl. *Herr-herr-herrrrrr,* it said.

Where I grew up, owls were only in storybooks.

The door opened beside me, and Zara stepped out. I held my breath while she locked up. The second the key was retrieved from the lock, I stepped out of the shadows and grabbed her wrist.

Dark eyes darted to mine. But she didn't say a word.

"Hi," I said, my voice husky. "You didn't have a lot to say to me tonight."

"When do I ever?"

I laughed, and the sound seemed loud in the quiet night air. "Good point, gorgeous."

She took her wrist back. "You want to stand here and converse now? Is that your plan?"

As if. I stepped into her personal space and stole my first kiss of the evening. Had to. Watching her move for an hour made me crazy. And *hell*. Every time, I felt a jolt of energy when we came together. The heat of the stars and sun were inside me when she was nearby.

Zara sighed in a way that sounded as if she didn't approve, even as she softened under my mouth. I deepened the kiss, treating myself to a taste, but just a quick one. "Come out with me tonight," I said, breaking it off. "Just this once." Usually we went upstairs to her place.

She stepped back and raised those dark eyes to mine. "Out where?"

"Outside. Not far. I only get one more night to look at the stars. Want you to come with me."

Zara considered this, her hands wandering up to land on my pecs. She had a thing for my chest. And I was smart enough never to point that out, because I was pretty sure she'd never touch me the same way again if she knew I'd noticed.

My favorite girl was a prickly one. But that only made us more compatible, I supposed.

"We don't go places together," she reminded me.

"Only because there's nothing open after you get off work," I pointed out. "But the stars are open. And I want one last, good look at them. You won't come?"

She looked at my rental truck standing by itself in the lot. "You're breaking the rules."

"Nah," I said softly. Zara loved her rules. Sex only. No sleepovers —she'd kicked me out every single time. We talked more now, though. I was going to miss her irreverent sense of humor. "You're not afraid of me, though, right? If I thought I was making you nervous, I wouldn't be a dick about it."

She lifted an eyebrow. "What if I'm *not* scared of you, but I have other objections?"

"Then I will be a dick about it."

She laughed suddenly. Zara's laughter was a rare and perfect thing—a husky burst of joy that tapered off quickly and was over practically before it began. "Fine," she said, her face already serious again. "Let's go see some stars." She sidestepped me and walked toward my truck with her typical efficiency.

As usual, her mind had turned on a dime, leaving me to catch up and follow her.

The hilltop where I'd chosen to go stargazing was a little farther away than I'd thought. But Zara turned on the radio and rolled down her window. She looked content enough beside me, gazing into the night.

I didn't know the right word for what we'd been to each other this summer. It wasn't a *relationship*. Neither of us wanted one of those. Zara would call it a series of one-night stands. But that wasn't quite right, either. A *tryst,* maybe?

But every single time I came to see her, Zara made it clear that she wasn't a sure thing. She always let me know she was doing me a favor.

I ate this up, too. Usually, getting sex was easy as a snap of my fingers. There was a certain type of woman who loved hockey, and loved hockey players. I never had to work hard to find my fun.

In spite of all the nights we'd spent together by now, Zara still didn't know I was a professional athlete. We didn't swap life stories—that was another one of her rules. I was just a guy in her bar. And I liked this arrangement just fine, because she *liked* me as just a guy in her bar. I didn't have to be that star and impress her. She never asked me if I knew Tyler Seguin or Henrik Lundquivst. She didn't want war stories or anybody's signed jersey.

She just wanted me.

Even if there was no word for it, the thing between us had been great. Every three or four nights I'd gone to the bar alone before closing time, waiting while she finished up, mostly ignoring me.

I'd thought I'd get a warmer greeting as time went on, but my girl made it clear that we only knew each other after all the customers had left. I was her dirty little secret, apparently.

Best. Thing. Ever.

Even though I teased Zara about her long list of rules, I liked them just fine. There was no pressure on me to pretend we had a future together. Our conversations weren't burdened with expectation. We were free to talk about our favorite movies. (Zara's was *Kill Bill,* mine was *The Blind Side.*) We talked about where to eat in Vermont and who made the best ice cream.

There was chatting and wild sex. Upstairs in her room I'd had some of the best sex of my life. And—another first for me—it just kept getting better as we spent more time together. It was a revelation, too. I thought I knew everything there was to know about pleasing a woman.

Not true.

I hadn't expected that knowing Zara a little better each time made it more interesting. It was like the playoffs—a seven-game series meant figuring out some things about the other team as the games piled up. We came together with passion reinforced by familiarity and—dare I say it—a kind of respect that I'd never felt before.

Who knew? It was knowledge I'd probably never use again, though. Our odd little temporary matchup was coming to a rapid conclusion.

Just like the playoffs.

She knew it, too. I'd been careful to tell her exactly when my time was up, and that I'd probably never be back. "Who says I'll miss you?" she'd asked last week.

Right.

Now I pulled onto a winding road that took us to a hilltop lookout. When I parked at the top, we were the only car in sight. "Come on," I said.

She got out of the truck, and I grabbed a quilt and a little cooler I'd brought. "Carry this?" I asked, handing her the quilt. I grabbed my binoculars, too.

"Look at you! Mr. Prepared. Were you a boy scout?"

"Nope."

She didn't ask any follow-up questions. Not my Zara. Other women might start the inquisition, trying to learn about my past. Zara just marched into the field ahead of me, chose a spot for the quilt and flung it onto the grass. Then she lowered her elegant self onto her knees and looked up into the heavens.

I joined her a moment later. "Now this is what I'm talking about," I whispered. I sprawled out on my ass, then pulled her nearer so she could lean her head against my chest and look up. "Want to see the half-moon?"

"Sure." She snuggled a little closer. Her words were prickly, but her body language could never manage the same level of reserve.

And I liked it in a way I never had before. Cuddly to me was always synonymous with needy. But Zara wasn't the least bit needy. Her physical affection was an unexpected benefit, demanding nothing of me other than pleasure. I got a quick whiff of the coconut scent of her shampoo. Hell, the scent of coconuts would probably always make me hard after this.

I lifted the binoculars to the sky and focused them. The craters came into view, especially along the receding edge where the earth's shadow hid half the moon. The detail was especially sharp there, where brightness faded into pitch dark. It was breathtaking. Before last month I had never known I could see it for myself.

"Okay, here you go." I handed the binoculars to Zara.

She made a soft sound when she found the moon. She was very still, taking her time, not saying a word. Pure Zara. After a contemplative silence she handed them back.

I set the binoculars on the quilt and couldn't resist stroking her hair with one hand. "That's Jupiter. The big bright thing."

"That's not a star?"

"Nope. A planet. If we had a telescope, we could see some of its moons."

I ran my hand up under her skirt, my fingertips skimming the smooth skin of her thigh. With any of my other hookups, this would be a Big Move. A signal. A transition from conversation to sex. But I touched Zara because I liked the way she felt under my fingertips.

The word *intimacy* had started to take on a different meaning for me than it had before.

Zara lifted the binoculars again and focused on Jupiter. I was moving around too much for her to lean on me anymore, so she wriggled away from me and lay on her back, using the earth as a brace to get a steady view.

Propping myself up on my elbows, I kissed the strip of skin where her T-shirt rode up. I nuzzled her bellybutton with my nose and then kissed my way upward, toward her breasts.

Still focused on Jupiter, Zara shifted her hips, as if she just couldn't help herself. She was easily the most responsive woman I'd ever fucked. To be honest—she made me feel like a sex god. Her words were standoffish, but her body couldn't keep up the act. When she forgot to push me away, she became cuddly and affectionate.

And I ate it up. I wasn't used to affection. Who knew it felt so good to touch someone all the time?

Now I kissed my way up, pushing her shirt out of my way. Wrecking her stargazing, I reached underneath her body to unhook her bra. She had small, perfect breasts, and I bent down to suck on their tips. I'd recently proven that she could come just from nipple stimulation. Or almost, anyway. I liked to suck on her until she was begging for it. Then, if I slid quickly inside, she'd come immediately, pulsing on my cock and moaning up a storm.

Hottest. Thing. Ever.

But tonight I had a different plan. Her short skirt had given me ideas, and my mouth was watering with anticipation. I kissed my way back down her belly and lifted the skirt. As I began to trace patterns with my lips on her thighs, my bare lower legs were spread out on the cool grass, and the night breeze kissed my skin.

My tongue traced the line of her panties as an owl hooted in the distance.

"Come here," she whispered.

"No. Busy." I tugged the elastic down, but she didn't help me get her panties off. "Up, baby."

"You want to do that here?"

"Yes, ma'am. There's nobody around." And I was hungry for it. My heart thudded while I tugged on her panties again. After a beat, she lifted her hips and let me slide them off. With a groan, I nudged her legs apart and began to drop kisses at the juncture of her thighs.

I've had a lot of sex in my life, in various places. Hotels around the country. The bathroom of a jet, once. (Totally uncomfortable and not a great experience.) And I've had as many partners and as much variety as any guy ever needs.

None of it came close to feeling as debauched as pushing Zara's skirt up a blanket on that hilltop and then rubbing my lips gently back and forth against the softest part of her body. She groaned, thinking I was teasing her. And I was, I guess. But the truth was that I'd rarely gone down on anyone before Zara.

This summer had made me realize that I had less experience with women than I'd thought. Because it was an *experience* to make the same woman shudder for the tenth time, because you knew exactly how she liked to be touched. It was an experience to memorize the cat-like shape of her smile.

It was absofuckinglutely an experience to get comfortable enough with someone that you couldn't wait to drag your tongue across her clit while she dug her fingers into your scalp.

The breeze whispered along with Zara's whimpers. She fought me a little. Being hyperorgasmic meant she would often try to delay it. "It's better when I can wait," she'd explained once, panting underneath me.

But I wasn't in the mood to wait. I pinned her hips to the blanket and tongued her. Then I caught her clit in my lips and sucked gently.

The result was a breathy cry and shaking hips. Christ, it was the sexiest sound I'd ever heard, and I nearly came in my shorts as she suddenly got wetter under my tongue.

That's when I heard the car.

Shit.

I sat up fast and saw the headlights of what would turn out to be a police cruiser coming slowly up the road.

Zara was still sucking oxygen into her lungs as I tucked her skirt into place and lifted her into my lap. I leaned her back against my chest and picked up my binoculars as a car door slammed and footsteps could be heard on the gravel.

"Evening," the policeman said from behind us.

"Evening," I answered cheerfully, raising my binoculars in the air. "Is there a problem? We're just looking at the stars here." I looked over my shoulder at him, and so did Zara.

"No problem, no." He smirked. "New hobby, Zara? Didn't know you were into..." He paused. "Astrology?"

Oh, buddy. Really?

"Big hobby of mine, *astronomy*," she said, then sighed.

"Is it, now? You two have a good night." He chuckled. Then he turned slowly and walked back to his car. Then we heard the crunch of gravel under his tires as he reversed the car to drive away.

I kissed Zara's neck, but she stiffened. "Something wrong?" I asked.

"Nothing new," she said quietly. "He was in my brother Alec's class in high school. Now he'll have something fun to tell the guys at poker night this week. Slutty Zara is still hanging out on Jasper Hill with the boys."

"Oh, fuck him!" I grumbled. "He's driving around in a polyester uniform and a car that smells like whichever drunk last puked in it. Gossip is all he's got. You've got the moon and the beer I brought you." I pointed at the cooler we hadn't touched.

Her slim fingers stroked my bare knee absently. "It's fine. It's just a small town. Nothing ever changes. My reputation in high school was well deserved, anyway."

I swept my hand down her dark hair, which was shiny in the moonlight. Zara had hardly ever confided in me before. "I was a total slut in high school," I admitted to her. "Isn't that what high school was for?"

"Sure—if you're a guy." She tipped her head back onto my shoulder and looked up at me. "The girls are supposed to keep their legs pressed together. But I didn't. My brothers would punch anyone they caught talking smack about me, but I didn't do myself any favors."

"You know what, though? You probably terrified those boys. I'll bet you were a knockout in high school. They were probably all praying you'd notice them and devastated when you shot them down. Including Mr. Nightstick, there." I pointed toward the road where the cop had come and gone.

"I gave him a hand job once under the bleachers during a homecoming game." She delivered this confession while looking me straight in the eye, daring me to judge her.

It made me roar with laughter, instead. Then I kissed her. "He's probably still dreaming about it."

Zara sighed. "Is it okay if we leave now? It's late. I should get some sleep."

"Sure," I said, disappointed.

seven
zara

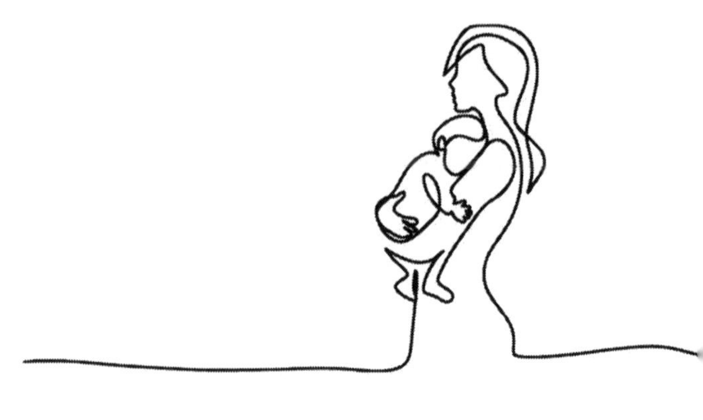

I KNEW I shouldn't have let it bother me. The arrival of Officer Brown—or Butchie Brown as we used to call him—was neither surprising nor consequential.

But it just reinforced my bigger problem. Dave was leaving, and I wasn't going anywhere. Tomorrow he'd go back to his rich-guy pad —wherever that was—and I'd still be the bad girl who hadn't quite figured out what to do with her life.

And now I'd done it *again*. I'd gotten spun up about a guy I couldn't have. He was leaving, and I would miss him so freaking much. And it made me so mad at myself that I couldn't even enjoy my last hour with him.

Would I ever learn?

Signs point to no, as my Magic 8 Ball used to say.

We drove back in silence, my poor attitude filling the interior of his rental truck. When we pulled into the lot behind the Goat, he cut the engine. The only sound after the engine died was the low, lonely grunt of a single bullfrog. And I smiled in spite of myself, remembering Dave's disbelief when I told him what peeper frogs sounded like.

And—damn it—the sound of frogs on a summer night would probably make me think of him for the next several *years*.

Time to cut him loose.

I put my hand on the door. "It's been fun. And I know you didn't really get what you, uh, came for this time, but I think it's better if we just call it a night."

He reached across the gear box and caught my hand before I could make my escape. "Not so fast, prickly girl." His thumb massaged the palm of my hand. Since our first night together he'd become more sensuous than rough.

Don't get me wrong—he was still hot and bossy in all the best ways. But he liked to linger over me now. And I should have enjoyed it, but instead I felt like Dorothy when she'd been locked up with the giant hourglass, counting down the minutes until her bitter end.

Emphasis on bitter. "I don't know what you want me to say," I admitted.

"You don't have to say a damn thing," he rumbled. "Just kiss me goodnight at your door."

Getting out of the car, I assumed he'd try to talk his way inside. But I was only half right. Instead of talking, he put his hands on either side of the door, then leaned in to kiss me senseless. It wasn't long before I whimpered into his mouth, because I have no self-control. And he took the keys right out of my hand and opened the door, following me upstairs with my hair curled around one of his big hands, because he knew that made me hot.

For a pleasant hour, I didn't even bother trying to pretend I wanted him to leave. I let his big body have everything it asked for—my skin, my mouth, every sound of my pleasure.

My very soul.

At last we fell, sated, onto the mattress. He curled an arm over me and held on tightly. I hated how good it felt and how badly I wanted to curl in closer. I counted out a minute, and then two. I was exhausted from the stress of his imminent departure, and I needed him to leave me alone to process it.

But I didn't want to be a jerk about it. I'd give it five minutes and then kiss him goodbye for the last time.

And that would have happened, except, for once, I fell asleep.

Since I wasn't used to having anyone in my bed, I opened my eyes when my digital clock said 3:07.

Fuck.

I had one leg thrown over Dave's, and we were holding hands in our sleep. The peaceful sound of sleepy breathing came from his side of the bed.

Closing my eyes again, I let him be. Only a total bitch kicks a sleeping man out of her bed at three in the morning.

Yet I'd been difficult all summer. "Prickly as a porcupine," he'd said once with a big smile. He'd just seen his first porcupine that day. "In a tree!" he'd told me. "I didn't know you guys climbed trees."

It wasn't a bad analogy. Like a porcupine's, my prickliness was there for self-preservation.

"You sure make me work for it," he'd also said more than once.

"Your other dates don't? They should."

He'd given his head a shake. "I don't date. Not cut out for relationships. Hanging out with you is the closest I ever got."

"Because there's an expiration date," I'd pointed out. "You don't have to look for the exits because you already have one foot out the door."

He'd snorted. "Are we going to psychoanalyze each other now? If so, I'd like to know why a country girl is afraid of spiders."

"It was just the one! I walked face-first into the fucking *web!*"

"Dave!" he'd mock-screamed. *"Is it in my hair?"*

"Yeah? I'll put one in your bed, and then we'll see how funny it is."

He'd only laughed and then kissed me.

Sometimes, during our longer conversations, I'd forgotten to keep my guard up, and I'd caught myself smiling back at him. It was easy enough to fall headlong into his green eyes, and laugh at his jokes. "A giggle!" he'd said once. "Alert the media. Zara giggled like a schoolgirl."

"I don't giggle. You must have imagined it," I'd said, staying in character.

"Uh-huh," he'd said, and then tickled me. Nobody had tickled me in a decade.

So here I was smiling into the dark at three o'clock in the fucking morning, feeling nostalgic over a hookup.

What a dumbass I was.

It wasn't easy to go back to sleep. Because I'd gone and done exactly what I shouldn't have done—I'd gotten hung up on Dave, the ginger hottie.

I must have drifted off. Because there was light seeping into my windows when I became conscious of Dave kissing me on the neck. "It's morning," he whispered. "I'm going now."

I closed my eyes and kept them shut tight.

"What a summer it's been," he whispered, landing a kiss on the underside of my jaw. "Hands down you're my favorite person in Vermont." Another kiss.

It wasn't easy to feign sleep; I hadn't tried it since high school when I'd had to share a room with my twin brother for a time.

But I persevered, not giving Dave an inch. I hated goodbyes.

"All right." He chuckled softly. "If that's how you want to play it. Goodbye, beautiful."

He fit his lips to the back of my neck and gave me a soft, slow kiss.

And then—finally—he left.

I waited, listening. His footsteps were achingly slow as he walked down my staircase. My heart was in my mouth at the sound of the door opening and shutting behind him. The sound of his rental starting up gave me a shiver.

If I sat up and opened the window right over my head and waved, he would see me and stop. God, I wanted him to stop and kiss me goodbye.

Wait! I wanted to yell. *Don't go.*

Fuck.

My heart thudded with unhappiness, but I didn't move. He wasn't going to stay in Vermont, even if I humiliated myself. He had a life somewhere else. And he hadn't asked for my number.

I don't date, he'd said.

It was the same thing Griff had said right before he and Audrey became a couple.

The truth was that men didn't date people like me. I was the girl they "hung out with," as Dave had put it last night. The bartender was a good time and fun in bed, but not a forever girl.

My heart hammered as Dave's truck backed up slowly. I heard the sound of his wheels pivoting in the dirt and the purr of the engine as he stepped on the gas.

Maybe sixty seconds later, he'd driven far enough away that I didn't hear the engine at all.

I lay there in my bed for a long time after that, the sheets smelling like his aftershave. Maybe another girl would have cried, but that wasn't my style. Sadness didn't come leaking from my eyes. It settled into my heart instead, like a weight.

An hour later I struggled upright, hoping to shake off my blues. But the first thing I saw was Dave's shiny watch on the bedside table where he'd accidentally left it. I crawled over and looked closely enough at it that I could hear it ticking.

Well, hell. I couldn't keep it. It was too pricey to be a guiltless souvenir. Instead, it would become something to add to my to-do list —find Dave from Brooklyn and FedEx his watch.

What I didn't know that August morning was that finding him would prove impossible.

I also didn't know that six weeks after I started searching, I'd realize that Dave had left something far more valuable than a luxury watch behind in Vermont.

And he wouldn't be back for either one.

part two

july, 2017

eight
zara

Two Years Later

"I REALLY SHOULD HEAD HOME," I said for the third or fourth time.

But it was so pleasant here on the Shipleys' front porch, in a rocking chair, with my daughter in my arms. We'd just eaten a big meal. The Shipleys usually threw a dinner party on Thursdays at their farmhouse. As Audrey's business partner and a friend of the family, I had a standing invitation, along with my daughter, Nicole. And we rarely missed a Thursday Dinner.

I should be inside washing dishes with Zach and Lark. But, as always, Nicole was a sleepy weight in my lap, and so the Shipley clan gave me a free pass on cleanup.

It was a pretty summer night in July, and the sweet weather made me wistful. I'd always loved Vermont summers, but July was the month when I'd met Nicole's father. Two years had gone by, but it felt like just yesterday.

On the porch swing beside me, Audrey stretched her arms overhead. "That second piece of pie might have been a mistake."

"Don't feel well?" Griffin reached over and palmed her stomach, giving it a gentle rub.

"I'm fine," she said quickly. "But I have my final fitting tomorrow. If the seamstress has to alter the dress again, she'll scold me."

"You're paying for her trouble, though," I pointed out.

"An excellent point," Griff agreed.

I gave Audrey a once-over. She'd let slip that she'd gained a few pounds, and I thought I knew why. *When can we all just acknowledge that you're pregnant?* But I held my tongue, because I knew firsthand what it was like to face too many questions. And Audrey would tell me when she was ready.

"Do you want company tomorrow?" I asked instead. "We'd have to leave Kieran alone at the counter, though." Griff's cousin was our part-time employee. He was a hard worker, but not super friendly to customers.

"That's never a great idea. Do you want me to pick up your dress while I'm at the shop?"

"Nope. I picked it up on Monday. It's hanging in the closet, ready to go." Audrey had chosen simple sheath dresses for her bridesmaids, which I appreciated. The fabric was cotton with an apple-blossom print. When she'd first shown the design to me I'd said, "Cutest bridesmaid's dress ever," and meant it.

Then she'd floored me by asking me to wear one.

Saying yes had been a no-brainer. A lot had happened in the two years since she'd rolled into town. When we'd first met, I'd really wanted to hate Audrey. I'd had some unresolved anger at Griffin for rejecting me. It had stung and had led to some self-destructive behavior on my part.

But several things happened to change my attitude. First, Audrey had won me over with her sunny attitude and big ideas. We were business partners now, as well as friends.

Second, I'd stopped being hung up on Griffin and transferred my obsessions to someone equally unavailable, with predictable results. That man was long gone. But his fifteen-month-old daughter was now the light of my life.

So, two weeks from now, I would happily stand in front of a row of apple trees at Shipley Orchards, bearing witness to the marriage of my ex-hookup and my best friend. We lived in a small town. There would be people in the audience who would find it titillating. *Remember when Griff was banging Zara? Before she got knocked up by a mystery man?*

But I'd hold my head up high. The past two years had shown me that the difference between dignity and disgrace was more than just an extra syllable. It was my attitude that mattered. Nobody could make me feel inferior without my permission. I'd made my peace with single motherhood, and it didn't matter what anyone said behind my back.

On the lawn in front of us, Griffin's younger siblings Dylan and Daphne were throwing the Frisbee around and somehow turning the game into a death match. The sky began to deepen. I needed to get the baby to bed. I'd lingered long enough.

"I need to go home," I said once more, but this time with more conviction. "Anything you need to know for tomorrow morning?"

"Hmm." Audrey shook out her golden hair. "Do we still have currants?"

"There's one more batch. I dried them this morning."

"Groovy. Currant scones tomorrow and blueberry muffins."

"Sounds good. See you around ten thirty? Then you can head for the dress shop."

"Roger, Roger." Audrey turned in her chair to look at us, and her face went soft. "Aw. She's really conked out now."

Even though I couldn't see Nicole's face, I knew she was asleep. Her body was limp against mine, trusting me to hold her while she rested. "That's my cue, then." I slid my butt forward on the rocker's seat, hoping to stand up without jostling her.

"Can I take her for you?" Griff asked, getting up from the porch swing and leaning over us.

"You can try," I said. "If she wakes up and cries, I won't hold it against you. Much."

He grinned. Then he scooped my sleeping daughter into his big hands. I stood, expecting him to hand her back. But instead, he tucked her against his chest, walked slowly down the porch steps, and then toward the driveway where my car waited.

"Aw," Audrey sighed, watching him.

"Cute, right?" There was a pregnant pause while Audrey seemed to glow with maternal expectation. I hoped she wasn't set on keeping her pregnancy a secret. It was so freaking obvious. "Night, toots," I said to her.

"Night!" Her eyes were on her man. Someday (very soon) Griffin would make a great daddy. I could say that now without feeling jealous of Audrey. When I looked at him, I didn't see a man I'd once wanted for myself. I saw Audrey's other half.

I hustled to overtake Griffin and opened the back seat of my car, where the baby seat waited. I yanked the straps out of the way and stood back. "Let's see if you can stick the dismount."

Chuckling, Griffin leaned down to try his best. Nicole's thatch of red hair was a shock against his black T-shirt. The bright shade of her hair—like a new penny—was both a blessing and a curse.

On the one hand, her red hair meant there weren't any rumors around town about the possibility of Griffin fathering my child. A glance between the two of them pretty much guaranteed that they didn't share a gene pool. On the other hand, that distinctive hair color meant that I thought of her daddy every time I spotted her sweet little head.

It also meant that every ginger who came into my brother's bar got the side-eye.

I hadn't been very forthcoming with anyone, including my family. Griffin and Audrey never pestered me for details about Nicole's origins, but my brothers and uncles weren't as easygoing.

"Hey, I did it," Griffin whispered as he eased his big body out of the way.

Lying in her car seat, Nicole shifted in her sleep. She let out a whimper but her eyes remained closed.

"Not bad," I whispered back. "The Russian judge took a couple points off, though."

Griff rolled his eyes, then he gave me a quick, one-armed hug and said goodnight.

I buckled both Nicole and myself into the car, then started home.

Several hours later I was still awake, listening to the gurgle of the river through the open window and the muted voices of bar patrons heading to their cars.

Although it had been more than a year since I'd stopped tending bar, my body refused to give up its night-owl ways. Maybe it was because I still lived over a bar—not The Mountain Goat, but a bar nonetheless.

There were only five hours left until my toddler-sized alarm clock would wake me up. I should *really* close my laptop and go to sleep. But many miles from here, my brother Benito was still up, too. The green dot next to his name on my messaging app was lit up.

I liked to think it was a twin thing—we were always awake when the other one needed someone to talk to. But it was also possible that we were both just lousy sleepers.

Either way, he was awake somewhere in New York state, where he'd been working on a case with other federal drug-enforcement agents. He'd told me he was coming back to Vermont within days, though. And I was eager to see him.

Zara: *Hey. You're up! Everything ok?*

Benito: *Sure thing. Just have a lot to plan before I come back to town. You?*

Zara: *I can't sleep. I'm making a list of all the things Audrey and I have to do before her wedding. And I've been thinking about you, too! I'm going to try to rent an apartment and get out of your place.*

Benito: *You don't have to do that! Stay where you are.*

My brother kept urging me to stay on in his apartment. But the truth was I needed to pay my own way in life. Staying in his nearly renovated bachelor pad had only made sense when he couldn't be here himself. Now that he was coming back to town, I needed a new plan.

Zara: *Nicole needs a yard to play in. This will be best for us.*

Benito: *And you can find an apartment with a yard?*

He had me there. The only rental space in town that I could afford was in an old house that had been divided into three units. The yard was a bit of a disaster.

Zara: *I hope to.*

Benito: *Take your time, tho. I haven't even decided if it makes sense to stay in my loft when I come back. That spot might be too public for me if I'm undercover.*

Zara: *But you could still be renovating it. That takes months.*

There was a pause before he replied. And then:

Benito: *Whatever, Z. Stay if you want. That place isn't in the top 20 of things I'm thinking about right now. And I'd just as soon hole up at the orchard for a while.*

Our uncles lived on our family farm, raising pear trees and poultry. There was a big old rambling farmhouse where we had briefly lived when I was in grade school, before my mother moved us into a too-small trailer in the woods. Ben would be welcome to stay at the farm. We all were.

The shape of our family was a weird sort of echo in time. My mother had two older brothers. And I had *four* older brothers, if you counted Benito's seventeen-minute head start.

My mom had a total of five children with a man who hadn't really wanted children. He'd finally split for good when I was in third grade. Last we'd heard, he'd been working in British Columbia on an oil field. Even his Christmas cards had stopped when Benito and I were in high school.

I'd given birth to *one* child whose father was absent. And there the echo would stop. Nicole would never have four brothers. She wouldn't even get one.

Benito: *You know, if a yard is what you want, there's always room at the orchard for you.*

Zara: *Shut up.*

Benito: :) *Thought you might say that. Can't wait to see you and Nic! We'll go to the snack bar and introduce her to double chocolate ice cream.*

Zara: *Double chocolate for a one year old? Think again. But you and I can eat it when she's napping. Later gator!*

Benito: *In a while crocodile.*

His green dot disappeared.

I closed my laptop in my darkened loft. Correction: Benito's loft. Apparently our family had a thing for apartments over bars. This space was nothing like my shabby little room over the Goat, though. It was fancier, as was the bar beneath it.

My oldest brother Alec had bought a five-acre riverfront property at auction—with a set of prewar buildings on it. But Alec didn't have enough cash to fix up all the buildings at once. So Benito had invested in a share, securing this apartment space for himself. When he got around to finishing the renovation, the place would be awesome. The building had once been a mill, so it had high ceilings and exposed brick walls. Thick, old wooden beams ridged the ceiling.

It was groovy. But it wasn't mine.

Downstairs was Alec's bar, The Gin Mill. And across the parking area was the coffee shop I co-owned with Audrey. Alec owned that building, too.

At least I paid rent on the coffee shop. In Ben's apartment, I was a freeloader.

I could sit up all night and worry about this, and sometimes did. But tonight I would try to get some sleep. Setting the computer on the coffee table, I crossed the room silently, pausing to poke my head into the tiny bedroom where my daughter slept in her crib. She was on her tummy, her legs tucked up beneath her, diaper butt in the air. Her sweet face was turned away from me but I could picture her round cheek against the sheet, her eyes shut tight, as if sleeping required great concentration.

Before I got pregnant, motherhood had not been very high on my to-do list. I hadn't thought of myself as a very maternal person, I guess. But Nicole had changed me. She'd made me into a parent.

Some people said gushy things about their babies—*The moment she was placed into my arms I swooned with happiness! My mission in life became complete!* That sort of thing had made my eyes roll. Hard.

I loved my daughter fiercely, and I would do anything for her. But the change began in me before I ever saw her face. When I'd felt her kicking for the first time, I'd realized everything was going to be different than I'd planned. My old problems had suddenly seemed small. Old jealousies and slights dried up and blew away like dust.

There was a child inside me, and I was all she had. We were going to be a team, and I was never going to fail her. Never.

And I'd kept that promise. She was healthy and always cared for by people who loved her. I'd given up my job managing The Mountain Goat for uncle Otto. I'd opened the coffee shop with Audrey, so that I could have a job that didn't keep me at work until three in the morning.

One of these days I'd learn to go to sleep before midnight like a normal person, too.

I tiptoed over to shift the summer-weight blanket onto Nicole's small back and forced myself to walk away from the crib and out of the room. My love for her burned brightly as I climbed into bed. In five hours or so she'd roll over in her crib and begin to babble until I roused myself to pluck her off the mattress. The two of us would get back into my bed where she'd nurse for a half hour or so, her little starfish hand exploring my face while I dozed.

We were a team of two, and a good one. And I'd do anything for her—even move back to my uncles' farm. I'd told Benito I wouldn't, but that was just bluster. If my business didn't thrive, or if I couldn't find the right apartment, I'd endure a little too much family togetherness to give my baby girl whatever she needed.

There was time, though. She was only fifteen months old and didn't need much space to run. Not yet.

Living with Otto wouldn't be easy. He was a difficult man, prone to giving everyone his opinion whether they solicited it or not. When I'd managed The Mountain Goat, at least his advice had been less personal. He'd had strong opinions about how to organize the cash register and which brands of liquor to stock. As the sole manager for three years, I knew far more about running the place than he did.

Now on Sundays, when our extended family ate together, I was frequently treated to his thoughts on Nicole's thumb-sucking habit and feeding schedule.

This from a childless man.

So I already knew that living under his roof would be a real trial, since every bit of his advice was laced with judgement. "Shame she doesn't have a daddy," Otto sometimes said.

"Good thing she has four uncles and two great-uncles," my mother always said, chiming in on my behalf.

One blessing of single motherhood still surprised me—my relationship with my own mother had bloomed. This was the woman who'd spent my entire youth trying to make me more ladylike. We'd fought over the length of my skirts, my curfew, my hair, and my music.

But that had all stopped the moment I'd found the nerve to tell her I was pregnant. To my surprise, she hadn't shed a single tear (except the joyous kind) at my "situation," as Otto called it. Instead, she'd greeted her first grandchild with nothing but excitement.

It had floored me. But after a time I'd understood why Mom always had my back. She knew how painful everyone else's opinions and advice could be, because she'd spent my whole life hearing it herself.

I got it now.

Hardly a Sunday lunch with my family went by without someone mentioning the unusual russet color of Nicole's hair. "Her daddy is a redhead. Must be," Otto had said more than once, hoping I'd spill the story.

But Nicole's parentage was private. Someday when she was old enough to hear the truth, I'd tell her the story of meeting the stranger who became her daddy, and how I'd searched for him when I'd figured out I was pregnant. I'll tell her he was a good man, but just passing through. Nobody deserved to hear that story before Nicole heard it herself.

And, by then, maybe there would be another good man in my life. A girl could dream.

"You deserve someone," Benito would say sometimes. "We both do."

"Then where are my guy and your woman?"

"They're out there somewhere," he'd insist.

Most days I didn't really believe him. Dating wasn't practical for someone with a toddler. I didn't even let it bother me.

As for Benito, he'd been in love once. And I'd wrecked it. If he was right that there was someone out there for everyone, I was sure he deserved it more than I did.

In the meantime, Benito was my only confidante. He knew the details of my life-changing hookup, because I'd needed someone to help me search for Dave when I'd learned I was pregnant. Since Ben was in law enforcement, he was a good choice.

Also, for all his flaws, my twin was a vault.

As the clock ticked toward morning, I allowed myself the briefest memory of Dave's chiseled face and the feel of his taut muscles beneath my fingers.

Then I slept.

nine
dave

"GOD, I LOVE VERMONT."

I said this as my rental car took another curve along a beautiful winding road. I had the windows down, and, out the passenger's side, I saw a grassy hillside where honest-to-God sheep were grazing. "Look! You see that?"

"Baa-aaa," my teammate Leo Trevi answered from the passenger seat. "Seriously, this place is like driving through a travel magazine. Who chose this trip, anyway?"

"Me—this time. But two years ago we rented a cabin up here for eight weeks. I forget whose idea it was. Bayer's, maybe? I saved the card from the rental company so I could find it again." I slowed down to make the turn toward Marbury and flipped on the turn signal. A reflex—there were no other cars in sight. And the sheep didn't really care if I signaled.

Yesterday I'd come back to Vermont for the first time in two years. I'd thought maybe the place wouldn't look as good as it did in my memory. I shouldn't have worried. This rugged little corner of New England was just as great as I'd remembered.

Vermont was just the same. Even if I wasn't. "I needed this vacation, badly," I admitted. "And last year the guys talked me into going golfing in the Carolinas. So this year I stepped up and made these plans so Castro wouldn't force me do that again."

The rookie snickered. "Not a big golfer?"

"Nope. You?" I didn't know Trevi all that well. He'd joined the team less than six months ago. He was a good guy, and I liked him. But we didn't have a whole lot in common. He was a college boy from Long Island. I was a ruffian from the wrong side of Detroit. Also, I had seven or eight years on him.

"I'm from Long Island. Everybody golfs. I could take it or leave it."

"I knew I liked you."

"This is going to be great. You said there was fly fishing?"

"Yeah, and I hired us a guide for tomorrow. Can you picture O'Doul in waders? It's a sight."

The rookie laughed. "I saw those pictures on somebody's phone. Are we going to have fish for dinner?"

"Depends on what you catch. If nothing's biting, we'll go to the bar instead."

"Tell me about this bartender," Leo prompted. "This woman—Z… Zoe, was it?"

"Zara. But she doesn't work there anymore."

"Bummer."

It really was. The guys still liked to hassle me about how many nights I'd disappeared that summer to spend with Zara. If they knew I'd gone straight to The Mountain Goat last night looking for her, they'd laugh their asses off.

But Zara hadn't been at the Goat last night. I'd walked in to find some younger kid tending bar. And when I'd asked if she still lived upstairs, he'd said it was his place now. "Ask her uncle, the owner," was his suggestion.

Now there was an awkward conversation. *Two years ago, your niece and I liked to get together for sex. Could I get her number?*

Leo fiddled with the radio, since we were losing the station. That always happened in Vermont because mountains blocked radio signals. The cell phone service was spotty, too. And I *loved* that about Vermont. You had to unplug up here. There was really no choice.

This year I'd taken control of the unofficial team getaway, and I'd be the only one staying up here the whole time. Quite a few of my teammates—Leo included—had gotten coupled up these past two years, and they wanted to vacation alone with their wives and families. Leo had just come back from his honeymoon, in fact.

I didn't have a wife or family, and never would. So I'd set myself up as the organizer of this trip. I'd rented the cabin in my own name, and my plan was to hike and fish with whichever teammates showed up.

Yesterday afternoon I'd opened up the cabin myself. Then I'd gone shopping for some groceries and taken myself out for a beer at The Mountain Goat. This morning I'd gotten out early for a little hike to a waterfall where I ate a takeout lunch beside the rushing water. Then I'd driven to Burlington to see a new physical therapist who would work on my shoulder this summer. That was the deal I'd made with the team—that I'd keep up my therapy.

After that, I'd gone to the little Burlington airport to grab Leo. Two more of our teammates were driving up together tonight. And tomorrow's fishing expedition was all planned out. We were going to have a great time.

"Hey, how is that place?" Leo asked suddenly, as the road curved to show us the Winooski River.

I looked up to see a couple of roadside businesses that hadn't been there two years ago. "Actually, that's new." There was a big new bar called The Gin Mill. And—also useful—a coffee shop called The Busy Bean.

"Can we stop?" Leo asked. "I could use a little somethin' something."

"Sure." I braked and turned into the gravel parking lot. Pulling up to an empty spot between the bar and the coffee place, I killed the engine. When I got out of the car, I groaned at the stiffness in my legs.

"Everything okay over there, old man?" Trevi teased me.

"I'm good," I said quickly. I used to be like Leo, who had no idea what achy joints felt like. At thirty-two, after two decades of massive athletic endeavors, my body didn't always behave like I wanted it to. I grabbed my phone and peeked at the reception. Four bars—almost unprecedented in Vermont. "You go ahead inside, I gotta call Bess."

"Give her my love." Leo shut the car door.

"I will." Although Leo was agented by someone else, everyone knew my younger sister, Bess. As an agent, she was loved and feared by her clients as well as acquaintances. She had a big personality. And I owed her a call.

As Leo disappeared, I tapped her name on my phone and waited for the ring. Bess had left me three messages while I'd been hiking. I hadn't called her back yet because I was worried about the news she'd give me, and I hadn't wanted to spoil my hike.

Waiting, I whistled to myself, wondering who was going to get cut off when my call came in. I knew she'd ditch whomever she was on the phone with to talk to me, for two reasons. A) I was one of her biggest clients. B) She was my little sister.

"Davey!" she squealed. "How's the vacay?"

"It's great," I told her. "You should try it sometime."

"When? There's always a sport in season, and some asshole athlete doing his level best to make my job more difficult."

"Who's on your shit list today?" I asked, stalling.

"Michaels. That idiot got a DUI last night."

"No!" I said. I didn't follow her baseball clients at all, but the DUI would give my sis a headache. Right in the middle of their season, too.

"So there goes my week. But before I fly to Chicago and kick his ass, I have some numbers for you, big brother."

Gulp. "Are they decent?" I was man enough to admit that I was nervous to hear what kind of contract extension the league had offered me. At thirty-two, I was getting up there in years. And during the post-season I'd had an injury that had kept me out of several crucial games.

My team had made it all the way to the Stanley Cup finals. And then lost it in game five. While I'd watched from the seats. So that was a giant bummer.

Before my injury, my stats had been excellent. They were,

however, just a hair less excellent than the last time we'd negotiated. And even if thirty-two wasn't old for a hockey player, it was headed in that direction.

"Yeah, the numbers are decent," Bess said. "But you're going to have to think this one over. They're offering you two years at ten million even. Or three years at twelve mil."

"Twelve?" I yelped, offended. "I'm worth *sixty* percent less two years from now?"

"Good job with the math, big brother. But that is *not* what that means," she said firmly. "It's their job to be strategic, okay? Hugh is a smart man, and he has to be nimble with his salary cap. It makes him nimble to get you to sign a two-year. And if you take the three-year, then he just saved himself some coin. But it's your choice, D. I want you to think it over."

"You think there's no chance we can get him to three years at fifteen?"

My sister's sudden silence said it all. Not to mention that my last contract had been for *four* years. Getting old sucked.

"I obviously pressed for fifteen," she said eventually. "But this is the best they're going to do right now."

Ouch. When my sister said she'd "pressed" the general manager, it meant she'd already twisted the guy's arm so hard it hurt. Nobody was a tougher negotiator than Bess.

"You don't have to decide anything today," she said, her voice soft. "Take some time, think about your goals. And Davey—you know better than to take this personally, right? The new owner is doing everything he can to return the franchise to profitability, and the team has—"

"A crap-ton of expensive talent," I finished. "I get it." I really did, too. There had been many frustrating years when I'd wished for more depth on our bench. Now we finally had it, and I shouldn't whine too loudly if my paycheck was suffering.

What a dick, right? With either contract, I would make more money than most people made in a lifetime.

"Things are *good*, honey. You're mostly healthy, and you're entering your eleventh year of major-league play. Your coach appreciates you and your teammates do, too."

Mostly healthy. My recent shoulder injury was going to weigh on my general manager's mind. He was probably worried about a recurrence. Fuck, I hated having a weakness.

"You're a lucky man, Davey," my sister said.

"I know," I said, eyeing the door of the coffee shop, wondering if Leo was ready to go. Grumpy now, I wasn't interested in spending a couple of my rich-guy bucks on a cup of coffee and a cookie. "I'll think it over, Bess."

"Don't brood."

"I won't," I said, laughing. "Promise."

"Did you make it to your PT appointment today?"

"Of course I did. You don't have to nag."

She made a clicking noise with her tongue. "Fine. Go enjoy your vacation."

"You could join us, you know," I pointed out. "If you get a free weekend, grab a flight from Detroit to Burlington. There's one every day. I checked. And we have room."

"I would if I could. But there are fires to put out and deals to make."

Summer was her busy season, which was half the reason we never saw each other. Summer was my only time off. "Take care of yourself."

"Love you, too. Later!" *Click.*

I pictured my sister in her Michigan office, her headset on. She'd undoubtedly clicked off my call and directly onto another one. Always busy, that one. She was three years younger than I. And even if the prospect of someday retiring from hockey gave me the cold sweats, the one benefit would be spending more time with my only family member.

Leo came out of the coffee shop eating a cookie. "Hey!" he said with a smile. "You need one of these. I'm not sharing."

"I'm not into sweets."

"You say that, but you haven't tasted this. It's oatmeal raisin." He took a sip from the cup in his other hand. "And the coffee is killer."

"You ready?" I said, too grumpy about Bess's news to care about coffee.

Leo stopped a few feet from the car. "You're seriously not going in there?"

I shook my head.

He frowned. "I think you should."

"Why is that?"

"Well..." He glanced at the door of the coffee shop and smiled mysteriously. "Can you maybe just trust me on this? Go inside and buy a coffee."

"Why?"

Leo shrugged and gave me that weird smile again. "I'm willing to let you think I'm insane. Just go. The shop is really cool, anyway. You should see it."

That was a lot of pressure from the rookie. I was irritated, but intrigued. Somehow my feet pointed toward the door of The Busy Bean, and I walked away from him.

A bell on the door jingled when I walked inside the lodge-like building. And Leo had been right about one thing—it *was* cool in here. The coffee shop had big old leaded-glass windows looking out on the river, and antique mismatched tables and chairs arranged on wide, pine floorboards.

The style was both comfortable and a little wacky. The walls were painted a warm brick color, but the beams were black like a chalkboard—and someone had spent a lot of time decorating them with cartoon figures of coffee drinkers and sayings. The one I spotted first read: "Unattended children will be given a double espresso and a special-needs puppy."

Hilarious.

The coffee bar itself was topped with a thick, zinc counter that looked like something out of one of Brooklyn's hipster cafes. And there were glass display cases filled with cookies and pastries.

But then I glanced across the room and forgot all about the decor. Because Zara was *right* there behind the counter. The moment I recognized the sweep of her hair against her long neck, my body flushed with unexpected heat. Then she turned, and I could see her face.

And, *wow*. She was just as beautiful as I remembered. No—more. The late afternoon sunlight streaming through the windows made her expression gentler than I remembered it. Her thick hair was tied back in a ponytail, and she was humming while she stacked paper cups beside the cash register. She looked…softer than the last time I'd seen her. The word *lush* came to mind.

"Zara—no way!" I sputtered, too surprised to be casual. I crossed quickly to the counter, and she lifted her eyes. "I'm back in town, and I looked for you at The Mountain Goat." *The second I arrived in Vermont,* I might have added. "Didn't know you worked here now. We should exchange numbers."

That's when I noticed her face going pale. Her eyes widened, and her mouth gaped open. It was clear that she recognized me. But a long beat went by before she said anything. And when she finally did, it wasn't what I expected. "Do you…have a b-business card?"

"Uh, sure?" I dug into my wallet and pulled one out. I handed it over automatically, still trying to figure out why she was looking at me as if she'd seen a ghost. I was still good at two things in life—scoring goals and reading people. And what I saw on Zara's face didn't make any sense to me.

Fear.

I didn't get a chance to figure it out, because she took my card and turned from me. Then she walked quickly away, disappearing out a side door I hadn't noticed before. It slammed shut behind her.

For a second I just stood there like an idiot, wondering what the hell had happened. And if she was going to come back.

"Can I help you?" asked another voice.

"Um…" It took me a beat to turn to face the other woman. She was a pretty blonde who wore a smile, but was also sneaking looks at the door where Zara had just disappeared. "Well, sure?" It took me another moment to shake off my stupor. "I'll have a small French roast."

A minute later she put a cup of coffee in my hand. She looked a little familiar, and I was sure I'd seen her somewhere before. I handed her a five-dollar bill and instructed her to keep the change. Then I left by the front door.

Leo was leaning against the rental car, sipping his coffee. "Back so soon? Wasn't it her? I heard the blonde call the dark-haired beauty 'Zara,' and I thought I'd found your girl."

I weighed the car key in my palm, still trying to process the odd interaction I'd just had. "It was her. But she didn't look too happy to see me."

Leo's face fell. "Shit. I'm sorry, man."

So was I. But I was also really freaking curious. "Can we take a walk for a minute?"

"Of course." He shoved the rest of his cookie into his mouth and followed me as I headed toward the river bank that was visible between the bar and the coffee shop. These buildings had obviously been part of an old mill. They were situated to take advantage of the river below.

The river bank was a well-kept piece of land, the neatly mown grass stretching to the distant waterline. There were clumps of flowers planted here and there. Once we reached the river, we turned to walk along the bank.

The water curved around groups of rocks in its center. And, in the distance, an angler wearing waders cast his line into the shallows.

When the river hooked around to the right, I got a new vista. And sure enough, the most beautiful sight in Vermont was about fifty yards away. Zara sat on a bench alone, her chin tipped downward as she studied the business card in her hand.

"There she is," Leo whispered.

"Yeah. She asked me for my card and then bolted out the door."

Leo stopped walking. "That's kinda weird."

"No kidding." It didn't make a lick of sense.

He put a hand on my shoulder. "I'm going to have a seat." He pointed at a flat rock on the riverbank. "I'll check in with Georgia. You can try to talk to Zara, maybe?"

"Yeah. I'll do that." Usually I didn't chase after women who didn't want to see me. But the way she was studying my card—as if the secrets of the universe were written there—definitely piqued my curiosity.

I made my way across the lawn. She hadn't spotted me yet. By design, there was very little on that card I'd given her—just a business email address that my sister checked on my behalf, and a phone number that went to Bess's office. It was a card designed to blow off people who didn't deserve my private attention. I would have given Zara my real number to add to the card, but she'd run away before I got the chance.

I slowed my steps as I approached, because she seemed so lost inside her own head. "Hey there."

She startled, and when she turned that gorgeous face up in my direction, her eyes looked damp.

I stopped a few feet shy of the bench, not wanting to crowd someone who looked so shaken up. "Are you okay?"

Zara swallowed hard. "No. Not really." Trust Zara to answer that question honestly.

"I'm sorry to hear that. Do you want me to go away?"

Slowly she shook her head. "I need you to sit down for a minute. Unless you're dashing off somewhere."

"I've got some time," I said slowly.

She took a deep breath, which came out shaky. "This won't take long. Sit down."

I sat.

"Didn't expect to see you walk into my coffee shop today. It was a shock." Her slim hands pressed my business card between them, and I was taken back in time two years. I'd had those hands all over my body, their comforting sweep across my chest after we'd made love. I'd never enjoyed anyone so much as I'd enjoyed her. Not before, and not since.

But something was wrong now. I could feel it.

"Is that your coffee shop?" I asked, trying to bring myself back to the present. "You don't manage the Goat for your uncle anymore?"

She looked up quickly. "Good memory."

"Who could forget?" I smiled at her, hoping to diffuse whatever tension was eating at her.

It didn't work, though. If anything, her face only became more serious. "I don't tend bar anymore because I need to be home at night. The coffee shop's hours are a better schedule."

"I'll bet." A sweet breeze drifted off the river, chasing tendrils of her hair across her face, and I itched to reach out and sweep them away. But something held me back.

"Look," Zara said, reaching into her pocket for her phone. "I need to tell you something."

Even then, I didn't see it coming.

She tapped on the screen. Then she took a deep breath and looked me square in the eye. "This is Nicole. She's fifteen months old."

Even though my brain wasn't doing the math yet, I took the phone. On the screen was a photo of a baby clutching a blanket. She had hair the color of a copper penny.

Just like mine had been when I was small.

That's when I understood. My throat closed up suddenly. The world went a little haywire, and I heard the sound of my pulse in my ears. "You..." I stuttered. "You can't mean..." My stomach bottomed out. I pushed the phone toward Zara as if I could make the truth disappear just by avoiding that photo.

"I'm so..." She made an audible gulping sound. "Sorry. Springing it on you..." She swallowed with difficulty. "I never thought I'd see you again. Didn't even know who you were."

"But it's *not* possible." My mind spun. A child. A *child?* This could not be happening. "We used condoms." Even as the words left my mouth, I knew how stupid they sounded. Condoms failed all the time.

Zara's expression darkened. "Sure we used them. *Mostly*."

Goosebumps broke out across my back. "Okay," I said slowly, still trying to catch up. This had never happened to me before. Or really to anyone I knew. I remembered that once a teammate had been in a situation like this, but it had turned out to be a false alarm. "So…" I swallowed hard. *Think*. What would Bess do right now? "I, uh, have a lawyer. He'll know about paternity suits. DNA tests. I'm gonna call him." Just saying those words made me feel cold everywhere. I could not be someone's *father*. What an insane idea.

Beside me, Zara made a small noise of surprise. "I don't need your lawyer," she sputtered. "I'm not suing anyone. That's not why I'm telling you this."

"Why then?" I asked without thinking.

Her eyes got wide. "Because it's the *right thing to do*. I spent nearly two years fending off my family's questions. I wouldn't tell them who her father was, because nobody had a right to know before you did." She stood up quickly. "You're welcome."

While my mouth was still hanging open, she got up and ran off, disappearing into the trees.

ten

zara

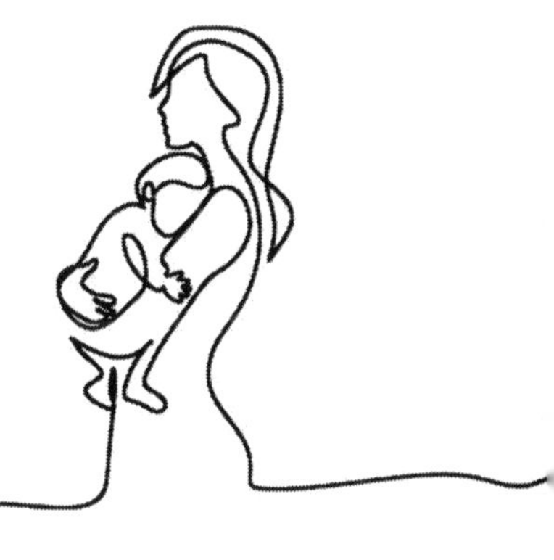

I RAN home as if someone had lit a fire under my ass. The motion helped shake off my tension and terror. Lengthening my strides, I ran along the road until I came back to my brother's property. Running felt different now than it had before I became a mother. For starters, there was more of me than there used to be. As I neared The Gin Mill, I crossed my arms under my breasts to stop the bouncing.

So many things had changed in the last two years. And now I was terrified that another tectonic shift was underway, and I hadn't seen it coming.

Breathing hard, I went around to the side of The Gin Mill building, where the private entrance was. But after I let myself in the door, I stood there at the bottom of the stairs, taking deep breaths. My mother was upstairs with Nicole, and they were expecting me. But I couldn't go up there and panic in front of my child. And I was too stunned to level with my mother.

I sat down on the third stair and tried to calm down. The business card was still in my hand, so I studied it one more time.

David Beringer
The Brooklyn Bruisers

There was a line-drawing of a hockey stick and a puck. And a phone number and an email address. Benito—after all his efforts to help me search for Dave—would be fascinated to know how the hell my onetime hookup actually spelled his last name.

How unreal it felt to be holding this information in my hand. When I'd woken up this morning, it was with the belief that I'd never see Dave again. The moment before he'd walked into the coffee shop, my mind was on a dozen other things.

The last person I expected to see today was the one whose green eyes could always stare right through me. For a second there, I hadn't even trusted my eyes. *Two years*. That's how long it had been since I'd seen him last.

That first fall, when I was pregnant, I used to look for him in crowds. Whenever the door to The Mountain Goat opened during my bartending shifts, I'd felt a little flutter of expectation. I'd scan the men entering the bar, looking for a flash of red-brown hair and a sexy smile.

It never came. And eventually I'd stopped looking. Switching jobs broke me of the habit. I finally accepted that he wasn't coming back, and I made my peace with it.

My family never did, though. They hated that I kept the details to myself. My older brothers and two Italian-American uncles—they all wanted to know whom to kill. Everyone wanted to take a piece out of the guy who'd "knocked me up," as my uncles put it.

That phrase made me want to scream.

Dave had gone, and even Benito—my only confidante—hadn't been able to find him. All we had was a first name, my crappy memory's feeble attempts at his last name, and Brooklyn.

There are two and a half million people in Brooklyn. Quite a few Daves, too.

And anyway, getting pregnant by a stranger had been a pretty stupid thing to do. But it was *my* stupid thing. I forgot about Dave. Or—even if I couldn't truly forget him—I'd stopped expecting him to reappear. As time wore on, I'd made my peace with the idea that he'd never know his child, and that a surprise child wouldn't be welcome.

Seems I was right about that last thing.

Here I sat in the stairwell, going a little insane, while upstairs my child waited for the parent who loved her.

I stood up, shoving the business card in my pocket, and took one more deep breath. Then I climbed the stairs to the second floor. I opened the door to my brother's mostly finished dwelling to find my mother seated at my kitchen table with Nicole in the clamp-on chair. There were Cheerios and carefully cut-up grapes on the plastic mat in front of the baby.

"Mama's home!" my mother sang as I stepped into the room. "Say, '*Hi, Mama!*'"

My baby girl opened her mouth and shrieked with joy.

"That also works," Mom said with a laugh.

Even though Nicole was fifteen months old, she hadn't spoken yet. I was starting to get worried, honestly. But the pediatrician said to wait a few more months before panicking.

The sight of my daughter's face relaxed me. The tension I'd been carrying in my shoulders fell away as I walked across the room to kiss her on the top of the head. She lifted chubby arms to me, and I glanced at my mother. "Did she eat enough?"

"This one always does," Mom said cheerily.

I tucked my hands under Nicole's arms and pulled her up to hug her. Since it was summertime, bare toes wiggled happily against my waist. "Hi, lady," I whispered. "Did you take a good nap for Grandma?"

"Good*ish,*" my mother said. "Forty-five minutes."

"Ah, well." She'd be grumpy later, but then pass out promptly at bedtime. "Thank you," I said to my mom. "You were a lifesaver today."

"Stressful day?" she asked.

"Yeah." *You have no idea*. But Mom was referring to the fact that The Busy Bean had lost electrical power that morning. Audrey and I had spent the day worrying about our refrigerated goods and leaning on friends for help. The problem hadn't been resolved until an hour ago.

Silly me, I'd thought a power outage would be the most stressful thing that could have happened today. Then Dave showed up.

I felt like a jerk for not telling Mom about Dave's sudden reappearance. The card he'd given me was burning a hole in my pocket. But I wasn't ready to talk about it. I'd just given that man the shock of a lifetime, after he'd given me the same by walking into my coffee shop.

We were both allowed some kind of cooling-off period, right?

The fact that Dave had brought up a lawyer right away chilled me. I'd almost bit the guy's head off. But people don't always say the right thing when they're in shock. I was going to keep telling myself that. *Please don't be a dickhead,* I privately begged. *And if you are, it had better not be genetic.*

My mother was wiping up bits of Nicole's dinner from the table. "I'll get the floor," I said quickly. After each of Nicole's meals, my kitchen looked as if a small food grenade had gone off in the proximity of her seat at the table.

"I got it," Mom said, bending to swipe a wet paper towel across the wood floor. Mom had raised five children, mostly as a single mother. And now she put in more than twenty hours a week babysitting Nicole.

"Thank you," I said with a sigh. I was looking forward to the day when my family would no longer have to do so much for me. I owed Benito for letting me live here until now. I owed Alec for renting me The Busy Bean at a below-market rate, and I owed Alec and Mom for many hours of free babysitting every week.

I was tired of owing my family. But I'd rather owe them forever than lawyer up and chase down Mr. David Beringer (spelled with an "e," damn it!) for child support.

"Zara," my mother said gently. "Is everything all right?"

I chased the scowl off my face. "Long day."

"If you need more time, I could..."

"Nope, I'm good. Thanks for your help." I bounced Nicole on my hip. One of her little hands was feeling up my left boob already. My baby wanted to nurse. I carried her over to Benito's L-shaped sofa and sat down in our favorite corner.

"All right," Mom said, grabbing her purse off the counter top. "Then I'm going to get to the post office before it closes."

"Bye, Mom. Say, 'Bye, Grandma!'" I prodded Nicole, hoping she'd give us a word at last.

Instead she grabbed at my shirt, on a mission for the boob.

My mother smiled at us and took her leave.

I tugged up my shirt and unclipped the cup of my nursing bra. "Have at it, champ."

Nicole grabbed my boob in two hands and clamped herself on, her little mouth working immediately. Her eyes closed, and she leaned her soft cheek against my arm.

With wonder in my heart, I stared down at my baby girl. She drank milk out of a sippy cup now. Nursing wasn't necessary anymore, really. But I wasn't ready to give it up yet. In the early days, when I'd been so scared and tired and sure that I'd stink at motherhood, nursing was the thing that always made me feel calm. My child took daily sustenance from my body. And with the milk I gave her, she grew like crazy. And when she fussed, I'd bring her to my breast, and everything would be okay.

It still was, too. *Nothing has changed,* I reminded myself. It was still Nicole and me (and a half-dozen family members) against the world. Even if I never saw Dave again, we were still okay.

eleven
dave

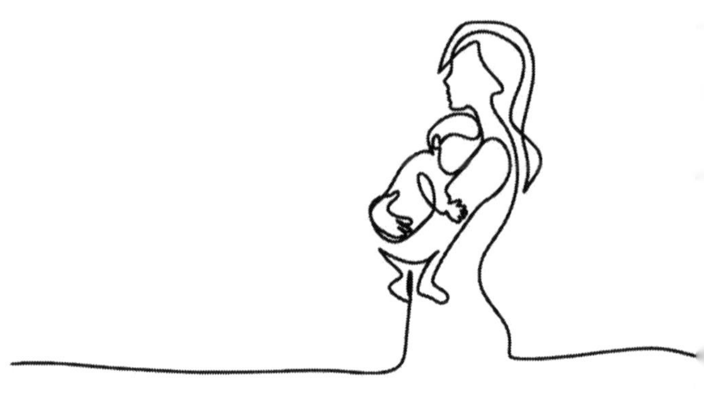

"BERI."

"Hmm?" I looked up quickly. That's when I noticed we were sitting in front of the cabin already.

The dashboard GPS picked that moment to announce, "You have arrived at your destination!" And its mechanical voice sounded accusatory.

Leo had shut off the engine, but he hadn't gotten out of the car yet. He was watching me carefully. "What can I do for you?" he asked quietly.

"Nothing," I croaked. "I just need…" The sentence died on my lips. I just needed…what, exactly? To rewind my life to the point where I hadn't fucked up? "An hour ago, my contract negotiation was the biggest thing on my mind. Now I have a problem that money can't fix."

"I suppose not," Leo said, leaning back in the driver's seat. "Did she ask for money?"

I shook my head. "I'd pay it, though. That's really not the problem."

"Right." Leo reached across the gearshift and squeezed my shoulder. "Let's go inside. You can call your sister."

"Oh, fuck. I'm not ready." Bess was going to flip her lid. And usually I was such a trouble-free client.

Leo laughed. "Fine. You said you went grocery shopping. Got some sandwich stuff?"

"Yeah."

"Great. I'll make you a sandwich while you strategize what you're going to say to Bess. Did she know about Zara?" He opened his door and got out.

"No," I grunted, unclipping my seat belt. I got out of the car and took yet another deep breath. But it didn't quell the panic. "There was nothing to tell. We had a lot of sex and went our separate ways."

Or I thought we had. But Zara had spent the last two years with my...

Panic rolled through me again. I hadn't *ever* been this flattened. Not even when the doctor had said that I had to sit out the Stanley Cup finals last month.

We went inside. I took a couple more deep, yoga breaths.

True to his word, Leo puttered around the cabin's kitchen, whistling to himself and rooting around in the fridge. "Wow, Beri—you weren't fooling around at the store. I don't even know what to pick. Turkey and swiss sound good?"

"Sure."

"Mayo? Tomato?"

"Thanks, rookie," I grunted.

He set several items on the counter and then stopped to study me. "I know you're freaking. But it's going to be okay. If it's true that you have a child, you'll deal."

"I can't be somebody's daddy." The word would hardly form in my mouth. I sat down heavily on a bar stool.

"Why not? I mean, nobody is demanding that you marry her and carve the Thanksgiving turkey every year."

The ridiculous image made me let out a bark of laughter. "Can you imagine?"

Leo made a point to survey all the food I'd purchased and then organized in our shared kitchen. "Thing is, I can. You play the lone-wolf role pretty well, but I'm not sure I buy it on you."

Jesus. The kid was being nice to me, but I wasn't in the mood for his theories. Buying groceries had nothing to do with raising a family.

"Now, if Zara isn't the girl for you, there's no reason to pretend she is. The child won't care if you're married, so long as you show your face sometimes. You know you can't leave your kid hanging in the wind."

I groaned, because that was the whole problem. I'd spent my entire life hanging in the wind. Whatever a decent father was supposed to look like, I had never had one. "My dad was the biggest asshole on the planet, Leo. Showing my face? I don't even know how to do that. At a bare minimum I'd need one of those yellow how-to books. *Fatherhood for Assholes,* or whatever."

"*For Dummies,* you mean? Because that's what you are. A dummy. Not an asshole."

"I'm so flattered," I said in my best asshole voice.

The rookie rolled his eyes. Then he pushed a plate toward me with a well-made sandwich on it. "You're allowed your freak attack, Beri. Today, at least. But tomorrow you gotta strap on the pads and deal."

"I'll need the pads just for Bess." I took a bite of my sandwich, trying to predict what my sister would say. She was going to be pissed as hell at me for causing drama during contract negotiations. Bess always told her athletes, "This is the month to be on your best behavior."

Shit. She was going to rip me a new one and then kick me into next Tuesday.

"When are the other guys getting in?" Leo asked, opening a bag of chips.

"Uh..." It was hard to believe that only a few hours ago, I'd been in vacation mode. "Couple hours, maybe. Doulie and Castro are driving up together."

"Eat your sandwich. And then call your sister after you're done. Get it over with."

I grunted at the rookie. But I knew he was right about making that phone call. Even if it was going to be awful.

"Say that again?" Bess whispered.

I swallowed hard. "A baby, Bess. You heard me. Fifteen months old."

"Fifteen...months." The quiet calm of her voice was scarier than screaming would have been.

"That's what she said." I cleared my throat. "The math checks out, too."

"This is that bartender? Long black hair. Funny name?"

"Christ, Bess. How do you know this shit about me?" There were some things you don't tell your sister.

"You talk about her every time you're *drunk,* Dave!" she yelled. Finally the yelling had started. "Three different times at least! You just left out the part about the BABY!"

"Didn't know," I argued. Still, I felt oddly better now that she was screaming. Sometimes Bess's anger had to burn itself out like a brushfire.

"You said once that if you ever settled down with someone, it would be someone like her. And I said—*why don't you give her a CALL AND SEE HOW SHE'S DOING?*"

I held the phone away from my ear to avoid permanent hearing loss. Across the room, Leo gave me a sympathetic look and then got up and went outside to give me some privacy.

"I know I fucked up, Bess." Not to mention that I didn't ever remember telling her anything like that. Wisely, I kept that argument to myself.

"You didn't ever give her your NUMBER? What kind of asshole does that?"

"She didn't *want* my number." I scrubbed my palm over my face. "She was really clear on the subject. Can we get past the details of how it happened, and get to the part where you tell me what to do?"

"I need to talk to your lawyer."

"Right." *Thank you.*

"I'll deal with *you* later. Text me the address where you're staying. Do it now. The lawyer will send you some documents." *Click*.

My sister actually hung up on me.

Jesus. I hung up the phone and stood up fast. The cabin walls seemed to be closing in on me. I stomped outside. Leo was sitting in a hammock strung between two trees, drinking a beer and poking at his phone. "The cell service is for shit here. I can barely check my email."

"Welcome to Vermont. That's why I used the land line."

Leo dropped his phone onto the grass beneath the hammock. "What did Bess say?"

"Just some yelling." I flopped down on the grass. The yelling wasn't as bad as her *disappointment,* though. I hated disappointing Bess. "She's going to call our lawyer and get some advice, I guess. I dunno. I'll call her back tomorrow or the next day after she's calmed down."

"She'll calm down." Leo lifted his hand and looked at the wedding band on his finger. "I'm still not used to wearing this."

"Would Georgia freak if you took it off?"

"Nah. But I don't need to." Leo worried the ring on his finger. "I'm not used to it yet, but I don't mind it at all. Sometimes it catches the light and surprises me. I think—that can't possibly be mine."

"I'll bet it's weird saying, 'my wife.'"

The rookie laughed. "I like it. 'My girlfriend' sounds like we're sixteen, you know?"

"Yeah," I said, although I didn't really know. I'd never called anyone my girlfriend. Not even when I *was* sixteen. Leo was what—twenty-four years old? Wearing a ring and happy about it. If Georgia got pregnant, he'd probably dance a jig. "You two going to have kids?"

"Sure. As soon as I can talk Georgia into it."

"She doesn't want kids?"

"Oh, she totally does. But she feels like it's too soon. She wants another year or two in her seat as the co-head of PR. And that's cool. We have plenty of time."

"True." My teammate was awfully enthusiastic about procreating. Then again, Leo had a nice family. His parents showed up at home games, smiling in the hallway outside the lockers to greet him after games. Family made more sense to a guy like Leo than it ever would to me.

"What are you thinking so hard about over there?" he asked.

"How I promised myself I'd never be someone's deadbeat dad. And now I've managed to be one without even knowing it."

"You can fix that, though." Leo was quiet a moment. "You think you already failed?"

"Is there any other way of looking at it?" My plan had always been to keep things casual with women. I was a one-and-done kind of guy because I knew long-term entanglements were never going to work out for me. Accidentally creating a child wasn't something I thought could happen.

The universe should really know better.

"This baby is a year old, right?" Leo asked. "She probably can't even *say* daddy. Declaring yourself a failure now would be like having a rough couple of games during the preseason and giving up on making the playoffs."

I snorted. "But hockey is a game I know how to play, kid. The Beringers don't do parenthood." A terrific understatement. My mother overdosed on cocaine when I was five. Then my father beat the crap out of me for nine more years, until people started to notice. He lost custody of Bess and me. We lived with our indifferent but nonviolent grandparents until Bess graduated from high school.

Bess turned out okay, although she didn't have a husband or a family. Bess thought men were great as long as they were paying her fifteen percent of their major-league paychecks. She was married to her job.

Having a family? Like me, she didn't seem to see the point.

A memory of Zara chose that moment to smack me right over the head. It had been one of the first times we were together—that night the crazy asshole threw a beer glass at Zara, and I almost had to break him in half. But Zara had handled him. And then we drank a lot of tequila together. That night we hadn't even made it up to her room. I'd banged her on a bar stool until she'd screamed my name.

Jesus. I remembered it like it was yesterday.

After, though, I'd been holding her, locked into an embrace right there in the bar, breathing hard. She'd suddenly asked, "You're not married, right? You don't have a family you're fucking around on?"

And I'd said, "Fuck no. And I never will."

Now I lay back in the grass and put my hands over my face. "I used to be such a cocky bastard, Leo. I think I still am."

"One day at a time, big guy," Leo said, crossing his legs in the hammock. "Today isn't the day to make a lot of important decisions. Give yourself a minute, okay? And let your teammates get you drunk tonight."

"Sounds like a plan."

"It's what we do," Leo said, looking up into the canopy of the trees.

"That's right," I agreed. My team was the only kind of family I understood. And when one of us had trouble, the rest of us were good at circling the wagons around him. I guessed it was my turn to be in trouble.

"Love you, man," Leo said. That's the kind of guy he was—the kind who could say things like that.

"You're a good kid," I said in return. Because I wasn't the kind of guy who did endearments. Never had been, and never would be.

A few hours later we were sitting like ducks in a row on barstools at the new bar, The Gin Mill. Me, Leo, and our two new arrivals—O'Doul, our team captain, and Castro, another chipper youngster.

"To Beri!" my team's captain said, lifting his shot glass. "We've got your back, man."

"Thanks, O'Doul. I really appreciate that." My teammates had decided we needed to go to a bar to properly christen this new complication. So here we were.

"You guys want to run a tab?" the bartender asked, leaning on the bar in front of me. He looked a little familiar, but I didn't think I'd met him before.

"Sure," O'Doul said, pulling a credit card out of his wallet.

"Ooh! The captain is springing for drinks. Somebody got a nice contract extension," Castro said.

The bartender took the card but then paused. "It's Vermont night, but you need to show a driver's license to get the discount."

O'Doul shook his head. "We're not local. Charge us the full freight."

The bartender left us alone, and Castro gave a happy sigh. "All problems are more easily solved in a bar," Castro declared.

"Not sure that's true, man." I took a sip of my beer. "But it's good to be here with you guys, anyway."

To their credit, neither O'Doul nor Castro had laughed or made a big fuss about my crazy news. They both hit me with one-armed man hugs, slapping me on the back and asking what they could do to help.

Maybe I was the world's biggest asshole, but I had some awesome friends.

"You're right," Leo said, tracing the condensation on the outside of his beer bottle. "Since this whole thing got started in a bar."

"So we've come full circle." O'Doul chuckled. "Drink up, men."

Castro, O'Doul, and I tipped our shot glasses back and swallowed. Leo had appointed himself the designated driver, so there was no tequila for the rookie.

The tequila burned my throat in a good way. And, damn. I hadn't chosen the drink, but it sure as hell reminded me of Zara. Whatever poetic randomness had put tequila into O'Doul's head when he'd ordered our shots, I wouldn't question. But it made me nostalgic for that more carefree time. When Zara had thought I was a fun fling. Before I'd helped derail her life.

Easy, I coached myself. She was going to be okay. I'd make sure of it. It couldn't be easy being a single mother and a business owner, though. I wondered how she did it at all.

I wondered a lot of things.

"This is a great bar," Doulie said, glancing around at the exposed brick walls. "Good vibe. And it's nicer than that little place we hung out last time we came to Vermont. The Mountain Lion."

"The Mountain *Goat,*" I corrected.

The dark-haired man behind the bar grinned as he set a bottle of beer down in front of Doulie. "I'm definitely giving the Goat some competition." He put a fresh beer in front of each of us. "You boys need anything else right now?"

"No thanks," I said.

"Guess we can't go to that other bar, anyway," O'Doul offered. "It would be like returning to the scene of the crime, right, Beri?" The captain laughed at his own joke.

"She doesn't work there anymore," I said to shut down that particular discussion.

The bartender gave us the side-eye as he wiped down the counter. His mouth got weirdly tight, and he studied me in a way I really didn't like. But I was probably just being paranoid.

"Anyone want to shoot some pool?" I asked, hoping for a change of subject.

"The tables are busy," Leo said, jumping off his stool. "I'll put some quarters down to get in line."

"Good rookie." O'Doul chuckled. "He snaps to attention. You should be more like Leo," he said, teasing Castro.

"Oh, please," Castro said with an eye-roll. He was a fun kid. A party animal and witty in a way that women enjoyed. "Nobody can kiss ass like Leo. There's no point in trying."

"Thing is," I said, taking a sip of my beer. "Leo isn't an ass-kisser. He means all the shit he says. He's really *that* nice."

"Not all of us can jump over the bar if it's set that high," Castro argued. "Maybe you should try to lead by example."

"I'm nice," I argued. "Nice*ish*. I'm at least as nice as Doulie, here."

"But I hit people for a living," O'Doul pointed out. He was our team's enforcer as well as the captain. "If I was too nice, they'd fire me."

"Excuses." Castro shook his head in mock disbelief. "And now you've gone and gotten yourself a girlfriend, too. Making the rest of us look bad. And Leo is married at twenty-four. That leaves me and Beringer to be the wild men. And he knocked up a local girl already, so there's no topping that."

"Castro, Jesus," I muttered. He was only trying to be funny, but hockey players could be pretty crude.

"The *fuck?*"

The bartender was staring at us with a strangely electric intensity. No—staring *me* down. He had both hands planted on the bar, and he leaned in like he might jump over the thing and take a swing at me.

And now I knew why he'd seemed familiar. This guy was the older, macho male version of Zara—all dark eyes and fire.

The hair stood up on the back of my neck, and I heard Castro's chuckle die in his throat. "Aw, shit," my teammate whispered. He might be crude, but he wasn't dumb.

"Something the matter?" O'Doul asked slowly.

"I need to know who it is *you* think you're joking about." The bartender pointed a finger right at Castro's chest. Then he lifted his chin in a challenge.

O'Doul lifted his chin in a matching gesture. "We're just teasing my teammate here. A little gallows humor." Nobody knew how to square off for a fight like O'Doul. I felt myself growing wary.

"*Gallows humor,*" the bartender spat. "About a local woman? That's low."

Nobody had said a single word against Zara. But this guy wasn't in the mood to go over the finer points of our banter. "Sorry, man," I said slowly. "We'll take it down a notch."

"You've been around here before?" the guy asked, turning his angry eyes back to me.

"Not to your bar, no," O'Doul answered for me.

The bartender's eyes didn't leave mine. "I'm talking to the redhead. You're not local?"

I shook my head.

"Been to Vermont much? You know Zara Rossi?"

"Oh, shit," Leo breathed, rejoining us.

"Oh shit is right," the bartender echoed. "You got a name?" he asked me. "How about a phone number."

"Slow down, now," O'Doul intervened on my behalf. "You want to be pen pals with my teammate or do you have any real business with him?"

I reached a hand out and palmed O'Doul's puffed out chest. "It's okay, Doulie. Maybe our new friend wants to tell us who he is to Zara, and we can have an actual conversation and not a pissing match."

The man scowled at me. Then he turned his head and barked out a command toward the other bartender at the far end. "Smithy! Cover for me a while." Then he stalked to the end of the bar and hopped over it, dropping to his feet beside Leo. He stalked closer and stood in front of me, his arms crossed over a puffed-out chest. "You and me are going to have a talk."

"We should have gone to a different bar, maybe," Leo mumbled.

"You're her brother," I said, stating the obvious. "She has four of them."

"Four?" Castro yelped. "You're in deep shit now."

"Come with me," Zara's brother said, turning toward the door.

Doulie put his beer down on the bar and followed the guy, uninvited. I didn't need my guys to trail me outside. In fact, it would have been easier if they stayed out of it. But there was no point in saying so, because that's what teammates did. O'Doul wouldn't let me take a punch alone whether we were wearing skates or not.

"I don't get to finish my beer?" Castro asked. "What a rip."

But he was just trying to lighten the mood. He set his bottle down and moved toward the door, too. I had to hurry to get there first. I pushed the door open into the Vermont summer night. It smelled so freaking good here. I'd never get used to it.

"What, do your friends follow you everywhere?" Zara's brother snapped when O'Doul stepped outside after me.

"Depends," I said. "You seem to want us out of your bar, anyway."

"You're not leaving until you tell me your fucking name."

"Do you have one, too?" I asked. "Let's all share."

That must have come out extra snarky because the guy launched himself at me, grabbing my shirt.

About a half-second later, O'Doul had pulled him back, trapping him in a hold. "Calm the fuck down, okay?"

"Whoa!" another man said, stepping out of the shadows to join our tense little gathering. "You want to let him go? I'm off duty right now, I haven't seen my brother in three months, and it would be a pain in the ass to arrest you."

"It all depends on whether your brother's gonna lunge at my teammate again," Doulie said calmly.

"Alec, don't lunge," the new guy said, sounding bored. This was another Rossi brother—a younger one. *Ben.* His name leapt into my mind, because I'd seen him before. He and Zara had gotten into an argument right in front of me once.

Fuck my life.

"But you all have ten seconds to tell me what the fuck is going on," Ben added.

O'Doul loosened his hold, and Alec shook him off. "They were at the bar talking some smack about getting a local girl pregnant. Look at *him*," Alec said, pointing at me. "Tell me I'm not crazy."

The newcomer's eyes widened. He gave me the same quick scan I'd given him a minute ago. "What's your name?" he asked me.

"David Beringer," I said immediately, just to piss Alec off.

"Spell it."

"B-e-r-i-n-g-e-r."

"With an 'e'?" He tipped his head back toward the stars. "Fuck. An 'e.' Why didn't I figure that out?"

"*Benito*," Alec demanded. "What the hell are you talking about?"

"We searched for him," Benito said. "We searched through a whole lot of Davids from New York City. Barrister. Barrier. Barer. Currier. Carrier. We never got the name right."

"But Zara knew my name," I argued. "I put my ID in front of the security camera..." The sentence died away as I tried to figure out how to finish it. *Before we banged for the first of many times.*

Benito gave me a stare. "Took Zara a couple months to realize she needed to know who you were. That footage was long gone. We tried rental-car records and cabin rentals, too. No name like yours came up anywhere."

"I rented everything," O'Doul grunted. "His name wasn't anywhere."

"We figured it was something like that," Ben said with a sigh.

But his brother Alec still looked like a bomb waiting to explode. If possible, he looked even angrier at his brother than he'd been at me. "You were *looking* for him? Zara told you his name?"

Ben put a hand on his shoulder and squeezed. "Yeah. She didn't want to talk about it, okay?"

"Except to *you*."

"I'm in law enforcement," Ben said quietly. "Who would you ask if you needed to find someone?"

Alec's jaw remained clenched.

Ben, who I had decided was the calmest member of the Rossi clan, turned his attention back to me. "So now you're back in Vermont?"

"For a few weeks, yeah."

"Did you, uh, see Zara yet?"

I smiled in spite of my tension. "This afternoon. Walked into the coffee shop and there she was." I cleared my throat. "We talked for about sixty seconds. The shock hasn't worn off."

"I'll bet." He crossed his arms, rocking back on his heels. "Come around back and have a beer on the house. We'll talk."

"Hey!" Alec argued.

His brother turned on him. "You really want to start off like that? I know you're pissed off for your little sister, but she wouldn't want you to be such an ass to the father of her child."

Father. The word sent a fresh chill down my spine.

"Do we really know how Zara feels?" Alec challenged. "Maybe she hates his guts."

Benito rolled his eyes. "The evidence suggests she liked him at one point."

Alec clenched his fists and growled.

"Go back to your customers." Benito pointed at the door. "I'm going to sit on the deck and ask Mr. Beringer a few questions."

Without another word, Alec stomped back inside.

"Well," Ben said, holding out a hand to O'Doul. "I'm Benito Rossi. You've met my brother Alec."

"And it was a pleasure," O'Doul said drily.

Benito shook everyone's hands. Then he waved us around the side of the building toward the deck. "I'll be right out to sit with you," he said before following his brother inside.

"He's loading the shotgun and calling the minister," Trevi joked as we walked toward the deck.

"What's your ring size?" Castro teased.

O'Doul just chuckled. "And to think we almost stayed home tonight."

I said nothing. We all took a seat at a round table with a hurricane candle on it. The air was cool and the frogs were singing their tune. I'd forgotten about the frogs.

"Nice place when people aren't trying to kick your ass," Trevi said.

"Be nicer if I hadn't abandoned my beer," Castro complained.

"So go inside and order a round," O'Doul suggested. "I'm running a tab."

But before Castro could make it through the sliding glass doors leading into the bar, Benito emerged with a tray, a full pitcher, and five glasses. He sat down with us and began to pour. "So what do you all do for a living?"

"Hockey," I said.

Benito handed me the first glass with a thoughtful frown. "How's that?"

"We play hockey," I said. "For the Brooklyn Bruisers. I play left wing."

Benito looked around the table. "Professional hockey players?"

"Yup," O'Doul said.

Benito snorted and shook his head. Then he raised his eyes up to the sky. "Oh, Zara. Really?"

"She didn't tell you?" I asked, and then I realized. "She didn't know."

Ben shook his head slowly.

"She didn't *know?*" Castro yelped. "What did you tell her you did for a living?"

"I didn't ever say."

"Why the hell not?"

I gave my head a shake, and Castro clamped his mouth shut. They wouldn't understand that Zara and I had experienced a rather unique month-long tryst. Sex, conversation, and very few personal details.

Benito ran a hand through his hair. "So you just happened to come back to Vermont for another vacation. And you ran into Zara?"

"That's right." I dug another business card out of my pocket. "Does somebody have a pen?" When Castro handed me one, I wrote my cell phone number on the card. "Here." I handed it to Benito. "I didn't get a chance to give Zara my number today. The conversation we had was really, uh, short."

Ben studied me, his dark features appraising. "Where did you two leave it?"

"How big a dick were you?" Castro clarified.

Thanks, buddy. "Just, I dunno. Medium-sized." Everyone laughed, even Benito. "I was just surprised. And so I said I'd call my lawyer." Benito flinched. "That's all. Zara bolted after that. I'll apologize to her when she's ready to hear from me. You can give her that number on the card. The printed one goes to my agent, so I added my own."

He nodded, tucking the card into his back pocket. "All right. She's my next call." He took a deep drink of his beer. "But before I go, there's something you need to understand about my family."

Beneath the table, Castro nudged my knee. His face said, *Here it comes!*

"Zara has four brothers," Benito said. "And two uncles. And we're horribly overprotective of her, even though Zara is the toughest girl alive." He smiled fondly. "But when Zara got pregnant, she didn't tell a soul what had happened. So that led to a lot of speculation. Some of it really *bad*."

"Why?" I wondered aloud. "Why not say that she and I had a fling for a while, but we were shaky on the details?"

Benito shrugged. "She's fiercely private. You kinda have to be in my family. It's a self-defense mechanism. But also she was embarrassed. I mean—she insisted that there was nothing awful about the story. That she wasn't protecting anyone. But my family has more testosterone than most, so it only gets you so far."

"Okay?"

"I just wanted you to know that there's been a lot of speculation."

"So he won't be too surprised when the next brother slugs him?" O'Doul asked, his question dripping with skepticism.

"Something like that." Benito smiled again. "I haven't seen my sister in way too long. So if you'll excuse me, guys." He drained his beer and stood up.

"Good night," Trevi called before he walked away. "That coulda gone worse," he said when we were alone again.

"The man brought us beers," Castro pointed out. "And I haven't seen a shotgun yet."

"The night's still young," O'Doul said, and everyone laughed.

twelve
dave

THERE'S A BABY CRYING. *She's wailing. Hard. But I can't see her. She's in another room. Even so, I can hear her anguished screams and the ragged gasps she makes between them. It's a horrible sound. Suffering.*

I need to fix it. I would do anything to make that sound stop.

But I can't. I can't move. Every new wail is like a fresh stab of pain. My head aches, and my pulse is too fast. But my feet are rooted to the floor. There's something terrifying in front of me. I can't lift my gaze because I'll see it again. I can't look.

Still. The screams. She needs me.

The carpeting beneath my feet is dirty. It's a dull gray color, but it used to be white. And there is a sick, green stain near the toe of my sneaker. It's the color of...

I sat up fast, almost nailing my head on the reading light affixed to the wall. For a moment my eyes darted around, taking in the details of my room in the cabin. Meanwhile, my chest heaved as I tried to take in oxygen.

Kicking off the covers, I swung my legs over the side of the bed and stood. My sweaty body needed space. It helped that I'd left the window open overnight, and the sweet Vermont air was good for breathing deeply.

I closed my eyes and inhaled all the way to my diaphragm, the way my yoga teacher—O'Doul's girlfriend—encouraged us to do. Then I exhaled the last of my panic.

What a fucking dumb dream. Crying babies? My subconscious had gone right for the cheap joke.

I raised my arms overhead and then bent slowly at the waist, hanging my head, stretching out my back. There. My panic was receding, leaving me with a calmness that was much more me.

Another day. Another chance to get it right. Nobody became a veteran NHL player without being able to center himself. Every professional hockey player worth his paycheck could shake off the prior day's disasters and start fresh.

Standing up again, I took stock of my day. I'd reserved some gear and hired a guide for a fly-fishing expedition in the very river that ran past Zara's family's businesses. But my teammates could go without me. I'd need the day to call the lawyer and learn a few things about my legal obligations to Zara's child.

A man takes care of his people first and goes fishing with his buddies later.

I found a pair of shorts in my suitcase and pulled them on, listening to the quiet chatter of my teammates' voices elsewhere in the house. I'd taken the upstairs master suite for myself, of course. The guy who planned the expedition always got dibs. My teammates weren't doing so badly downstairs, though. O'Doul had a queen-sized bed with its own bathroom, and Trevi and Castro were doubled up in a bunk room.

"Oh man," Trevi had complained last night. "I see how it is. The rookie gets the bunkbed."

"That's right, college boy," O'Doul had teased. "You're used to dorm rooms. You and Castro. This will be like memory lane."

"You shoulda given the single guy his own room," Castro had grumped. "If I hook up I'm gonna put a bandanna on the door handle, Trevi. If this bunk bed is a rocking, don't come a knocking."

It had just been smack talk, though. We'd all come home from the bar together last night.

Now, as I descended the stairs, I heard Castro's chuckle. Then I was startled to hear a feminine giggle. And not just any feminine giggle. Holy…

I rounded the corner at the bottom of the staircase and walked into the great room to find the giggle's owner. "Bess?" I yelped. "What are you doing here?"

My sister stood up and squared off against me, her face losing every trace of humor. "What am I *doing* here? That is the dumbest question you've ever asked me in your whole freaking life. And that's saying something."

Right.

Okay.

One more deep breath.

"I know I caused drama," I said in my calmest voice. "But I'm going to handle everything that needs handling. You can go back to your other PR disasters, okay? This isn't a DUI. I didn't do anything wrong, and it's not going to end up in the paper. I'm a big boy, and I know how to clean up my own messes. I got it, Bess. I'm going to do the right thing. All of 'em. Whatever the lawyer tells me."

For some reason, Bess looked even more upset at the conclusion of my rambling little speech. Castro turned his face aside, as if bracing for impact. I couldn't figure out why. And then Bess stepped up into my personal space, her eyes pinched. Her cheeks red. She lifted her hands and clamped on to my shoulders. "You moron! I'm *here to meet my niece*. Our only living relative! My brother's *child…*"

She actually began to shake me, and I started to lose it a little. We did *not* touch each other in anger. I stepped back and caught her hands in mine. "Bess…"

"What?" she gasped. "This is *big,* Davey. I get that it's easier for you to go into macho damage-control mode right now. But your life just changed for the better. And I hope you're not too stupid to figure that out."

That left me pretty much speechless, while my teammates looked at their feet, their hands. Anywhere but at me. "So what is your plan?" I finally ground out. "Just barge in there and ask to inspect the kid? What if we're not welcome?"

Bess lifted her chin. "You have rights. You can sue for visitation. But first we're just going to ask nicely."

"Uh…" O'Doul said with a chuckle. "If I could make a suggestion? First we're going to take a deep breath and eat breakfast."

I wanted to hug him for breaking up the most intense conversation I'd ever endured before my first cup of coffee. "Right. First things first," I said. "Time for bacon and eggs."

I fried up two pounds of bacon and then whipped up a big frittata. Then, leaving Bess in charge of making toast for everyone, I snuck out onto the porch to dial Zara's coffee shop.

"You've reached The Busy Bean, this is Audrey speaking. How can I help you?"

"Hi, Audrey. My name is Dave Beringer. I'm a friend of Zara's. Is she available by any chance?" Audrey was Zara's co-worker. I was pretty sure.

"Negative," Audrey said. "Hang on a sec." I heard her ask a customer whether they wanted cinnamon or cocoa on their latte. Then she came back. "Sorry. The morning rush is upon us. But this is Zara's morning off. You should try her phone."

"I, uh, don't have that number. I came in yesterday, though. You might remember me. I said hello to Zara, and she took off like she'd seen a ghost."

"Hmm." There was a silence on the line. "And now you need to reach her?"

"I'd like to see her this morning. Is there any way you could text her my number? She'll know what it's about."

"Okay," Audrey said immediately. "Just let me grab a pen."

thirteen
zara

WHEN THE KNOCK came on my door, my heart shimmied for no good reason. And when I opened it, Audrey stood there alone. "Good morning!" she said, looking cheerful. "I brought you a bag of mini muffins and a message."

"Muffins?" my twin brother muttered from a prone position on the sofa where he was drowsing.

"They're not for you, Benny Boy," Audrey said, handing me a bag. "They're for the mystery man who wants to visit Zara." Audrey squinted at a note in her hand. "Dave Beringer. This is his number."

My heart shimmied again. "What did he say?" I asked with a squeak.

"Nothing, babe. Just that he wanted to see you, and that you'd know why."

I didn't, though. Yesterday he'd protested the very idea of having a child. And even though Benito had managed a calmer conversation with him last night, it still seemed unlikely that he'd suddenly warm up to having a daughter. "I'll call him. Thanks for the message. You'd better get back downstairs." Kieran Shipley would be manning the counter, unnerving the customers with his broody stare.

But Audrey didn't budge. She leaned on the door frame and studied me. "Who's the guy? I wouldn't ask, but you're clearly freaking out. Why is that?"

I hesitated, as if Nicole might overhear me. But she was asleep in her crib in the other room. "It's him," I said with a sigh. "Nicole's sperm donor."

Audrey's eyes lit up. "I *knew* it! Zara that man is *hot*. That red hair? Those muscles?"

Ben snorted from the sofa.

Audrey ignored him. "Gah! No wonder you couldn't resist him."

"It's not like I tried very hard," I pointed out.

"How'd he take the news?"

Slowly, I shook my head. "Not so well. But Benny met him last night at the bar, and he seemed to be getting his head around it."

"Good!" Audrey said, clapping her hands.

But I wasn't so sure. "Is it? I spent two years wondering if I'd ever see him again. But now I wonder if he should have stayed away. A bad father is worse than no father."

"I wouldn't know," Audrey said, and I mentally kicked myself. She had an *actual* sperm donor for a father. "But maybe it will all work out. And meanwhile, you can admire his pretty face."

Now it was my turn to snort. Dave wasn't pretty. Rugged was a better description.

Audrey dropped her voice to a near whisper. "The sex must have been amazing."

"As if I can even remember," I lied. Then I put a hand on her shoulder and nodded toward the stairs. "Go save our business from Kieran's stormy face. If there's news, I'll let you know."

"You'd better!" she whispered back.

After I shut the door I pulled out my phone to call him. Then I walked over to the sliding glass door and pulled it open, stepping out onto Benito's unfinished balcony. I shut the door again, so Benny couldn't eavesdrop.

There was nothing but an ancient, oversized lounge chair out here, and I sat down on it, stalling. I needed to call him, but I was a chicken. So I texted him instead.

Zara: *You were looking for me? —ZR*

David: *Good morning ZR. Can I call you?*

Gulp.

Instead of answering, I dialed him. He answered on the first ring. "This is David," the low voice said right into my ear.

An involuntary shiver climbed up my back. "Hi." We'd never spoken on the phone before, and I was suddenly self-conscious. "I know I gave you quite a shock yesterday."

"You sure did. I'm sure sorry if I was abrupt with you. Never had a conversation like that before."

"So..." I cleared my throat. "Do you have any other children?"

"God, no." He chuckled uneasily. "Anyway, I've had some time to get over myself. My plan for today had been to start researching things like child support. But then my sister surprised me by showing up in Vermont for a couple of days. And she was really hoping we could meet your little girl while she's here."

One hundred butterflies converged in my stomach. "Are you sure you want to do that before you confirm paternity? You seemed a little hesitant about that yesterday."

"Zara." His voice was low and steady. "Is it my child?"

"Yes," I whispered.

"Then even if my lawyer insists on confirming paternity, I already know what the test will say. And my sister is probably only here a day or so."

"Okay." I swallowed hard. "This is my morning off," I said, feeling like my life was rushing forward at a speed out of my control. "Nicole is napping right now, but she'll probably wake up around eleven."

"Then we'll come at eleven, if that's all right."

"Sure," I agreed, although the idea filled me with panic. I wasn't at all sure that having David walk into our lives was a good idea. "We're in an apartment over The Gin Mill. There's a separate entrance on the left-hand side. I'll see you at eleven."

"See you then."

With a shaking hand, I pocketed my phone. And then I did what anyone in my position would do. I went inside and kicked my sleepy twin brother in the thigh.

"Ow," he said, opening tired eyes. "What's the problem?"

"Dave Beringer, with an 'e,' wants to bring his sister over to meet Nicole."

"And you said yes?"

"Yeah. So get up. We have work to do."

"What kind of work?" He sat up and yawned. We'd sat up late into the night talking, and then he'd slept on his couch until Nicole got him up at six. Now they were both ready for a nap.

"We're panic cleaning."

"Bummer," he said. But he stood up to help me.

"Can you make that stack of toys look less trashy?" I asked, waving at the corner of the big room. "I'll tackle the kitchen."

There were breakfast dishes in the sink. I rinsed everything, and was just sponging down the countertops when I looked at the time. "Heck, I've got to change my clothes."

"Why?" Ben asked, opening the dishwasher to load it. "You don't need to dress up for this guy."

Seriously? Had my brother ever *met* a woman? I wondered what Dave would see when he looked at me. In the first place, I was heavier than I used to be. Nursing made me hungry all the time, so I hadn't lost all the baby weight. Also, I probably looked tired, because I was always tired.

And what would his sister see? I looked down to give myself a cursory scan. "I can't wear this T-shirt to meet his sister." It featured a drawing of a maple tree, with the words, *I'd Tap That*. "This shirt says, 'I sleep around.'"

"Nah!" Ben argued. "That shirt says, 'I'm from Vermont and I don't mind dorky jokes.'"

Either way, I wasn't taking any chances. "I need a quick shower. Will you listen for Nicole?"

"You think I'd just let her howl from the crib? Go already."

I was halfway out of the room when he delayed me with a question. "Hey, Z? Do you want me to stick around for this little visit?"

"Would you?" I begged immediately, even if it made me a chicken.

He grinned. "Anytime. I'll try to make my overflowing suitcase look less like a hobo's while you're in there."

"I really shouldn't care," I said.

He waved a hand. "Go do whatever it is you do when you're trying to impress your baby daddy."

"New rule. Never use the phrase 'baby daddy' again."

Benito laughed while I ran for the shower.

By eleven o'clock, I was showered and wearing my newest top, as well as lipstick and the barest hint of mascara.

"Makeup?" Ben said from the sofa. "You must have really liked this guy."

"Shut up." I would never admit that I had, in fact, really liked Dave Beringer. Who knew I'd been banging a professional athlete? "I'm just trying to look less like a trailer-park mom, here."

"Zara, we spent some years in a trailer park. Mom still lives in one. There's no shame in it. Nothing wrong with not having money."

"I know that," I groused. But who wouldn't want to put her best foot forward?

"I peeked in the bag Audrey brought. There's cookies." Benito pointed at a bag on the counter. "And, like, tiny yellow muffins. They're delicious."

"You can tell that just from looking?"

"Well…I tasted them, too."

"Uh-huh." I grabbed a plate out of the cupboard and opened the bag. I was arranging them prettily after starting a pot of coffee when someone buzzed from downstairs.

My stomach did a somersault, and I actually thought I might be sick. I hadn't been this terrified in a *long* time.

"Do you want me to go let them in?" Benito asked.

"Would you? I was just…" *having a nervous breakdown.*

My brother opened the apartment door and disappeared into the stairwell. My hands began to sweat, even though I knew I was focused on all the wrong things. I shouldn't care that seeing Dave again would be an ego-bruising experience. The real terror here was letting someone else into my child's life.

While I often felt guilty for robbing Nicole of living in a two-parent household, it was undeniably easier to be the only one in charge. In spite of my bossy family, the parenting decisions were all mine.

In principle, I knew that Nicole's father had a right to be involved with his child. Yet I knew I'd have trouble if anyone—no matter how well-meaning—wanted to tell me what to do.

My worry train was interrupted when the door opened and Dave himself stepped through—all six feet odd inches of him, those broad shoulders making Benito's apartment look smaller than it had a moment before.

And, damn him, he was every bit as attractive as I remembered. Maybe more so. He had a model's cheekbones, and a wide, full mouth. His expression was as serious as I'd ever seen it. "Hi, gorgeous. Thank you for letting us drop by."

Gorgeous. I never thought I'd hear him say that again.

"It's my pleasure," I said quickly. Then I wanted to kick myself for the breathy way it came out. And was I supposed to step up and hug him? Shake hands? What was the protocol for greeting your baby's father?

"I have to apologize in advance for my sis…"

"Move your butt, Davey!"

My eyes widened as a woman with hair even more red than Dave's pushed past my one-time hookup. In her arms was clutched a giant stuffed animal. A dog. And it too had red hair. "Is that an—"

"Irish setter!" Dave's sister said with a smile. "It was either that or the Great Dane. But he was even larger. And I didn't want you to hate me too much."

"You only want her to hate you a little bit," Dave said dryly.

His sister hip-checked him. "Introduce me, big brother."

"I'm Zara," I said in a hurry, taking care of the introductions myself. "And you met my brother Benito."

"I'm Bess." Suddenly my hands were full of a giant dog, and she'd wrapped her arms around me. "It's an honor to meet you."

An honor? After she let me go, I set the stuffed animal down on the floor beside the sofa, where it assumed a lazy position, its cute chin on its paws. "Nicole is going to lose her mind over the dog," I said, swallowing hard. Who could resist a giant stuffy? "Thank you. That was really sweet."

"I'm just getting started," Bess said, rubbing her hands together.

"Bess," Dave cautioned gently. Then he sighed.

She *was* a little terrifying, even if I knew she was only being enthusiastic. I gestured toward the kitchen. "Would you like some coffee? I also have muffins and cookies. In fact—take one now because I'll probably make them disappear when Nicole wakes up. I don't really let her eat sugar." I was babbling now. *Awesome.*

"I would love a cup of coffee," Dave said. He gave me a little smile, as if trying to tell me that he knew this was awkward as all hell.

Sprinting to the other end of the room, I poured a couple of cups of coffee and grabbed the plate of baked goods.

But when I carried the mug to Dave, I realized I didn't even know how he took his coffee. "I have milk and sugar."

"Black is just fine," he said in a quiet voice. "Do you want us to come back another time? If she's napping..."

"She'll wake up really soon," I said. "The big nap happens later in the day."

Bess waved off the coffee, so I handed it to my brother, who was quietly watching this drama unfold. Bess took a tiny lemon muffin off the plate and took a bite. "Yum! Are these from your coffee shop?"

"They are. This is Audrey's recipe. I'm more of a chocolate girl."

"It must be hard to run a business and take care of a baby," she said, nibbling on the muffin.

"I like being my own boss," I said quickly. "And my family has been really great." Single-motherhood was exhausting, of course, but I was never admitting that to Bess. *Aunt* Bess, really.

Weird.

"This is a cool apartment," she said, glancing around with a smile.

"It will be when it's done," I said, hating the half-constructed look we had going on in here. The floors were already gleaming, and the old leaded windows had been restored to their former glory. But the kitchen was a work in progress. The cabinets were new but the countertop was currently a big piece of plywood. "This is Benito's place, and you can see that he's still putting on the finishing touches. Nicole and I have been staying here because he was away for a few months."

"But it's yours for as long as you need," my brother added quickly.

"It's been great to be close to my business." The tension was killing me, and I couldn't stop talking. "My mother takes care of Nicole while I'm working. And this way I've been able to pop in during my work day. But I'm looking at houses up the hill in town. Nicole needs a yard to play in when she gets bigger."

Gah. Somehow I clamped my jaw together and shut the hell up. My housing woes weren't something I wanted to draw attention to.

"Davey," Bess prompted. "Please give Zara that bag in your hand."

He looked down at the shopping bag he was holding as if he'd never seen it before. "Of course." He stepped forward and handed me the bag, which was from BabyGap. "My sister shoots first and asks questions later. But she brought you a few things just for fun."

The bag was surprisingly heavy in my hand. She must have bought out the entire store. "Wow," I said, sitting on the sofa. I opened the bag and pulled out a pink snowsuit with bear ears on the hood. Size 2T. "This is adorable."

"The Detroit store had all their fall stuff out already," Bess said. She was practically bouncing up and down at the other end of Ben's L-shaped sofa.

I dipped into the bag again and came up with three fall outfits for Nicole, each one more beautiful than the last. She was going to be the best-dressed toddler in Vermont. "Thank you so much," I said for what felt like the hundredth time.

"She's just really excited," Dave said, sipping from his mug.

"We don't have any family," Bess said. "Except each other. So, sorry. You're it."

I was just trying to get my head around that when I heard a squawk from the other room. And for some reason I leapt out of my seat at Nicole's first sound—as if jumping to attention would advertise what an excellent parent I was. "Excuse me a second," I said, grateful to get away for a moment from the unbearable tension.

Sprinting into the bedroom, I looked down at Nicole's grumpy little face. She was sprawled out on her back, her chubby legs propped up on the crib's bars. Even though I had a fan running at low speed in here, she looked hot.

Midday naps in July, though. What can a baby expect? "Come here, sweetie," I whispered.

She raised her arms but did not roll over. I leaned over the side and tugged her off the mattress, lifting her into my arms. "We have visitors," I said quietly, moving her to the changing table. I swapped her diaper for a dry one and finger-combed her feathery hair. The color was coppery, brighter than her handsome father's.

The fact that he was sitting right in the living room made my stomach twist with uncertainty.

He'd better love you, baby girl, I thought, even though it terrified me to share her. *Because you're the best there is.* My baby was dazed from her nap, but she was still the most beautiful person I'd ever seen, and surely the best thing I'd made of my life. She yawned, showing a line of tiny, perfect teeth, her soft arms stretching on the changing pad.

I lifted her again, holding her against my chest. And I paused for a moment in the privacy of the tiny bedroom, praying that our lives weren't about to get too complicated.

fourteen

dave

I ATE a mini muffin while I waited to see my daughter for the very first time.

This morning, while Bess had been refreshing her makeup, I'd actually Googled "fifteen-month-old," because I had no clue what size child that was. The sites I'd found had taught me that at this age, they're still babies. But some of them can walk or say one word at a time.

If there was a more clueless man in the world than I was, I hoped I'd never meet him.

So there I sat, listening to my sister make small talk with Benito while I tried not to panic. After a couple of long minutes Zara emerged from the little hallway to the back of the apartment. Against her chest, she held a small person with chubby arms. The baby's cheek lay against Zara's shoulder, so I couldn't see her face.

But that *hair*. Suddenly I was four years old again, watching my angry mother stomp around our little shitbox of a house with baby Bess wailing in her arms.

I fought off an honest-to-God shudder.

Nobody seemed to notice my distress. They were all watching the baby. Zara sat down on the sofa beside her brother, her daughter settling into her lap. And Bess made a little gasp of excitement.

"There she is," Zara's brother said in a low voice. "Hi, princess."

The baby turned slowly toward her uncle's voice, and I saw her face for the first time. She had pink cheeks and sleepy eyes.

The room was silent as Zara adjusted Nicole on her lap. "That's Bess," she said, gesturing toward my sister. "And Dave."

I swallowed hard, hoping nobody could sense my terror. But the baby didn't even look in my direction.

"And your crazy Uncle Benito, of course."

"Nicole!" He encouraged. "Say…Uncle Ben!"

"Baba-ba!" The baby said. Her soft little voice made chills rise up on my arms.

"Almost!" Zara's brother grinned. "You could try for just *Ben.* I'm not picky."

He was making jokes, while I sat over here having an out-of-body experience. What was, after all, the proper reaction to meeting the child you never knew you had? I noticed how the width of her shoulders was about the same as the length of my hand. And that her elbows dimpled in a baby-like way.

She was seriously cute. I wasn't a heartless person. I was just way, way out of my depth here.

Benito reached for his niece, taking her onto his lap, and she leaned against his chest as if he were her own personal cushion.

Zara smiled, looking more relaxed, finally. As if watching her brother with her baby was the best thing in the world. And maybe it was. I never meant to throw a wrench into Zara's life, but it comforted me a little bit to know she had her family around her.

"Ben has been out of town for three months, and that's a fifth of her life," Zara was saying. "I'd been worried that Nicole wouldn't remember him. But when she saw him this morning she ran over and gave him a look that basically said, 'Where ya been, man? Let's party.'"

Benito put a hand on the baby's back and patted it, as if it were the easiest thing in the world.

"Oh, Zara," my sister said, swallowing hard. "She's so *beautiful.*"

I didn't say anything. I didn't trust myself. I'd never doubted that Zara's baby would be beautiful. But it sure wasn't because of me.

My sister got up and fetched the plush dog from its spot on the floor. "Hi, Nicole," she said, kneeling down on the rug beside the coffee table. "I've got someone here who wants to meet you."

Nicole lifted her still-sleepy face from Benito's shoulder. When she spotted the dog she began to wiggle toward the floor.

Ben set her down on her feet, and Nicole put one chubby hand onto the coffee table. Then she began to move, clutching the table in one hand, waddling around it toward Bess and the big stuffy.

"Look at you! Walking like a big girl!" Bess's eyes were shiny.

In order to reach my sister, the baby had to pass me. And I was so trapped inside my own head, just trying to take it all in, I didn't realize that my knees were blocking her way around the coffee table. She stopped, put a surprisingly warm little hand on my bare knee and turned to look up at me.

When I got a look at her expression, a small bark of shocked laughter escaped from my throat. Her face was miniature, but it was all business. *Outta my way, mister.* And her *eyes*—dark brown, with an intensity that was all her mother. The familiarity stole my breath.

I moved my knees in a hurry, and she toddled past.

"Isn't the likeness amazing?" My sister asked.

"Yeah, to her *mother*." I looked up to where Zara sat on the sofa. "She just gave me a...Zara glare."

Zara's eyes widened. She gave me a smile that was a little less terrified than before, and I felt my chest flood with an emotion I had no name for.

When she made her way over to Bess, Nicole sort of flung herself onto the dog, which was at least twice her size. My sister laughed, and I saw tears in her eyes. Bess put a tentative hand on the baby's soft hair and whispered something sweet to her.

I swear to God I'd never seen my sister fuss over a baby before. Didn't know she liked babies. Then again, I'd never really asked her.

And, crap, my own eyes began to feel hot.

I took a deep inhale and let it out slowly. *My baby.* I tried the words out in my head for the first time. Those impossible words.

But she was right there on the rug, her little arms squeezing the stuffy.

Deep breaths.

While Bess was focused on the baby, I snuck glances at Zara. I couldn't imagine what was in her head right now. Did she even *want* me to meet her child? She was probably just humoring us. She'd never wanted anything to do with me outside of the bedroom. The Zara I'd known before would have kicked us out already.

But I had to admit that this new Zara seemed different. She was tentative. Watchful. I hated to wonder if that was my fault, if I'd knocked her off her game by showing up here again.

Her eyes suddenly met mine, and I realized that she'd been sneaking looks at me, too. We both looked away at the same time.

Meanwhile, Nicole was becoming more comfortable with my sister. More animated. She stood on her stubby legs and gathered the dog's floppy midsection into her arms. Then she tried to walk with him.

It didn't work out so well. She stumbled twice, Bess catching her each time. Bess got closer, trying to hold the stuffy so Nicole could grip it better. And I saw Nicole raise her eyes to Bess's, and then decide she didn't want a stranger's help. She looked around for her mother, wearing a suddenly cranky face.

"Right here," Zara said quickly.

The baby did her little waddle—butt out, hands up—back in her mother's direction. And when she reached Zara's knees, she was scooped into her lap. Then Nicole grabbed the edge of Zara's T-shirt and began to tug it upwards.

"Um…" Zara chuckled, looking suddenly uncomfortable. She used an elbow to pin her shirt down against the baby's attempts to lift it. "Benny? Would you grab me that afghan behind you?"

He handed over the blanket, and I watched her drape it over Nicole's head. The baby squawked, and I still didn't know what was going on. Zara reached underneath the blanket, wriggling to adjust something. "We're still nursing," she said, which finally clued me in. "It's probably time to wean, but I just haven't gotten around to it."

She gave me a nervous little glance, but I sure as hell didn't have an opinion about nursing babies. And I wouldn't have voiced one if I had.

Once again, Bess made small talk by asking Benito about the mill and by picking up our coffee mugs to take them over to the kitchen area.

"I got those," Benito said. "You sit."

There was movement under the blanket, which was suddenly flung away by one little arm. It was hard to blame the kid for pushing the blanket off her face on an eighty-degree day. But Zara's cheekbones flushed pink as her baby made herself more comfortable by baring Zara's breast. She'd put her little palm up against the swell of Zara's boob.

And—whoa. Zara had expanded in the chest department. She was curvy now.

The baby's hand wandered off her mother's breast and into Zara's hair, which she wrapped around her little fingers as she suckled.

I was witnessing something intimate and touching in a way that seemed entirely foreign to me. Goosebumps broke out on the back of my neck.

I'd never been in so far over my head.

fifteen
zara

SO THERE I WAS, tit in the breeze, Nicole slurping away like a starving baby while my brother laughed and my former lover averted his gaze.

If I'd learned anything the past two years it was that humility and motherhood were bosom buddies.

"Anybody heard any good jokes today?" I asked into the uncomfortable silence.

Bess dabbed at her eyes. "You're a good sport, Zara. Thank you for letting us come over today."

"It's my pleasure," I said, although it was a lie. I couldn't think of a more stressful moment in my life, including the scary day when I'd taken a home pregnancy test and had seen a plus sign.

Dave leaned forward and grabbed another of Audrey's mini muffins. "This is a cool old mill. When was it built?"

"In the 1890s," my brother said, rising from the couch. "From over here you can see the original hydraulic system."

Dave followed my brother out onto the terrace, and I could hear Ben's voice as he pointed to the old water wheel below.

Bess and I were left alone, and I let myself exhale.

"You must be freaking out," she whispered.

The observation caught me off-guard, and I laughed. "So much for my acting career."

She grinned. "Bumping into him must have been a shock."

"I don't know which of us was more stunned," I admitted. "I searched for him, you know. Benito did, too."

"Dave said."

I shrugged. "Never meant to drop a bomb like that on anyone. I was at least as afraid as him."

Bess sighed. "Dave said he was kind of abrupt."

"It was a shock," I said, dismissing it.

"Sure, but..." She glanced toward the terrace and back at me. "We had kind of a harrowing childhood. He has a pretty dismal view of family life."

Wonderful. I kept my face impassive, but she probably saw me flinch.

"Listen." She leaned forward. "He's a good man. He just might need a little time to get his head around the idea. He used to talk about you, you know."

"He did?" I failed to keep the surprise out of my voice.

"Whenever he got drunk and mellow. He'd say, 'I met this girl in Vermont. Did I tell you about Zara?'"

All the hair stood up on the back of my neck. The story I'd told myself was that Dave forgot about me the minute he left Vermont. And I'd sort of needed that to be true, so that I wouldn't think wistful thoughts about him. "We had a lot of fun together," I said slowly. "But that was a long time ago."

Bess's green gaze looked thoughtful. "I'm just saying, it meant something to him. He's freaked out right now, but he'll come around. He's an excellent caretaker."

"Of who?" I whispered.

"*Me*. He saved me." Her eyes got shiny. "When he was fourteen, he hit himself in the face with a wrench. Four times."

"God, *why?*" I gasped.

"So that someone would *notice*," she said quickly. "Our father only hit us where it wouldn't show. I got the worst of it, because I fought back more than Dave did. It was terrible. So he needed to make a point, that's why he beat himself up. That same week, the school intervened. Our grandparents had to step up and open their home. He broke his own cheekbone. But our father never hit me again."

"Jesus, Bess!" Dave hissed, re-entering the room. "Nobody wants to hear about that."

Bess flushed, but her eyes argued with him. And her brother stared her down, quietly threatening hellfire if she kept talking about their childhood.

It was almost like I could hear their argument flying back and forth through the air. Because I'd had those sibling standoffs, too. Benito and I had engaged in more silent battles than I could count.

My brother bailed them out of their argument by changing the subject. "Bess, have you been to Vermont before?"

"I can't say I have."

"When Nicky has had her fill, we can all get outside for a few minutes. I'll give you the nickel tour of the banks of the Winooski River. Or you and I could go down now."

"Great idea," she said, taking the bait. She rose from the sofa, not looking at Dave.

They were obviously trying to give me a moment alone with Dave, though I wasn't sure either of us was ready for one.

"We'll join you in just a minute," I said. "Nicole loves to get outside."

"See you down there." My brother headed for the door.

A silence settled over the room as soon as Benito and Bess exited. Avoiding Dave, I looked down at Nicole, where she lazily nursed in my arms. One of her chubby hands had found a lock of my hair, which she was twisting. When she'd been really little and nursing all the time, I'd had to pin my hair up or she'd tie me in knots.

A shadow fell over us, and then the sofa depressed under Dave's weight as he sat down beside me. I held my breath.

"She's beautiful, Zara." His voice was so soft I might have missed it if all my senses weren't dialed up to eleven. "Just like you."

"Thank you," I said stiffly. And Nicole chose that moment to pop off of my nipple and struggle to sit up. I swiftly tucked my boob away and smoothed down my shirt. The baby spent a moment studying Dave. My pulse pounded in my ears, and I waited to see if she'd climb into his lap. Nicole *loved* men, in spite of the fact that she didn't have a daddy. She gravitated toward their deep voices, and never showed any fear. Mommy's girl.

I wondered what he'd do if she approached him. Would he pick her up and smile? Or would that look of hesitation stay on his face?

And which of those two things did I want? I was at war with myself.

Nicole didn't approach him, though. Dave wasn't doing anything particularly entertaining—just watching her. So Nicole decided to wiggle toward the floor. I set her down and then found Dave studying me.

"Hey. I wanted to apologize again for being rude yesterday," he whispered as Nicole wandered back over to the giant stuffy Bess had brought. "I was shaken up."

"I can only imagine."

"I'll bet you're a little shaken up, too, though."

"Yeah," I said quickly, meeting his green eyes. And, wow. I never thought I'd be trapped in that emerald gaze again. "Yesterday was like seeing a ghost."

He smiled suddenly, and I felt a shiver of familiarity. Then his smile faded. "I'm sorry if I was a dick."

"It's okay. I get it." I cleared my throat. The tension between us was oppressive, so I changed the topic. "Your sister is great."

"In small doses," he corrected, and I laughed. "Your brothers really look out for you, too."

"That would be better in small doses, too," I agreed. "They love me, but my family is bossy as fu…*heck*," I corrected quickly.

He grinned. And then he did something even more unexpected. He reached over and pulled me into a brief, tight hug. "It's good to see you again," he whispered right into my ear. "I can't imagine the time you've had."

The next moment he released me, but it took a few seconds for my brain to catch up. I was still stuck on the feel of his hard chest against my body and the familiar scent of his aftershave. "I…" I stammered, my brain fogged. "It's been..." *Focus, Zara.* "I'm doing well. You don't have to feel guilty."

"I do, though." His voice was gruff.

"No," I shook my head. "Don't. A lot has changed for me these two years, but that's not a bad thing." It wasn't easy for me to explain. "Becoming a mother wasn't something I'd been considering—yet. I was kind of a wild teenager. I may have mentioned that."

He smiled broadly, and it changed his face into a more welcoming place. It was so easy to smile right back at him.

"Anyway... I didn't think I was a maternal person. So at first I was terrified. But then I realized that I was her *person*." I checked his face, and he was listening intently. "That sounds like a weird way to put it. But it was me or nobody, and that was bracing..."

Nicole pushed past me and toddled over toward the stuffed dog again.

I realized I was rambling. "I'm not expressing myself well. My brother Damien says that he had to become a soldier before he figured himself out. And for me, it was like taking care of a newborn was my own personal boot camp. I just dug in and learned how everything worked, and I did as good a job as anyone else."

"I'm sure you did," he said.

"The thing is—I loved it. She slowed me down. I used to spend time worrying about my lack of direction and all my mistakes. But I don't anymore. And now I co-own a growing business. Go figure." I took a breath and realized I'd been talking about myself for a long time now. So I sprang off the couch. "Shall we walk outdoors? It's a nice day."

Nicole looked up when I mentioned going outside. She pushed up onto her feet and headed for the door. I followed her and slipped some shoes onto my feet. Then I had a moment of wondering whether I should try to put shoes on Nicole. She'd prefer to be barefoot, and I'd prefer to avoid the wrestling match. But I didn't want to look like a hick who didn't dress her child appropriately.

My baby let out an impatient squawk, so I lifted her and decided she didn't need shoes. "Okay, toots." I opened the door.

Dave followed me downstairs and outside, where we spotted Benito in the distance, showing Bess the cornerstone of the Gin Mill building, laid in 1804.

"Nice place," Dave said to break the silence.

"It belongs to my brother, Alec. He opened the bar first. Then Audrey and I opened the coffee shop."

"Audrey is the blonde?" he asked.

"That's right," I said. "She's my business partner."

"Is she still dating your ex?"

I looked at him with surprise. "They're getting married in two weeks. How did you know that?"

"I remember her from the bar, that's all." He frowned at me. "So you own a business with your ex's fiancé?"

"Sure. She's my best friend now. It's not weird." My gaze challenged him to disagree.

His said, *Well, okay. If you say so*. Out loud he said, "I'm going to pay child support, just as soon as my lawyer educates me on how that all works."

"Dave," I argued instinctively. "I didn't ask you for money."

"Never said you had. But I can afford it, and there's no reason for you to object."

We stopped right there on the lawn, staring each other down. The familiar push and pull of our summer together seemed to have risen up like a spirit between us. I saw the same bossy spark in his eye, and it was so familiar that I couldn't look away. The masculine curve of his cheekbone. The determined set of his mouth. It was just the same.

And I *ached*.

"What do you want from me?" I finally asked.

He smiled. "I'm pretty sure that's my line. Lawyers can only tell me so much. I need to know what you want from *me*. How I can help you. I have a few ideas, but it's better if you let me know."

I turned away, walking slowly toward my brother and Bess again. Nicole had already made it to Benito, her little hand on his knee.

What did I want from Dave? *Nothing* was the first answer that popped into my head. There were already too many people I owed. My heart was a traitorous bitch, though. If I opened my mouth to say so, the word *everything* might come tumbling out instead.

And that wasn't on offer, and never would be.

"I'll think about it," I said stiffly. "How long are you in town, anyway?" By which I meant, *How often do I have to look at you and try not to remember how good we were together?*

"Until the second week of August. Then I go to training camp with my team."

"Oh. Okay." Six whole weeks. His offer of child support was something I would have to consider. I shouldn't turn down the money. Even I wasn't stubborn enough to refuse a college fund for Nicole.

Yet I wondered why he was so eager to pay, even without being asked. Maybe it was his way of soothing his conscience. If he sent us a check every month, he could tell himself he was a good dad. He could put some distance between us and still hold his head up high.

If that was his plan, I'd just have to be okay with it.

sixteen
dave

I HADN'T MEANT to get into a big discussion with Zara about money. But I hadn't known how else to bring it up. She'd pushed back at me as if on instinct. And when I saw the fiery look she gave me, it took me right back.

If we had ever been a couple—a real one—we would probably have been the sort that fights like crazy. If we'd even tried to have a relationship it probably would have flamed out and burnt up within months. Maybe that was a Beringer family trait. All I could remember of my parents together was the yelling, and my mother crying.

Zara fell silent as we grew nearer to her brother and my sister. The baby wandered a few feet away from them. She toddled through the grass, back toward us, her bare feet occasionally tripping her up. But she didn't seem to mind the occasional stumble. She steadied herself with her hands on the ground, then continued on her way.

Nicole stopped at my feet and put a hand out, steadying herself on my bare knee. I cleared my throat. "Well, hello."

She didn't look up, though. I was just a handy balancing place. Her gaze was in the distance.

A moment later, I saw why. A big, muscular dog was sniffing the grass some yards off. Nicole made a squeak of interest. And the dog looked up, lifting its gaze and spotting her.

And then I saw it happen as if in slow motion. The dog stiffened. Then he leaned forward in a burst of speed, running toward the baby.

I didn't even think. It was just a game-time decision. I bent over and plucked her off the ground. A moment later, I was holding a baby awkwardly by the armpits while an enthusiastic dog stood on his hind legs in front of me, trying to reach her.

Nicole squawked. She was heavier than I'd expected her to be. I lowered her a little ways, tucking her against my body, folding her legs against my chest so they weren't dangling. My arm shielded her from the damn dog.

At close range, her brown eyes blinked at me, surprised. My own heart sped up as I met my baby's trusting gaze.

She let out another squeak. It surprised me, and I smiled.

"Rexie, sit!" Zara ordered. "Dave, it's okay. He won't hurt her."

"Seriously?" I looked down at the slobbering beast on the ground. He was alternately sitting down and then popping up to bark.

"He's my friend Kieran's dog. He only *looks* like a beast."

I hesitated. "He's not very well-behaved." What the hell did people want with dogs, anyway?

Bess laughed, and Zara reached for her daughter, lifting the baby out of my arms and then lowering her to the grass. The dog stopped barking immediately. He knocked Nicole right off her feet and then licked her face. The baby retaliated by grabbing his floppy ears with both hands and laughing.

I was still experiencing a fight-or-flight reaction. Dogs bugged the shit out of me.

My sister made a clicking noise with her tongue. "Oh, Davey. Still not over your fear of dogs, huh?"

"They don't haunt my dreams, Bess," I grunted. "I just don't trust them."

She sighed, patting the spot between my collarbone and my shoulder. "A dog bit him when he was in sixth grade. He has a scar."

Zara and I locked eyes. And for a second or two we shared a glance of amusement, as we undoubtedly had the same thought—

that Zara was acquainted with that scar. I distinctly remembered her kissing her way across that shoulder on more than one occasion.

"Oh, Jesus," Benito said slowly. "The, uh, dog isn't the real threat right now. Heads up, Z."

Zara turned to look, and then made an exasperated sound under her breath.

"You want me to head her off?" Benito didn't wait for an answer. He began jogging toward the parking lot, where a car had just pulled in.

"Too late." Zara sighed.

A woman in a rather prim sundress got out of the car. She took in Benito and then Zara, raising a hand to wave. Then she started toward the group of us.

Benito headed her off, hugging her and then nudging her back toward the parking lot.

"Something the matter?" Bess asked.

"That's, uh, my mother," Zara said. "She doesn't usually come by on Saturdays. But Benito just got into town last night, and he hasn't visited her yet."

"And you haven't told her that I'd turned up," I guessed.

Looking guilty, Zara shook her head. "Didn't quite get around to it. Thought I'd get her drunk first." She put a hand to her head. "Pretend I didn't say that. I'm just a little stressed out right now. Alec must have ratted me out."

"Why don't Dave and I give you some space?" my sister suggested. "You've been very generous with your morning already."

"That's nice of you, but she's already overpowered the family law-enforcement officer." Zara sighed.

"*Mom,*" Benito said. "Just give Zara an hour to—"

Mama Rossi wasn't listening, though. She was already briskly walking in our direction. She lifted her chin in what I was now sure was a genetic Rossi trait and marched right towards me.

"Oh dear," my sister whispered under her breath.

Zara paled. The only person who was completely and totally at ease was the baby, who was now stroking the dog's silky ears while the beast panted lazily on its back.

"Zara," Mrs. Rossi said, somewhat breathlessly. "Is it true that introductions are in order?" Her sharp eyes grazed my sister and landed squarely on yours truly, narrowing as she looked me up and down.

"Mother," Zara said in a low voice. "I owe you a call, but it's been a really busy morning. Could we maybe not discuss this right now?" She pointed her gaze down to Nicole.

Mrs. Rossi leaned over and plucked Nicole off the grass. She smoothed down the toddler's hair and sighed. "Don't let the dog lick you, sweetie. Yucky." She tucked the baby on her hip and then she thrust a hand out toward me. "Maria Rossi. I'm Zara's mother. And you are...?"

I shook her hand. "David Beringer, ma'am. It's a pleasure to meet you." Although it wasn't, really. I could only imagine what this woman thought of me. In fact, I'm pretty sure that she summed up my whole life story in one glance. Rough kid. Loner. Not the marrying kind.

Not the *fathering* kind.

Maria Rossi dropped my hand and whirled on her daughter. "So it's true?"

"*Mom.*" Zara's tone was a warning. She and her mother regarded one another with laser eyes, as if thirty years of strife were ringing between the two of them. Zara had a fiery family. I would have been amused if I weren't so tense.

"Well," Zara's mother said in a tone that indicated she'd just decided something. "He'll come to Sunday luncheon next weekend. We'll have a nice opportunity to get to know each other."

Zara balked. "We don't know if David is free on Sunday next week."

"Oh, sure he is," my sister sang. Of course Bess had to pipe up. "He can make himself available."

Zara's eyes flared, and I wondered if a three-way cat fight was out of the question. I hadn't seen a gaze that murderous even on O'Doul during the playoffs.

"It's settled, then," Mrs. Rossi said. "Next Sunday, one o'clock. After church." She kissed Nicole on the head. Then she thrust the baby into Zara's arms, turned on her heel, and began to march away. "Benito!" she called. "Come with me."

Her son hesitated a moment. "I tried," he said to his sister.

"I know," Zara grumbled. "Go already."

When he left, it was just the three of us. No—four. The baby wiggled in Zara's arms, asking to be let down even though the dog had wandered off.

"I shouldn't have put my two cents in," my sister said to Zara. "I'm sorry."

Zara's mouth relaxed by a degree. She gave Bess a wry smile, then looked up at me. "You don't have to come to Sunday lunch. They're just going to interrogate you."

"I'm not afraid of your family," I told her. "If it makes your life easier for me to go, I'll go. If it makes your life easier if I stay away, then that's what I'll do."

"Hmm. It's a tough call."

She set the wriggling baby down, and Nicole took off across the grass. Zara turned to watch her, but Bess said, "I've got her," and followed the baby.

Zara faced me again. "If you show up, they'll interrogate you. If you don't show up, they'll interrogate me. But I'm sort of used to it."

"Maybe I should just let 'em get all their shots in at once," I suggested. "It's okay."

"It's your funeral," she said, and Bess laughed over her shoulder.

It was trippy to be standing in the sunlight with my sister, having a conversation with Zara. *My worlds collide*. "All right. Where am I meeting you next Sunday at one o'clock?"

"The Rossi Farm, on State Road 17. I'll text you a picture of the house, okay? GPS would send you to the neighbor's."

"All right."

"And you can still change your mind." Her eyes wandered to

Nicole and Bess, who were admiring some petunias. "Right now I should feed her some lunch."

"Hey." I put a hand on her shoulder, and she looked quickly up at me, startled. She felt warm and solid under my hand, and I gave her shoulder a little squeeze. "Hang in there. I'm sorry to cause drama."

She licked her lips. "I've been causing drama my whole life. My mother isn't wrong about that. Pretty sure this isn't your fault."

"Pretty sure it's both our faults," I pointed out.

She smiled, and more sparks of our former chemistry leapt between us. That kept happening. The urge to kiss her goodbye was strong. But Bess was watching me, and I didn't want any more commentary than I was already going to get.

"Later," I said, giving Zara a quick hug instead. She felt so fucking good that it was torture to release her.

"I'll text you," she said, turning away to collect her daughter from Bess.

"You do that."

We weren't in the car for twenty seconds before Bess turned to me with a giant smile. "She suits you."

"What? Babies don't suit me. You're high."

"I wasn't talking about the baby. Your baby game needs work, for sure. I was talking about Zara. It's obvious that you two are a good match."

My snort was loud. "A good match for what? Complicating each other's lives? Two years ago we had a lot of sex. I don't know why you're reading so much into it."

"How many times have you thought about her since then?"

Well, shit. That question was a big trap. The answer was many, many times. But just because the month I'd spent with Zara had been one of the most erotic times in my entire life, didn't mean we were soulmates.

"Your silence says everything, big brother."

"You can draw whatever conclusions you want. And you know I'm going to help her. But I can't imagine why you're so quick to assume that this changes anything for me. A week ago you gave me the speech about keeping my head down and focusing on my sport. And I'm good at that. Families are not my expertise. Why would you try to rewrite the script like I'm some Mr. Nice Guy?"

"Anyone can have a family, David. Do you really think it's not possible for you? You think you're some kind of mutant who could never be half of a couple?"

"Did you *miss* the part of our lives where our family life was a shit show?" My voice got all high and crazy, but my sister should really know better. "We did *not* survive that childhood with sunny ideas of family life. I don't see you settling down. You don't even *date,* Bess. Because we both know better than to try."

My sister made a choking noise. "I rarely date because I'm too busy building my empire to look for Mr. Right! Not because I'm fatally flawed! You really think I can't attract a well-adjusted guy? Thanks for the vote of confidence."

"It's not *you*. That's not what I meant."

"Then what did you mean?"

"The pattern. The history. We grew up assuming that everyone's mother turned tricks for her next hit. And every father slapped his kids around."

Bess didn't say anything for a minute. "I also grew up knowing that brothers were awesome, and that somebody always had my back. I don't see why you and I shouldn't end up happy, Davey. We deserve what everyone else has."

That shut me up, because of *course* Bess deserved the moon and stars. But our past had left me wondering if there was such a thing as a happy family. And if chasing the illusion only made you into a sucker.

I hated to be a sucker.

"Are you going to meet her family?" Bess asked. "I think it's important that you show your face. Right now Zara has everything handled, and your daughter is only a baby..."

Your daughter. The words still sounded like a foreign language.

"But meeting the family sets an important precedent. That you won't duck your responsibility to your child. Who knows what could happen down the road? If Zara hits a patch of trouble, they might need to know who you are."

"I'll go," I said quietly. "I'm not ducking anything."

She reached over and patted my arm. "I know. I wouldn't let you, anyway."

seventeen
zara

THE NEXT DAY I did not, in fact, text Dave the details of Sunday dinner. And then I didn't text them on the day after that, either.

For starters, I just couldn't picture him sitting down for ham and pasta with my family on Sunday, while my brothers and my uncles asked pointed questions.

But even if Dave was willing to withstand that sort of trial, I wasn't sure I wanted him there. I'd feel so exposed, sitting there beside him while my family looked on. Because the truth was that I'd often wished for a man in my life who would come to Sunday luncheon, drink beer with my brothers, and hold the baby.

If Dave was sitting there beside me, stepping into that role only for a day, I was afraid that everyone would be able to see right through me. Old yearnings would rise off me like mist.

My tough-girl cred would take a serious hit. I didn't want that. So I was stalling.

Wednesday morning it was my turn to open up the shop. I took three early days and Audrey took three. And we traded off on Mondays, which kept things even.

At five a.m.—per our usual routine—I tapped on my brother Alec's apartment door, which was right upstairs from mine. Still mostly asleep, Alec shuffled in his boxer shorts down the staircase.

Without a word, he went into my apartment (really Benito's, of course) and lay down on the sofa for the next leg of his slumber.

That's where I left him, as well as Nicole asleep in her crib. I tiptoed out again, heading down the stairs and across the lot to the bakery.

In an hour Nicole would wake up and babble to herself until her sleepy uncle managed to stagger into her room to greet her. They would hang out together for an hour or so until my mother arrived for her babysitting shift.

This was my patchwork support system. It allowed me to run a business. On the other days—when I went to work at ten or noon—Nicole went to a daycare in town.

Going to work at five in the morning wasn't ideal, but I enjoyed the solitude more than I'd expected to. The first thing I did was preheat the oven and stir together a batter for muffins. I enjoyed moving through the early morning stillness of the coffee shop routine, flipping on lights, warming the espresso machine.

There was tremendous satisfaction in owning a business. Every month Audrey and I learned a little more about what worked and what didn't. How to predict which days would be busy and which would be slow. How to price our products and how to entice clients to try new things.

Someday I hoped my daughter would go to college and be a scholar. I hoped she had her pick of careers. But I was going to show her what resourcefulness looked like. It looked like four-dozen muffin trays ready to go into the oven before six a.m.

July was berry season. So I stirred local blueberries into the first batches of muffins. Audrey had taught me the rudiments of baking, but I'd learned a lot myself. When fall came, I couldn't wait to try some new recipes with the pears from my family's orchards.

As the daylight strengthened outside the kitchen window, I cooled the muffins and took delivery of the bagels we sourced from a bakery in Montpelier. I measured out the dry ingredients for the cookies that Audrey would make when she arrived later.

Then I went into the front of the shop and patrolled the tables and chairs for cleanliness. I restocked the coffee grinder and checked our supply of milk and other mixers. I made coffee, its rich scent as familiar as breathing. I took the chalk to our signboards and listed blueberry muffins as today's seasonal pastry.

One of the beams where I wrote pithy sayings had been smudged, so I cleaned it with a cloth, then wrote a new saying in its place. *If I'm silent, I might be furious, or maybe I'm just chillin'. May the odds be ever in your favor.*

I loved improvising this way. Putting my own personality on the walls. It was tough to run a business, but also fun and freeing. Just like single-motherhood.

The first customers—as well as Kieran, my part-time barista—began showing up right after I flipped the sign to "open" at seven. Then the real hustle began. For the commuting crowd I made lattes and poured coffee. I sliced bagels and spread cream cheese while chatting about the weather and the Red Sox.

Kieran was a quiet presence beside me. He was a great worker, hustling to refill the platters of baked goods from the trays in the kitchen, pouring coffee orders, anticipating our customers' needs. He did everything well, except for small talk. Every day I watched various women try to catch his eye or engage him in conversation.

Good luck, sister, I'd think. But it never really worked.

Five hours went by in a rush, and I took off my apron just as Audrey came through the door. "Morning, sunshine!" she sang. "How's tricks?"

"Not bad. Do you need me to stay a little longer while you get the biscotti on?"

She looked around at our moderate crowd. "Nah. It'll only take me a few minutes. Go on. It's yoga day, right?"

"Sure. Thanks."

Audrey waved me away, looking unconcerned. She slung an arm around Kieran and greeted him. He gave her a quick kiss on the temple and then motored off to grab more bagels from the back.

And then I walked out the door. Going to yoga a couple of times a week always made me feel guilty. It was stolen time. I texted my mother from the parking lot. *Thinking about going to yoga.*

You should, she replied immediately. *The princess is napping. I'm reading the new Jill Shalvis. Go.*

All right. Thank you! I replied. The words "thank you" were the two most common in my vocabulary. I thanked my mom, Alec, Benito, my uncles, Audrey… The list went on forever. I was in debt to everyone, all the time. And I would steal this hour of yoga for myself because their assistance allowed it.

Since I'd worn my yoga bra and leggings under my clothes when I went to work this morning, I didn't have to go upstairs first. I jumped into my car and drove the ten miles to the Green Rocks resort community. It was a group of rental properties in the woods, with a lodge for community activities. I never went there except for yoga, but my mother played bingo at Green Rocks sometimes.

My mother loved bingo. She was like a Fifties housewife in a new-millennium body.

The day was warm but not unpleasant, and I made the drive with the windows down. I parked my little car on the gravel lot outside the lodge and retrieved my yoga mat from the trunk. My water bottle was only half full, but it would have to do.

"Let's get started in child's pose," Rayanne—the teacher—was saying when I slipped into the back of the lodge's great room. "Unless there's another pose that's calling out to you today."

Everyone else was already kneeling on their mats, their arms stretching out toward the front of the room, foreheads lowering to the floor. Not wishing to tromp around where my classmates were beginning to relax, I tossed my mat onto the floor in the back, hastily unrolling it. Then I shucked off my top and tossed it against the back wall.

"Welcome, Zara," the teacher said softly, and I smiled at her.

Another yogi's head swung around to look at me. And I froze when I realized it belonged to none other than Dave Beringer. His green, startled eyes took me in.

Then he smiled. And my insides went all warm and squishy. I

found myself smiling back. He winked, and then turned to face forward.

The spell was broken. I kicked off my skirt and settled down on the mat, wondering what the hell he was doing here.

"Let's begin by focusing on our breath," the teacher prompted. "Bring yourself into a place of presence on the mat. Inhale deeply through your nose. Open your mouth and sigh it out."

The whole room inhaled and sighed. But one of those sighs was his, and now I was listening for it.

Great.

I tried some deep breathing while my brain tried to catch up with the idea that Dave was on a yoga mat about seven feet away. Yoga? Really? I knew he was a professional athlete, but I pictured him grunting in a gym somewhere, not stretching in child's pose.

Maybe he had an injury, and had been advised to stretch? Or maybe he'd never been to a yoga class in his life before today and had decided to try it out.

Don't even think about him, Zara, I coached myself.

Yeah, right. As if I could look anywhere else. All his muscular glory was on display in a pair of black lycra shorts. They were neither thin nor very short. But no scrap of fabric of any caliber stood a chance against that musculature.

Seriously, his butt was a work of art. And I had a great view of it.

When the teacher asked us to rise to mountain pose, I could see that his T-shirt read, "You Ain't Nothin' But a Down Dog." When we were asked to dive down into a forward fold, he bent that drool-worthy body with such swiftness and grace that I clawed back a gasp.

My ability to focus only went downhill from there.

The man had obviously been to many, many yoga classes. His body in motion was a tremendous distraction. It was lucky that Rayanne always used the same poses during the first half of the class, because my attention was shot. I watched, enthralled, while Dave executed the sun salutation sequences as if he'd been doing them all his life. And every time he lowered his body slowly from a plank position to the floor, I pictured myself underneath him…

And here I'd thought this hour would be relaxing.

The only saving grace was that he couldn't see my distracted face perving on his posterior. Although, it was quite possible he could feel my hot gaze on his tight man buns. My gaze and everyone else's. It wasn't every day that a hot stranger wandered into the late-morning yoga class. It was mostly moms trying to get out of the house.

"Find warrior one. Exhale, hands to heart's center. One breath here. On the next exhale, twist toward the right."

Since I was a beat behind the asana, Dave turned before I did, his powerful arms locked in the prayer position, his bulky torso twisting over a surprisingly slim waist…

And he caught me staring. Green eyes bored into mine. And then he licked his lips, as if he were having a dirty memory.

Shit!

I twisted, finally. My body was an inferno as I struggled to do vinyasa yoga in the presence of my baby daddy. And revolved poses were not my strong suit, either. So I wobbled like a tourist on the bunny slope at the ski hill.

Just kill me already.

After that disaster, I tried to up my game. Rayanne brought us into half-moon, and I concentrated with everything I had, lifting my leg toward the heavens and balancing my fingertips on the floor.

"Feel the extension in all four directions," the teacher prompted.

I felt them. And I knew I'd be feeling them tomorrow, too. I'd pay later with muscle pain for trying to show off.

During the entire hour, Dave struggled with exactly one pose, and that was the standing split. And thank goodness. If that man had managed to do the splits while inverted in the air, all the women in the room would have crash-landed right onto the floor.

By the time we got to boat pose on our mats, every one of my muscles was quivering. But somehow I'd survived the hour. When the teacher brought us into Savasana for a rest, I was breathing like a sprinter and sweating through my sports bra.

Worse, I was more turned on than I'd been in two years. Lying there on my back, with my ankles gently spread… *God.* Every other time I'd assumed this position in Dave's presence, we'd been burning up the sheets.

And it had been so, so long since anyone had touched me.

When Rayanne finally asked us to sit up and join her in a single Om, I closed my eyes and listened for him. And there it was—his deep voice an octave below all the others, vibrating through my core.

"Thank you for joining me in your practice today," the teacher said softly. "If you began class by setting an intention for yourself, try to carry it with you throughout the day."

My daily intention was simple and yet still terribly difficult—to not think about David-freaking-Beringer.

Class broke up, and I dabbed my towel at my face in a vain attempt to look less sweaty. As a teenager, I used to get so mad at my mother when she emphasized the importance of behaving in a "lady-like" way. I'd hated that word, and everything it stood for. But now I almost understood. Sometimes, when you've been stripped bare by circumstance, and your personal travesties are known by every person in your small town, *ladylike* is all a girl has left.

Scraping my dignity off the floor with my tired body, I rolled up my yoga mat and attempted to slow my breathing.

"Afternoon, gorgeous," Dave said, standing over me.

Play it cool, Zara. I rose to my feet so I could look him in the eye instead of in the crotch. "Afternoon. Didn't expect to see you here." I hoped he knew that was true.

"The cabin we're renting is in this complex."

"Oh," I said slowly. That made perfect sense. Of course he'd rent in the most expensive spot in the county.

We headed for the door, walking out together. I didn't miss the appreciative looks the women gave him as they passed us, heading to their cars.

"So, yoga, huh?" I asked like an idiot.

"It's mandated by the team. Some guys hate it, but it works for me."

It sure does.

"Hey—can I pour you a cup of coffee?" he asked, pointing toward the circle of cabins against the forest. They weren't cabins, really. More like two-story luxury homes. "We're just over there."

"I do own a coffee shop," I pointed out. "I should probably get back to it." *Ugh,* that came out sounding bitchy. "Honestly, I don't want to meet your teammates when I'm this sweaty." *And reeking of desire.*

His smile was the panty-melting kind. "That's funny, because they see me sweaty all the time."

"Be that as it may..." I cleared my throat and tried to find somewhere to put my eyes. Dave was sweaty, too, and his eyes were bright. He looked exactly how I remembered him in the middle of sex. "If it's all the same to you, I'd rather meet strangers when I've had a shower."

And boy, did I need one. Cold, probably.

I tipped my water bottle up to my lips, but nothing came out. Another smooth move on my part. I'd drained the bottle within the first twenty minutes of class, just trying to keep up with Mr. Professional Athlete.

The corners of Dave's mouth turned up in a smirk. Then he offered me his own water, which appeared untouched.

"Thank you." I grabbed it gratefully and took a gulp, hoping it would squelch the fire raging inside me. As if.

"Don't mention it, yogi." He watched me take another sip, and I felt his gaze like a hot stroke of his hand.

As if I weren't already self-conscious enough, a drop of sweat chose that moment run out of my hairline and down the side of my face. Since I was holding my stuff in one hand and Dave's water bottle in the other, I made an awkward movement that tried and failed to wipe it off with my shoulder.

Dave's low chuckle reverberated in my chest. He stepped closer, into my personal space. His muscular body leaned close to mine. He grasped the water bottle and then slowly *kissed* the drop of sweat off my cheek. All my blood stopped circulating as his lips tasted and then teased my skin. Then they skimmed lower. He tortured the sensitive corner of my mouth, as every nerve ending in my body lit up.

If I turned my head a fractional degree, that full mouth would land on mine in a heartbeat. He'd tilt my chin just so and...

"Time out," I gasped, leaping backward.

Dave blinked at me through an aroused haze.

He looked so hot, so ready to do every amazing thing we'd ever done together, all over again. But we *couldn't,* damn it.

So I got angry. Because that always helps. "What the *hell* was that? I'm..."

"Sweaty," he finished. "I heard you the first time. Thing is, I never minded you sweaty."

"Dave!" I warned, as my heart rate doubled. "That is not the problem. You *cannot* kiss me." I was furious at both of us. At him for showing up here and reminding me how badly I'd wanted him. And at myself for being so fucking predictable.

"I can't?" He crossed his sculpted arms and stared me down. "Because I swear you've been staring at me with your tongue hanging out for an entire sweaty hour. So sue me for remembering exactly how good it was to get you all hot and bothered."

"Stop. It," I hissed, wondering if anyone was still inside the building behind us, listening through an open window. "Maybe *you* can still think with your dick, but things changed for me. You don't have the first idea what it's like!"

"I don't, huh?" His face flushed even redder. "I wonder why. You never answered a single question I ever asked you. 'Hey, did you grow up around here, Zara?' 'Shut up and take off your clothes, Dave.'"

His complaint had the sting of truth. Emphasis on sting. It ignited all my pent-up fear and frustration at once, and that's when I lost my ever-loving mind. My hand flew up, unbidden, connecting with his face. I heard a loud *smack.*

I'd actually slapped him.

Dave reeled back, as if the surprise hit him harder than my hand.

Horrified by my own actions, I stood there with my mouth open, my heart thundering with a toxic brew of rage, fear, and regret. I expected him to put a hand up to his cheek, which was reddening quickly. But he didn't. Instead, his expression just…dimmed. Like the lights went out inside. Then he backed slowly away from me, like I was a wild animal that needed to be watched.

I felt like one.

He turned and walked quickly away, disappearing a moment later behind the row of scrubby pines bordering the cabin property.

eighteen
dave

I BARELY NOTICED Castro in the hammock as I stomped into the house. "How was the class?" he called after me. "Worth going?"

He got no answer.

Quick strides carried me up the stairs and into my suite, where I threw my clothes on the floor and stepped into the shower. I stood there a while, letting the water sluice down over my body, wondering what the hell had just happened.

Kissing Zara had been a dumbass thing to do. Obviously. My lizard brain had bested me.

But—*Jesus Christ*. The attraction had been mutual. I wasn't crazy. And I didn't know why she'd been so fucking offended.

Oh right—because I'd gone and made a big deal out of it. I'd thrown her attraction back in her face, as if all the sex we'd had was something to be ashamed of.

It wasn't. Or it *shouldn't* be.

Shit. I'd never been more confused.

When the water finally ran cold, I toweled off and got dressed. Though our encounter still played on repeat in my head. The impulse to kiss her had been so strong. Then she'd gotten mad, even before I'd shot my mouth off. But feeling our old attraction rear up between us hadn't been a hardship for me. Honestly, it helped me to remember why we'd ended up making a baby in the first place.

Did she actually want me to pretend we were strangers who'd never felt a thing? I didn't think I was a good enough actor.

I didn't understand Zara at all. And maybe I never had. The Beringers were missing the gene for understanding how relationships worked.

Hopefully I hadn't passed that trait on to my child along with my red hair.

When I went downstairs, Castro was sitting at the kitchen counter, eating grapes and scrolling through his phone messages. "Hey, Beri. Your sister called."

Shit. "Did she say what she wanted?"

"Negative." Castro looked up. "Something wrong?"

"Other than everything?" I stole one of his grapes and popped it in my mouth.

He frowned. "That yoga class must have sucked, because usually it makes you all Zen and shit."

"Zara was there." I opened the refrigerator and studied its contents. Leo had gone home to Brooklyn, so Castro and I would be the only ones here for a few days. We were almost out of food. Time to do some shopping.

"Ah. That's why you're a grumpy bear?"

"I kissed her."

"During yoga?"

"No," I grunted. "After."

"Hmm. It didn't go over well?"

"We had words. I might have been a dick."

"Again?"

"Yeah." I chose a container of yogurt.

"Huh. Are you still invited to lunch on Sunday?"

"Good question. She never sent me the directions, so maybe I was never invited in the first place." Now there was a clue I should have heeded.

"Do I need to get you drunk already? Or can we still hike to that waterfall first?"

I grunted. "Sure."

"Call Bess and then we'll go."

Right.

I waited until Castro went into his room—he'd claimed the queen-sized bed that O'Doul had just vacated—before I dialed Bess from the landline. My sister had left Vermont, too—visiting clients on the West Coast somewhere, and it was just as well. She'd throttle me if she knew I'd caused drama for Zara.

"Davey," she said by way of a greeting.

"Bessie."

"How are you?"

"Fine."

"Then why do you sound all bitchy?"

"You can tell just from the way I say 'fine'?" I snapped, proving her point for her.

"Did something happen?"

"Nope," I lied. "Do you have any news about my contract?"

She was silent for a second. "No, honey. I just called to see how you were holding up."

Great. I'd walked into this trap for nothing.

"There wouldn't *be* any news, though," she said. "You were supposed to be thinking about whether or not you wanted to take the two-year or the three-year."

"I know that. But I thought maybe you'd had an idea for me. I was thinking about the no-trade clause. We could drop that for the third year, maybe. If they could trade me, they might pay me more."

She sighed. "Davey, we already dropped the no-trade in year three. That's how they're offering you a third year at all. Didn't you read the deal memo I sent?"

Awkward silence. "Not closely enough, I guess." I hadn't done a fucking thing since I'd come to Vermont except implode. "Never mind."

"Listen." My sister's voice went soft. "Maybe we don't need to renegotiate your contract early. You have a lot going on. We could tell management that you're having some unexpected family drama this summer and we weren't as ready to negotiate as we thought we were."

I groaned. "But they're not going to like me any better this winter. I should just sign the thing before we tell the PR department that I have drama."

"It's not news, though," my sister said immediately. "You have a child. Like anyone."

"Don't blow smoke up my ass, Bess. You told me yourself that we have to warn the PR department." If some internet rag decided to make Zara and Nicole into their next gossip nugget, I couldn't have team management caught off-guard.

"We're going to tell them about Nicole, but it's not a big deal to them. Do you want me to postpone the contract talks?"

"Don't say anything to them yet. I'm still thinking."

"Okay," she said softly. "Hang in there."

"Thanks," I grunted. We said our goodbyes, and I disconnected.

Then I whistled up Castro and took him hiking, hoping that the world would start making sense again soon. And in the meantime, I needed to go hiking and schedule another PT appointment in Burlington.

nineteen
zara

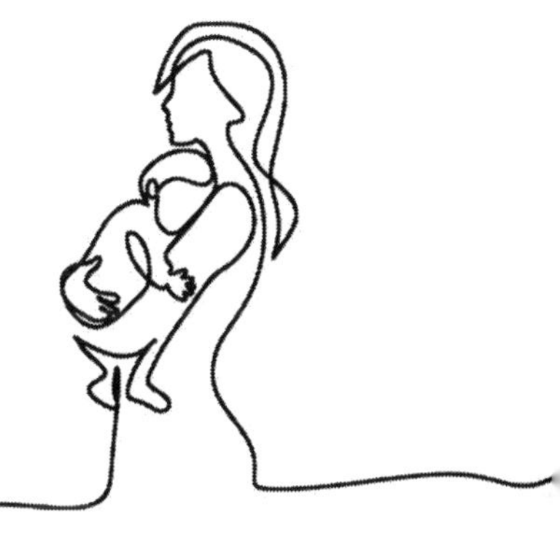

"WHY THE LONG FACE?" Audrey asked the next day as we stood behind the counter at The Busy Bean eating lunch. The lunch was chicken salad with grapes and blue cheese, and it was just as fabulous as everything else Audrey made.

"It's not the food," I said, shoveling another bite in. I could eat my weight in Audrey's chicken salad.

"Then what is it? Man troubles?"

"Sort of. I freaked out at Dave yesterday." That was a horrible understatement. I was too embarrassed to tell Audrey that I had actually slapped him.

"Why?"

"He kissed me."

Her eyebrows disappeared into her bangs. "Wow. Go, Dave."

"We *can't*, Audrey. Our days of wild sex together are over."

She blinked at me and then pinched her top between two fingers and fanned her chest with it. "Wild, huh? Like…really wild? Give me a visual."

"No way." Although since he'd come back to town, my dirty mind was full of them. "He'll never try it again, anyway. I can promise you that."

She made a sad face. "Time to apologize?"

"Obviously. But there's a text from him on my phone, and I'm afraid to look. I'm half afraid it says, 'Decided to go back to Brooklyn. Nice knowing you.'"

"I'll look." She held out her hand for my phone.

I took another bite of chicken salad. For courage. Then I unlocked my phone and handed it over.

Audrey tapped on the screen a couple of times, then smiled. "Aw!"

"What?"

She turned the phone around and showed me. It was a picture of Dave on the summit of a hill somewhere. I was temporarily distracted by the view of his muscular thighs emerging from his shorts. But then I noticed he held a handmade sign—marker on paper—which read: *Insensitive Jerk Alert*. And then in parentheses, *But he's sorry*.

"Well, shit," I sputtered. "He apologized first, damn him."

"That is freaking *adorable*," Audrey said. "Come on. We have to make your reply just as cute."

"How?" I wasn't sure I deserved to be cute. I'd been really out of line earlier and didn't know how to come back from that.

Audrey grabbed an order slip off the stack and slapped it onto the counter. Then she took a Sharpie out of our junk drawer and handed it to me.

What to say to this man who scared me so badly? I'd never given anyone such power over my emotions before. I hadn't meant for it to happen. But his appearance, disappearance, and subsequent reappearance had all wreaked havoc on my psyche.

I might as well turn my apology into something cute, because I was *never* going to tell him how I really felt.

The pen was heavy in my hand. Finally, I uncapped it and wrote:

Awful Drama Queen Alert
(She's even MORE sorry)

"That'll do," Audrey said. "Hold it up." But when I did, she waved me over to the side. "Stand there—in front of the wooden beam. That's cute. Now uncross your arms and look sexy."

"I don't know how to do that. Just take the damned photo."

"Smile, damn it."

I tried.

At long last, Audrey took the photo. "I'm hitting Send so you can't chicken out."

"Fine." I wouldn't have, anyway.

"You should go home," she said, handing back my phone. "It's my day to close."

It was. "See you tomorrow."

"Hey." She stopped me. "Can I drop off my wedding favors on Sunday?"

"Of course. Later!"

Audrey gave me another cheery wave, and I went home to find Benito on the couch with Nicole giggling on his chest. "No really," he said to my baby girl. "When are you going to talk? Just one word. Ben. B-b-b-ben!"

She howled.

"You think this is funny? This is serious business. Your mama is home."

Nicole gave a little shriek and climbed off my twin.

"You sent Mom home?" I asked, scooping her up.

"She went to get her hair done."

"Nice of you to step in."

"If you want to be the favorite uncle, you have to put in the hours." He sat up. "Hey—Audrey invited me to her wedding."

"Yeah? That was nice of her." I wasn't going to tell him that Audrey kept extra invitations in her purse because we lived in a small town and she'd invited pretty much everyone. The wedding had begun as a modest affair at the Shipley orchard, and then had morphed into a huge party at the Shipley farm. Multiple tents. Catered barbecue. Two different groups playing live music. Audrey's rich mother was footing the bill.

"She says you don't have a date."

"Like that's news?" Nicole started plucking at my T-shirt so I sat down beside my brother and lifted my shirt.

"I'll go with you if you need one. But I'd offered to tend bar that night for Smitty so he could go to the wedding."

"I don't need a date to Audrey's wedding." I made the baby comfortable and sighed as she latched on. "Mom is babysitting for me, so I can't stay late, anyway."

"Okay," my brother said slowly. "It's just that, well…"

"It's weird for me to be in Griff's wedding?"

He grinned. "Not weird. Uncomfortable."

I shook my head. "It's okay. That was a long time ago. It's not uncomfortable." Not much, anyway. "Thanks, though. You might as well tend bar."

"All right." He stood up. "You think I can toss the bottles around like Tom Cruise in *Cocktail*?"

"If that's your goal in life, have at it."

He left, and just after the door clicked shut, my phone vibrated in my back pocket. I fetched it carefully so as not to disturb the nursing princess. She was drinking in slow, lazy pulls.

Another text.

David: Don't apologize. I realize I shouldn't have assumed anything.

*Zara: Not a big leap, though. Historically. And I could have disengaged without violence! Seriously, that was not cool and I'm sorry. If I saw you hit someone I would *not* think it was okay.*

David: Not a hockey fan, then?

Zara: That's different. I think. Isn't it?

David: I'm not the kind of player who fights, generally. But I was just making a joke, Z. Let's just move on. I'm truly sorry I assumed things.

Zara: I'm truly sorry I hit you.

David: Serious question. Am I coming on Sunday or not? It's okay either way but Sunday is in 48 hours so I need some guidance.

What to do? I was anxious about the testosterone-fest that Sunday might be—my uncles and brothers, all staring him down. On the other hand, if Dave decided to play a part in his daughter's life, the uncomfortable gathering would happen sooner or later. Kindergarten graduation, maybe. Or Christmas?

The idea of seeing Dave a couple of times a year to facilitate visits with Nicole made my heart lurch with both excitement and dread. No matter how many years went by, I'd always look at his handsome face and think, *if only.*

David: You are thinking really hard over there.

I really was.

Zara: You should come. I'll text the details today. I promise.

Dave: Okay gorgeous. Now I should go. I'm standing in a river right now, trying to catch a fish.

Zara: Really?

He sent a selfie a minute later, and I laughed aloud. Shorts and waders was a pretty silly look. But, damn him, Dave was still hotter than a July afternoon.

That pang? It would never go away.

Zara: Funny, I'm doing exactly the same thing right now.

Dave: Seriously?

Zara: No. But it's nice to know you're so gullible.

I held up my phone and took a picture of Nicole and I nursing on the couch. Her eyes were half-mast, her little mouth slurping lazily at my breast. It was a hundred percent reality and not the least bit sexy.

After I hit send, I sent him directions to my family's farm.

twenty
dave

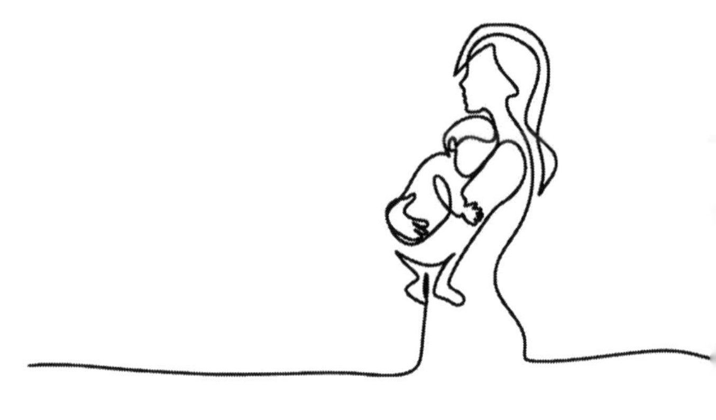

I DREAM OF ZARA. *Daylight. White sheets. Filtered sunlight on soft, bare skin.*

We're tangled up in bed together, her body under mine. I sink down into her curves. We're wound so tightly together that my hips move in shallow, inadequate thrusts. She makes breathy, desperate sounds. We're never going to stop. The wanting will never be sated. I grip her more tightly and moan. Our mouths are locked into one long kiss.

But then I hear it—the baby crying. She's wailing, and it's been going on a while. I just didn't notice until now.

I pull back, but Zara grips me even more tightly.

The baby lets out an agonizing cry and...

I woke up sweaty, my breath coming too fast. Also, I was really fucking hard.

Letting out an entirely different kind of moan, I threw off the sheets to get some air.

Really, brain? A mashup of the sexy dream and the baby screaming? It was almost funny.

Almost.

It was Sunday morning. I lay there a little while, waiting for both my body and my fucked-up mind to relax. When I picked up my phone, I saw it was ten a.m. I still had plenty of time to shower and get ready for the midday meal at Zara's uncles' farm.

The phone was open to that photo Zara had sent me. I didn't know how long I'd looked at it yesterday, but it was longer than I cared to admit. I was drawn to it, and I didn't know why. It wasn't meant to be a sexual shot. I wasn't perving on the nursing mother.

Okay, I was, a little. She was so casually voluptuous in the photograph. And her smile was cheeky.

But there was more to it than that. There was my sleepy baby's head in the shot, her face serene, her little hand curled comfortably around the fabric of Zara's T-shirt. The two of them so cozy and so *complete*. Like they belonged together.

And Zara's smile was wise. Like she knew secrets I'd never learn. One of us had grown up a whole lot in the last two years, and it wasn't me.

I put the phone down and rolled over in bed. But my hungry body imagined Zara underneath me—the Zara of two years ago, who'd wanted me only for sex. My cock thickened again, as it always did when I remembered those nights. I trapped my palm between the mattress and my dick and flexed my hips. Her body had welcomed me in. I'd fucked her so eagerly and then...

Gripping myself, I pictured spilling into Zara, planting my seed inside her as we slowly kissed, coming down from the high we'd given each other.

I took my hand away and wondered what the fuck I was thinking. We'd made a baby, and I shouldn't find that sexy at all. It was irresponsible. It was exactly the thing I'd never meant to do.

What the hell was wrong with me?

"Is that what you're wearing?" Castro asked me when I came downstairs a couple hours later, freshly showered and shaved.

I glanced down at my khakis and oxford shirt. "What's wrong with it?" I thought I looked fine.

"Where's the body armor?" He cracked up at his own joke.

"You're hilarious." I grabbed a banana off the kitchen counter and peeled it.

"Need a last minute pep talk? I think I should show you how to change a diaper."

"Why? I'm not babysitting. Her whole family will be there."

"It's not babysitting if it's your own kid," Castro pointed out. "Besides, I thought you wanted to make a statement that you can handle whatever gets thrown at you. Even if it's a poopy diaper."

My reluctance to be someone's daddy had *nothing* to do with diapers and everything to do with my pessimistic attitude. "The only point I want to make to her family is that I'm not afraid to show up and look 'em in the eye. But I'm not anyone's idea of Mr. Family Man. I'm not going to pretend."

"Thing is, you *are* a family man now. Whether you're just a check in the mail, and not a show-up-every-Sunday kind of dad, you're still in it forever. Just like I'm an uncle to my nephews forever, whether I'm a good one or not."

I scowled at him, because that was exactly what freaked me out. He'd just stated the problem in all its glory. "What is your point? I don't think a diapering lesson is going to make me into a good daddy."

"You gotta start somewhere. I learned, and I don't have a kid."

I ate the banana, getting grumpier by the second.

"Babies are so cool," he said, oblivious to my discomfort. "They will laugh at anything. For some reason, my sister's youngest thinks the top of my head is hysterical. All I have to do is lean over him and he grabs my hair and laughs."

It wouldn't be nice of me to wonder aloud if that was normal, right?

"And he'll, like, fall asleep anywhere. Even sitting up, with a toy in his hand."

"Hmm," I said, feigning interest.

"The first time I saw him, it was *love*," Castro gushed. He spotted the look on my face. "I guess there's one big difference, though. If my sister really needed me, I'd be there. But the truth is that he's not really my baby. I can just hand 'im back if he cries. All I have to be is the fun uncle. So he's real easy to love." My teammate reached across the counter and squeezed my shoulder. "Give yourself time, D. We gotta get that deer-in-the-headlights look off your face."

If only.

"So." Castro clapped his hands. "Let's talk about diapering. I'm gonna show you some skills. First you remove the old diaper. There are tapes that hold the diaper on."

"Tapes?" A fragment of a memory floated up to the surface of my brain. "I thought there were safety pins."

"Pins? Hell no. Too dangerous. Welcome to the twenty-first century. The tape is the multiple-use kind, so after you roll that wet diaper up you can close it again. If there's poop, you use baby wipes to clean it out of all the crevices."

"That sounds…alarming."

He grinned. "Baby wipes are awesome. Once when Mario had a poopsplosion I used a half a box of them. You could clean up, like, organized crime with those suckers."

"Good to know."

But he wasn't done talking yet. "The dirty wipes go inside the messy diaper. Then you tape up the whole mess into a little poop grenade. Most moms have a diaper bin thing to throw them into. You know those hazmat wastebaskets in the doctor's office? Like that."

"Right." I eyed the clock with a pointed look.

"Now, always put something under the baby before you change her. A baby boy can whiz *right in your eye* while you're working, so you gotta stay nimble. But a girl just makes a puddle, I think."

He *thinks*. We were the blind leading the blind. Or the stupid leading the stupider…

"Then you take the fresh diaper…" Castro grabbed a paper napkin and set it on the counter. He took the banana peel out of my hand and laid it on the napkin. "Just fit the front part between the baby's legs, and tug it upward…" While I watched, he began to bring the napkin's front and back corners together between halves of the banana peel.

"Whoa," a voice said behind us. "What the fuck are you two doing?" Our sleepy teammate—Silas, the backup goalie—shuffled into the kitchen, staring at Castro's banana diaper.

"You don't even want to know," I warned. "You just stay in your happy place."

"My happy place needs coffee."

"Tape 'er up, and boom!" Castro said, as if I was still listening. "Fresh kid. Easy peasy."

There was nothing easy about any of this. "Pour me a cup, too, Silas. This could be a rough day."

I wasn't dumb enough to show up for my beating at the Rossi farm empty handed.

With a little help from Silas—who had arrived after Leo and O'Doul went back to New York—I was well armed with a bouquet of flowers for Zara's mom.

And earlier in the week, Castro and I had waited in line for two hours outside a Montpelier food co-op to buy our allotment of the most decorated beer ever made. So I also had a case of coveted Heady Topper beer for Zara's uncles.

With my bribes in the back seat, I drove with the windows down along several winding dirt roads, following the instructions Zara had texted. I knew I was in the right place when row upon row of pear trees appeared out the window. The fruits were green and shorter than my thumb. But there were hundreds of them on every tree.

I found the sign for Rossi Farm and turned onto a gravel driveway. The rental car bumped along until a big house came into view. It was a white clapboard farmhouse with a gently sagging porch and a porch swing.

As soon as I parked the car, Zara came outside. My progress was halted momentarily while I took her in. She was wearing a sundress in orange and white that made her look... *Softer* was the word that came to mind. She looked more approachable than the bartender I'd met two years ago.

"Hi," she said shyly. Then she smiled like I'd done something funny.

"Hi," I echoed, walking toward her. I opened my arms to greet her, then hesitated. After our ugly moment earlier in the week, I needed to take care not to overstep boundaries. But then she came closer, allowing me to wrap her in the world's most awkward we're-just-friends hug.

I kissed her cheek quickly. She smelled like sunshine and perfume, and my libido shook itself awake.

No time for that, I reminded myself, stepping back. "Have your brothers loaded the shotgun, yet?"

"Oh." She waved a hand dismissively. "There's more than one shotgun. But lunch is almost ready, and they're more interested in my mother's cooking than in firearms. After lunch, though, you never know."

"Noted." I went to the back door of the rental car and popped it open. "These are for your mother," I said, pulling out a generous bouquet arranged in a basket.

"*Hello,* kiss-ass." Her face lit up with humor, and I found myself smiling back at her.

"Can you blame me? And these are for everyone." I hefted the beer out of the back.

"Nicely done, champ. You might live through dessert." She turned and carried the flowers toward the house and I followed her, trying not to notice her long legs in that dress.

Maybe this whole thing would be easier if I wasn't attracted to Zara. But there was no chance of that fading. She just *did* it for me. I couldn't even say exactly why. It was some heady combination of her looks and her take-no-prisoners attitude.

She reminded me of a female superhero from the comics I'd read as a boy. Put her in a bodysuit with a bow and arrow in her hands and ink in that dark hair and those piercing eyes.

Then look out, boys.

A half hour later I was no longer worried about surviving until dessert. I was, however, worried that I might kill someone. Because Zara's uncle Otto was a real dickface.

We were seated at the dining table in preparation for the meal, and he'd already made disparaging remarks about Zara's coffee shop, Alec's bar, and Zara's mother's menu choices. "Who puts sesame oil on broccoli?" he grumbled. "What, are we Chinese now?"

"I love sesame oil," I said immediately. "I put it on everything. Even eggs."

Otto snorted. Then he mumbled something about "arrogant city folk."

Whatever.

Zara's mother had just put about ten dishes on the long table in about as many seconds, two of which were giant pans of lasagna. "TV off, Benito!" she hollered. "And bring a corkscrew to the table!"

"Can I help you in any way?" I'd asked a moment ago, watching her make lightning-fast adjustments to the meal she'd prepared. Now I knew where Zara got her efficient demeanor.

Mrs. Rossi had given me the side-eye. "Do you actually cook?"

"Only bachelor food. Eggs. Burgers. Chicken. But I take coaching really well."

She'd sniffed. "I have everything under control. But it's good to know you're not completely helpless, like some of the men in this family." She'd turned toward an open doorway and bellowed, "ON THE TABLE! LET'S GO!"

Zara had set the flowers I'd brought in the center of the table. Now she was seated beside me. Her brother Alec was already seated as well, and shooting me grumpy looks. Another brother—Damien—had given my hand exactly the bruising shake that I'd give his if he'd gotten my sister pregnant. But now he was ignoring me from the seat beside Otto's.

Benito was the last to sit down. I noticed that Zara's fourth brother was missing, but I didn't ask why.

And then there were the uncles. Otto had an identical twin, Art. But I found them easy enough to tell apart. Otto was the sterner man, and his hair was grayer. Art had less to say, but he smiled when his sister put a lasagna down in front of him, and he didn't seem to want to kill me.

"So," I said, clearing my throat. "Twins run in your family?" I asked, thinking of Zara and Benito. I gave Zara's elbow a squeeze. "Only one at a time for you? Slacker."

"God, bite your tongue!" She laughed.

But then I heard Alec mutter under his breath. "Maybe you just couldn't get the job done."

You couldn't pay me to touch that comment.

"Thanks for these," Art said, cracking open a can of Heady Topper. "You'll have one, right?" he asked me.

"Sure, I'd love one." *Or ten.* "Want one?" I asked Zara.

She shook her head. "Can I have just a sip of yours? Nursing is literally a buzz kill."

Otto snorted. "Offer the nursing mother a sixteen-ounce beer at noon, whydontcha?"

"Right. Sorry," I said, feeling my neck heat.

Zara gave me a sympathetic look. I winked at her. Otto was a prick, and her brothers looked ready to pounce. But I honestly didn't care what they thought of me. I was here for Zara and the baby. They were the only ones who mattered.

Luckily, Zara's mother finally took her seat. "I'd like to say grace," she announced, so I bowed my head.

I always felt like a fraud at moments like this. Nobody had said grace at my house when I was a child. Hell, I couldn't remember ever sitting down to a home-cooked meal. Even when I'd lived with my grandparents, food sometimes appeared on the kitchen counter. And when it didn't, I heated things from cans for Bess and myself.

"Thank you lord for blessing us with this meal, and may we know thy everlasting grace—" A baby's squawk erupted from the other room, and she flinched.

"Sorry." Zara pushed back her chair and stood. "I knew she wouldn't go for a nap right now."

"Amen!" Otto declared, then reached for the spatula in one of the lasagna pans, and his nephews reached for their beers.

Mrs. Rossi raised her eyes to the ceiling. "I'm sorry, God. I tried. Thank you for these blessings. Amen."

Dishes were passed, and I waited for Zara to reappear. She came back with Nicole in her arms just as Benito offered me a piece of lasagna. I picked up Zara's plate instead, extending it toward her brother, who plated it up.

"No, you eat," Zara said when I offered her the plate. "I'm going to cut up a few things for the baby first."

Other dishes were passed, and my plate became loaded down with two different salads, a slab of ham, and cheesy potatoes. There were olives in a cut-glass dish and green beans topped with almonds.

"You must have been cooking all week," I remarked to Zara's mom. "This is delicious."

"Thank you." She smiled at me from the other end of the table, but somehow it still looked chilly. "I like to make a big spread for the family on Sunday. Then I walk out the front door and let Otto and Art deal with the cleanup."

"Totally worth it," Art said, helping himself to the ham.

Zara cubed a piece of meat into bite-sized pieces and cut several green beans in half. "Here," she said, bringing the plate closer to where Nicole sat in her lap.

But the baby pointed at the potatoes in their casserole dish and squawked.

"Hmm," Zara grumbled. "If you eat those, I'll probably be wearing that cheese on my dress." But she reached for the serving spoon anyway.

"Shouldn'a got all fancied up to try to impress your man, then," Otto rumbled.

Zara glared at him, and I developed a fascination with my lasagna, pretending I hadn't heard that comment.

"So what do you do for a living?" Art asked me.

Let the grilling commence. I was surprised I'd made it this long without being questioned. "Hockey," I said.

"That's not a job," he grunted.

"There's no desk, if that's what you mean," I said lightly. "But it pays, and it keeps me busy. I play eighty-five games during the regular season, and sometimes we make the playoffs. Keeps me off the streets."

"Did you go to college?" Otto asked.

Did you? my inner smart-ass wanted to fire back. But I reined it in. I'd basically come here to be grilled, not that it was fun. "I didn't finish college. The NHL signed me after my sophomore year. And I had bills to pay so it wasn't a tough decision to leave the University of Michigan."

I'd been a decent student before I'd dropped out, but the NHL paycheck had been impossible to resist, since it would allow me to pay Bess's college tuition and still feed myself. Who wouldn't make that choice?

"Still have your teeth?" Benito asked, smiling.

"Mostly. But my dental bill is pretty brutal." Like everyone else in hockey, I had a mouth full of crowns. Not my favorite topic. "I chew carefully now. It could be worse."

"How many years do you think you've got left?" he asked, watching me with a thoughtful expression.

"On earth? A bunch, I hope. In hockey, maybe five." Okay, that was probably a stretch. "Maybe less," I amended. "But I don't like to think that way."

Zara's mother piled on. "What's your Plan B?"

The questions just kept flying. And I hated that one. "Not quite sure yet," I admitted. "Some guys coach, some work in the media." I happened to hate sports-TV, so that wasn't really a good choice for me. But the Rossi family didn't get to hear all my secrets. I cut another bite of lasagna with my fork. "This is really fabulous," I said, and meant it. "I don't really eat carbs during the off-season but I am going to have to finish this, anyway."

"You drink beer," Zara pointed out.

"Yeah. That's why I don't eat carbs." I lifted another forkful. "During the season I can eat and drink almost anything, and I still drop weight. During the summer I have to be a little more careful. The Chinese takeout place knows me as that weirdo who doesn't want any rice with his order."

"That *is* weird," she said, offering Nicole a tiny bite of potato on the end of a spoon.

I glanced at her plate, which still held only baby bites of food. "Don't you get to eat?" I asked.

"In a minute," she said.

Well, then. It was obviously time to make the point I'd come here to make—that I'd stand by Zara and her baby if she needed me to. So I pushed my plate forward, out of the way. Then I offered my hands to take the baby. "Switch?"

The corners of Zara's mouth turned up in amusement, and I waited to see what she'd say. And everyone else watched us as carefully as a season finale on *Game of Thrones*.

But Zara's mother jumped out of her chair and came around to take Nicole herself. "Finish that lasagna," she ordered me. "I only make it a few times a year. And I'll take care of the baby."

She'd fired me before I'd even begun my job.

Alec got chatty as the meal wore on, taking some of the focus away from me. "I think all those emails I wrote to travel bloggers are paying off. The summer tourists have found The Gin Mill."

"It's either that or the fact that you're sleeping with that woman from the distributor," Benito teased him. "You never run out of the hard-to-get beers anymore."

Alec grinned, and Mrs. Rossi gave them both a stern look.

"Seriously, though. Business is good. If my cash flow keeps up I can renovate the mill kitchen and think about serving food."

"Don't get out over your skis," Otto grumbled. "The off-seasons'll kill ya. Running a bar is hard."

"Oh yeah?" I heard myself ask. "Do you run a bar?"

"The Mountain Goat in Tuxbury," he said. "Goin' on fifteen years now."

"Huh." I picked up my excellent beer and took a sip. "Two years ago I went there all the time. Never met you, though. Seemed like Zara was running the whole show—tending bar, managing the help, keeping the place orderly. Tossing out the drunks, too. You're right—looked like a lot of work."

Otto chewed slowly, staring me down. Maybe he was trying to decide whether or not I'd meant to call him out on if he'd put in hours at The Mountain Goat. Under the table, Zara nudged me with her knee. But I was pretty sure it was more of a solidarity tap than a plea to shut up.

Meanwhile, Benito hid his smile behind his beer can. At least somebody found me funny.

"This is a great meal, Mom," Zara said, deflecting. "Is the baby still eating?"

"She sure is. Another member of the clean-plate club. Takes after her daddy, maybe?"

Daddy. How wild that she was referring to me.

After lunch I tried to ferry some of the dishes to the kitchen with Benito and Alec, while Otto scowled at me.

"Guests don't help," Mrs. Rossi said sternly. "Have a glass of wine instead?"

"Or come outside to see the orchard," Zara suggested. "Nicole needs to run around a little and tire herself out."

"Sure thing," I said, grateful to escape the claustrophobia of the Rossi house.

The old farmhouse screen door squeaked (as a screen door should) as Zara carried Nicole outside. I followed her, trying not to admire her tanned thighs as she set Nicole onto the grass. "Let's show Dave all the pear trees," she said, pointing toward the first tidy row of orchard trees. I noticed that Zara hadn't used the word "daddy."

Nicole took off at a toddle, her chubby little feet bare in the grass. "Vermont is an awfully nice place to be a baby," I said. "Nobody can run free like that where I grew up in Detroit."

We followed Nicole between the row of pear trees, and it felt like entering a green tunnel. "Detroit, huh? You never told me where you grew up," Zara said.

"You never let me tell you anything," I said.

"That is true." She bit her lip, looking sheepish.

I felt like a dick for making that sound like an accusation. "The thing is, though, I probably wouldn't have shared much, anyway. It's not my favorite topic. Actually, my tolerance for sharing personal details would've only been slightly higher than yours."

"Fair enough." Her smile was wry. "Then ask me anything, and I'll answer. Go ahead."

I thought about it for a minute while we followed the baby down another row of pear trees. She could move pretty fast on those short little legs. "Did you grow up on this farm?"

"Not exactly." Zara shook her head. "We spent plenty of time here. I *wanted* to live here. And I did twice—for less than a year each time. Both times happened after my father left us. He did that a lot. One day he'd be at home, my mother fussing over him at the dinner table. The next day—gone. No forwarding address.

"My uncles always offered to share the house, but my mother wanted her independence. She kept us in successively smaller dwellings—I can't even say houses, because the last one was a trailer —rather than move in with her brothers. I was so angry about it. Sharing a room with Benito when I was sixteen made me insane. When I was a senior in high school I actually moved in with my friend Jill for a little while, just to get out of that trailer."

"Jill from The Mountain Goat? The one who caught her husband with the nanny?"

Zara stared at me. "You have a killer memory. You really do."

"I told you, gorgeous. I remember everything when it comes to you. That was the night we drank tequila before we went upstairs. Don't tell me you forgot the tequila."

Two pink spots appeared on her cheekbones. "I remember. I'm just surprised you got Jill's name from that crazy night."

I shrugged. "I loved The Mountain Goat, and hearing all the locals' gossip. Never saw your uncle's face once, though. Hope you don't mind that I said so."

She grinned. "That was the best part of the meal."

"No wonder your mom didn't want to live with him."

"Exactly," Zara agreed. "Otto never held back his opinion on my mother's life choices, just like he doesn't hold back on me. My mom just couldn't stand it. Living with him would have meant more space for us but less peace for her. And I get it now. My brothers are great. They're so much kinder than Otto. But even so, they're all up in my business."

"I can't imagine how you've kept it together," I said.

"It's been a chaotic couple of years." She laughed. "But there's something I want to explain to you."

"Yeah?"

"Two years ago I was in a dark place. I wasn't very happy with myself or anyone else. I wasn't always that nice to you."

I laughed, because that's not really how I remembered it. "You seemed pretty nice."

Zara's eyes sparkled. "I suppose I had my moments. But I was angrier at the world that summer. In spite of, uh, recent evidence to the contrary, I'm much happier now. I have a new business and a healthy kid. I'm feeling pretty optimistic. You don't have to worry about me."

"That's great. I…" Let's face it, I could not say the same thing for myself. "You found optimism, and I'm more of a wreck."

"Really? Why?"

"Well…" *As it turns out, I'm not invincible, and also stupider than I'd thought.* I wasn't used to sharing my thoughts with anyone. Let alone Zara. And where to start? My career seemed to have hit a rough patch. The future scared me, and everyone had tiptoed around me all season. "I had an injury during the playoffs that's still bothering me. That's the worst of it."

She made a sympathetic sound.

"Two years ago I felt like I had the world hanging off the end of my dick. Now I just feel like an old guy in a young man's life."

"You look okay to me," Zara said. And when I met her gaze, those spots of pink had returned to her cheekbones, and she looked away. "Still in Brooklyn?"

"Yeah. I own a condo that's only two blocks from our training facility. Bunch of guys live in the same building. It's great."

"I lived in Brooklyn once."

"Really? When?"

"For two years right after high school. That's where I learned to tend bar—in a nightclub in lower Manhattan. I used to take the F train home to Red Hook at four in the morning, and fight sleep so nobody could pickpocket me."

"Yikes."

"It wasn't a great life. When I came home to Vermont, I appreciated it a lot more. Otto let me tend bar, and within a year I was running the place."

Ahead of us, Nicole tripped over something in the grass. She pitched forward, and my heart lurched as her small body made the short trip to the ground. It wasn't the worst fall I've ever seen, but her shriek was almost instantaneous.

"Oh, baby." Zara ran and scooped her up off the grass. "You're fine," she said calmly. "It was just a tumble."

But the baby howled. Her little face turned red, and she wailed onto Zara's shoulder.

"Come over here for a moment?" She didn't beckon, since her arms were full of the child. But I followed her around the end of the row of trees, toward an outbuilding.

Square bales of hay were lined up against the outer wall, and Zara sat down on one of them, as if it were a bench. I sat down beside her, while the baby still cried.

"She's just tired," Zara said. "My brothers love to rile her up and then hand her back to me." She fumbled with the strap of her dress, tugging it off her shoulder. In a practiced maneuver, she freed her breast and the baby latched right on, going silent mid-shriek. Then her little body relaxed completely in Zara's arms.

"That's some powerful mojo you've got there."

"When it works, it works." She tipped her head back against the barn wood. "I have your watch."

I had no idea what she was talking about. "What?"

"Your wristwatch. You left it behind. I put it in a drawer. I thought I'd never find you, and someday I'd end up giving it to Nicole when I was ready to explain to her the real story of where she came from. But now I can return it to you instead."

For some reason I looked at my wrist, which was banded by a Timex on a canvas strap. "I wondered what happened to that. I thought I left it in the cabin. And when I called the rental company they said nobody had turned it in."

"I'll drop it off when I go to yoga again."

"Eh," I hedged. "I never really missed it. That thing wasn't really me. Just something I bought my first year making big money. Thought that's what you were supposed to do. You guys should hang onto it."

Zara didn't say anything, and I realized that I'd just validated her original plan—to use an overpriced chunk of metal to explain an absent father to Nicole when she was a teenager. It wouldn't go down that way now. I wasn't going to cut off ties with Zara again.

Although, when I tried to look a decade into the future, I saw... nothing. It was all a haze—my career, my relationship to Zara and her child. What the hell would I be doing in ten years?

The question scared the shit out of me.

"I got papers from your lawyer on Friday," Zara said suddenly.

"Really? That was fast. What do they say?"

"Standard paternity request. I take a swab from inside Nicole's cheek and mail it back to a lab. And that if I refuse to comply with the test, you can take me to court."

"That's just lawyers talking. You know I wouldn't really do that."

"I know." She cleared her throat.

"I think I got the same test by FedEx. Haven't opened it yet. I'll do it tomorrow. And if you don't like the tone the lawyer takes, I can ask him to back off."

"It's really okay. Somehow I don't think you're about to surprise me with a request for full custody."

We both knew that would never happen. But even I wasn't a big enough ass to agree too loudly. Instead, I reached for her hand and gave it a quick squeeze.

Her fingers closed around mine, and then I think she surprised both of us by holding on and interlacing our fingers.

We sat in silence for a minute while I admired this quiet spot in my favorite state. "So when are pears harvested? There's so many of them." There were hundreds on each tree, still small. "They get bigger, right?"

"Sure. And the tree will shed fruit over time. The harvest happens in August, but the fruit is still hard and green when it comes off the trees. Pears are tricky. They're not like apples—you don't wait until they ripen to pick them."

"Really? Why?"

"If you let a pear ripen on the tree, the texture is mealy at the core. They ripen from the inside out. So we pick them hard, chill them down to thirty degrees for a day and then ship them out."

"But how do you know when to pick them?"

"There's some guesswork involved," she admitted. "Some varieties are ready when the stem releases easily from the branch. Some never release easily, and you just have to go with your gut."

"Who knew?" She was still holding my hand, and I liked it way too much.

"Hey, Dave?"

"Mmm?"

"I'm really sorry I slapped you."

"I thought we were going to forget about that."

"But I just want you to know that the last person I slapped was Benito. When we were seventeen."

"He probably had it coming," I said mildly. "Pretty sure I got into some scuffles with Bess." I distinctly remembered locking her in her room when we were teenagers because she'd gotten into my stuff.

"Well." She cleared her throat. "I would never hit my child," she whispered. "Just putting that out there."

Wait, what?

I turned to find her watching me with sheepish eyes. "No kidding, Z. You're really not the type."

Her face softened, and it made her appear more vulnerable than I remembered her ever looking. Clear brown eyes blinked back at me from that pretty face, with those defiant cheekbones. She was so pretty in a way that was unforced. I'd bet she had no idea how far she turned my crank.

"Just wanted you to know that," she whispered. "Your sister told me that your dad used to hit you both..."

"That's different," I said quickly. We were not going there. "And anyway, my mother was a face slapper," I said. "But she would never..."

Shit. I couldn't talk about that parent, either. This was exactly why I wasn't a family man. My family tree was a fucking landmine.

"She what?"

"Never mind. I was going to say something dumb."

"Why? Where is your mother, anyway?"

Yikes. "She passed when I was small. Really, I barely remember her."

"You remember her hitting you on the face, though."

Point to Zara. "It wasn't a big deal." It didn't even make the top-ten list for things that went wrong during my childhood.

"How'd she die?"

"Zara," I warned. *Christ almighty.* She didn't really want to hear about this shit. She only thought she did.

"How?" she pressed, proving my point. "I thought we were asking each other anything?"

I sighed. "Drug overdose. I was five, Bess was one and a half. I'm the one that found her."

"Wow." Zara's eyes popped wide. "I'm sorry."

"It was a *long* time ago."

"But you still remember it?" she pressed.

Leaning my head against the outbuilding behind me, I closed my eyes. "Yeah, I remember that nobody had shown up at school that day to pick me up from kindergarten. This was not much of a surprise, and so I walked home by myself. I didn't think anything of it, even when I banged on our front door and she didn't open it…"

I pictured my five-year-old self standing there, waiting. And then the hair rose up on my arms as I remembered something else—the sound of Bess inside the house, wailing. Just like in the dreams I'd been having.

Shit.

And then I couldn't stop the memory from unfolding. I'd gone next door and retrieved the extra key from Mrs. Parker, the retired school librarian who was always out on her porch, watching the kids come home from school.

When I finally got into the house, I'd seen her. My mother. Laid out on the floor, a baggie of powder near her outstretched fingers. She'd been very, very still.

And I'd *known*. I'd known, but I hadn't known. My mother had been passed out in my presence before.

But this time I was afraid of her. I was afraid to touch her.

I knelt down on the rug while my sister screamed even louder. She'd probably heard the door open, and was making her presence known. I knew I had to get back there and show my face so she'd stop. But I was staring at my mother's body. Her eyelids were blueish. Her lips were ashen. Her hand lay on the rug in an ordinary way. But way too still.

Slowly, I stretched out my own hand, hovering an inch over hers, and finally lowering it to her fingers.

They were cold. And then so was I. So cold and so scared. Bess wailed on.

I rose from the rug. With a pounding heart, I stepped over my mother's outstretched legs and went into the bedroom I shared with Bess. My sister was standing in her crib, chubby little hands clenched around the wooden bars, her face bright red and tear-streaked. Her voice was hoarse from screaming. She didn't stop when I entered the room.

Getting her out of the crib wasn't going to be easy because I was too short. So I climbed into the crib and hugged her until she calmed down. She stank of urine...

Whoa.

With a gasp, I let go of Zara's hand and leapt to my feet.

"What's the matter?" Zara asked, sounding far away. Nicole popped off her mother's nipple and squinted up at me.

"Nothing," I wheezed, pacing in a circle. I'd just realized that Bess had worn cloth diapers. I remembered them now—they were held together with safety pins, and there was a plastic thing she wore over them. I remembered cupping her fat little foot as she stepped through the leg hole...

I'd changed diapers before. Quite a few of them. I'd done my first one that day in the damp crib, while my mother's dead body lay on the floor of the living room.

"Dave." Zara's voice was low and steady, and it broke through the fog of my panic.

"Yeah?" I forced myself to stand still for a second.

Deep yoga breath in...

"Are you okay?"

"Sure," I grunted. It might even be true eventually.

"Have you ever had perry?"

Breathe. "Who's Perry?

Zara's smile was the kind you get when someone was tolerating your strangeness. "Not who. What. Perry is pear cider."

"You can do that?" I watched her pretty face and tried to calm down.

"Sure. I'll show you."

Zara had already tucked herself back into her dress. Now she lifted a sleepy Nicole onto her shoulder and stood. The baby wrapped one chubby arm around her neck and tucked her face onto Zara's neck. "Let's walk the long way so this one gets lazy."

She pointed down a row of trees and I followed.

My heart rate descended back into the normal range as we walked slowly through the orchard. Nicole was completely zonked out on Zara's shoulder. Supporting her sleeping body looked cumbersome, and I realized I was basically letting a woman carry a heavy object while I walked beside her unaware. "Hey. You want me to take her?"

She stopped, turning to me with amusement on her face. "Sure?"

"Unless she'll wake up during the handoff."

"It'll work. Sleep is the deepest right after you go under."

Well, okay then. I held out my hands, and Zara grasped her daughter and turned her. I bent my knees and hastily brought her against me, tucking her head against my shoulder with one hand.

And then I was holding my sleeping baby girl for the first time.

"There you go," Zara said, looking more amused than absolutely necessary.

We walked on, coming to a fenced-in area where chickens pecked at the grass. Some were reddish and some had blond feathers. A single rooster walked towards us on his claw-like feet, cocking his head at me and blinking reptilian eyes. He opened his mouth and let out a loud crow of warning.

The baby on my shoulder did not stir.

"I think he's telling us to back off," I said, as the rooster crowed again.

"No way," Zara scoffed, giving the rooster a casual wave. "I think he's just showing off. 'These are all my wives. Aren't they pretty?' Just like a man, really."

Something tight inside my chest loosened up, and I laughed as the hens began to cluck. It was like a fucking storybook around here.

twenty-one
zara

WE WALKED BACK to the farmhouse while I snuck glances at Dave carrying Nicole. Any mom of a toddler is so used to toting the baby around that she practically wears the kid like a scarf. But Dave used both arms, cradling her head with one and her butt with the other. He held himself stiffly, as if she were easily breakable.

He looked awkward but so damn cute that I could not stop peeking at them.

Just as we reached the front porch, Griffin Shipley's truck rolled up the driveway and stopped beside Dave's rental car.

"Expecting more company?" Dave asked in a hushed tone, taking care not to disturb Nicole.

"Um…Audrey is dropping off a little project I'm helping her with." But she wasn't supposed to show until *later*. I'd told her four o'clock, and it probably wasn't even three. And the change of plans was almost certainly intentional.

Indeed, Audrey hopped out of the passenger seat looking gleeful. She took in Dave, the baby asleep on his shoulder, and her expression went straight to the same giddy look she wore whenever she watched puppy videos on YouTube. "Hi there," she said, a giant smile on her face. "You must be Dave."

"And you're Audrey, right? I'd shake your hand, but…" He was still holding Nicole as if she were a Ming vase.

Audrey's eyes danced. "Sorry we're early, but Griff finished up his errands already."

No way. The little stinker had come early on purpose. "Errands on Sunday, huh?" I asked, calling her on her bullshit. The only businesses that were open in Vermont on Sunday were restaurants and hotels.

"Busy, busy!" she said, unrepentant. "Nice dress, girly. Now where should we unload these?" She jerked a thumb toward the tailgate, where the cider bottles would be stacked.

Griff got out of the truck, pocketing the keys. He gave me a wave, but his eyes were trained on Dave. And he wore one of his Grumpy Griff frowns. If I wasn't mistaken, it was even ornerier than usual.

Lovely. Just what I needed in my life—one more oddly territorial man.

Wordlessly, Griff began pulling wooden wine crates out of the back of his truck. He carried the first two up onto the porch. When his hands were free, he came down to meet me. "Hey, Zara!" He kissed my cheek. "Thanks for taking care of this for us."

"It'll be my pleasure." I'd assigned myself the task of handling their wedding favors because Audrey seemed a little strung out. The wedding was only six days away.

But first, I needed to rescue Dave. "Why don't I lay her down, now? I'll take her inside and put her in the Pack-n-Play."

"The...?" He gave me a quizzical look.

"Portable crib. Here." I reached for Nicole and took her warm, sleepy body from him. "Back in a jif."

I was inside the house for all of sixty seconds. But that was long enough, apparently, for Audrey to do her damage. When I came back out onto the porch, Dave was holding a wedding invitation in his hand.

"We're having barbecue and swing dancing!" she bubbled. "You should totally come!"

"Sounds amazing," he said, because what else do you say to a bride who's invited you to her wedding? He tucked the invitation into his pocket.

Meanwhile, Griff leaned against the truck, arms crossed, trying to kill Dave with Jedi mind tricks.

"So let's unload some cider," I said, shooing Audrey off the steps. The faster I could get rid of those two, the better.

"I'll help," Dave said lightly.

We all pulled crates off the truck, and when they were stacked onto my uncles' porch, Audrey handed me a file folder full of labels and several spools of ribbon. "So, you're basically going to…"

"Stick on the labels and tie a bow onto the neck of the bottle," I said quickly. "Got it."

She narrowed her eyes. "Are you trying to get rid of us?"

"Never," I lied, and she grinned.

"Good. Because I thought we could get started on this project right now."

"Right now?" I hedged.

"Great idea," Griff said, slamming the tailgate of his truck back into place. "I'm ready to stick on a few labels. Let's do this." He came up the porch steps and thrust a hand out to Dave, the gesture as friendly as if he were brandishing a knife. "I'm Griffin Shipley. Nice to meet you."

Dave shook his hand, looking amused. "Sure. I remember you."

"From where?"

"The Mountain Goat." Dave's smile widened.

But Griff's frown only deepened. He hadn't been expecting that. And he didn't seem to like it at all.

Awesome. Nothing better on a summer Sunday than watching your two ex-lovers stare each other down. And for what? I'd always assumed that men would save their macho bullshit for *women they were actually interested in.*

"Guys," I said. "Who wants a glass of perry? I was just going to pour Dave his first taste."

"He's a perry virgin?" Griff yelped, and even Audrey rolled her eyes.

"Sit," I ordered. I slapped the folder of labels against Griff's chest. "Make yourself useful."

Five minutes later, four so-called grownups were seated on the porch, sipping glasses of Uncle Otto's perry.

"The taste is amazing," Dave said. "It really reminds me of apple cider."

Griffin made an exaggerated choking sound. "It does *not* taste like apples. *Jesus*. Perry has a much lighter mouthfeel and the color is completely different."

Dave blinked. "Right. How could I have been so blind?"

Audrey smirked, and Griff scowled.

Poor Dave. The truth was that pear cider tasted shockingly like its apple cousin, having much of the same tang. But a snob like Griffin could go on until a week from Tuesday about subtle differences in tannins and acidity.

Audrey met my gaze. She was obviously restraining a giggle.

"Pears have distinct tannins and a higher sugar content than apples," Griff went on. "The fermentation process happens at a completely different rate."

"Okay. Just going out on a limb here," Dave said drily. "But are you involved in cider-making?"

I couldn't hold in my laughter anymore, and Audrey joined me.

"As a matter of fact, I am," Griff grumbled.

twenty-two
dave

SIPPING perry with the bearded farmer, I helped Zara and Audrey stick labels on a couple hundred miniature wine bottles.

"What's in here, anyway?" I asked, smoothing down another label. The label read only "Audrey," with last year's vintage.

"The best hard cider Griff ever made," Zara said. "It won a big award. The Stanley Cup of cider tastings."

I knocked my knee into hers. "Look at you, with the hockey terminology."

"You run a bar, you learn a few things. Business was always crap during the finals."

"Ah." I conjured up an image of The Mountain Goat in my mind, which wasn't hard, because I loved the place. "There was no television in your bar. It's like the last bar on earth without a TV."

"I know. I liked it that way. I don't want to live in a world where everyone is pasted to a screen."

"I hear you." I stuck on another label. "But I have to run, now. Literally. I have to get a workout in to pay for that big piece of lasagna I ate."

"And the pie," Zara pointed out.

"That, too."

"I'd give you a bottle of Audrey," said Audrey. "But you have to attend my wedding if you want one. Saturday. Five o'clock."

"Got it." I chuckled. "Nice seeing you again, Audrey."

Zara walked me inside, where I thanked her mother for lunch. Mama Rossi had softened up just a little towards me, I decided. Because she said, "Goodbye, honey. Come again anytime." Or maybe she was just looking forward to grilling me some more.

I was spared from having a final discussion with Zara's grumpiest uncle, because he was busy arguing with Griffin Shipley. As best I could tell, Griffin wanted Otto to sell him part of his pear harvest. "I can't get cider pears anywhere else," he argued. "And you aren't monetizing them at all."

But Otto didn't sound too keen on the idea of selling part of his harvest, and for some reason it made me happy to see Zara's ex fail to get his way.

I shouldn't have cared, though. It had nothing to do with me.

On the porch, I gave Zara a hug and kissed her forehead. "Thank you for lunch, beautiful. Text me if you want to get together."

"I will," she said. "But it's going to be a busy week."

"That's my fault!" Audrey said cheerfully. "Last-minute wedding prep is brutal."

"Maybe I'll see you at yoga, then?"

"Maybe?" Zara said, giving me a wave as I walked off the porch.

I could feel her friend Audrey's eyes on me as I got into my rental car. The minute I pulled away, I knew they'd be talking about me. And I wished I were a fly on the wall. Zara was hard to read. I shouldn't care how she felt about me, but I did anyway.

While the engine warmed up, I found four missed calls on my phone, all from Bess. And when it rang again through the car's Bluetooth as I drove along the hilltop, I answered it.

"How'd it go?" Bess asked at once.

"Just a flesh wound," I said in my best Monty Python accent.

"No, really."

"Fine. Of course it went fine. I got all the standard questions. Zara's uncle is a tool. But I don't mind being grilled about my career. And after lunch I spent some time with Zara, and that was nice."

"What about the baby? Did you play with her?"

"Wait, is that something you're supposed to do?" I'd meant it as a joke, but playing with babies wasn't really part of my repertoire.

"Dave!"

"Just kidding. We went for a walk, and when she fell asleep on Zara I carried her home."

"Yeah?" The sound of optimism in my sister's voice was pretty hard to miss. "I wish I could have seen it. Did anyone take a picture?"

"No." It hadn't occurred to me. Carrying Nicole wasn't a photo op. It was just something I'd done for Zara, who had "carried" her in one way or another for two years. Though I hadn't minded the feel of her warm weight on my injured shoulder. Babies smelled like strawberries, apparently.

Bess let out a deep, wistful sigh, which I found mildly alarming. My sister's sudden attack of baby fever was freaking me out a little. So I changed the subject. "Zara's mom cooked a feast. I'm gonna have to run an extra three miles to work it all off."

"Were her uncles hard on you?"

"Nah. They were just letting me know they were paying attention." Though I'd never be the guy they wanted for Zara. Maybe nobody was. No man alive would ever be good enough to impregnate *my* sister, so I didn't expect Zara's family to like me, either.

But I'd wanted to make Zara more comfortable, especially after our fight. And I'd done that. She'd hugged me goodbye with a secret smile.

I'd take it.

"Can I come back next week?" my sister asked suddenly.

"To Vermont?" The request surprised me.

"Of course to Vermont. I'm trying to clear a couple of days so I can visit again. You invited me, remember?"

"You're always welcome," I said quickly. "When you pick a flight, text me." I loved my sister, but a couple of hours' notice would be nice. "Hey—Bess? I had a weird memory today. You wore cloth diapers with safety pins on each side. And this plastic thing that went over them."

She was so quiet for a second that I thought maybe the call had cut out. "There's no way I could remember that, Davey."

"I suppose not." And I didn't really want her to. Our mother's death had been awful. But it hadn't been the most awful part of our childhood. Our widowed father's punches had been worse. And I knew for sure that Bess remembered those.

"What's next with the lawyer?" she asked.

"Um…" I tried to bring my brain back to the present. "I'll do my paternity-test kit and send it back. He'll draft a child-support agreement. Then I'll have to have an awkward conversation with Zara about how she wants to be paid. She'll get a lump sum up front, of course. For back payment. But I could advance her more money if she wants to move into an apartment with a yard."

"Or," my sister said. "You could just buy a house with a yard. A house in that town can't cost much."

I thought about that for a second. "You're right. Then she wouldn't have to spend the child-support money on rent."

"And you'd have an investment."

"You're pretty smart for a girl."

"Davey!" she shrieked at the insult, while I cackled. There were things I said only to rile up my sister. It was painfully clear that all the women in my life were smarter than the men.

Just spend five minutes in our locker room, and you'd be convinced.

"Gotta go," I told her. "There's no cell service when I get close to the cabins."

"Later, turd."

"Later."

twenty-three
zara

WHEN I'D TOLD Dave I was going to have a busy week, it wasn't stretching the truth.

There were last-minute preparations for Audrey's wedding. And I needed to line up extra childcare for the week following the wedding. Griff and Audrey were taking a honeymoon in San Francisco, which meant that I'd be working twelve-hour days.

Meanwhile, Audrey wasn't fully present at work. She was focused on wedding details and relatives who were arriving in town.

Also puking. Poor Audrey spent part of her coffee-shop hours ducking into our bathroom to dry heave. We weren't discussing her pregnancy yet. She hadn't come clean. But when she wasn't puking, she was shoving bread in her mouth. Oh, and she'd given up coffee. Either the Apocalypse was upon us or the girl was preggers.

I was excited for her. But needless to say, this week I did all the heavy lifting in the shop.

So it wasn't exactly a good moment to get a call from Dave, asking me to meet him at an address in town. "Can I have just a half hour of your time?" he asked. "I need your opinion about something."

"Today?" I cringed when the question came out bitchier than I'd meant it to.

"Well…I could probably schedule a different time. But today would really be best."

"What is it, anyway?" I couldn't imagine Dave needing my opinion on anything important.

"I'd rather show you than tell you."

Right.

Sigh.

Even if I hadn't been so busy, the vague answer would have been irritating. But Dave was my Kryptonite. "Okay," I caved. "I'll meet you at eleven. Before the lunch rush, I guess."

"Thanks, gorgeous." He repeated the address and we hung up. And an hour later I drove up the hill toward town. If I hadn't been in a hurry, it would have made a lovely ten-minute walk.

The address he'd sent me belonged to a single family house on the hill situated between the river and the tiny downtown area. It was only a mile from my coffee shop. When I pulled my aging car into the driveway, Dave stood beside his rental car, talking to two people. One was Mrs. Godfrey, a real estate agent friend of my mother's. The other was a man wearing a tool belt. A van was parked at the curb. *Karl's Construction* it read on the side.

It was all very odd.

"Hi," I said warily as I stepped out. "What are we, uh, doing here?"

Dave beckoned me over. "I need you to take a quick peek inside this house." He pointed at the white one with a long porch on the front. "And also that one." He pointed at its neighbor—a brick Tudor with a peaky roofline.

"Why, exactly?" I wondered aloud. Mrs. Godfrey beamed and the contractor just looked bored.

"You have to pick one, so I can let the contractor know," Dave said. "Both houses need work."

"The colonial needs a new kitchen," Mrs. Godfrey put in, as if her opinion was useful right now. "New counter tops and appliances, at least."

"And I don't like the electrical in there." The contractor jerked a thumb at the white house. "Gonna need an upgrade if you want a dual fuel range." He looked at me as if I knew what he was talking about.

I really didn't enjoy being confused, and my natural response was to get snippy. "David," I barked. "Come here a second." I marched out of earshot of his new friends and over to a nice lilac bush in front of the Tudor.

He followed me, and when I stopped, he put his hands on my shoulders. "Sorry, Z. I didn't know everyone would show up at once. But I need you to take a look at these two houses and pick one."

"Why?" My pulse fluttered, because it sounded like Dave was planning to buy a house in Vermont. Although that couldn't be right. The man got paid a lot of money to play hockey in Brooklyn. But my foolish heart wished for it anyway.

He didn't help matters by stepping closer to me and giving my shoulder muscles a squeeze. I looked up into his green eyes at close range and held my breath.

"For you," he said, in a low voice. "And Nicole. You said you were looking for a house on the way into town. With a yard. There are only two houses for sale that fit that description. These two."

Wait.

"For me?" I squeaked. "I'm not in the market to buy a house right now." Maybe five years from now I could afford to think about it. Not now.

Dave stood back, and I lost his broad palms on my shoulders. "You know I have to go back to New York in a few weeks. So we need to do this sooner rather than later."

"Do *what* now?" I said, losing my battle with patience. "I can't just buy a house today because you got the urge to think over my real estate issues."

"I'm buying the house," he said.

"Why? For who?"

"For you and Nicole!" He squinted at me as if maybe I'd lost a few brain cells this morning.

I hadn't, but I might if he didn't start making more sense. He couldn't just buy someone a house. "When you asked me what I needed from you, I don't remember mentioning a house."

"But you *did* mention it. You said you were looking for a new place, just like these. And it's a simple decision, okay? Because there are only two. Personally, I think Number 12 has the better yard. But if you have a thing for fireplaces, Number 14 has three of them. You'll have to make up your mind in the next week, so the contractor can get the place ready for you. He had a cancellation."

"He had a cancellation," I repeated in a brittle voice.

"Right." He crossed his big arms and stared down at me. "Would you please look at the houses? Silly me, I thought you might enjoy it."

Bitch mode kicked into a higher gear. Because I would enjoy looking at houses, if it didn't mean *owing* him. My heart thumped speedily against my rib cage, and I fought to downshift from bitch to grump. And didn't quite manage it. "Fine," I snapped. "Show me, already."

"The previous owner opened up the kitchen to the dining room, converting this to a lovely family floorplan," Mrs. Godfrey gushed as I walked around the pretty space once again.

Both houses had three bedrooms and two bathrooms. Tons of space for one prickly woman and her toddler. First we'd toured the white colonial. As advertised, the kitchen was about thirty years out of date. But the Tudor was lovely inside, with cozy family spaces and a big cherry tree with a swing in the backyard. Like a storybook.

I loved it.

But I hadn't said so yet. Because I was still trying to wrap my head around the idea of moving into a house that Dave had purchased. I'd never been the kind of girl who'd clipped photos of her dream house. But somehow I was standing in it, anyway. I'd always been the type who'd clipped pictures of the dream guy, instead.

He was here, too. But not really. He was offering to mend my bank balance, but not my heart.

"What do you think?" Dave asked me when Mrs. Godfrey finally stopped talking. "It's okay if you can't decide today. I can give the contractor a deposit and send him home. You could take a few days to think it over."

Mrs. Godfrey stared at me, waiting for an answer. But I didn't like the pressure. So I stared her down until she got the message, saying, "I'll leave you two to chat."

"You don't have to do this," I said when she finally walked away. "I was doing all right on my own."

He didn't call me on the lie. He just parked his hip against the doorframe to the dining room and sighed. "I never said you weren't doing okay. But it's easy for me to help you like this. I'd feel better knowing you had a plan for the coming year. And, hey, your brothers think this town is a good investment. They said so several times on Sunday."

I blinked at him. *An investment.* It sounded so clinical. Not that I should care.

But that was the whole problem. I did care. He was standing about four feet away, and I could smell his woodsy scent and see the faded freckles at his hairline.

He was *right there*. And it was torture.

Since the moment he'd reappeared, I'd been trying to figure out what the future held. Would he leave again on August first, and not show his face for another few years? That was completely possible. He wanted to set us up in this house like a sea captain setting off for his next adventure. He could ship out without worrying too much about us. Heck, if only the house had a widow's walk in the attic, I could stand up there and watch for him, like a freaking loser.

I'd never wanted to be like my mother, damn it. She'd spent my childhood watching for signs, the way other people watched the weather. If my father brought her flowers, maybe he planned to stick around.

Dave wanted to buy a house for me to live in. Was that *more* encouraging than flowers, or less?

Fuck.

"I want to pay rent," I said, swallowing hard. Because he definitely hadn't thought this through. What if, a year from now, I met someone who really wanted to be with me? It wasn't completely impossible—at least I liked to think so. Living in Dave's house rent free would make me beholden to him. I needed nice, clean boundaries.

Clearly I should have thought about that before we'd gotten naked and had mostly-but-not-always-protected sex.

"We can work something out," he said, and I couldn't help but think it sounded patronizing. "Which house are you leaning towards?"

"Are the prices the same?" I asked.

He shrugged. "Close enough. One's cheaper, but needs more work. It's probably a wash. Do you want to tour the other one again? I could keep Mrs. Chattypants away from you."

The nickname made me smile in spite of myself. "I don't have time, but it doesn't matter. Both houses are fine, of course. But these brick fireplaces are yelling my name."

"They're pretty cool, right?" He smiled at me, and I felt it everywhere. "I'm going to catch the contractor before he drives away. Meet me outside?"

"All right."

His footsteps echoed in the empty house. After he left, I did another slow tour of the front parlor, with its inlaid wooden flooring. I passed the fireplace that made me want to curl up in front of it with a book. Then I walked slowly up the staircase. It was a bit narrow and steep. I'd need a baby gate for a little while, until Nicole was big enough to handle the stairs.

There was a big, sunny bedroom I'd give to my little girl, so she'd have a nice place to play with her toys. And the rear bedroom looked out on a big oak tree and a yard with a picket fence around it and lilac bushes along the back.

I wanted to live here, damn it. But not as Dave's pity case. I wanted to buy a house with a man who couldn't wait to fuck me in front of that fireplace while the baby slept upstairs. A guy who'd stand in the kitchen with me on Sunday mornings drinking coffee and making pancakes.

I might as well wish for a pony and front-row tickets to Pearl Jam.

And I really did need to get back to work. My brother Damien might have scared all the customers away by now. When I traipsed down the front steps, I was ready to tell Dave that I would like to live in the Tudor if I could make a meaningful contribution to the costs.

However.

By the time I got outside, Mrs. Godfrey was adding an "Under Contract" label to the sign in the front yard of the *other* house. And just like that, bitch mode was reactivated. Dave hadn't even waited for me to decide? Who does that?

"Who does what?" Dave asked, turning to watch me storm across the yard. So I must have said it aloud.

I marched right over to him. *No hitting this time.* "Are you *kidding* me?" I squeaked. "You told me to take my time? And five minutes later, you just pick anyway? What the hell?"

Heads turned, and I knew I was shouting. But seriously! This man and his ego!

"Beautiful, look." He actually caught my chin in his big, callused palm and turned it a few degrees. That made me even angrier, because he'd used those bossy, macho moves in bed, and it had driven me crazy. He'd overpower me and then thrust so slowly until I—

GAH!

Now I wanted to kick him in the shins *and then strip him naked.* So irritating! Finally, though, my eyes focused on the other sign—the one in front of the Tudor.

It too had an "Under Contract" label on it.

"Wait," I said stupidly. "*Both* of them? Why?" I shook off his hand and gave it a shove, while he chuckled as if he could hear my dirty thoughts.

"Yeah, I'm buying both houses. Your brothers think this town is a good investment, right? I'm getting in on the ground floor. We'll rent the one you don't pick. And if you're hell bent on making a contribution, you can take charge of renting out the spare house and acting as superintendent. That way I won't have to hire a property manager. And also, you can choose your own neighbor."

I looked up at the Tudor, picturing Nicole looking out the front window on an autumn day, as the leaves began to turn red and yellow. Then I swung my chin in the other direction, toward the white Colonial, which could be fixed up and rented out.

Dave-freaking-Beringer. He was still in charge. And we weren't even naked.

He lifted his hand a final time and gently nudged my chin upward, closing my gaping jaw. "Catching flies there, beautiful. Now didn't you say you needed to go back to work?"

twenty-four
dave

"WHEN I TOLD you to buy a house for Zara, I meant that you should *ask*, first." My sister delivered this bit of advice while we sat on the front porch of the cabin eating waffle cones after a late lunch.

"The real estate agent had me all spun up. 'Act now. They could both be gone tomorrow.'"

Bess rolled her eyes. "It's good to remember that there's a reason I negotiate on your behalf."

"You weren't around," I said, defending myself. "And the houses here just aren't very expensive. You could buy eight or ten of them for the price of my two-bedroom condo in Brooklyn."

"Be that as it may," my sister complained, "since you went all Tarzan on Zara, she isn't returning your calls. So I don't get to see my niece?"

"I don't remember Tarzan investing in real estate."

Bess giggled in spite of herself. "Still. You could have eased her into the house idea. Not everybody shops the way you do. How many apartments did you look at in Brooklyn before you bought your condo?"

"One."

"One other one?"

"No. Just the one."

My sister laughed. "Why can't you be that decisive about your contract extension?"

"Why didn't you get me a better contract extension?" I fired back.

"It's better than anyone else could have gotten you." My sister had never lacked confidence. "Text her again. I want to hold that baby."

"Maybe she's busy," I pointed out. "Her friend is getting married today. I think it's today." I wasn't going to pester Zara just because Bess was Little Miss Eager. Lately, every time Bess said Nicole's name, she looked a little possessed.

"Please?"

I pulled out my phone and tapped out a message. *Hey, Z. Bess is still hoping to see Nicole before tomorrow night. But if you're busy with the wedding, we'll understand.*

"I *won't* understand," Bess argued.

"Bess..."

My phone rang in my hand. Zara's number. "Look, pushy," I said to my sister. "Maybe it's your lucky day." Then I answered the phone. "Hello, gorgeous."

"Hi," Zara said, sounding out of breath. "I am sorry I didn't get back to you and Bess, but I'm having a *day*."

"It's no problem," I said, making myself sound as chill as possible. Because maybe I really had behaved like a bulldozer about the house thing. "Isn't that wedding today?"

"Yeah. And I'm in a bit of a situation. It is totally fine if you two are busy, but I have a wild little favor to ask."

"Name it," I said. "We're sitting on the porch doing nothing."

"Well, is there any way I could drop Nicole off with you for about ninety minutes?"

"Sure." Bess would probably wet herself with excitement. "Are you having a babysitting emergency?"

"My mother's friend fainted at the hair salon this morning, and Mom took her to the ER. They've already decided it's not serious, but they waited a long time to see a doctor and they're not back from Burlington yet..."

"Come on over," I told her. "It's fine. We'll watch her."

Beside me, Bess let out a little shriek of joy. And, hey—if I could make my sister smile and do Zara a favor at the same time, that made two women happy. That's two more than usual, so I was counting it as a win.

Twenty minutes later, Zara's crappy little car pulled up beside my rental. She emerged from the driver's side, full of apologies. But I missed the first few things she said because I was too busy admiring her in a sleeveless, flowered dress. Not only was she showing some very kissable skin, but her hair was loose and wavy, and she was wearing a little more makeup than usual, so her brown eyes looked enormous.

I had the same damned reaction to her that I always did—pure, burning lust.

"Milk doesn't need to be warmed. It's a hot day. I don't care how many of those crackers she eats, either. All my plans are blown to bits today, so just keep her happy. If you can." Zara cringed. "Once she wakes up and realizes I'm not here, she might howl. I'm sorry."

"It will be *fine*," Bess clucked. "We can take it. I brought toys."

Of course she did.

"Okay." Zara let out a deep breath. "I have to get back for the ceremony before Audrey has a coronary. The handoff would have been easier if Nicole hadn't conked out in the car, but..." She opened the back door, and there was the baby, strapped into her car seat in a checkered dress, rounded limbs flung out in every direction, eyes pressed closed.

"I'll pick her up," I offered, but Bess beat me to it. She carefully unclipped the harness and fit her hands under the sleeping child. Supporting her head, she lifted the baby out of the car.

"Hey, listen," I said to Zara, realizing something. "If you need me to bring her to you at the Shipleys' farm, I'm going to need the car seat."

"Oh, jeez!" Zara slapped a hand across her forehead. "You're right. There goes another ten minutes. I have to show you how to secure it..."

I pulled out the keys to my rental and offered them to her. "Let's just switch."

She hesitated less than half a second. "I owe you big, hockey man."

"Hockey man?"

She shrugged, handing me her set of car keys. "I'll text you the address as soon as the ceremony is over. I really appreciate this!" She jogged around the car, heading for mine.

"Take a breath, babe. Everything is fine."

That's when Nicole let out a wail.

"Uh-oh," Zara said, hesitating, her hand on the door.

Go, Bess mouthed, rubbing the baby's back.

Zara bit her lip. Then she jumped in my car and drove away.

Unfortunately, Nicole was quite determined not to join the list of females I'd made happy today.

Woken from her nap to find herself with strangers, she would not be soothed. If anything, the wailing got louder.

Bess tried everything. She offered the kid a bottle of milk and a handful of crackers. She fetched a toy she'd brought from a specialty shop in Michigan.

Nope, nope, and nope. Nicole's face had turned bright red, and I didn't know how one small person could make so many tears.

There was nothing wrong with my child's lungs, that was for sure.

Poor Bess paced the house with the baby in her arms. "Shhh, honey," she said. She tried singing a couple rounds of "Twinkle Twinkle Little Star." But nothing worked.

I didn't know I'd have to step in until my sister began to look tearful herself. "I know I shouldn't be offended," she said. "She only wants her mother."

Uh-oh. Sad sister. It was time for an intervention.

"I'll take a turn getting yelled at," I told her, scooping Nicole out of her arms. "You relax for a minute." *Maybe find some ear plugs.*

Nicole howled at me when I took her. She opened her mouth so wide I could see her tonsils rattling as she cried. Like the baby on *The Simpsons*, except cuter.

"I know, girl," I said, just in case she was listening. "You want your mama. We're going to see her in a while. She's pretty great. I understand how you feel."

The crying really seemed to bounce off the walls of the cabin, so I pushed open the screen door and went outside. The breeze had kicked up, tossing all the leaves on the branches. The baby's cries became a little distracted as she followed the movement with her big brown eyes.

"How do you feel about hammocks?" I asked her. Did other people ramble on to babies like this? Probably. It would be rude not to ask her opinion. "This hammock is my favorite thing about the cabin," I told her, sitting carefully down in the center of it. I rocked for a moment. And when the crying didn't get worse, I tilted until I was lying down in the hammock, one foot anchored on the ground for stability.

Nicole turned her body, struggling a little until she was lying in the crook of my arm. That took some effort, so she had to stop crying to do it. She began making little snuffling sounds, her back hitching with each shuddery inhale. Then she let out a big, resigned sigh.

"Sorry you're stuck with me," I whispered, and she listened. I nudged the ground with my foot, and we swung gently.

One little hand suddenly gripped my thumb, but she didn't complain.

"It's nice here," I pointed out. "Not too hot, not too cold. If you want to finish that nap you started, now might be a good time. Just sayin'."

Small fingers sifted through the hair at my wrist, and I rocked the hammock gently again. We had a view of the treetops, where the breeze whispered. Out of the corner of my eye I saw Bess's face appear in the window of the cabin. She was probably wondering what I'd done to stop the crying. But she was smart enough not to come outside and ask.

The baby was a warm weight against my ribcage. The breeze was sweet on my face. The July day held its breath for me, and the baby didn't start crying again.

I must have dozed off. The next sound I registered was the faux-shutter noise of a phone snapping pictures. I opened my eyes to see Castro standing over me, grinning away, tapping the screen repeatedly. I gave him a glare. *Don't wake up this baby or I will end you.* Nicole was passed out, her little face turned into my chest, her eyes screwed shut.

Grinning, Castro backed away, then handed the phone to Bess who was lurking nearby. They fled when I gave them another glare.

I lay there a while longer. Parts of my body were numb, and my healing shoulder was stiff. But a twenty-million-dollar signing bonus wouldn't have been enough to make me move.

Who would even recognize me right now? Two weeks ago I'd driven to Vermont with very different ideas about how my vacation—and my life—were supposed to go. Whatever Castro had captured on that camera was a shot I'd never expected to pose for. It was madness. I knew this.

Weirdly enough, I didn't mind all that much just now.

Eventually Nicole woke up from her nap, this time in a better mood.

Bess spread a blanket on the lawn, and the baby deigned to sit on her lap, snacking on strawberries, while I did some stretches on the grass and watched my sister. She'd brought Nicole a wooden school bus with little painted peg people that fit inside the top. The bus rolled on its perfect wooden wheels, but the baby seemed to like taking the people out and then putting them in again, one at a time.

The toy looked handmade, and I wondered where Bess had gotten it, and what she saw when she looked at it. Bess and I never had anything that nice to play with, ever. I remembered loving the

Head Start program my mother had dumped me in when I was four because they had toys there, and I could touch them whenever I wanted to.

Jesus.

The worst thing about the last two weeks wasn't the stress of finding out I'd fathered a child. And it wasn't getting yelled at by a baby or my sister. The worst part was a brain full of shitty old memories. No lie—every tense conversation with Zara was easier than five minutes alone with my own head.

I pulled out my phone to distract myself. There were texts from Zara, with an address for the farm. Her mother was scheduled to arrive at the wedding during the ceremony. And Zara would text me when it was over, probably around six.

It was almost six now.

I knelt beside the spot where Bess sat with Nicole. "I'm going to change. Don't want to walk through someone's wedding wearing this." I pointed at my gym shorts and T-shirt.

"Good plan," Bess said without looking up.

But when I got up to go, Nicole squawked. Then she raised her short little arms up to me.

"Wow, Davey." Bess put a hand on her heart and smiled. "The lady wants your attention."

"I'm just going upstairs," I said to Nicole. "I'll be right back."

That apparently wasn't good enough. She put her little hands on the ground and pushed herself into a standing position. Then she came for me.

"Fine," I said, caving. I didn't want her to cry again. "Let's go find a nicer shirt for me to wear." I scooped her up and carried her indoors.

Upstairs, my bed was unmade. So I awkwardly tugged the comforter up while holding Nicole in one arm. "Okay, little miss." I deposited her on the bed. "Let's see what we've got." I opened the closet to locate the button down I'd brought to Vermont. I grabbed my T-shirt and pulled it off. Then I tossed it at Nicole, and it came down on her head.

She giggled from underneath.

I hastily buttoned up the clean shirt and pulled my nicer pair of khakis out of a drawer. But then I hesitated. Nicole had shrugged off the T-shirt and was watching me. So I turned away like a prude and changed my pants facing into the closet. If she had an opinion on the color of my boxers she did not express it.

When I turned around again, she had crawled to the edge of the bed and was leaning down, head first. So far down that—

I lunged, catching her by the waist just as she nearly executed a face plant onto the wood floor.

She squawked as I moved her back onto the bed.

"Everything okay up there?" my sister called. She must have been hovering at the bottom of the stairs, waiting for me to fuck up.

"Yup! All set!" *Except I'd thought the baby might know better than to dive to her own doom.* My heart was pounding from the near miss. I could just picture handing Nicole back to Zara with a giant bruise on her face and a possible concussion.

Note to self—don't take your eyes off the kid.

Tucking in my shirt in record time, I scooped Nicole off the bed. "Try not to scare me like that again," I whispered. "At least not until I figure out what the hell I'm doing."

"Ba-bah-de-da," she said, as I carried her into the bathroom to do the worst one-handed tooth-brushing job ever. It was a mystery to me how Zara ever got anything done at all. Single moms must develop some kind of ninja skills just to get through the day.

By the time I carried her downstairs, Zara had texted to say that the ceremony was over and that I could bring the baby to Shipley Farm. "She says her mother will be there shortly," Bess added. Then she looked up from my phone, and her face lit up. "Holy cow. You are hilarious."

"What?" I looked down at myself, wondering what I'd done.

"You're twinsies! I need a picture. Stand on the porch." She snapped her fingers.

When I looked at Nicole, I saw what she meant. The pattern on the baby's blue checkered dress was awfully similar to the one on my blue and green checked shirt.

"Adorable," my sister said, aiming her phone at us, as I tried not to roll my eyes.

After the photo, Bess took Nicole out of my arms for one more squeeze. "You are my favorite baby," she said to Nicole. "Please don't get much bigger before I find a way to see you again."

The look on Bess's face was one I'd never seen before. Pure yearning. She carried the baby to her car seat, strapped her in, and put the wooden bus on the seat beside her.

"You could drive over there with us," I offered.

Bess shook her head. "You go. Spend a few minutes with Zara. I'll start dinner with Castro. I told him I'd try out a recipe for peach pie."

Huh. My sister wasn't much of a cook. Eating a pie she made might require some diplomacy. "All right. See you in a bit."

Zara's car was a piece of shit, I noted as I drove away. It had a hundred and eighty thousand miles on it. But one feature was nice—she had an extra mirror clipped to the rear-view, and when I glanced at it I could see Nicole's face in the back seat.

Another single-mom innovation.

Finding Shipley Farm was easy. There were a hundred cars lining the otherwise sleepy dirt road. I added Zara's car to the end of the line and climbed out. "Okay, girlie," I said to Nicole. "Let's go find your mommy."

Nicole smiled so widely that I found myself smiling right along with her. I took stock of both of us. My fly was zipped, and my shirt was tucked in. "You look like a big girl in this dress," I told Nicole, smoothing it down. "Very appropriate for a wedding."

I carried her the quarter mile or so up the long driveway, past rows of apple trees not unlike the pear trees on Zara's family farm. Only this place seemed bigger.

So this was Shipley Farm. It was a nice spread, I had to admit. I wondered what Zara thought about this wedding. If she'd gotten her original wish, it might have been *her* wedding, right? If Griff hadn't ended things, she and I would never have had our fling, and Nicole wouldn't be propped onto my right hip as I approached a wide, oval lawn where guests stood in clusters.

Would an outcome featuring Mrs. Zara Shipley have been better for everyone?

Ten days ago I would have said yes. But now Nicole was a very real weight on my arm. Bess was deeply in love with the baby, and I had to admit that Zara seemed happy—if not with me, then with life in general.

Besides—nobody had asked me, anyway. I was starting to realize that getting older was just a lengthy exercise in getting schooled on all the ways you weren't in charge of your own destiny.

The baby wiggled in my arms as we approached the wedding guests. She wanted to get down and run across all that green grass. But I couldn't give in. There was a cocktail hour in progress. Caterers circled with trays of drinks. I scanned the crowd for Zara, but other women wearing the same exact dress kept fooling my eyes.

Someone pointed at me—a stranger who whispered into his date's ear. I felt eyes on me, but I didn't really care.

There was only one person here that I needed to find.

twenty-five
zara

MY GOD, weddings were stressful. Maybe it was actually a *good* thing that I would never have one of my own.

"Is there anything I can bring you?" I asked Audrey for the seventeenth time. "Maybe something bland to put in your stomach?"

"Sure," she whispered.

We were standing behind the caterers' tent, where Audrey had just puked into a wastebasket. I was holding a stack of napkins, handing them to her one at a time.

"I'll be okay now," she said with a watery smile. "I think." She took the glass of water from my hand, rinsed out her mouth, and spit.

"Here's the lipgloss." I offered it to her from my purse.

She shook her head. "The fake cherry smell isn't helping."

"Oh, honey. I'm so sorry."

"Don't be." She took a deep breath and let it out. "I knew this was a risk."

"You're a trooper. And I'm sure Griff will be great about it on your honeymoon."

"He's over the moon about the pregnancy."

"Oh, I'm sure." He would be, of course. Before today, Griff and his mother were the only two people who'd *officially* known about Audrey's pregnancy. They'd been trying to reach the twelve-week mark before announcing it. But morning sickness was still hitting Audrey hard, and this morning I'd stopped pretending I didn't know she was pregnant. Instead, I'd held her hair and her dress out of the way every time she'd barfed.

"You're my hero," Audrey had whimpered more than once already.

She'd held it together during the ceremony and the receiving line, but when I had seen her dart away from Grandpa Shipley and run behind the tent, I'd followed with the water and the napkins.

"This gets better, right?" She dabbed at her watery eyes.

"Absolutely." I was faking this knowledge, though, because I'd never thrown up when I was pregnant, whereas Audrey had puked four times already today. I had no clue when she'd start to feel better. "If it's any consolation, you really do look beautiful right now. I hate you just a little bit that you can yarf and still look put-together."

"I've been a very tidy barfer today. There should be a trophy."

"What sounds better—a bit of bread, or sparkling water?"

"Fizzy water. Definitely."

"Coming right up."

Audrey pasted on a smile and went back to her guests. I brought her a drink and then got a glass of soda for myself. Today had been long already, and I was looking forward to eating some barbecue and then sneaking out before it got very late.

Outside the bar tent I found May Shipley—Griff's sister—as well as my friends Lark and Zachariah. The three of them were standing in the sunshine together, eating from a bunch of grapes that May held on a plate.

"Where's Nicole today?" Zach asked me after I'd greeted them.

"She's"—I'd never said these words before—"with her father for a couple of hours. My mother was supposed to be my babysitter, but she got stuck at the ER with a friend of hers. In fact..." I pulled out my phone and looked for my mother's last text. There wasn't a new one, which meant she was still en route.

"Wow," Lark said. "Does that feel strange to see them together?"

"You have no idea," I said, taking a pull of my soda. "I'm not used to it yet." *And probably never will be.*

Time for a subject change. "Did the wedding give you any big ideas?" I teased Zach, cuffing him on the arm.

He laughed and glanced at his girlfriend. "What's the count up to?"

"Eight," Lark said. "Eight people in twenty minutes."

"As if the topic had never occurred to me before." He wrapped an arm around Lark's shoulders.

"I'm sorry!" *God.* Open mouth, insert foot. "I should be the *last* person to tease you about popping the question. Social convention and I don't really get along very well."

Lark smiled at me from inside Zach's embrace. "And yet *you're* not the one who spent a couple of months at the mental hospital. So you have that going for you." She held up her beer and we touched glasses. "Cheers!"

I liked these two a lot. They gave me hope, because they'd both been through a lot, and now they were so happy together. I scanned the rest of the crowd and saw a lot of smiling faces. A girl shouldn't breathe too deeply here today—the wedding was off-gassing optimism right along with the smell of barbecue smoking on the grill.

And I was happy in spite of the odd circumstances. I'd just stood up for Griff and Audrey's wedding, keeping my Joy Face intact the whole time. It hadn't even been that hard, because I really did feel joy for the two of them. The way Griff looked at Audrey while reciting his vows—with every promise echoed by the expression of love in his big brown eyes—gave me hope for the future of the human race.

This was a *good* day. I was going to keep telling myself that.

"Whoa," Lark said suddenly. "Is that your…? *Wowzers.* I wouldn't kick him out of bed, either."

And then my eyes found the man who'd made her say that. Hell, the crowd parted like the Red Sea for Dave Beringer as he came toward me with my daughter in his arms. Their two coppery heads were inches apart, and I was startled by how much like a matched set they really were.

Seriously, I forgot to breathe there for a moment. My reaction was swift and strong—a tug in my belly and a quickening pulse.

Okay, who knew that the sight of the two of them would be ten times harder to watch than Griff's wedding? My gaze snagged on Nicole's chubby arm resting casually against Dave's chest and her serene face. Just like any little girl being carried by her daddy.

My throat got tight even as I straightened my spine and prepared to greet him. This was so much worse than the wedding, because my yearning for the picture in front of me was fierce.

"Damn," May murmured. "He's dreamy."

That he was. *Dreamy* was exactly the right word, because dreams weren't real. He was smiling at me, causing another hormone spike throughout my body.

"Hey there," I said in greeting as May and Lark moved over to give him the space to approach me. "You guys look cute together. Your tough-guy rep is going to take a hit."

The baby chose that moment to dive for me, but both Dave and I were ready.

With a chuckle, he transferred her weight to my arms. "I think she missed you. But I promise she didn't cry the *whole* time."

"I should have brought you ear plugs," I said. "Have you met May, or Lark and Zach?" I introduced them, and when Dave leaned forward to shake Zach's hand, May made a comical fanning gesture in front of her chest.

He's so hot, she mouthed.

Yeah, I'd noticed.

When Dave stepped back, he put a polite hand on my shoulder, his touch cordial. "How are you?"

"Great!" I said a little too brightly, aware of all the people looking our way. Dave's reappearance had been widely discussed, but few people had set eyes on him. Several dozen were taking that opportunity right now.

Naturally Nicole picked that moment to put her hand right between my boobs, down my dress. "Abah!" she babbled, which surely meant, *Whip out the boobs, Mom.*

"Well..." I chuckled nervously. "Since your grandma is deep in discussion with Father Peters, you and I can sneak off for a few minutes. I should nurse or she'll be cranky for my mom."

"I'll come with you," Dave said.

"You don't have to." I'd expected him to bail immediately.

"It's okay." He pointed into the catering tent. "In there, maybe? There're chairs."

I didn't want to be nursing while they ran around me setting the tables. "No, this way." I led him to the side of the cider house. On a work day, Zach and Griff might be washing or filling cider barrels here. But today the concrete slab was empty of people, and I sat down on the bench against the wall.

Immediately, Nicole tugged on my dress.

"Hang on there, champ," I said, trying to wriggle an arm out. My efforts weren't working.

"Want me to hold her for a second?" Dave asked.

I looked up at him in surprise. We'd come a long way in two weeks. And every time he did something fatherly my insides turned to mush.

Danger!

"Well... Could you unzip me?" I steered my knees away from him in order to expose the back of my dress.

"Any day of the week." He chuckled. Then his hand landed at my shoulder, the palm warm, while his other one slid my zipper down.

I bit my lip as a sizzle ran through my body. Just the brush of his fingertips against my skin was enough to remind me how much I'd enjoyed being undressed by this man.

Stop it, Zara! We're not going there.

Slipping an arm out of one side of my dress and bra, I set the baby up to nurse on the right side. Tired—and probably cranky from dealing with strangers—she naturally tried to get at my *other* breast.

"Nope, sorry. You have to go with righty today." I was trying to preserve a few shreds of my dignity by exposing only the boob furthest from the party.

"She has a preference?" The bench creaked as Dave sat down

beside me. He angled his big body the other way and was actually blocking for me now.

"Yup. She prefers the left side. I think she's going to be left-handed."

"I'm left-handed," he said suddenly. "Is that genetic?"

"No idea. Although Alec once made a joke about loading the shotgun for any left-handed redheads he met."

Dave snorted. "Of course he did. Your brother hates me."

"He hates the *idea* of you," I corrected.

"Whatever. I can take it."

We fell into a companionable silence as the baby nursed and the sun sank behind the distant hillside. Dave was people-watching, while I gazed down at my daughter. "How'd it go with her?" I asked. She looked as peaceful as ever.

It had been incredibly hard to walk away from her earlier—to just hand her over even though I'd known in my gut that Bess was as avid a babysitter as they come. Even though I knew Dave well enough to say he was a good guy who cared about people.

It was still hard. For Nicole's sake, I wanted Dave to stay in our lives. But sharing her might be the hardest thing I'd ever tried to do.

"It went fine. She freaked out when you left, but then she fell back to sleep and woke up in a better mood."

"I should have brought you the portable crib," I said, feeling guilty. *Here, watch my screaming kid without any of the gear!*

"It was okay. We took a cat nap together in the hammock."

"Really?"

"Sure. I like a nap as much as the next guy."

The mental image was almost more than I could take. Nicole curled up in a hammock with Dave? Was it awful that I was a little jealous of both of them?

At the sound of a bell being struck, I looked over Dave's shoulder to see Dylan Shipley—Griff's younger brother—walking through the crowd with a dinner bell which he tapped with a fork.

"Can I offer you a plate of barbecue for your efforts today?" I asked, tucking my boob back into my bra. Nicole sat up on my lap, swaying like a little drunk. She had that blissed-out look she always got after nursing.

"Sure?" he said. "I hadn't planned on staying, but I'm always happy to hang out with you."

"And Audrey invited you," I reminded him, brushing aside his compliment. As if it didn't light me up inside to hear him say it.

"Let me zip you up," he said.

With my face warming, I turned to give him access to my back. The man must have zipped and unzipped a few hundred women in his life because he knew to hold the two sides of the fabric together to let the zipper run smoothly.

I popped up off the bench. "Is everything where it ought to be?" I asked, looking down at myself as best I could with a toddler in my arms.

Dave's eyes heated. "Everything is exactly where it should be."

My pulse kicked up several notches. "Come on. Let's find my mother, and then some food."

We handed the sleepy baby off to Grandma, who thanked Dave politely and then took her home.

In the catering tent, Dave and I fixed plates for ourselves and sat down at a table of familiar faces. This wasn't the sort of wedding with assigned seats. Audrey had wanted to keep things casual.

With us sat Zachariah, Lark, and May Shipley and her girlfriend Daniella. It was a good crowd. My friends would all be sweet to Dave. It was a typical Shipley gathering in many ways—good food and teasing. We were hard on Zach about the notecards in his pocket.

"But I never give speeches!" he said. "This is my first one!"

Of course it was.

The only awkwardness at dinner came from Daniella. She was

already tipsy, and she didn't wear it very well. She dominated every conversation and gave out too many bold opinions. And generally made an ass of herself.

"Professional hockey is a brutal sport," she slurred. "It probably contributes to domestic violence. Society idolizes the masculine warrior. Long live the patriarchy."

"Uh-huh," Dave said cheerfully. "Did you know there's a pro hockey league for women now? They're warriors, too."

But Daniella ranted on.

Poor May gave me a weary smile as the band tuned up outside. "My brother has just tapped a keg for a toast," she said, pointing to a table where Griffin stood passing out glasses. "Has Dave tried the cider, yet?"

"I don't think so," I said, putting a hand on his arm. "You need to try this, since you helped paste labels onto a couple hundred bottles the other day."

He pushed his empty plate away and stood up. "I'm game. Shall I bring over six glasses?"

"None for me," May said, standing up, too. "But I'll help you and grab a ginger ale for myself."

"May doesn't drink," Daniella sneered. "We weren't together back when she was actually *fun*."

There was a long, awkward silence while we all cringed for May. Her family had been patiently waiting for her relationship with Daniella to end. But it was going on seven or eight months, now.

"Well, I guess it's showtime," Zach said, rising to pull his notes from his pocket.

After Dave and May brought back the drinks, Zachariah gave a short but funny speech about Griffin as a grumpy bachelor. There were several adorkable *Star Wars* references. And then everyone in the tent raised a glass to Griffin and Audrey.

"Tonight, enjoy the music and the cider," Zach urged. "Here's to the only couple I've ever met who made their own hooch for the wedding!"

There were cheers and catcalls as Audrey and Griffin kissed. But my eyes were on Dave as he tasted the cider. "Goddamn," he said immediately. Then he took a second sip, his throat working. I used to suck on that neck…

I cleared my throat and looked away. "I know, right? This cider is their prizewinner. It's called 'Audrey.'"

"It's amazing." He put his nose over the glass and inhaled. "I may have underestimated your favorite farmer."

"Don't tell him," May said. "My brother's ego is already unmanageable."

"It'll only get worse," Daniella slurred. "He got his wife pregnant. That'll make 'im beat on his chest."

"Shhh!" May hissed.

"Wow, already?" Dave said lightly, pretending to check his watch. "The man works fast."

I gave him a good-natured kick under the table, and he smiled at me over the rim of his glass. And that smile was potent. "You know," I teased him. "This cider is rumored to have special powers."

"Mmh?" he asked.

"What do you think it tastes like?"

He closed his eyes. "I'm not sure. It's musky and dark."

"Sexxx," Daniella said. "Griff's cider tastes like a long night of dirty sex."

Dave didn't say anything. But the smile he gave me said, *No wonder I like it so much.*

I drank deeply of my glass, too, enjoying its heady aroma. I wasn't going to nurse again tonight, so I was free to enjoy a glass. It was, as always, delicious. But I couldn't vouch for its aphrodisiac powers because I'd basically wanted to jump on Dave since the moment he'd appeared.

Outside, a dance floor had been laid on the lawn. The band kicked into a swing tune. Guests began to clap as Griffin and Audrey took the first dance. No silly slow dance for them—Griffin whirled Audrey around, and I wondered how her stomach was holding up.

"Wow," Daniella said. "I wouldn't have guessed Griff could dance."

"He used to be fun, too," May said drily.

More to the point, he used to be a football player before he became a farmer. The man could move. I knew this from ogling him at high school dances my whole life. The crowd cheered when he dipped his new bride. It was quite the spectacle.

After their two minutes of solo fame, the music slowed by just a hair as other couples took the floor.

"Let's go!" May said to her girlfriend. "I love swing music."

Daniella wrinkled her nose. "You go ahead. I'm not feeling it."

May's face fell, and I had to bite down on my tongue from wondering aloud who was the fun one in their relationship. I'd give Daniella a piece of my mind in a heartbeat, but I didn't want to embarrass May.

"Then I'll dance with you," Dave said, standing up and offering his hand to May.

"Really?" She grinned up at him.

"I love swing. Come on."

She took his hand with an apologetic glance at me. "Is it okay if I steal your date for a few minutes?"

"Of course it's okay. You kids have fun." The chance to watch Dave swing dance? I'd pay cash money to see that any day of the week.

And I wasn't disappointed. Holy hell. The moment Dave stepped onto the makeshift dance floor, I couldn't stop staring. His stance loosened as he took May's hand, his hips beginning to move with the tempo. He gave my friend a nod and a smile and then guided her into a basic swing step.

Maybe all athletes could dance?

But no. Dave was *spectacular*. His feet moved quickly, his steps light. And even as he wowed me with his prowess on the dance floor, he and May chatted. When she gave him a nod, he spun her, picking up the pace, weaving in a circle around and through the other dancers on the floor.

They were showing off, really. But who could hold it against them? May didn't have quite as many moves as Dave, but she was a great sport, following his lead.

Mine wasn't the only head that turned to watch them. Which meant that everyone saw my brother Alec cutting in a moment later. He tapped a whirling Dave on the shoulder, a grumpy look on his face. Then he said something curt. Dave's eyes widened at the interruption, but he stepped back immediately. The song changed just as Alec took May's hand.

I watched my brother begin to dance and cringed. He wasn't terrible, but Dave was a tough act to follow.

A moment later, Dave dropped into the seat beside me with a smile.

"That was fun to watch," I admitted.

"Is it your turn?" He asked.

"I'm sorry to say that swing is not part of my repertoire. I'd trip over my feet."

"I doubt that," Dave said kindly. "So I guess your brother has a thing for May?"

"Nope." I laughed. "To be honest, they're not really even friends. Alec owns a bar, and May is a recovering alcoholic. Not a lot of overlap there."

Dave chuckled. "So your brother hates me enough that he feels the need to break up a swing dance with one of his acquaintances?"

"I guess so. But don't take it personally. He's had two years to hate you and just a couple of weeks to think about getting past it."

Dave crossed his arms. "So I think you should dance with me. Consider it exposure therapy for your brother."

"I told you. I don't swing."

Dave tapped his foot in silence for another minute, watching the dancers move. And when the song changed, he stood up and held out a hand to me. "Slow dance! On your feet, beautiful."

"You smug bastard."

He smiled, his palm waiting for me.

I stood up slowly, suspecting this was a terrible idea. As my hand folded into his bigger one, I was sure it was.

"Come on, everybody can slow dance," he said, mistaking the reason for my hesitation. "Just pretend it's a high school dance, and they're playing 'Stairway to Heaven.'"

I followed him onto the dance floor, putting my hand on his shoulder. We were too close now. With his hand at my waist and the smooth scent of his aftershave enveloping me, wistfulness made me blurt out a trashy reply. "If this were a high school dance, we wouldn't be dancing. I'd probably be blowing you under the bleachers."

He threw his head back and laughed. "I knew I liked you." He pulled me a little closer. I liked the feel of his hand wandering onto my back better than I cared to admit. But at the same time, I felt eyes on us.

"People will talk," I said, straightening slightly to put another inch of respectability between us.

"And say what?" He grazed the shell of my ear with his lips.

Goosebumps rose on my back. "I can't decide if my scarlet letter dims or shines more brightly since you came to town. I have to live here after you go back to Brooklyn, you know."

"Sorry." He was quiet for a second, guiding me around in a slow circle. "Respectability has never been my forte. But I don't want to tarnish yours."

"It's blackened already, I guess."

"What a pair we make." Dave skimmed his lips over my eyebrow, then he pulled back an inch or two and gave me a potent smile.

My defenses were weakened, damn him. So I didn't look away. I just let his heated look shine all over me.

It was a bit of foolishness on a summer night. Swaying to a love song under a Vermont sky that was turning purple, it was hard to deny that I wanted this—the dance and that dangerous smile. I wanted him. Before he'd showed up this month, I'd made my peace with never seeing him again. But now here he was.

And I *ached*.

The music swelled, and his eyes fell shut. He kissed my forehead so tenderly I wanted to die. Because moments like this didn't last.

The brew of music and sex-cider that had claimed my better judgement was obviously affecting his, too. I forgot to care about eyes on us. I put my head on his shoulder and let him pull me closer—just for a little minute. Maybe two.

He turned his chin and kissed the corner of my mouth.

That's when reality set in. "You can't kiss me here," I said quickly.

"Then where *can* I kiss you?" His voice was pure smoke, and my tummy tightened up instinctively.

Thankfully, the song ended just then. I stepped back and lifted my chin, looking him straight in the eye. "I should go home. My mother has had a long day." That was really just an excuse. My baby girl was undoubtedly asleep in her crib. My mom's feet were probably up on the coffee table as she read one of her romance novels on Benito's sofa.

He raised his cayenne-pepper eyebrows. "You're bailing on Audrey's wedding before the cake is cut?"

"You bet," I said with more cheer than I felt inside. "I did my duty, and now I'm going to play the mom card and go home early."

"Then I'll walk you to your car, since I'm the one who knows where it is." Dave took my elbow and guided me off the dance floor. "But you'll have to help me find my rental."

"Of course." I let Dave steer me away from the festivities. I could feel Alec's eyes boring a hole in my back as we walked past where he stood drinking a beer and talking to May.

But I ignored him.

By the time I found Audrey and Griff to wish them well, it was fully dark. "You're parked over there," I said to Dave. "I'll show you."

"Uh-oh." He pointed to his rental car beside the farmhouse. "Looks like that Rav4 is parking me in. Don't suppose you know whose car that is?"

"Oh, crap." I had no idea. "Everyone in Vermont drives a Rav4. I'm so sorry."

I stopped and looked back at the wedding in full swing. The only way to sort it out would be to write down the license plate and ask the band's front man to make an announcement. And I didn't want to interrupt the festivities to announce my departure.

"What if I drop you at home?" I asked instead. "Tomorrow morning I could get my brother to retrieve your car." *While I run the bakery single-handedly.* The next ten days were going to be brutal.

"Sure," Dave said. "Bess has a rental car. She can just run me back here tomorrow."

"You guys have done so much already." I sighed. Today I'd added Dave and Bess to the long list of people I owed. But, hey—what was two more?

Because Dave had arrived after the ceremony, my car was literally the last one in a long line on the gravel road. He bleeped the locks, but then stalled in his tracks, his hand on my back. "Wow. See that?" His voice was full of awe. He'd lifted his chin skyward and was gazing at the stars.

Of all the details I'd memorized about Dave, I'd somehow forgotten this—his love of the starry sky. Instead of looking at the stars, too, I watched him. Fascination softened his features. It was hard to keep up my cynical view of men in general and Dave specifically as I watched his gaze dance around the summer sky.

Eventually he caught me staring. "What?" he whispered, the corners of his mouth quirking into a smile.

"You're just..." I paused, because there was no way to finish that sentence that didn't reveal the hold he still had on me.

"I'm just what?" He squared his body toward mine and took my face in both of his hands.

And maybe weddings *did* make people crazy. That's the only excuse I could think of for why I leaned forward and kissed the corner of his mouth. Just a sweet little touch of my lips against his.

He made a sexy grunt of surprise and pulled me in toward his body. When our chests collided, he angled his head and kissed me for real. His mouth was salty sweet and his kiss so tender that my heart expanded in my chest.

Big hands spread out across my back, their grip possessive. He took over the kiss, his bossy tongue coming out to play with mine.

Oh, damn. Why did I have to like it so much? Why?

On a groan, I broke it off. But instead of stepping back, I put my cheek against his shoulder and sighed. And the bastard *hugged* me.

Naturally, I liked that a whole lot, too.

"Weddings make people crazy," I mumbled into his collar. I thought he'd laugh, but he just ran a kind hand down my hair. He smelled wonderful. Like pine needles and clean shirts. "Time to go home," I said a little more firmly.

Some sort of self-preservation instinct kicked in, because I finally stepped away from him and fumbled my way into the car.

Not well enough, though. By the time we were rolling down the road, I realized I was sitting in the passenger seat of my own car, while he drove. Dave's kisses were obviously more mind-bending than strong liquor.

My temporary incapacitation must have been pretty obvious, because he drove me to the Gin Mill building instead of to his cottage. When he pulled into a parking spot outside the bar and shut the engine off, I had to finally look him in the eye.

"Beautiful," he said in that smoky voice. "Let's go upstairs and have a whole lot of sex."

What?

I blinked at him for a long moment. "Who says that? It was just a *kiss*," I managed eventually.

"No." He shook his head. "With you and me, it's never just a kiss."

"What does that even mean?" I asked in a quiet voice.

He sighed, then broke our gaze to look out the window. "I know you think everything is complicated. But when you look at me with those big, hungry eyes, it all seems pretty simple."

I didn't want to have big hungry eyes, damn it. "We can't. And the kiss was a mistake."

"You started it." He turned to me again and smiled.

Ungh. That smile was probably the reason I was a mother. This man's sex appeal had probably been studied in a laboratory. And if it hadn't been, it should be.

"You keep that wolfish grin zipped up," I said, scrambling for the door handle. “My mother is upstairs. You can’t just walk in with me, like, ‘Hey, Grandma! Just here for some more casual sex!’”

He snorted and then laughed.

“Go home, Dave.” With that as my parting shot, I hastily opened my car door to make my escape.

twenty-six
dave

I WAS SMILING up at her, a big old grin on my face. I was going to argue.

But I lost my train of thought as Zara was suddenly illuminated. Her pale dress was brightly lit from the back, and her hair shone. *Beautiful* was my only thought just before my synapses fired rapidly enough to clue me in on what was happening.

Those were headlights. And they were moving fast.

I think I lunged even before I heard the squeal of tires. I thrust my body sideways, jamming the gearshift into my ribcage as I grabbed Zara's body with both arms, yanking hard on her hips with all the torque I could muster.

Pulled off kilter, she tumbled back toward the seat. Her head and neck got caught on the car's roof, and there was a sickening split-second when I wasn't sure if I'd done it.

But then all of Zara came crashing into my arms. Her shriek was deafening as a pickup truck barreled alongside the car, snapping off Zara's open passenger-side door as it zoomed by.

I heard the sound of skidding tires as the driver tried to stop and then a sickening crunch as the back corner of the truck's bed swung into a telephone pole.

The truck finally stopped. But a moment later it leapt forward again, fishtailing in the gravel, then accelerating away.

"He...!" Zara said. Another beat went by. She wriggled free of me, mouth open, one hand at her jaw. A big red mark was forming where it had hit the door frame as I'd yanked her back inside. "I..." She tried again to speak. But then she gazed outside again, trying to make sense of the gaping hole where her car door had been.

All I could see now was the mark on her jaw. And I realized I was still clenching one of her hands in a death grip. I made myself let go, and raised my hands to gently cup her head. "Are you—"

"Yeah, it's just—"

"Is your..." I brushed a thumb across her jaw as gently as I could.

"You... You really—"

"Shh," I said, pulling her to me again, even though the gear shift was in the way. She started to shake. Or maybe we both did. I could feel her heart fluttering against mine, like a little bird's.

Some amount of time passed. I spent it trying not to think about the glow of the headlights on Zara's hair as the truck had accelerated toward her.

I became aware that nearby voices were raised in excitement. "What the hell happened?"

"Jesus Christ."

"Zara? Holy shit."

She pulled away from me to look up at her brother Benito. "I'm okay."

"The door of your car is *gone*. It's, like, fifty fucking yards away."

Nausea rolled through me as I pictured Zara standing against that door a few seconds before the truck hit it. "Someone call the police," I said, my tongue thick.

"They're on the way," Benito said.

During the next few minutes I worked out that Benito was managing the bar that night. Someone else who'd seen the speeding truck had gone in to fetch him.

My brain remained a little fuzzy. Shock would do that. I got out of the car and stood there, holding Zara's hand, leaning against the wrecked side of the car, waiting for the police, and just trying to hold my psyche in check.

Eventually the cops came. They let Zara speak first. "I didn't see the driver. I barely saw the truck. I didn't even know why Dave yanked me back into the car until I heard the truck crack off the door."

There was talk of calling the paramedics, but Zara waved them off. "I need to get upstairs."

At some point they let her go on up.

Watching Zara walk away splintered something inside me. There was a baby upstairs in her crib who'd almost lost her mother tonight. I felt sick every time I pictured those few seconds. It was a miracle she hadn't been hit. Hell, even if she'd left one leg outside of the car…

I shuddered again. "Sorry, what was the question?" I asked the cop who was trying to talk to me.

"What color was the truck?"

"Uh. Dark. Black, or at least dark gray."

"Model? Any idea?"

"Well…" I hadn't gotten a good look. "A really ordinary pickup. Maybe an F-150. Not fancy."

"We have cameras on this parking lot, Johnny," Benito offered. "I set 'em up myself."

"Yeah? That was gonna be my next question. Can we go see 'em?" the cop asked.

"Follow me," Benito said.

twenty-seven
zara

"WHAT HAPPENED?" my mother demanded the moment I stepped into the apartment.

"Everything is fine," I said in a shaky voice. "There was a truck. Drunk driver, maybe. He didn't hit anyone." *Because Dave pulled me out of the way, first.* I didn't go into detail because I didn't want to scare her.

"Why are the cops here?"

"Slow crime night in Vermont?" Sass was so ingrained in my personality that I could snark even when numb. And I *was* numb. My hands were cold and my knees felt unsteady. Not in a good way, either. "Go on home, Mom. Thanks for putting her to bed."

"Four picture books," she said with a smile. "She didn't want to go to sleep. Did she have a late nap?"

"Yeah," I mumbled. Dave had told me. But I could swear that conversation happened a week ago, not just a few hours ago.

"Get some sleep." She patted my cheek. "You're going to need it to make it through the next ten days."

"I know. Thanks again," I said by rote. "See you in the morning."

She left, but I didn't go to sleep. I spent some time staring out the window, watching the cops talk to Dave and then to my brother Benito. Then all the men disappeared from my view, possibly inside the bar. I stood there at the window for a minute longer waiting for them to reappear again.

They didn't.

I was still wound up. I toed off my shoes and tiptoed into Nicole's room to check on her. She'd kicked away her cotton blanket, so I pulled it up. She'd probably kick it off again the moment I left. It was midsummer, and the only one who was cold was *me*.

I stood there a long time, just watching the rise and fall of her little chest. What would Nicole's life be like if I were run down by a truck?

It was enough to give me another round of chills.

As I watched her sleep, I tried not to hear the terrible crack of the car door wrenching off, right after Dave's arms had yanked me violently into the car. My jaw ached just at the base of my skull where I'd gotten hung up on the door frame. Tomorrow I knew my neck would be stiff, too.

Whatever. I was still here. That's all that mattered.

So why was I still shaking?

The door buzzer sounded, startling me.

Not wanting the baby to wake, I scurried out of her room, eased the door shut, and then ran to press the lock button. I heard footsteps climbing the stairs at a rapid clip. I opened the door and there Dave stood, his expression intense.

"Are you okay?" he asked. He didn't wait for an answer. He pushed inside the apartment and pulled me to his chest.

Strong arms locked around me. The door thunked closed.

My nose met the V of skin where his top button was undone. I took a deep, steadying breath of him. He was warm and solid and I exhaled with shameless gratitude. The shaking didn't stop, though. It actually got worse for a second, as if my subconscious allowed itself to come fully unhinged in the safety of his arms.

He made a noise of distress, deep in his throat, and held me even more tightly. He kissed the top of my head. Then he did it again. Big hands smoothed their way down my arms, bringing much-needed warmth to my chilly limbs. "Are you okay?" he whispered gently. His hands swept up my back, until one wide palm cupped the back of my neck. "Are you hurt *anywhere?*"

I shook my head, but then his fingers skimmed my bruised neck and I flinched.

Dave tilted my head to see what had probably become a bruise. He made a hissing sound, and his fingers became more gentle as he probed the area. "Are you sure we shouldn't get you checked out?"

"No need," I choked out. I wasn't really injured. Just terrified.

His thumb traced my roughened skin. Then he bent down and placed his mouth over the hurt spot. I whimpered as soft lips comforted that spot. Unbidden, my hands dug into his shirt. And I turned my head a fraction of a degree to give him better access.

He let out a sound that was half groan, half growl, and I felt it everywhere. I turned my face again, this time to find his mouth with mine. And we came together in a way that felt completely inevitable, our lips sealing together just right on the first try. "Oh," I breathed against his mouth, parting my lips. And then his tongue stroked against mine. He tasted like man and warmth and everything I'd ever needed.

Yes. This. Finally.

I rose to my toes and wrapped my arms around him, leaning into all that solid weight. My poor, terrified heart had a better reason to race now. It was impossible to fear for my life when I was kissing the most intoxicating man who'd ever walked into it.

And he didn't miss a beat, folding me closer to his body, those strong hands dipping down to my ass, yanking me against him. His kiss was fierce and desperate. Seconds later, he turned us around, pressing my back against the door. He cupped my chin in one hand and held it there, kissing me with great focus and fire, while his other hand wandered my curves, cupping my breast, slipping down over my hip.

All the restraint I'd shown these past few weeks flew right out the window. Gone. I undid the top button of his shirt before abandoning that tedious work to caress his stomach instead. He groaned and I moaned and everything was a heated blur.

He lifted my dress.

I tugged at his belt.

His mouth found my throat.

My fingers fumbled to unzip his fly. And then his cock lay in my hand, hard and heavy.

"Fuck," he cursed. Then I heard a tearing sound—stitches giving way. A second later my panties fell off, and thick fingers forked between my legs, finding slickness. *Yes.* I bore down on that sweet friction and whimpered as my body lit up everywhere.

He took my mouth in another hard kiss.

Artlessly, I hooked a leg around his hip. He tugged on the fabric of my dress, lifting it further. Then finally he lifted me off the ground by my hips.

Oh, yes please.

My legs closed around him as my back connected with the door again. I panted into his mouth as we struggled to align ourselves for what we both needed. But it wasn't easy. Desperation and coordination didn't always go together.

They had earlier tonight, though, when Dave had yanked me into the car *right* before that truck could—

I shuddered in his arms.

"Hey, I got you," he ground out.

And he did. The blunt tip of his cock found me and the breach was swift and shocking. "Ah!" I cried out as he filled me completely. I was impaled on him, pinned against the door, heart thudding.

We were nose to nose. Everything stopped for a moment, except for my racing pulse and our heavy breathing.

Clear eyes blinked into mine. "Zara," he breathed. "Sweetheart."

I closed my eyes and lunged into a kiss. I levered my shoulder blades against the door and thrust my hips. *Move,* my body said to his. *Fuck me.*

With a groan, he did. Bracing me against the wall, he set a hungry pace. I wrapped myself as tightly around him as I could and took it. There was no room to maneuver, and I didn't care. I just held on and let him bounce me on his cock. It was wild and ugly and beautiful and exactly what I needed.

We *consumed* each other, and I forgot to be afraid.

It was fast and crazy, and his groans let me know that it wouldn't last forever. Every thrust was more feverish than the last, and his desperation was contagious. I felt it building, and I opened my eyes so I wouldn't miss a thing. His rugged jaw tightened, then he looked right into my soul. His hands dug into the flesh of my ass, and he groaned again.

My body answered him. The first clench of my climax made me gasp. He covered my mouth with his own and then shuddered, planting himself deeply one more time.

I felt his cock pulse inside me, and it turned my limbs into liquid, helpless things.

Dave made a deeply satisfied sound just before I buried my face in his neck and burst into tears.

Dave

Zara was crying and shaking and clearly we'd both lost our minds.

I eased her to her feet and disconnected us. "Hey, now," I whispered. "You're all right." But I don't know which of us I was trying to convince.

After hastily tucking myself back into my unzipped pants, I scooped Zara up into my arms. Then I carried her farther into the apartment, finding her darkened bedroom and setting her on the bed.

She buried her face in her hands and tried to sob more quietly. Her dress was hanging off her shoulder, so I unzipped the back of it and eased it off her body. Then I pulled down the quilt and nudged her to get into bed.

"I'm...okay," she gasped.

"I know," I said soothingly. I was ninety-nine percent sure she wasn't upset with me, but rather with the scare she'd had. And then ninety-nine became a hundred when I kicked off my pants and shoes and lay down beside her. She pulled me into her arms and then buried her face in my shirt collar.

Having no better ideas, I held on tight and let her cry. And eventually she began to calm down.

"I'm…sorry," she hiccupped.

"Don't be sorry," I whispered.

"I'm such a *girl* tonight."

"I like girls." I kissed her, and she tasted like tears. So I wiped her cheeks with my thumbs and kissed her again.

She took a deep breath and tried to let it out slowly. "It doesn't even make sense to panic about something that didn't even happen."

"Not sure fear ever makes sense," I argued. "I'll be seeing those headlights for a long time whenever I close my eyes."

Her teary gaze met mine. "Thank you for pulling me out of the way."

"Anytime," I said, then gave her a smile.

She returned my smile, but hers looked embarrassed. "Thank you for the comfort fuck up against my door."

"Anytime," I repeated. Then I rolled on top of her. "If you're still crying, though, maybe I didn't do a thorough job of it. Maybe I'm slippin'."

"Not hardly," she whispered. Then she tugged my face down for a kiss.

I got a little sidetracked then. I forgot myself in her kisses. Got lost as her tongue stroked against my own. Time slipped. Soft hands unbuttoned my shirt, and I shed it. I kicked off my boxers and climbed under the quilt with her.

That's how I found myself lying naked on top of Zara for the first time in two years, making sweet love to her neck. My body hummed with need, even though I'd just come like a fountain in the living room. But with Zara, there was no "off" switch for me.

She moaned into my mouth, and once again, everything was heat and wonder. She lifted her knees to hug my hips, and I groaned. I couldn't resist turning my chin to find her hot mouth with mine.

"Ungh," I slurred against her tongue. Then I actually chuckled.

"What's so funny?" she panted.

"I feel like a teenager. You kiss me and I just want to come everywhere."

"So do it," she whispered, then captured my lips in another kiss.

I moaned and pushed her down into the mattress, my erection against her belly. "Want you so bad. But I don't have a condom." I hadn't had one in the living room, either. I had to get off of her right now or we'd end up doing it again.

She grabbed my elbow to keep me right where I was. "It's okay. I have an IUD now."

"Yeah?"

She smiled at me, dragging a thumb across my lip. Goosebumps broke out on my back. Then, beneath me, she spread her legs with an unmistakable invitation.

"Fuck," I whispered, and it came out sounding hoarse. "Missed you, baby." I lifted one of her knees and pushed inside. "So much," I ground out, too stupid with lust to keep that to myself.

We tumbled into another kiss. And when I began to move, it was a sensory overload. Her soft body under mine, my hungry tongue in her mouth. I tried to slow down and relax, but my body fought for more. My hips pumped, and her long legs wrapped around me tightly. Again.

For the second time tonight, it was burning madness—all muscle and motion, and her brown eyes boring into mine. Then her hot gasps turned vocal—as if the pleasure were too much to keep inside. I'd been fantasizing about this for two years, but the real thing was even more intense than I'd remembered.

I pinned her hips down to the mattress with firm hands. She was panting now, her head thrown back, stomach muscles tight. "Give it to me," I begged, fucking her in long strokes. Maybe I was turning into a sap—someone I barely recognized. But taking her in her bed again felt like coming home.

Afterward we lay there, ruined. Our breathing was loud, and my heart was trying to beat its way out of my chest. She closed her eyes and turned her face away, as if it were all too much. Her first impulse was—as always—to put a little distance between us.

"No, baby." I wasn't having it. I reached out an arm and rolled her over again, halfway onto my body. "You're not gonna shake me off so easily. You're not kicking me out of your bed tonight. I'm staying."

"This was a bad idea." She pressed her cheek against my shoulder and sighed. "We probably should have had tea and kept our clothes on."

"Tea instead of a doubleheader?" I chuckled. "No fucking way."

She kissed me on the pec. "Am I at least allowed to visit the bathroom?"

"Only if you come right back."

She slid from the bed, and I admired her bare backside as she disappeared from the darkened room. She spent a few minutes out of sight. I heard the toilet flush, and footsteps as she walked around, shutting off the last lamp.

When she slid into bed again, she said, "Won't Bess wonder what happened to you tonight?"

I snorted and pulled her closer. "Nice try. Bess can use her imagination. You don't really want me to leave, anyway."

"Says who?" she challenged.

"Says the marks all over my back. A few minutes ago you were clinging to me like that girl on the Titanic."

"*You* watched *Titanic*?" She poked me in the chest. "Big tough guy like you?"

"Bess made me," I lied.

Zara laughed out loud, and I loved the sound of it.

twenty-eight
dave

I WOKE up to a kiss from Zara on the side of my face. "I have to go bake scones," she said.

"Okay," I mumbled, pressing my eyelids closed, trying to remain unconscious.

"Nicole will wake up in about an hour. Here's the monitor." I opened one eye to see that she'd placed a plastic device on her empty pillow. "When you hear her cry, will you get her out of the crib?"

"Of course," I slurred. Did she think I would just let the baby cry?

"When she's up, you can either go upstairs and knock on Alec's door—he'll take care of her. That's usually his shift. Or, if you'd rather do it yourself, I left you a note on the kitchen counter."

"I'll handle it." Even in my sleep haze, I knew I'd never ask Alec for help. Fuck that noise.

"Fine." She kissed my cheek one more time. "I'll leave my phone on. Text me if you have any issues."

"Sure."

She stood up to go, but I caught her wrist. "You doing okay?"

"Yeah." Zara gave me half a smile. "I'm all right. I do have to get moving, though."

"Okay, gorgeous." I rolled onto my back and stretched. "I'm just going to lie around naked in your bed for a while, wishing you were here."

That won me a full smile. But then she gave me a little wave and disappeared. I heard the door click shut a moment later.

On any other day, I would've fallen right back to sleep. But suddenly *I* was the responsible adult in the house. Given that, the best that I could manage was a light doze for the next hour.

When the squawk finally came, it was so loud that I didn't even need the monitor. I heard Nicole in stereo and sat right up to look around for my boxers. "Kap-Pah-Dis!" she demanded as I struggled into my underwear and then hurried into her room.

When I got there, I found her standing on the crib mattress, her hands wrapped around the slats, like a jailed criminal rattling the bars of his cage. When she spotted me in the doorway, her eyes narrowed. Clearly I was not the personnel she'd expected.

"Hey," I said, my voice scratchy. "How you doing today?"

She babbled an answer that I'm pretty sure would translate to: *I'd be doing a whole lot better if you got me out of this cage, dummy.*

When I approached the crib, she lifted her chubby arms toward me. And I'd be a liar if I said it didn't affect me—that simple motion of trust.

"All right," I said, lifting her to my chest. "Let's figure out this diaper thing."

And there was really nothing to it. I unsnapped her baby PJs. Then I removed her heavy, wet diaper and threw it away. Zara had all the fresh ones in a stack beside the changing pad, so ten seconds and a couple of tapes later we were done and on our way.

But I did have one problem. I hadn't stopped by the bathroom myself, and now I was dancing a jig. I carried her into the bathroom. "Avert your eyes," I said pointlessly, peeing one-handed and then flushing. Then I washed one hand.

Zara must do everything one-handed. Huh.

In the kitchen, as promised, there was a note.

1. She will want the bottle in the fridge. Nuke it for fifteen seconds and then swirl the contents because microwaves create hot spots. Then run the

nipple under warm water for a few seconds so it isn't icy.

2. You can turn on Sesame Street and hold her on the couch while she drinks it. Channel 49.

3. When the milk is gone she can have a small bowl of Cheerios.

There was an arrow on the page pointing at a small plastic bowl that I was supposed to use for the Cheerios, which had also been left out on the counter.

Zara had idiot-proofed my hour alone with Nicole.

The baby was pretty excited about the whole thing. She made impatient noises while I got her bottle warmed and carried her over to the sofa. I forgot to find the remote for Sesame Street, but she didn't seem to care. She made herself comfortable on my lap and leaned her head back on the arm of the sofa. I lifted the bottle for her, but she grabbed it with her own two hands to guide it to her mouth. *Give me that, rookie. I'll take it from here.*

And that was it. For now, that was the whole job. I sat there, propping up the bottle, behaving as her very own human lounge chair for ten minutes or so, while she took long, luxurious pulls from the bottle. Her eyes went half-mast, and one of her hands drifted over to my wrist, where her small fingers sifted absently through the hair there.

My phone was on the coffee table where I'd abandoned it the night before. When Nicole gave up on the last bit of milk in the bottle, I reached over to trade the bottle for my phone. There were text messages from Bess. *Where are you?* And then another one an hour later. *Never mind, I retract the question.*

There was also a text from my lawyer earlier in the evening. *Just got the DNA test results back. As you'd assumed, you are the father.*

I dropped the phone onto the sofa and lifted a startled Nicole slowly into the air and then lowered her onto my lap again. She smiled at me, so I did it again. "Looks like you're stuck with me," I told her. "I don't know whether to congratulate you or apologize."

Her response was to point at the darkened television screen and babble a complaint.

I found the remote and turned on the television to her station. Then, while she was staring at the screen, I went into the kitchen and poured a baby-sized bowl of Cheerios from the box beside the note. I added some milk from the fridge. Given Zara's level of detail, it was sort of surprising that she hadn't left a spoon out for me, but I found a pink plastic one in the drawer.

Then I carried the whole thing over to the coffee table, along with a paper towel in case of accidents.

Nicole slid feet-first off the sofa and gave her bowl of cereal a look. Then she turned her Zara glare on me.

"What? The note says you like this." I spooned up a couple of Cheerios and lifted it toward her.

The baby's expression was blatantly accusatory. In response, she plunged her little hand right into the bowl and grabbed a few pieces of cereal, then lifted them, dripping, to her mouth.

"I like my way better," I said, grabbing the paper towel and catching the milk that was dripping down her arm. "But you gotta be you."

Luckily it was a small bowl of cereal, because Nicole made a royal mess of it. And she was a slow eater. She got distracted by Elmo on the television, which gave me time to clean her up between every handful of cereal.

When she'd eaten almost all of it, the apartment door banged open, startling us both. Zara's brother Alec stood there in a pair of shorts—one level up from the boxers-only outfit I was wearing—looking sleep-drunk and pissed off. "What the f…fudge are you doing here?" he demanded.

Buddy, you really don't want me to answer that.

Wordlessly, I wiped another milk slick off Nicole's hand.

Alec's face reddened as he did the math. When he opened his mouth, I was sure I was about to get an earful about how I wasn't good enough for Zara. But instead he said, "Zara gives her the Cheerios *dry*."

"Oh," I said, slowly. The note had said "a small bowl of Cheerios." There had been no mention of milk, come to think of it. "I guess that makes sense."

Alec made a rude snort, then staggered over to the couch and flung himself down. "This is my shift. You can go now."

"Nope," I said. "I'm good. You can go back to bed."

Alec glared at me and didn't move.

I didn't move either.

Nicole gave up on her cereal, and I scooped her up in one arm and took the sticky bowl with my other. I carried her over to the kitchen sink and turned it on. "How about you rinse off your hands?" I suggested.

Miraculously, she stuck both hands under the faucet.

"Good work," I said, and the praise sounded alien to my own ears.

Actually, everything about this moment was weird. Alec had given me the chance to drop Nicole in his lap and be done. But I hadn't taken him up on the offer. Sure, it was partly just stubbornness on my part. But so what? I could hold the baby for a couple of hours just as well as Alec could. And Zara had left the job to me. I wasn't about to let her down.

Truthfully, there were moments when I still felt in my bones that I wasn't father material. But it was dawning on me that fathers were made, not born. You held the baby and you figured out how she ate cereal. You learned to prevent her from doing a header off the bed. You just *dealt* with whatever came up.

Before now I'd convinced myself that my own shitty childhood meant I'd never understand this. But my parents' ghosts didn't hover today. It was just me and a little girl who needed her hands dried on the dish towel.

When that was done, I carried Nicole into Zara's bedroom and found my clothes. We sat down on the bed while I pulled on the khakis I'd worn to the wedding, and then the shirt, unbuttoned.

I didn't let Nicole near the edge of the bed. I kept her close, and she climbed into my lap and put her little hands on my chest. When I lifted her up suddenly, she squealed with glee.

My phone chimed again from the coffee table in the living room. I grabbed it when the baby and I sat down again. The text was another from my lawyer. *This paternity test means the judge will grant you visitation if you want to ask for it. You're the father with 99.999+ percent certainty.*

That was not the least bit surprising, but it still felt strange to see those words on my phone. "See? You're stuck with me," I whispered to Nicole.

She gave me an appraising squint.

"Can you say daddy?" Those were words I'd never expected to say in my life.

"Dah-dah."

I laughed so suddenly her eyes widened. "Did you really just say it?"

"Bah-bdah," she babbled.

"Huh. We'll revisit that later."

Alec was glaring at me from the other end of the sofa. I didn't know why he didn't just go upstairs already. Was I really expected to fuck up so spectacularly that he'd need to save the day? Or, worse, was he intending to make me so uncomfortable that I'd just leave?

Leaning back on the couch, I made myself comfortable.

Nicole was a little bored with me so she crawled out of my lap toward Alec. He picked her up, looking smug. "Look," he said to me. "I think you should stay away from my sister and Nicole."

Ah, there it was. "That's not your call," I pointed out. "And you don't know me. So I don't know why you'd even say that."

"You're not what she needs."

"Really? And what does she need?" I asked.

"A guy who lives in the same area code, for starters."

I didn't even know what to say to that. And luckily it didn't matter, because the door swung open and Zara stepped through, carrying a cup of coffee. She took in the sight of the two of us sitting at opposite ends of the sofa, and her face turned wary. "I thought you could sleep in today," she said to Alec.

"Woke up at six in a panic that I hadn't heard you at the door," he grumbled. "That coffee for me?"

"Nope." She crossed the room and handed it to me.

"Thank you. Very thoughtful," I said.

Alec rolled his eyes.

"You can go back to bed, big brother," she said. "Especially if you're here to judge me."

"He's here to judge *me*," I said. "I'm pretty sure."

Alec stood, the baby in his arms. He gave her a kiss on the cheek. Then he handed her to Zara and left without a word.

She flinched as the door closed with a bang. "Sorry. Was he an ass to you?"

"Eh. I've seen worse."

Her smile made an appearance. "Of all my brothers, his case of macho bull…crud is the most stubborn. How did you two get along?" she asked, pointing between Nicole and I.

"Just fine. You left good instructions." We could just gloss right over the cereal disaster.

Nicole began to wiggle in Zara's arms, so she set the baby down. Nicole waddled off to see her toys in the corner of the room.

"You need to go," Zara said, shutting off the TV.

"Ah, there's the Zara I remember," I joked.

She gave me a sheepish look. "My mother is on her way over, okay? Unless you want to explain your presence, take the cab that's downstairs for you, and run for it. I'll get someone to help me fetch yours later."

"I'll do it," I offered. "If you give me the keys to my rental, Castro will help me."

"The keys are in it," she said. "Are you sure?"

"Of course." I crossed the room to stand right in front of her. Already I felt a certain distance between us. Like she wanted to be rid of me and not just because her mother was on the way.

That was my girl. "I'm going," I reassured her. "Right after you kiss me."

She straightened her spine, but bit her lip. "Listen, Dave..."

"Hey, are you really going to give me a speech about how last night was a fluke, and we should never do it again?"

"Well..." She cleared her throat.

"Honey, don't let your mouth write a check your body can't cash." I reached out and cupped the back of her neck, rubbing a thumb against the muscle at the base of her skull. Her eyes fluttered closed, as I knew they would. "You've been through a lot and you need me to go now, and I'll go. But this isn't over. I'm still drawn to you, Zara. Don't see why that's such a bad thing. I like you. Always have."

"I like you, too, you jerk. But I have responsibilities."

I raised my hands in supplication. "You can tell me all about them the next time I see you." I pulled her against my chest, and she came willingly, wrapping her arms around me. "Hey." I stole a kiss. "I'll see you real soon." I kissed her again.

"Soon*ish*. I have to work more hours in the next ten days than I have in my life," she said, looking up at me. "Don't be too surprised if I'm not easy to get ahold of."

"Okay. Then this will have to hold me." I stroked my thumb down her nose and then leaned over and kissed her a good one. She sighed against me and let me plunder her mouth.

Until somebody grabbed my knee and squawked.

We broke apart, looking down at the little person who was frowning up at us.

"No way! Look who's jealous." Zara leaned over and scooped Nicole up off the floor.

"Thanks for putting up with an amateur," I told my baby, then kissed her wispy forehead. "Goodbye for now." I hugged Zara, too.

"Wave bye-bye," Zara said.

They watched me with matching big brown eyes as I let myself out the door.

twenty-nine
zara

THE FOLLOWING week was longer than a washed-out country mile.

With Audrey away on her honeymoon, there was no backup at the bakery. I worked the longest hours I'd worked in years, while my family pulled extra shifts with the baby. I couldn't even get extra hours from Kieran Shipley, because that man had three jobs already.

The hardest hours of the day were the early mornings. I discovered that the difference between getting up before dawn three days a week versus six days a week was worse than I'd predicted. I felt like crying every morning at quarter to five when my alarm clock went off. Alec felt the same. He grumbled loudly when I went upstairs to drag him down to sleep on my couch.

Usually, Audrey closed the bakery on the days when I went in early, and vice versa. But now I both opened and closed, sneaking away in the middle of the day only briefly before Kieran left at two.

"You need a full-time employee," my mother said as I dragged myself through the door again after the third day.

"Too expensive." I sighed. Audrey and I often did the math on hiring someone else. But a full-timer would be entitled to benefits. And we were afraid to take on liabilities this early in our business development.

"If Audrey's pregnant, you're going to need someone, whether it's expensive or not."

"Who told you she was pregnant?" I asked, lifting my shirt for Nicole to nurse.

My mother waved away the question with one of her carefully manicured hands. "The bridge club was all over that last night. I know I missed the ceremony, but apparently Audrey was a lovely shade of green during her vows."

"That's not nice," I said, even though I'd noticed it, too. Although Audrey wouldn't give a rip what the bridge club said, the gossip still bothered me. Small towns were brutal. "What does the bridge club have to say about Dave turning up at the wedding with Nicole?"

My mother gave me a cat-like smile. "Do you really want to know?"

"No," I grumbled. "I guess not."

"They thought you looked lovely together," she reported anyway. "And the fact that he's buying two houses on the hill hasn't escaped notice, either. There's a rumor that he's going to knock one of them down to make a double yard with an ice rink."

"That is *not* true," I pointed out. "Where do people get these ideas?"

My mother just shrugged. "You picked the Tudor, right? Jana Godfrey said it was prettier."

"Yeah." I sighed. "It was." I'd been trying not to think about the house, or about Dave in general. But it sure wasn't easy to put him out of mind. I'd gotten texts from him asking when he could drop off some paint chips and see me.

And by "see me" I was sure he meant "see me naked."

Sleeping with him had been a mistake I shouldn't repeat. And yet every time I lay down in bed for my precious few hours of rest, I imagined him there beside me. My traitorous body craved his touch, and not just at night. When I was standing in the bakery alone at five thirty in the morning, I thought about his green eyes staring down at me while we—

Unngh.

I didn't know how to stop wanting him. I'd always promised myself I wouldn't do what my mother had done—wait around for the father of her children to turn up again and love her. But now—even if I was determined to avoid the same mistake—I finally understood how she'd spent two decades of her life bamboozled by a man who really didn't care.

I got it now, because I had it *bad* for David Beringer. I couldn't imagine ever wanting another man as much as I wanted him. And even if he ended up treating me poorly, I didn't think the yearning would ever go away.

Now, if I *really* felt like torturing myself, all I needed to do was take another look at the photo Bess had texted me yesterday. It was a shot of Dave and Nicole asleep in a hammock, their ginger heads relaxed beside one another, their eyes closed peacefully. *Hello, hormone rush.*

Like I said, it was a long week.

By the sixth night, I was questioning all my life choices. Lucky for me, Benito brought takeout wrap sandwiches from the little place in Colebury. After putting Nicole to bed, he and I collapsed together on the couch.

I was too tired to even pretend to watch the cooking show that was on the television. I just ate my sandwich and counted the minutes until I could reasonably fall into bed. From her crib in the next room, Nicole was still talking to herself.

Please go to sleep, baby girl. Mama can't take anymore.

"How's it going with you, anyway?" I asked my twin, trying to summon the energy for conversation. Between the coffee shop and Benito's brand new undercover work, we hadn't seen each other in over a week.

"Interesting times," he said. "This is confidential…"

"Duh." We'd always kept each other's secrets.

"Okay. You remember Jimmy Gage?"

"How could I forget him?" He had been our next-door neighbor in the trailer park when we were teenagers. Back then he was a cop —the dirty kind. And a mean drunk. I'd been legitimately afraid of him, even before that weird showdown at The Mountain Goat. "I don't think I ever told you about the night he sat at my bar and tried to humiliate Jill Sullivan."

Benito tensed. "Was this recently?"

"No! Two years ago. I gave him some lip and he threw his beer bottle and stormed out. That was the end of it."

"Well…" My brother rubbed the back of his neck. "He hasn't gotten any better behaved. Gage is responsible for the worst of the drugs in this county. I'm going to take him down. Really shouldn't talk about it, but if you see his face anywhere you are, I want you to leave the premises and call me."

Shit. Now I was sorry I'd asked about his job. "Well, I guess I'd better change my sign to read: Open, Except for Jimmy Gage."

Ben snorted. "Does he come into The Busy Bean?"

"No. I haven't seen him for months." But still, I was uneasy. I hated the idea of Benito tangling with him. Jimmy Gage had just replaced my near death experience at the top of my late-night worry list. Not only was that dude scary, but he made me remember an uncomfortable time in my life—my rebellious years, when I'd punished everyone. Including Benito. I'd been so angry at everyone all the time.

Now I was just tired.

"It's gonna be okay, Z." He squeezed my wrist. "I'm going to nail his ass to the wall and send him away for twenty to life."

"You could have become a tailor. Or a candlestick maker. Just sayin'."

He laughed. "If I were a tailor, you'd still find something to worry about. Needles or shears."

That might even be true. "But still. Jimmy Gage?"

"He'll get taken down," Benito assured me. "He's running a lot of product, and he isn't careful. People talk. And customers are dying from his shit. I only have to catch him once."

And he only needs one bullet to kill you, my worry-brain added.

"How's it going with your man?" Benito asked, changing the subject.

"He showed up today in the coffee shop," I said casually. Hopefully Benito didn't have truly creepy telepathic twin powers. In the first place, that would be unfair. And secondly, I didn't want him hearing everything in my brain. Not the dirty parts.

"To see you?" Benito asked.

"For coffee. And to drop off paint chips—apparently I have to choose colors for the Tudor before the weekend."

"Ah. That's nice, right?"

"Definitely." Dave was always nice. That didn't make it any easier to keep my head on straight when he was around. Today he'd bought a cup of coffee from my surly part-time employee. Then he'd come back into the kitchen uninvited to give me a kiss so hot that I blamed it for the batch of cookies I'd burned. "He wants to hang out," I told Ben.

"Hang out, huh?" He smirked.

"Don't judge me." *Even if I totally have it coming.*

"Fine. I liked him okay when he pulled you from the path of a speeding truck. But I liked him a little less when Alec said he spent the night after the wedding."

I groaned. "*One,* Alec has a big mouth. *Two,* weddings make people crazy."

"That's why I avoid them," Benito agreed.

"Let's plan yours," I said, just to rib him. "Black tie or no?"

He snorted. "Have you met me?"

"No tuxes? Jacket and tie, then."

"No *wedding*. You're a pain." He took my soda can out of my hand and drained it.

"We are both going to be single forever." At this rate, I was never getting married. And since I'd ruined the great romance of Benito's life when we'd been eighteen, things didn't look so good for him, either. "Between the two of us we have almost sixty years of bachelorhood," I pointed out.

"But not virginity."

"Well, duh."

He nudged my ankle with his. "At least someone broke her recent dry spell."

"About time, too. My dry spell was two years. But you can't possibly be doing that badly. Any hotties in your training course?"

"We're not supposed to sleep with other agents. And since the training facility is in the middle of the Adirondack mountains, the talent pool was thin."

I snickered. "Thinner than here?"

"No joke."

"Ah, well. I need to climb back aboard the celibacy train myself. Sleeping with the father of your child is pretty much the epitome of a bad idea."

"Probably true," he said.

I immediately wanted to pinch him for agreeing with me. So I did.

"*Ouch*. What I meant was—I have no opinion about you sleeping with McHockey."

"That's better."

My brother yawned. "I'm going home."

"You are home," I grumbled.

"Yeah, well. I heard somebody was getting a three-bedroom house on the hill after it gets a coat of paint. So I expect to be slumming it here over the bar in a few short weeks."

"I don't even know what to think about the house," I admitted.

"It's complicated," my brother agreed. "Especially if you're sleeping with him. Or maybe that makes it less complicated?"

"Nothing was ever made less complicated by sex."

"Except for conception."

I pinched him again and he laughed.

Unfortunately, the week had more punishment in store for me. The real low point didn't hit until the day before Audrey's return. In fact, she was probably in the air over the Great Plains when the power at The Busy Bean went out.

Again.

I wanted to wail. Instead, I called my mom, asking her to leave Nicole with me and to please go buy some fuel for the generator. Audrey and I had *meant* to do that after our last incident, but I'd put it off, damn it. And I was *not* about to lose all the dairy products and food in our walk-in refrigerator.

Then—even though I'd promised myself I would make it ten days without asking anyone at the Shipley farm for help—I'd called the farm and asked for Zachariah. He was the one who had diagnosed our electrical problem the last time this happened.

"I'll be right over," he said.

"Thank you!" I said, since *thank you* was still my mantra. Now I owed Zach on top of everyone else. But Audrey would've wanted me to call him, because it cost us a hundred and fifty bucks to get a repair man just to walk through the door. And I didn't know if I needed the heating and cooling guy or the electrician. Meanwhile, Zach would hook up the generator for me, making sure it kept our refrigerators on.

With Griffin out of town, the Shipley farm was probably experiencing a series of chaotic, short-staffed days, too. But Zach turned up a half an hour later, gave me a hug, then disappeared into the back to try to diagnose the problem.

Kieran stayed an extra half hour, sweeping up the kitchen and the dining room for me. But then his dark-eyed gaze found mine, and he gave me a wry smile. "I have to go to my other job. But if you need somewhere to stash the cold stuff overnight, text me and I'll see what I can fit in my fridge."

"You're the best." I pointed at the door. "Now go. I've made you late enough already."

He gave me a quick grin and disappeared.

That left me minding the store alone with Nicole strapped into the baby carrier on my chest. She was cranky about the confinement.

Meanwhile, I poured iced coffee and served baked goods to customers perplexed by the unlit bakery.

Also, it was hard to keep Nicole around baked goods without sharing. She kept pointing at cookies. "Look," I said, removing a biscotti from a jar. "If I give you this one, that's it, okay? Just one."

"Appa-da-bah."

"Right." Out of the corner of my eye I saw two men walk into the store. "Hey guys," I called. "Our power is out, so there aren't any espresso drinks today. But I have iced coffee and whole lot of cookies."

"Oh, man," a familiar voice said. "Rough day?"

I looked up into the sea-green eyes of David Beringer, and my heart flipped over, as it always did. "Hi! Yeah." Once again, I'd forgotten how attractive he was in person, and it made me babble like Nicole.

"Sorry, baby." Then he gave Nicole a smile. "Hi! Remember me?"

"Dada!" She shrieked.

"That's a girl! You said it again."

If jaws could literally hit the floor, mine would have done so. "She did *not* just say that! That was a lucky babble."

Dave's teammate stepped up to the counter, too. "I don't think so. That sounded real to me. Hi Nicole!" he said to my baby girl. "Who's that?" He pointed at Dave. "Is that *daddy*?"

"Dada!"

"Yeah, baby!" The younger teammate took Nicole's hand in his and high-fived her. "Job done!"

You could have knocked me over with a feather. "Seriously? You decide to say your first word today of all days, and it's…?"

"Dada," my little girl said. Then she held out her hand for the cookie.

I gave it to her, because I knew when I'd been beaten. "You know you have to say mama next, right?" She gave me a drooly smile around the cookie.

"Could I have a cookie, too?" Dave asked. "I'll be a good boy."

"Likely story." I gestured toward the case. "Pick your poison."

"Chocolate chip. And Castro wants—" He glanced at his teammate.

"Oatmeal raisin. And a double-shot cappuccino."

"Without electrical power, I can't make…"

Castro winked. "Just kidding. I'm a pain like that. If you still have iced coffee, I'd love some."

I poured coffee and handed over baked goods. Then I waved off their payment. "Your money is no good here."

"Aw." Dave's eyes were worried. "Seriously, are you okay? You need anything?"

"I called a friend to come look at the generator and to tell me which repair guy to try next." Just as I said that, the lights came back on.

"Zara? You got power?" Zach called from the back.

"I do! And you're the best thing ever!"

"Then don't sell all the cookies!" he yelled back.

"Is that Zach?" Dave asked, taking a bite of his cookie.

"Yeah. Good memory." He'd only met him at the wedding.

"I pay attention. But really—is there anything I can do to help?"

I glanced around the bakery. "Not really. Now I wait for the electrician."

"You want me to hold the baby?" Dave asked. "She looks kinda squirmy in that thing."

"Sure? Actually, if you want to save the day, take her outside for a few minutes. She'd love to run around in the grass. Unless you two were on your way somewhere."

"We were going for a cheater's hike up Skaggs Hill," Castro said. He was an attractive guy in his mid-twenties. "We can walk around here instead."

I lifted Nicole out of the baby carrier. "Hey, Dave? Watch that she doesn't run straight for the river."

He grinned at me. "Really? Babies in the river are a bad idea?"

"Well, I just…"

His smile grew. "I know—I'm the rookie. But I won't take my eyes off her."

"Me neither, ma'am," Castro said. "I won't take my eyes off either one of 'em."

"I'm sold." I set Nicole on the floor. "Want to go outside with your daddy?" It was the first time I'd referred to Dave like that out loud in front of him. It felt weird rolling off my tongue.

Nicole didn't have a problem with it, though. She bolted around the counter and kept on toddling toward the open door.

"There's a shot on goal!" Castro said, just as Dave leaned down to head off her break for freedom. "But the keeper makes the save."

"You two should take that routine out on the road." I lifted the Bjorn off my tired body and tossed it onto a hook on the wall. "Thanks for doing this."

"It's my pleasure." Dave came closer to the counter and then beckoned. I leaned forward and he kissed my cheek sweetly. I felt my neck heat with pleasure. "We'll run her around for a while. How long until you're done here?"

"Depends when the repairman shows up." I was exhausted, and also starving because I hadn't had a lunch break. I'd probably end up eating cookies for dinner, which always made me feel rundown afterward.

"Okay. Then I won't rush back."

"If she starts wailing, you might rush back," I said, trying not to get lost in those green eyes. "My mother said she didn't have a great nap."

He turned to go, Nicole held in his bulky arms. "I'll take my chances." He winked, and turned to walk out.

My heart seized up at the sight of her disappearing with him. "Wait!" I called, feeling like a loon. What my heart meant was, *Wait for me.*

He turned patiently, and both he and Nicole waited calmly. I was the only one having heart palpitations. "She needs her hat," I said, unsticking myself from the spot behind the counter and running to grab it out of my bag. "She sunburns easily."

"Ah," Dave said. "I'm familiar with the problem." He pointed at his own hat—a Brooklyn Bruisers cap.

"Your team color is purple?" I asked, crossing to the two of them.

"Yeah. Don't judge." His eyes were smiley. I trusted him. I really did. But it still weirded me out to see him holding my baby girl.

I fit Nicole's little white fisherman's hat onto her head, and tucked the elastic below her chin.

She grunted unhappily about it.

Dave kissed me on the cheek one more time. Then I watched them walk out the door, feeling sad that they were leaving me and giddy that he offered and exhausted and every other human emotion, all at once.

thirty
dave

"YOUR LADY IS STRESSED OUT," Castro said as we watched Nicole climb the wrong way up a tiny plastic slide behind the bakery.

"Yeah," I agreed, noticing that I didn't mind very much that he'd referred to Zara as mine. Hell, I could even think "my baby" pretty easily now without panic. Not *much* panic, anyway. "Castro, is the baby gonna do a header off that thing?" I asked.

He shook his head. "That's kinda the point of the baby slide—to learn your limits. Do you think your mama grabbed your little butt off the baby slide?"

I snorted. "My mama was probably getting high in the bathroom with the door locked."

"And yet you survived," Castro pointed out quietly.

"Still. I'd rather not add to Zara's stress today by bringing her back a bruised kid."

"Mmm. You two going to be a couple after all?"

Now that was a fine question. "I really don't know." Though I liked that idea a whole hell of a lot more than I'd ever expected to.

"Zara's the best there is," Castro said, even though he'd only just met her.

"Yeah, I know," I agreed.

"And you chased plenty of tail already, player."

"That I have. But with me it was never about variety. It was about avoiding expectations. And not *owing* anyone. If Zara and I became a couple she would probably end up resenting me. I'm not going to quit playing hockey."

"Some day you will," the younger man pointed out.

I grunted. That idea made me even queasier than fatherhood. This summer would forever be remembered as the one where both my age and my overconfidence caught up to me. *Hello, humility.*

Castro finished his coffee. "I'm gonna throw away my cup. Yours too?"

I handed it over.

"Be right back."

He went into the bakery. When he came out a minute later, Zara was with him. She jogged across the parking lot and up into her apartment.

"What's up?" I asked him.

"I asked if she had a baby pack. We can go for a walk, after all."

"What's a baby pack?"

I found out a couple of minutes later when Zara returned with it. The pack had a metal frame, a baby seat and a five-point harness.

"Perfect," Castro said.

"Here's some water for her. Come back if you have a diaper issue." She passed Castro a sippy cup and then ran back inside.

"Will do!" Castro called over his shoulder. "Nicole, baby. Want to go for a ride?" He showed her the pack.

She slid down the slide on her belly and came over to investigate.

"You've ridden in here before, right?" Castro had an easy way of talking to the baby. "C'mere, princess." He lifted her into the pack and strapped her in. "Now I'm gonna pick this up…"

"I'll do it," I said, stopping him. I lifted the pack, while Nicole watched me with big eyes.

"Your shoulder gonna be okay with that?"

"Sure. She only weighs twenty-odd pounds." Castro was a great guy, but if anyone was going to carry my baby in a pack, it was going to be me.

"Suit yourself. Here—I'll hand her off to you." He took the pack by its frame while I pulled the shoulder straps on. "Clip that chest thing," he said.

So I did. Nicole let out a string of babbling and kicked her feet, shaking the pack gently. "Let's walk, and we'll see if she's down with this."

"Awesome. Let's go downriver?" He pointed.

I looked around. "No—that way. She needs shade or she'll burn."

"Look at you being the dad!"

"I have pale skin, too."

"Castros don't burn," my friend pointed out.

In three more weeks, neither would I. There was no sunshine in the hockey rink. *Three weeks*. That was all the time we had left before training camp. Inconceivable.

Carrying Nicole on my back was an unfamiliar experience. I could feel the warmth of her body where it rested against mine. And, as I walked, a little hand explored my hairline. I reached back and caught one of her stubby feet in my hand, and she giggled.

She babbled as we walked upriver, following the grassy bank.

"Hey, cool rock. How deep do you think it is here?" Castro asked, pointing at a giant boulder in the middle of the stream.

"No idea, man."

"Hang on a second, then." Castro kicked off his hiking shoes and socks. He turned up the cuffs on his shorts.

"Showing me some leg? Sexy."

He gave me the finger.

"Don't curse in front of the child."

He made another rude gesture, and I laughed.

Wading out into the river, he began to laugh, too. "It is so freaking cold." But he made it to the big rock in the middle without much trouble. "There are tiny fish nibbling my toes."

"They don't know any better. Do you want me to take your picture on that rock? That will impress the ladies. Or at least your sisters."

"Good idea."

I took out my phone to take his picture, but Nicole started to fuss.

I took a couple of shots, put the phone away, and then reached back for her toe, which was kicking madly. "Everything okay back there?"

"She wants to go wading, too." Castro picked his way back toward me.

"Zara said to stay away from the river."

"She said not to let the baby *walk* into the river. But it's mean if we don't let her get her feet wet. I won't set her down."

I took the pack off, and the baby wriggled to get out. "Go ahead," I said, lifting her out of the pack and onto the grass. "But if this goes badly, tell mommy it was his fault."

"Come here, little cutie," Castro said. She ran to him. He lifted her up over the water, then swung her gently, allowing her toes to dip into the shallow water.

She hooted with laughter.

"Whee!" Castro did it again and again. Nicole laughed until her face was red, and her whole body was shaking. When he stopped, she fussed. So he obliged, dipping her toes into the cool water a dozen more times.

Then, for no discernible reason at all, she began to cry. Tears streaked down her cheeks.

"It's okay," Castro said, tucking her onto his hip and wading toward the shore. "I've got you." He tried that thing where you jiggle the baby gently against your body.

But she howled. Her face turned red. She opened her mouth wider and screamed.

"You broke her. Let me." I took her back from him, trying to decide what to do. Last time I calmed her down in a hammock. But there wasn't one here. Maybe some more walking in the pack?

"She's probably just tired," Castro said. "Didn't Zara say she didn't get a nap?"

"Guess so." I set her into the pack with the predictable result—more yelling. I felt like a dickhead strapping her in as she screamed. But I didn't know what else to try. So I picked up the pack and set off up the path. Castro ran to join me, hustling to fall in step.

As we walked, he told me a funny story about the time his sister was on the freeway when her little boy started to throw up in his car seat, and she couldn't pull over to help him. "They had to get that car detailed the very next day."

Nicole's cries had quickly begun to sound less insistent, and then they stopped entirely. She leaned to the left, toward the river, maybe watching something in the water.

"What's she doing back there?" I asked.

Castro looked and then laughed. "She's passed out cold. Looks like you on the team jet after a four-game road trip."

"Very funny."

"Funny 'cause it's true!" We walked in silence for another minute. "You still afraid of the baby?"

"No. She's not very fierce."

"Wait'll she's sixteen and telling you her current curfew is too early, and that she needs your car."

There was nothing about that scenario that I could picture. Fifteen years from now sounded like another epoch in time.

Thinking back, I tried to picture Bess at sixteen. She'd never given anybody sass. Neither of us had. We lived our teen years on tenterhooks, hoping that the scowling grandfather who'd taken us in wouldn't find us to be too much trouble. "Hey, Castro?"

"Yeah?"

"Have you ever thought you were on top of your shit? And then you realize you really haven't dealt with your shit at all?"

"Wait—what kind of shit are we talking about here?"

"Baggage. History."

"Maybe? I used to lose it whenever someone in the minors would use a slur against me. But mostly I'm over it now. I'm like—take that, fuckers. I made the big league and you didn't. But once in a while a fan will say something stupid, and I realize I'm *not* really over being the only brown guy on the ice. Is that the kind of shit you mean?"

"Pretty much. I thought I was really over mine. But every night lately I'm dreaming about my dead mother or my asshole father." Last night I'd been standing in our old house while my father swung his fists at me. And while Nicole cried from another room. Not Bess,

Nicole. All my baggage was swirling around in my mind, in technicolor.

The only night I hadn't had at least one weird dream was the one I'd spent in Zara's bed. Go figure.

"That's just your brain trying to scare you into doing better," Castro said. "Like when I have that recurring dream about showing up to practice without my pants on."

I laughed and tipped my head back to feel the sunshine on my face. Nothing about this summer was happening like I planned. But maybe it wasn't a bad thing.

We walked for a good ninety minutes. The baby slept for only a little while, but she woke up in a better mood. I felt small hands playing in my hair as we moved through the forested path at the river's edge.

It was after five o'clock when we headed back toward the coffee shop, and my phone pinged with a text from Zara. *I'm all done here. Heading up the hill to find a burger for dinner. Want one?*

Yes, I replied quickly. *Can we eat them in the Tudor? I want to give you a set of keys. The realtor left them in the mailbox after closing.*

You bought the place already? She fired back.

Sure did. Meet me there?

Twenty minutes later I arrived at the house. It was just me and Nicole. I'd sent Castro home. I found Zara inside, walking around the empty rooms, looking thoughtful.

Nicole squealed with delight at the sight of her mother. And I didn't blame her at all. I felt like making happy noises every time I set eyes on the woman, too. Not waiting for an invitation, I walked right up to Zara and kissed her on the neck. "Did your electrician show up?"

"He did," she said into my ear. "He replaced something that I've already forgotten the name for, but swears it will do the trick." Her hands caught my stubbled face before I could kiss her more thoroughly. "Let's eat, okay? I'm dying."

I followed her into the kitchen, still wearing the baby. When I removed the shoulder straps, Zara eased the pack off my shoulders and unclipped her babbling little girl. "Did you have a good walk? I have some food for you!"

Nicole ran away. We could hear her toddling around the empty living room, her squeals echoing off the walls.

"Come here, baby girl," Zara said, calling her back to the kitchen. "I brought your clip-on chair."

Zara had suspended a baby seat off the stone countertop, but it took Nicole a few minutes to be convinced to sit in it. Zara set down some bites of chicken and French fries on a placemat. When the baby saw the food, she agreed to be confined again.

"Thank the lord," Zara said, clipping her in.

"Long day?" I asked, putting a hand on her lower back. I ached to touch her. The night we'd spent together hadn't gotten her out of my system at all. It had made me crave her more.

"Long day. Long week," Zara said, dipping her hand into a paper bag and pulling out a foil-wrapped burger. "Here you go. You don't strike me as the picky type, so I got you one with everything."

"Thanks. That's perfect." It was bonkers that Zara and I had only had dinner together a couple of times—the wedding and her family's Sunday lunch. Standing at the counter side by side, we ate in silence for a few minutes, while Nicole stuffed her face, too, with great enthusiasm.

"Still like the house?" I asked, admiring the way the late afternoon sun slanted through the room.

"I love it desperately," she said immediately.

Swear to God, that made me feel ten feet tall. "Glad to hear that. You didn't seem so sure about the whole idea before."

"It wasn't the house," she said quietly. "It was *owing* you. I owe everyone in my family. No—everyone in my *life*. I didn't want to add you to the list."

She said that with her spine straight and her dark eyes boring into mine. And that's the moment when I finally understood that I loved her. I'd probably loved her a long time, but I'd been too chickenshit to use that word, even to myself.

"You don't owe me anything, baby," I said softly. "I want you to have this place. In fact..." I stepped across the roomy kitchen, opening empty drawers until I found what I was looking for—an envelope with a copy of the deed inside. "Here. This copy is for you."

Zara opened the envelope and pulled out the document. Her frown deepened as she flipped through the pages. "Both our names are on here?"

"That's right." My lawyer had known what to do. "Joint tenants with rights of survivorship. If anything happened to either of us, the other one gets the house automatically."

Her dark lashes lifted, and her gaze met mine. "You could have just willed it to Nicole."

I shrugged, because I supposed she was right. But I wanted Zara to have a house. Hell, I wanted her to have *everything*. "It makes me happy to do this for you, gorgeous. I hope you like the house. And I hope you'll let me visit."

"Thank you, Dave." Her cheeks stained pink. She took the last bite of her burger and then crumpled up the wrapper. "I got fries, too," she said, changing the subject. She set the bag between us, like a deep-fried barrier.

Fuck that. I pushed the bag aside, leaned in and kissed her jawline.

Never one to beat around the bush, she captured my face in one of her sleek hands. Turning her chin, she kissed me once on the mouth. But then she pushed my face away. "I can't, Dave. I want to, but I can't."

"Why not?"

She glanced over at her chewing baby before looking me straight in the eye again. "Once upon a time, you and I were wonderfully, gloriously casual with each other," she said. "It was a temporary thing, and that was *fine* with me."

"Right." I chuckled. "I haven't forgotten that you threw me out every night."

Her smile was sad. "The thing is, I can't even do that anymore, because now we're not the only two people involved. I have someone else's feelings to consider."

"Okay," I said, trying to understand. "You don't want me hanging around because you don't think I'm good for Nicole?" Didn't she see I was trying?

"That's not it." Zara shook her head. "And I love having you around." She sighed, as if it had cost her to tell me that. "But what I want isn't very important anymore. I can live with all kinds of uncertainty in my life, but I won't do that to Nicole. I'm a big girl. She's not."

"Okay. I get it." *Sort of.* "It's just that I missed you like crazy, and I don't see what it hurts to let you know. I don't mind remembering why I liked you so much, or how we ended up having a child together."

"I missed you like crazy, too," she whispered. "But the other day you asked me what I needed from you. And I didn't give you an answer."

"Yeah? Lay it on me."

"Okay. I need you to decide if we're really on your list, or not."

"My...list?" Now I definitely wasn't following her.

Zara picked at invisible lint on her sleeve. "When I was a little girl, sometimes my father was around, and sometimes he wasn't. My mother was way too patient with him. He strung us along. And then eventually he went away for good. The last time I saw him I was fourteen."

Oh. Now she was making sense. My own childhood was my least favorite topic in the whole entire world. Judging from the expression on Zara's face, this wasn't a fun chat for her, either.

But she went on. "Nicole is just a baby, and, when she's bigger, she won't remember the summer her father showed up for two months." She took a deep breath and met my eyes. "You can swing by and let Bess visit for an hour, and it doesn't mean a thing to Nicole. Even if Bess buys out every baby outfit in Detroit."

Which she might.

"But it's like this—someday Nicole is going to turn ten. She has a spring birthday—May seventh..."

We both glanced over at our daughter. And I tried and failed to imagine our baby girl as an auburn-haired fifth grader.

"Audrey will probably make her a cake with Wonder Woman on it—or whatever is trending that year." Zara gave me a fragile smile. "Right here in this kitchen, maybe." She tapped the counter top.

"Right." I was still following. "Okay."

"But here's the thing I want you to think about." She let out a shaky breath. "On her birthday, she should already know where she stands with you. You're either in her life, at that point, or you're not."

Oh.

She reached out and grabbed my hand. "Don't make her *wonder.* Don't make her sit there and stare at the phone, unsure if you're going to call her to say, *Happy Birthday.*"

Zara turned her face away. But before she did, I saw the tears in her eyes. And my heart broke for her in a way it hadn't before. Maybe I had a thick head, but it wasn't thick enough to prevent me from understanding that this little scenario Zara had spun was deeply personal to her.

I reached for her hand, then lifted one of her palms to my mouth and kissed it.

She swallowed hard, but didn't look at me. "A kid can do fine without a dad in her life. Really." She let out a shaky breath. "You don't have to stick around, Dave. But do *not* make my little girl sit there by the phone and *hope* she's been a good enough girl that year to get five minutes of your time on her birthday."

Fuck. My throat was tighter than it had ever been. "Okay, sweetheart," I croaked. "I get it." I didn't plan to do that to Nicole. But listening to Zara describe her pain, I could totally understand how she wore those scars.

That's when I finally understood how complicated we really were as a couple. If things didn't work out between us, it could break three hearts, all at once.

"You..." She swallowed hard again. "You don't need to be her daddy. She has a lot of family already. If you don't want to be involved, I'll understand. But I need you need to figure it out before she's old enough to ask me if she has a dad or not."

"I can do that," I whispered.

Finally, she turned to look at me again. "It's only been a few weeks. You're probably still reeling. She won't remember this summer, Dave. But she won't be a baby forever."

"All right," I said gently. I reached for her, and pulled her into a hug. "I hear you. I'm not going to do that to her. I promise. Can you trust me?"

She wiped her eyes with the back of her hand. "I can. But I need you to take some time and figure yourself out. A lot has happened in the last few weeks. You've been great. But you're still on vacation. Everything is always better on vacation. It's not real life."

It felt pretty fucking real to me, and I opened my mouth to say so. But she beat me to it.

"All I want is for you to think things over. When you go back to New York, your life will swallow you up, right?"

"Well, sure, but…"

She held up a hand. "Go back. Do your thing for a while. Think things over. Figure out how much of yourself you can give your daughter. It's important to me, because I know it will be important to her."

"Okay," I whispered. Her hand was shaking in mine. "Come here." I tugged her closer.

She came willingly, resting her cheek against my collarbone. She sighed, as if wrung out from getting all that off her chest.

I kissed her forehead. And her skin felt so good against my lips that I did it again. I held on tightly, pulling her closer. I wanted to press away her fear and her pain—extinguish it between our two bodies.

But that's when Nicole decided she'd had enough food and began to flail her arms and squawk for freedom.

"Right," Zara said gently, stepping out of my embrace to gather food scraps from where they'd fallen beneath the baby chair. "Real life calls."

Real life was pretty great, though. I leaned over the counter, unclipped the baby, and pulled Nicole out of her seat. "Okay, baby girl. Let's go outside and try out your new backyard."

thirty-one
zara

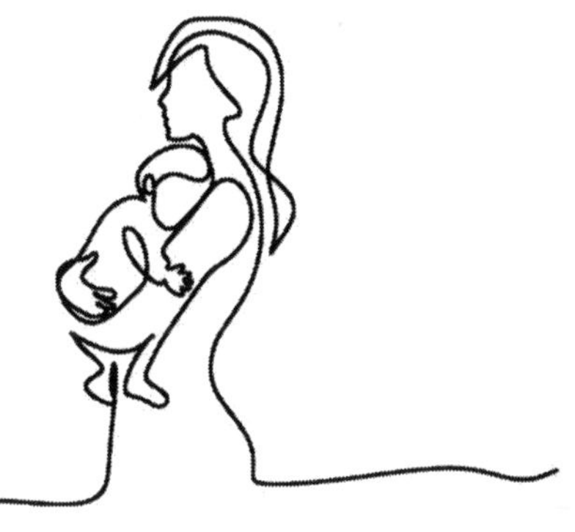

WE TOOK NICOLE OUT BACK, where she buzzed around like a little bee on the lawn. I pictured the two of us playing out here next summer and the summer after that, while she grew into an even more active toddler and then a leggy preschooler. I could push her in the swing. I could even put a sandbox right here outside the kitchen window where I could watch her while I made lunch.

Dave sat down on the grass, running a hand over the green blades beside him. “Grass is getting a little long. We’ll have to find someone to cut it.”

“I’ll ask Benito for a recommendation,” I said quickly. “Next summer I’ll get a reel mower and do it myself.”

Dave glanced at me, his face thoughtful. But he didn’t say anything. He didn’t call me out for the way I’d just cut him out of the picture, assuming that he wouldn’t be around to cut the grass of the house he’d just bought, or its neighbor next door.

But would he? My gut said no. He’d get back to New York, realize his bachelor life looked pretty good, and cross Vermont off his travel plans for the foreseeable future.

I couldn’t plan on him returning. I just couldn’t even think about it.

When Nicole began to tire herself out, I gathered her up and corralled her back into the house. “Time for stories,” I whispered in her ear, and she squirmed because she knew that stories meant bedtime.

Dave gathered the trash from our meal, the clip-on chair, and the baby pack.

"I'll drive you down the hill to your car," I offered, and he quietly agreed.

He hadn't said much since we'd talked in the kitchen. And he was silent in the car as we practically coasted down Main Street toward the river. I pulled into a parking space between two other cars—I was still too freaked out from the near-miss to stop anywhere that wasn't protected—and killed the engine.

I cast a glance at Nicole, who was looking downright sleepy.

Dave laid a hand on my arm. "Just a minute, gorgeous. There's something important I need to ask you."

"Mmm?" My mind was on the baby and whether I could get her teeth brushed before she started fussing.

"Let me be with you tonight," he whispered.

"Wait, what?" I brought my focus to his heart-stopping face and the heated expression there. Had he even been listening in the kitchen? "Didn't you hear me when I said I needed you to take some time to think?"

"Every word." He took my hand and raised it to his stubbled face, kissing my palm with such sweetness that I held in a gasp. "You said Nicole won't remember this summer. But I know *you* will. And I sure as hell won't ever forget it."

"And?" He caressed my hand, which was very distracting.

"*And* I already promised I'd go back to work and think about my situation. But I'm asking you the opposite favor—not to think at all until I go back. Don't think. Just be."

"Be...with *you*," I clarified. "In what way?" I asked, even though it was a stupid question.

His voice dropped low. "Let me love you tonight."

"And what would that solve?"

"If you can't figure that out, then I can't really help you," he said quietly. Then he reached across the gear shift to cup my cheek. "But I'm pretty sure you won't be sorry."

His fingertips brushed my skin so lightly that I shivered. "How do you know I won't be sorry?" I was pretty sure I *would*. Not tonight, of course. Tonight would be wonderful. But I'd just be digging the hole deeper for my poor, broken heart.

"You asked me not to toy with my daughter's affections." Those green eyes stared me down, and I couldn't look away. "And I won't do that. But you just told me you were a big girl who didn't worry about knowing the outcome of the game before the hand was dealt."

Fuck me, I *had* said that. What a giant lie it was, too. "Maybe you're not what I need right now, though."

"Aren't I?" His hot gaze called me on every last one of my lies. "Why don't you let me convince you that I am?"

"Convince me," I snarked. "With your…" I didn't want to say *dick* in front of my child, so I dropped my eyes to his lap.

He grinned. Then he tugged my hand, drawing his big body closer to mine, and kissed me once on the corner of the mouth. He slid one rugged cheek against my face as a shiver climbed my spine. He whispered in my ear, "I'm very persuasive. Not just with my cock. But also my fingers. And my mouth."

I took his face in my hands and moved it where I could look him directly in the eye. "I don't know what to think," I admitted.

"Then *don't* think," he whispered. "Take me upstairs with you." He leaned forward and kissed me then—a real one. He pulled my stubborn self closer and crushed my objections with his satin lips and then his pushy tongue.

He was going away in a matter of weeks, and I'd have to get over him *again*.

And I was going to let it happen anyway.

But first, the bedtime ritual. "Hey," I said, breaking a kiss that threatened to last about an hour. "Before you get your jollies, your daughter needs to be put to bed. And since you're here, you get to help."

For that, I got a devastating smile. "Let's do that," he said. "Educate me."

Twenty minutes later, I lurked on the sofa, listening to Dave read a second picture book to Nicole. I couldn't make out the words, but his low, easy voice had a soothing cadence. After a while he stopped reading, and there was only silence. Then I heard him clear his throat in a way that was meant to summon me.

Leaping off Benito's couch, I trotted down the hallway. When I stopped at the door to Nicole's room, I beheld the sort of scene that lit up my ovaries like a pinball machine. Nicole was passed out on Dave's chest. He sat in the rocking chair, his big arm holding her pajama-covered diaper butt. There was nothing like the sight of my daughter's trusting face cradled against his muscular body.

"Man down," he whispered.

The sight was so distracting that he could have been referring to me. "She didn't nurse," I said stupidly.

He cocked an eyebrow. "Yeah, I'm not equipped for that."

It was odd that she hadn't fussed for me, though. When I was at home, she always demanded it. And if I wasn't at home, she gave my mother a hard time about falling asleep. But not tonight.

Maybe my baby was ready to wean. Was I, though?

I gave myself a shake. "Okay, well then that's easy. Just lay her on the mattress."

"On her back?" he asked, rising slowly, supporting her weight against his big body.

"Yeah, but it's not that important at this age. She'll just roll over if she doesn't like where you put her."

Clearly my little hormone surge wasn't finished yet, because I couldn't help but ogle Dave's biceps as he laid our child gently on the mattress. Dragging my eyes off his perfect form, I grabbed the blanket off the side of the crib and covered her lower body with it.

"That's it, huh?" he whispered.

"Job done," I agreed quietly. He followed me out of her room, closing the door behind himself with a click. "I usually leave it open a crack," I argued, leaning around him, reaching for the door knob.

"Is that right?" he asked, still whispering. He plucked my hand from the door knob and then backed me up against the wall. As he trapped my hands in his, my heart began to flutter. Then he leaned down until his lips grazed the shell of my ear. "Didn't think you'd want her to hear how loud you get when I make you come."

I shivered as that dirty mouth moved down, beginning to drop soft kisses on my neck.

You are a smart man, I thought as my fingers laced with his. He obviously knew better than to give me time to think about whether or not this was a good idea.

My body made my decision for me. I melted into the wall, angling my chin away so he could kiss his way into my cleavage. He hadn't even undressed me yet, but those hot kisses on my chest had me buzzing with desire. "God, I'm so easy." I laughed quietly.

"You say that like it's a bad thing," he mumbled between my boobs. He lowered himself to his knees and lifted my top, his lips finding the soft skin of my belly just above the waistline of my jeans. He popped the button and undid my zipper. "Take these jeans off," he ordered.

Jesus. That tone of voice set me on fire. Every. Freaking. Time. My shaky hands began to shove the denim down off my body.

"Get on the bed," he ordered. "On your back. Go."

This I did so quickly that he was only unbuttoning his third button when I'd positioned myself the way he'd asked. I watched him unbutton the shirt, and he did it *slowly,* that fucker, because he knew me. He played me like a good hand of cards.

I didn't even care. I'd always been good at living in the moment, and this was a pretty good moment to live in.

Dave cast our clothes onto a chair and undid his belt slowly, my hot stare on his body. Then he lifted his eyes to mine and pulled out his cock, shoving his boxers down so I could get a good look. "See anything you like?" he asked, giving himself a slow stroke.

"Come here," I demanded, trying to balance the scales of power.

"When I'm ready," he said, playing right into our old groove. Push and shove. Call and response. "Lose that little top and those panties. Lovely as they are, I want to see you."

I grabbed the fabric of my tank, but then I paused.

"Disobedient already?" he teased, misunderstanding my hesitation. He was stark naked, his hand gripping his erection. His body was *so freaking perfect.*

I appreciated the view. But still I couldn't bring myself to strip in front of him. Two years had elapsed since we last viewed each other so critically and I got a little stuck thinking about it. "You look fantastic," I said slowly.

"As do you, beautiful. But you're still wearing too much clothing."

I leaned back against the pillows and stared up at the ceiling. "Dave, I gained ten pounds and pushed out a seven-pound baby. Things aren't all in the same places now."

"What?" he asked stupidly. I guess I wasn't the only one addled by lust, because it took a couple of beats for understanding to dawn across his masculine features. "Fuck that noise. You're every bit as hot as you used to be. Just with bigger tits."

I lifted my hands to my very full breasts. "You can't even suck on these or you'll get a face full of milk."

His smile turned wicked. "Strip, lady. Or don't. Whatever. Just keep touching yourself." He put a knee on the bed and thrust his hips, slowly fucking his own hand.

I groaned at the sight, then took a deep, slow breath. "Jesus."

"All this can be yours," he teased. "Spread your legs. And take off that fucking top before I take it off you myself."

The rasp in his voice gave me a full body shiver. I forgot to care whether he'd notice the stretch marks on my belly, and I lifted my little tank top over my head.

As a reward, Dave dropped down onto his forearms and nosed into my pussy, his lips grazing the lacy strip of fabric there. He kissed the juncture of my shaking thighs, then opened his mouth over the lace and let out a hot breath.

I shuddered mightily.

"Can you come like this?" he asked, pressing his lips against the little panel of lace, dropping kisses. "Or maybe..." He tugged the fabric aside and licked my clit without preamble.

"Oh!" I gasped, my fingers slicing through his hair.

He pressed the flat of his tongue down and then moaned, and the sound lit me on fire. I became shameless, spreading my legs further and canting my hips toward his mouth. One thing apparently hadn't changed about me—my ability to heat up in no time at all. I quickly grew soaking wet, and my nipples tingled with warning.

Whoops. I pressed my palms against my breasts, wary of my milk suddenly letting down.

Dave looked up at me with heated eyes, his mouth busy. His eyes darkened as I writhed under him, clutching my tits.

He ran out of patience all at once, sitting up suddenly and yanking my panties off completely. He did a military crawl up my body, lined himself up and filled me. All in one aggressive pass.

"Oh!" I gasped against the lovely intrusion, gripping his shoulders, my knees lifting to his body instinctively.

"Ungh," he agreed, tipping his forehead down to mine. "That's what I'm talking about." We regarded each other at point-blank range, and I expected him to buck right into high gear.

But he didn't. Not yet. He gave me a quick kiss, and then startled me with a question. "When do you think we made Nicole?"

"What?" I rubbed his back because I couldn't stop touching him. All that skin against skin made it hard to think.

"When did it happen?" he whispered. Then he closed his eyes and circled his hips, giving a low groan. "Fuck. Who knew the idea of getting you pregnant would make me so horny?"

"It does?" I panted, rocking my hips to meet his. I knew exactly what he meant. One summer night I'd lain beneath him just like this, while we made a baby. My foolish, romantic heart liked the sound of that.

"When do you think?" he pressed, slowly thrusting. "The first night? The last?"

Then he picked up the pace, and all that sweet friction made it hard for me to think. "Tequila," I said on a gasp. "That night. When Jimmy threw that glass, and we sat together and drank tequila."

"Yeah?" His lips grazed over mine. "Why that night?"

I kissed him instead of answering, so he relaxed again, torturing me with a slow slide. "Because…" I whispered eventually. "That night you *teased* me." I craned my neck to reach his mouth for more of those hot kisses.

But he moved out of my reach. "I teased you how?"

"Mmm," I said, remembering it. "On the b-barstool. You made me c-come with your cockhead," I gasped, straining for more contact.

He smiled before kissing me again. "Like this?" He propped himself up on an elbow and reached down to disengage. Then he dragged his swollen, rounded cockhead across my clit, and I cried out. "Like that, huh? And you think that's what did the trick?"

"There was no…c-condom," I breathed. He was torturing me. Actually, he was torturing both of us. I could see the hungry grimace on his face. So I angled my hips and fit him inside me again, and he went for it, gratefully. Smiling again, too. I'd forgotten that—how he used to smile at me during sex. Like we'd shared a secret.

No wonder I'd fallen hard for this guy.

"That's right," he whispered. "Turning you into a needy girl is my favorite thing in the world." With a chuckle, he pinned my hips to the mattress with firm hands. I threw my head back, my stomach muscles tight. "Give it to me," he begged. "Let me have it."

Then he leaned down and captured my mouth in another bossy kiss while his hips pistoned rhythmically, and his muscular chest flexed above me.

Who could resist that view or this man? I arched off the bed with a sob, feeling a groundswell roll blissfully through me. He gave a grunt of victory and rode me through it, while I closed my eyes to hang on to the sensation a few seconds longer.

"Oh. Fuck," he grunted with surprise. "*Christ.*" He threw his head back and shuddered, his arms locking up as he groaned out his release.

That's when I noticed all the wetness trickling down my breasts. It was *milk*. The orgasm had triggered a milk letdown. "Oh, geez." I clapped my hands over my nipples. But there was milk everywhere. So I reached under my pillow and produced my nightgown, using it to mop myself up quickly. "What a mess."

"Whew." Dave shook his head. "No lie, that the was sexiest thing I *ever* saw. Let me." He took the cotton and dabbed my skin, but it was already mostly dry. Leaning down, he licked my sensitive breast, then licked his lips, a wicked expression on his face.

"No more of that." I pushed his face aside, the way you'd redirect a dog who was nosing where he shouldn't. "You'll make it worse."

"You're so sexy. I can't help it." He nuzzled between my breasts, just to be a pest. Then, still connected to me, he lowered his body onto mine and kissed me. "Damn, Zara. That ended way before I was ready. I'm losing my touch."

Not with me, my heart murmured. If anything, I felt the pull more strongly every time he was near me.

I'm so fucked, I thought, even as he kissed me.

We didn't get much sleep at all. My body was exhausted, but my brain wouldn't shut down and let me sleep. I was having the perfect night, and I didn't want to miss a minute of it.

Dave didn't either. He never stopped touching me. Caressing me. It led to more sex, and then more cuddling. We lay there in the dark afterward, and I assumed he'd fallen asleep.

"Tell me about being pregnant," he whispered after a while. "Were you freaked?"

"Yes and no," I said to the faint dusting of hair on his chest where I'd laid my head. "When I realized I was pregnant, part of me wasn't even surprised. I'd been a wild teenager and didn't really tone things down for years. I thought, 'Okay. So this is where it stops.' It's almost as if Nicole turned up to tell me that enough was enough already."

I lifted my head off his chest. "It wasn't the softest landing into adulthood. But it wasn't so bad. And the pregnancy itself was easy for me. I didn't even puke."

"Well that's good news. I don't like to think of you all alone and scared." His big hand sifted through my hair, and I practically melted into a puddle.

"I'm not that easily scared," I said, trying to cover up how much his words meant to me.

"Didn't say you were. It's a big deal, though."

"It is," I admitted. "I definitely felt like a screw-up for not knowing who you were. I wondered what you'd think about the whole thing." I was still wondering, I supposed. "I took these child-birth classes—the kind where they teach you how to breathe."

"Yeah?"

"It was all couples. And me. My mother offered to go with me but she had four kids and didn't really need to learn. And I didn't want to drag her there just because I was the only one in the room who didn't know her baby's father's last name."

He chuckled, and I heard the sound right against my ear, through his chest. It must've been how Nicole heard everything. She was always using someone for a pillow.

"You know," he said at a whisper. "I looked back in my calendar to see where I was on May seventh a year ago. But it was after the regular season, and we didn't make the playoffs. And I didn't take a trip with the guys until June. It weirds me out thinking I was probably lifting weights at the gym while you were busy having our baby. What was it like?"

Again he'd made my poor little heart go pitter-patter. I never thought I'd be lying in the dark telling him about the biggest day of my life. "Well, I don't remember most of the exciting parts," I joked. "So I guess I can't fill you in."

"No?" His arm tightened over my back. "The drugs were that good, huh?"

"The drugs were probably responsible for part of it. But also I was just so exhausted. She took a good eighteen hours to arrive. I was practically speaking in tongues by the time they handed her to me."

"Who was with you at the hospital?"

"My mom was with me the whole time. And the rest of the brat pack was out in the waiting room. My brothers. My uncles. Audrey and Griffin." I yawned. "You know what's funny? I thought Nicole was the most beautiful baby I'd ever seen. Really perfect."

"She is."

"She is *now*. But on her first birthday, my mother gave me a photo album of her first year. And in the newborn photos she's red and wrinkly, and looks like a skinny old man."

We both laughed. And then I got up and fetched him that photo album, so he could see for himself. At two in the morning we looked at those pictures. It was a lovely, ordinary thing that most mothers had always done with their babies' fathers.

And it was every bit as wonderful as I always expected it to be.

Dave

In my dream, a baby was chattering.

Wait, no. That wasn't a dream.

I opened my eyes to see sunlight streaming in Zara's windows. Beside me, Zara groaned sleepily, but her eyes were still closed.

"Bah bip ta-da!" Nicole demanded from somewhere nearby.

I swung my legs out of bed, pulled on my boxers and stuck my head in her room. She stood in the crib, waiting. "Da-da!" she yelled when I appeared.

The clock on her wall said 6:45, but it felt earlier. I scooped her out of the crib and changed her diaper, even though my eyes were only half open. When I carried her into the hallway, I heard Zara say my name.

"Don't make a bottle," Zara murmured from the bed. "My boob is about to explode. She hasn't nursed since yesterday morning."

Nicole lunged for her mother, but this time I anticipated it, lowering her safely down. She wasted no time snuggling in beside Zara and clamping her mouth onto a nipple. They both closed their eyes and relaxed together.

Watching them, that unfamiliar emotion returned—the one I didn't have a name for. A warm spot in the center of my chest—some kind of sentimental yearning that I wasn't used to feeling.

I stepped away to use Zara's bathroom and splash some water on my face. Then I lay down beside the two of them and dozed, trying not to do the math on how soon I'd have to leave Vermont again.

thirty-two
zara

EVERY SUMMER there came a moment when the season began to turn. And this year—like every year—the moment took me by surprise. The next afternoons were sunny and warm, but the June bugs had stopped smacking into the window screens at night. The frogs stopped singing in the ponds, falling silent.

And when I stood outside the coffee shop one afternoon, turning the sign on the door from OPEN to CLOSED, I heard it—the first cicada. Its hum rose up to fill the air, and it was quickly joined with its friends' songs.

That's when I knew. Summer was practically over. Fall would soon paint the leaves red. Busses full of leaf-peeping retirees would crisscross Vermont. There wasn't a freaking thing I could do to make summer linger.

And this year that hurt me a little more than it had last year. Go figure.

The days after Dave gave me the deed to the house on Main Street were bittersweet. Audrey was back, so I had some much-needed time off. "Go!" she'd say, shooing me out the door of the cafe on more than one occasion. "I'm back, I'm feeling better, and you put in your hours already. Go play with your baby and visit with your man. I'll see you at Thursday Dinner."

The thing was, I hadn't been to Thursday Dinner in a really long time. Dave had distracted me, and Griff and Audrey's honeymoon had upended me.

Should I go? And more importantly, should I bring Dave?

Still unsure, I called Ruth Shipley to offer her a half-bushel of my uncles' earliest pears, and to ask if I could bring a guest to Thursday Dinner, just this once.

"Of course, sweetie!" she said. "Bring him every time."

If only.

Lately, Dave and I had been spending almost every night together. Every morning I woke up to find him in my bed, usually with his hand lying possessively over my hip. I let myself enjoy it. On the mornings when I wasn't opening the bakery, we all woke up slowly together, snuggling in the bed after Nicole woke up.

I didn't know why she'd picked this moment in time, but my baby stopped asking to nurse. She still wanted cuddles, of course. But she drank her milk out of sippy cups and stopped reaching under my shirt.

That meant there were *two* things lingering in the periphery of my consciousness, threatening to break my heart. Dave's departure, and my baby not needing me as much anymore.

And he was leaving in a matter of *days*.

The Thursday night we all got into his rental car to go to the Shipleys', he was down to less than a week in Vermont. We didn't talk about it. Neither of us wanted to. But the number of phone calls he had with the team staff went up, and sometimes when I glanced at him, I knew his mind was elsewhere.

I bit my lip and said nothing. What was my alternative?

When he parked the car beside the Shipley farmhouse, I popped out and unbuckled Nicole from her car seat. Then I fetched the peach tart that I'd made. By the time I had balanced it on one hand, Dave was already carrying Nicole on one arm and a half-bushel sack of pears in the other.

"She could walk," I pointed out. "I'll hold her hand on the stairs."

"I got her," he said mildly. He walked up onto the porch while I admired his muscled ass in a pair of khakis, and then he somehow managed to hold the door open for me, too.

I held back a sigh of longing and followed him through to the dining room.

"Well hello there, little lady!" Grandpa Shipley boomed at Nicole. "Who did you bring with you tonight?"

Nicole, who loved a crowd, bounced on Dave's arm. "Dada!" she crowed.

I swear, all the women in attendance got a little starry-eyed. Even Griffin looked a little less grouchy at the sight of Dave carrying Nicole into the room.

Audrey rushed over and relieved him of the pears. "Ooh! These are fantastic. Have they been chilled off?" she asked. Pears needed a few days at a near-freezing temperature to ripen properly.

"Yes they have," I assured her. "I took them out of the cooler yesterday, so give them two or three days in a bag. Or refrigerate half of them if you don't want them all to ripen at once."

"I can't wait," she said, hustling toward the kitchen door. "I'm going to make a pear and goat-cheese salad with balsamic vinaigrette."

"And bacon!" Zach called from a seat at the table. "I think bacon goes with that."

We were shown to seats on the bench that stretched along one side of the huge table. Dave greeted Zach and Lark, and was introduced to Jude and Sophie and the Shipley twins, Daphne and Dylan.

I took a seat next to Kieran. "You need to hire a full-time employee," he said without preamble.

"Good evening to you, too," I said, unfolding my napkin as Ruth and May put the last dishes on the table.

May's bitchy girlfriend seemed to be missing tonight, and I couldn't help wonder why. Dare I hope they'd parted ways?

"Audrey's going to have this baby," Kieran continued. "And you have your hands full with Mr. Hockey, here…"

Dave gave him an amused glance, and then accepted a glass of cider from Griffin. "This tastes just like perry," he said with a wink.

Griffin rolled his eyes and moved on.

"...and I can't give you more hours," Kieran finished.

"I know you can't," I said, patting his arm. "And I appreciate the advice, but every month we put it off is another bunch of money saved."

"No, it isn't," he argued. "If someone else was cooking you could do more catering orders."

"He's right," Griffin said from across the table. "It's time to hire someone. If a business is going to work out, you have to invest, even when it's scary."

"And I have the gray hairs to prove it," Ruth added, taking her seat beside Grandpa at the head of the table. "Can we say grace?"

I grabbed a warm roll out of the basket and handed it to Nicole to keep her busy. Then I joined hands with Kieran and Dave and bowed my head.

Dave stroked my palm with his roughened fingers under the table while Grandpa dove into a recitation of our blessings.

It took a while, because there really were so many. Even with my eyes closed I could feel the presence of this circle of friends, each one dearer to me than the next. My heart split right open like an overripe peach from all the goodness in my life.

I'd spent a long time feeling like the girl who had less than everyone else. I hadn't known it would ache just as much to feel blessed.

After the "amen," we settled in to enjoy Ruth and Audrey's cooking. There was pork loin with plum sauce, garden carrots, a version of potatoes au gratin, and piles of roasted cauliflower.

"Wow," Dave said, helping himself to another portion of the potatoes. "I shouldn't eat like this until next month, but I don't think I can hold back."

My poor little heart trembled at this mention of his departure.

"Off to New York?" May asked. "When do you go?"

"Tuesday," he said, setting down his fork.

The food I'd eaten settled heavily in my stomach.

"But you'll visit soon, right?" Audrey chirped.

"I'll sure try," he said. "I'm hoping Zara and Nicole can visit me, too."

"See?" Griff said. "You two need an employee. Stat."

"All right, already," Audrey grumbled. "You and Kieran can stop mansplaining our business to us now. We've been a little busy running the shop, cooking your dinner, and gestating your heir."

I had to laugh. Trust Audrey to break the tension knotting inside my chest. I cut more little cubes of meat for Nicole, and the conversation moved on to cidermaking, as it often did at this time of year.

After dinner, I left Nicole on Dave's lap and helped with the dishes for once. Dessert was served, and my peach tart praised. I drank a second glass of wine—another first. "Nicole doesn't nurse at bedtime anymore," I told Ruth and Audrey. "So I guess I can have another drink."

"I hope I can figure out nursing," Audrey said, settling into a chair with a cup of herbal tea.

"Of course you can," I said, drying another pan.

Audrey hooted. "You were, like, the *perfect* earth mother. But I've heard horror stories from other people. Bleeding nipples and babies who can't latch on."

"It will be fine!" I assured her.

"You made pregnancy look like a cakewalk," Audrey complained. "Seriously. My ass has already doubled in size, and I just spent the last three months puking. You looked like a string bean concealing a soccer ball under your shirt, and you wore *heels* behind the bar until you were eight months' pregnant. Who could compete with that?"

"They weren't spike heels," I pointed out, but Audrey, May, and Lark all groaned and laughed.

"Wish I hadn't missed that," Dave said leaning in the kitchen doorway, Nicole in one arm and a glass of wine in his hand. His green gaze was warm, and it was aimed right at me. "Wish I hadn't missed a lot of things."

The kitchen got quiet. *You're about to miss a lot more,* I couldn't help but add silently. There was no help for it.

"We should get home," I said instead. My baby girl's eyes were shut where she lounged on his shoulder.

"Probably true," he said, then finished his glass.

thirty-three
dave

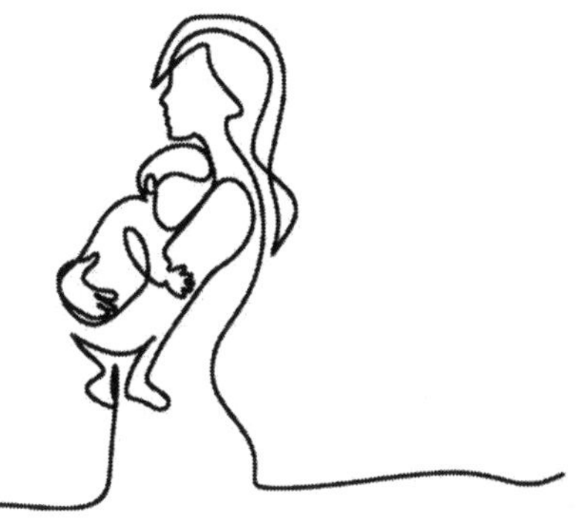

WE SAID our thank-yous and goodbyes. I put Nicole into her car seat without waking her up. A month ago I couldn't have imagined doing that, but it wasn't even hard.

It turns out that holding on to your child wasn't that difficult. Holding on to your moody woman, on the other hand, was a little tougher. Tonight I could feel all Zara's barriers going up again. When Griff Shipley's sister had asked when I was leaving for New York, Zara had put on the bullet-proof mask that I used to know so well, and she hadn't taken it off again all evening.

The ride back to The Gin Mill parking lot was a quiet one. We were both lost in our own worries, I guess. But that was the problem. We'd never had the chance to talk to each other like a real couple, and I'd never done that with anyone in my whole life.

On the ice, when my teammates and I were struggling in a scrimmage, Coach Worthington would yell, "Talk it out, men! I can't hear you." And I knew what to say in that kind of situation—how to save my teammate's ass when a competitor was bearing down on him.

I just didn't know what to say to a prickly girl who was too used to getting by on her own.

"Baby," I tried, as we sat there listening to the engine cool. "I printed out my fall schedule."

"Sorry?" She turned to me, surprised.

"My game schedule. I printed it out at the copy shop so we could try to figure out when I'm going to see you again. We can look at it after we put the baby to bed."

Zara bit her lip. "Dave, you have twelve games in October and ten in November. Then fifteen in December. All over the fricking country. How is that even possible?"

I blinked as this little explosion of words hung between us for a second. "You looked at it already?"

"Of course I looked," she grumbled, bumping her head back against the headrest. "I know you have to go, Dave. It means a lot to me that you want to see us. But it isn't going to be easy."

"I do have to go," I said slowly. "For a lot of reasons."

"You don't have to explain."

"But what if I want to?"

She swallowed. "Okay. Go ahead."

"There's a lot of people depending on me. And they pay me a shit ton to show up and stay sharp."

"Your whole life is there. Your career. I get it. Vermont is just a vacation for you."

I reached across the gear box and took her hand. "It's more than that, prickly girl. I love you."

Zara's eyes widened. "You don't have to say that."

"I *know* I don't have to." It came out sounding almost angry. But, damn. She was never going to let me in if I didn't kick down the door. "I didn't say it out of obligation. And I've never said it to anyone before, unless we're counting my sister. So don't throw it back in my face when I tell you I love you and I wish I could wake up in your bed every day."

Zara put her elbow on the passenger door, then rested her cheek in her hand. But the fingers of her other hand curled around mine. "I'm sorry. It's just that I find it hard to trust you."

"Okay." I snorted. "I'll try not to take it personally."

"You didn't *choose* this. You didn't choose me." Her lovely, proud chin turned in my direction again. "Let's face it—your vacation fling got a little complicated. But I refuse to be that girl who tries to pin you down. Been there. Have the T-shirt and the scars."

"Nobody's pinning me down. Unless you want to ride me when we go upstairs." She gave me a glare, and I had to chuckle. "That was just a little joke to shake you loose." I picked up her hand and shook it gently. "If you don't love me, you can say so. But don't make me out to be a guy who can't figure out what's important. I'm a slow learner, but I'm not an asshole, Z."

She sighed. "I don't know what to think. You have to leave, and I have to stay here."

"For the record, if you ever wanted to spend some time in Brooklyn, I have a sweet apartment." It was a long shot, but I didn't want her to think she wasn't welcome there.

"Can't," she said simply. "I have a business to run. I can't bail on Audrey. I lease space from Alec. My whole family is here. I can't just fritter off to New York because you're a lot of fun."

"At least you'll admit that I'm fun," I said, squeezing her hand. "It's a start. If I'm lucky, you might even admit you like me a little."

"I do like you. A whole lot," she added grudgingly. "But I have obligations, and I can't run off on a wild hair. I have to protect my child."

And myself. She didn't add those words, but I heard 'em anyway.

Clearly I was going to have to wait her out.

A half an hour later, I carried two glasses of wine out onto the condo's balcony. This arrangement was my suggestion. There weren't many summer nights left for me, and I wanted to sit under the stars with Zara. She followed me out, sliding the screen door closed behind her and setting the baby monitor down on the deck boards.

I sat down on the only piece of furniture, which was a giant metal lounge chair—wide enough for two people. The cushion on it had clearly seen better days, but I didn't care. We could hear the river in front of us, and the gentle sounds of conversation rising up from the bar down below us.

"This is a great spot," I said, moving over. "Sit down, prickly girl. Drink some wine with me and stop worrying. I can practically hear your gears turning in there."

She gave me a sheepish smile. "I was just wondering why Benito still has this weird chair. He used to keep it in the woods behind the trailer where we lived in high school."

"Huh," I said, taking a sip of my cabernet. "Maybe it was his hookup spot. Good thing it's dark so we can't see the stains."

"Ew, no." Zara laughed. "I think he used to just sit out there and think. We Rossis are a brooding bunch."

"I noticed that." I put an arm around her shoulders. "But maybe he only kept this thing because it's comfortable."

She tucked herself in beside me and took a sip of her wine. "All right. Point taken. This is a nice spot."

"Hey—do you own furniture?" I asked her, wondering about all those empty rooms in the Tudor we now owned.

"I'll be fine."

"Zara," I said, dropping my voice. "I asked you a question, and that's not an answer."

"It's a reflex," she said grumpily. "I don't like to complain. No, I don't have furniture. Not for adults, anyway. Nicole is all set, though. Her crib is the kind that will convert to a toddler bed later, and she has a dresser and a rocking chair. I'll buy a mattress for myself next week. And that's really all we need for now. I'll work on getting some living room furniture this fall."

"Don't suppose you'd let me help you with that..."

"Nope," she said quickly. "A girl's got to pick her own furniture."

"Right." I smiled into the darkness. "But if I manage to get up here to visit you this fall, we're gonna need a nice big bed. King size. And a couch in the living room and maybe another one in front of that fireplace off the kitchen, so if I visit in the winter we can sit there in front of the fire and watch it snow outside." I gave her a little nudge. "Am I allowed to assume you'll open the door if I visit?"

"You know I will." She sighed. "But I was serious when I said you need to do some thinking before you do more planning."

"I will. And I'm not dumb enough to get between a girl and her furniture. But you're going to need a bed frame and whatever else goes in a bedroom. Oh—and stools for that counter in the kitchen so I have somewhere to park my ass while we're making dinner." I was on a roll. "And a table. I forgot the table and chairs. I have to eat during my visits. When I'm not playing with Nicole or fucking you right into that king-sized mattress."

"That all sounds nice," she said, "especially that last part. But it sounds like you're angling for a long-distance relationship. And this from a guy who said he'd never had a relationship? What if you hate it? What if you realize that once a month isn't enough exercise in that king-sized bed?"

"Doesn't matter." I rubbed her palm with mine. "The minute I leave Vermont, I'll be thinking dirty thoughts about you in Brooklyn. Lying in bed, stroking myself, wondering when you're going to come and visit me."

"That's just the horny talking."

"Yes and no," I said truthfully. "You bring out a different kind of horny in me—the kind that wants to buy furniture as well as fuck on it. The kind that would rather be a patient man. Because you're worth it, honey."

She went still beside me. "That's the nicest thing anyone ever said to me."

"Well, I meant it. I've been single a long time. And it's not because I need to have a lot of casual sex with strangers. It's because I didn't know I could be part of something better." I was laying it on pretty thick. But I meant every word. And I'd rather say these things in person, even if Zara wasn't quite ready to believe me.

"You have to remember how it looks from where I sit," she whispered. "One time I asked you if you had a family—because I was really hoping I wasn't unwittingly half of an affair. You said 'Fuck no. Never have been and never will be.' So forgive me for being a little skeptical now."

Beside her, I flinched. "Yeah. Not the most encouraging attitude, right?"

"No."

Well, shit. I'd already given Zara every reason to think I'd leave her. Not only had I done so for two years, but I'd sworn up and down that I was a no-strings guy. There was no way I could take all that back. My only move was to *show* her I meant business. And that meant going back to Brooklyn without any promises from her.

"Still love you," I said quietly. "It's just that I'm like those green pears you brought Audrey. You had to pick me before I was ripe."

Zara actually choked on the sip of wine she had been trying to take. One hand over her mouth, she started to sputter. And then to laugh.

I whacked her on the back. "Breathe, gorgeous. It wasn't that funny."

"It was…too," she gasped.

"I'm a slow learner, that's all."

Zara clutched her wineglass and giggled, and I had to kiss her to calm her down.

thirty-four
zara

MAYBE IT WASN'T Dave that I didn't trust, but happiness itself. As we kissed, my eyes burned with emotion even as my body heated up. Strong arms encircled me, and I straddled him happily.

It was so very good between us tonight. But could we really survive a lengthy separation?

In my gut, I just didn't trust it.

Dave lifted my skirt right there on the lounge chair and pulled my panties down. Wordlessly, I unzipped him. It wasn't two minutes later when I pressed up on my knees so he could line up his cock beneath me. But instead of filling myself with him the way that I wanted to, I teased him mercilessly, lowering myself centimeter by centimeter. It was torture for both of us, and I eased myself with kisses.

He groaned into my mouth. "Quit this teasing and fuck yourself on me." He grabbed my hips, but I clenched my thighs and stayed strong.

"The way I see it," I whispered, "You just volunteered for a lot of self-torture this fall. Now's your chance to practice." I slid down another fractional inch.

He leaned his head back on the chair and sighed. "Is it all gonna feel like this? Maybe I won't mind at all."

It wouldn't, though. We both knew it. So I wrapped my arms

around his neck and kissed him. I lowered my body over his until I'd taken him as deeply as I could, and then paused as we stared into each other's heavy-lidded eyes.

"Need you, Zara." His voice was strained. "Nobody else but you."

Oh, wow. Those heated words were impossible to ignore. I kissed him deeply, and my hips set a pace that pleased us both. "Sweet-talker," I murmured against his lips.

"It worked, right?" he panted, then smiled at me.

That smile, damn it. I missed him already.

"Don't think," he whispered, punctuating the command with a kiss. "Just feel."

It was good advice, so I did.

I opened the bakery the next morning. Now that Audrey had been back a little while, it was a pleasure because I wasn't so tired. Griffin had sent over the first half-bushel of early apples, so I peeled and diced them into muffin batter that I'd seasoned with ginger and cinnamon.

The kitchen smelled wonderful.

I wasn't the only one on the early shift. Dave and Nicole would wake up together again today, as they'd done several times lately, sparing my brother Alec the early morning babysitting shift.

I had hoped Alec appreciated it, but he'd never said so. He still hadn't said one nice thing about Dave.

Because I didn't enjoy drama, it was still my habit to leave Kieran in charge behind the counter and relieve Dave of babysitting duty just before my mother showed up for her babysitting shift. If my mother had wondered why I was waiting for her instead of Alec, she didn't ask.

But this morning we'd had a rush of espresso orders. As Kieran and I hurried to shorten the line of caffeine junkies at the counter, I'd lost track of time. I was late getting out the door—late enough to bump into my mother in the parking lot as she got out of her car.

Whoops.

"Morning, sweetheart," she said, tucking her keys into her bag. "You need something upstairs?"

"Well, no." I cleared my throat. "I was just going to say goodbye to Dave before he goes."

"Oh," she said, stepping backward suddenly. Then, "I see." And a sigh. "Are you sure that's what you want?"

Do you really have to ask? "If I didn't want him upstairs, he wouldn't be there."

"Yet he's leaving in three days?"

"Yes. For now. We're probably going to make some plans to see each other soon." I hated the hopeful sound of those words as they came out of my mouth. "I know it won't be easy. Maybe I'm setting myself up for disaster."

She lifted one perfectly tweezed eyebrow in question. "Like your foolish mother?"

"I didn't say that."

Mom actually rolled her eyes. "You said that quite a few times. Loudly. So did all of your brothers. When you were teenagers you were so mad at me for waiting around for your father."

Oh, good lord. I didn't want to have this fight again. "I'm sorry for whatever horrible things I said at seventeen. Trust me, if I could redo that decade of my life, I would. And fate is obviously having a chuckle at my expense right now."

My mother tossed her purse onto the hood of her car and sighed. "Maybe not, sweetheart. Dave might surprise us both. He's already put a roof over your heads, which is more than your father ever managed."

"He *is* a good man," I said, realizing that I'd never doubted that. What I doubted was his ability to love me the way I wanted to be loved. "Maybe our issues are entirely different from yours."

"Maybe," she admitted. "I just don't want to see you get hurt. And when Nicole is grown and pining for some unavailable man, you'll know just how it feels."

"Ouch," I said. "Touché."

She shook her head. "My point is that you'll empathize, whether hers is a good man or not. My heart breaks for all my children. And I will try not to look at your man and see your father. Dave is a hard worker, I'll give him that. There's no way to succeed in professional sports without a lot of self-discipline."

"That's true." And Mom had just become the first Rossi to say something nice about Dave.

"Your father couldn't stick to anything," she went on. "He never held down a job, because he was too easily offended if the boss didn't like his work. And everything that went wrong was someone else's fault. Usually mine."

I flinched, because it was true. "I'm sorry, Mom."

"Me too, honey. Me too." She grabbed her purse again. "I guess we can't choose who we love. So I will go up there and be civil to him and hope for the best."

"Thank you," I said, as I always did. But this time it meant a little more. "Thank you for giving him a chance."

She gave me a rueful smile and marched toward the private entrance.

And I went back into the coffee shop to make more espresso drinks.

The following day, Benito agreed to sit with Nicole for the evening so Dave and I could go out together. "Date Night!" Benito teased me.

But that's exactly what it was. Strangely enough it was our *first* date. We'd done everything backwards.

We decided to start Date Night at a furniture store in Burlington, as if we were an old married couple. Dave made me laugh by testing all the mattresses. "This one is nice," he said. "Lie down."

"They're all the same," I complained. "Can you really tell the difference?"

He tugged me down one-handed. "I can. I like this one, but do you think it's too firm?"

"It's fine," I said, just like I had for the last five he'd tried.

"Okay. Sold." Then he rolled over and gave me a kiss. A hot one.

Embarrassed, I wiggled away. "We'll try it out properly *after* it's delivered."

He gave me that smile that I'd do anything for.

After picking out a coffee table—but not a couch, because I didn't like the choices—we went out to dinner at Hen of the Wood, one of Burlington's finest restaurants. Dave draped his arm over the back of his chair, looking like a satisfied king, while I admired him in the candlelight.

"When are you going to move in to the new house?" he asked me. "I wish I could help you."

"Benito will help me," I promised him. "He wants his apartment back."

Under the table, his leg rubbed against my ankle. "Don't tell him we broke in that deck chair."

"I would never!" I yelped, and he laughed.

His phone beeped. He glanced at the text but then put it away. Unfortunately, it beeped again during dessert, and then rang in the parking lot.

"Sorry," he sighed. "But I don't think they're going to let it go."

"Who is it?"

"The team doctor's assistant."

"At this hour?"

"Yup." He tapped the screen. "There are no regular business hours in professional hockey. Let me just return her call."

I watched his face as a female voice spoke rapidly into his ear. "Tomorrow?" he asked warily. "I'm five hours away, though."

The yapping went on, while his frown deepened, and my stomach dropped.

"Okay," he said with a sigh. "If that's the way it's gotta be."

He ended the call a minute later and looked at me, his face grim. "I'm sorry, baby."

"You have to go *tomorrow?*" That was two days early. I'd been counting on those days.

"I do. They got me an appointment with a specialist to talk about my shoulder."

"And it has to be tomorrow?" I could hear a note of hysteria in my voice.

"Yeah." He cringed. "They'd told me it would be this week, but I didn't know they'd schedule it for before training camp began. It's partly my fault."

Can't you tell them you're busy? The argument was on the tip of my tongue. But I wasn't going to say it, because I knew in my gut that Dave would stay two more days with me if he could. Somehow I'd gotten myself to a place where I could at least be sure of that.

Hallelujah. I was learning.

"Okay," I said slowly. "When do you need to leave?"

"Well…" He looked at the Timex on his wrist. "I have to pack. If I drive away from the cabin at four-thirty, I can make it back in time."

"Four-thirty…"

"In the morning," he said with a grimace.

"Okay," I said more firmly than I had before. "I'll help you pack."

"Really?"

"Of course." If he and I were going to consider a long-distance relationship, I might as well get used to it.

Benito looked up from the television when we walked in the door. "Good dinner?" he asked.

"Yeah, but don't get up," I said. "Would you stay here tonight with Nicole?"

He blinked. "Okay."

"I'm changing the sheets on your bed," I said, walking away before he could make a snarky comment about why I might need to do that for him.

After that little task, I looked around the room for Dave's things. He'd left a shirt and a pair of flip flops.

And his fancy watch. It was still on the bedside table where we'd left it after I'd showed it to him. "Never really liked that thing," he'd said with a chuckle. "Except it taught me that spending money on bling wasn't really my style."

I left it on the bedside table like a talisman, and grabbed my nightgown and toothbrush to spend the night at Dave's cabin.

Dave was not in the living room when I went back out there. Nor the kitchen.

I found him in the baby's room, standing quietly in the dark, looking down at his sleeping child. While I hovered in the doorway, he bent down to lift the blanket over her sprawled out body, and whisper something I couldn't hear.

Tears sprang into the corners of my eyes, and I left the doorway quickly to blink them away.

"Okay," he said when he joined me in the living room. "Shall we?"

"When are you coming back?" Benito asked, his eyes on the Red Sox game.

"He's shipping out at four-thirty," I said. "So I can come back whenever."

Benito looked up. "Oh. Fuck."

Right.

He stood and held out a hand. "Hope to see you back here again."

"You can count on it," Dave said to me as much as to Benny. "Thanks for the babysitting. You know, for the last sixteen months."

Benito grinned. "It was really my pleasure. I'm the favorite uncle for sure. Got the trophy and everything."

He waved us off, and I followed Dave out the door.

thirty-five
dave

THE MINUTE I told Zara I had to leave, everything began to feel wrong.

She was a trooper, though. My Zara put her game face on and did what needed doing. I fell a little more in love with her as she straightened her spine against yet another disappointment and followed me in her crappy little car to the cabin.

We made quick work of packing the place up. There wasn't much food in the kitchen because I'd been spending so much time with her. "What about the keys?" Zara asked. "Can you just leave them here on the counter?"

"Sure can," I said. "Place looks fine, right? We're done."

She gave me a sad smile. "We are. Let's get you some sleep. You're going to be driving in just a few hours."

"Sleep is overrated," I said, catching her around the waist. But my smile felt fake, and there was an unfamiliar tightness in my chest. "God, I hate this," I said suddenly. "I hate leaving you. Both of you."

Zara's stalwart expression slipped. "I know," she said softly. "It sucks."

Then she kissed me to shut me up, and it totally worked.

We lay a long time in the dark together after making love. I couldn't sleep until I felt Zara drift off. And then I slept the anxious slumber of someone who knows his alarm clock is going to go off way too early.

And then it did. I lay there groggily, trying to summon the will to sit up. And I thought back to the last time I'd left Zara on my way back to New York—when I'd slept in her bed uninvited. "You'll say goodbye to me this time, right?" I rasped.

"Yes. I promise," she said into her pillow.

I trailed my palm over her hair, then her long neck, and then onward down the silky skin of her naked back.

How did people do this?

She reached out and gave me a shove. "Take your shower, honey. Push the button on the coffee pot. Go on."

I went.

Thirty minutes later I was behind the wheel of my car, driving slowly out of Green Rocks on a gravel road, startling a doe and her fawn in the pre-dawn gloom. There was very little traffic in Vermont at any hour. So as I made my way to Interstate 91 before five a.m., I felt like the last man alive. On the highway there was nobody but the occasional big rig and me.

I drove all those hours thinking about Zara and Nicole. The goodbye kiss I'd finally gotten. Zara's hug—a tight one, like maybe she didn't expect to ever get another—and her words of endearment in my ear. "I'll miss you," she'd whispered. "We both will. Take care of yourself for us."

Those words cut me. Having her and Nicole was a gift, and I wasn't sure I deserved them. I was committed to doing right by them, but it was really hard to picture how the next three years were going to work.

Would she really wait for me? If I were her, I don't know if I would.

I got to New York in time to turn in my rental car and eat a late breakfast in a midtown diner. My only companion was my giant duffel bag, sitting across from me in the booth.

Afterward, as I walked toward the specialist's office, the traffic noise was startling to me. I'd forgotten how loud it was here—something I never used to notice.

The specialist took me back into her exam room right away, where she took a series of images with some of her cutting-edge equipment, then proceeded to prod my shoulder for a while, chatting away with a medical student who was observing that day.

"And you've been doing PT all summer?" the doc asked.

"I sure have."

Then she disappeared.

While I sat waiting, I checked my phone. Zara had sent me a photo of Nicole in her clip-on high chair, smiling up at the camera with yogurt on her face. The text read, *Guess who finally said MAMA?*

I laughed out loud. That's when I realized I'd been waiting kind of a long time for the doctor to review my data. Maybe the news wasn't good. If they sent me back for another ten weeks of therapy...

That idea would have made me vomit at any other point in my career. But the first idea that popped into my head was that I could spend more time with Zara if I wasn't going to play at training camp.

The door popped open and the doctor walked in. "Congratulations, Dave! Good work on your shoulder. I see no reason why you can't get back on the ice."

She held out her hand to shake, and I took it reluctantly. "Really? That's it? Am I doing more PT?"

"Nope." She shook her head. "I mean—if you suddenly develop any more pain, make sure you report it. But the joint is nicely mobile, and the tendons seem strong. Well done."

"Thank you."

And that was that. I walked out of there feeling a little numb, probably from lack of sleep. This was the good news I'd been waiting for.

In the elevator I texted Bess. Then I stuck my phone in my pocket and went out into the noise of Manhattan. There was a subway stop a few blocks from the doctor's office, and I headed in that direction. But when I got to the turnstile, it wouldn't let me through.

Card expired, the machine complained.

Well, fuck. That was just the kind of welcome home that New York dished out.

Both MetroCard terminals were spoken for, so I waited, wishing I'd taken a Lyft instead. Although sitting in bridge traffic to Brooklyn would probably take even longer.

Not that I had anything to hurry home to.

"Hey! Aren't you Dave Beringer?"

I swiveled carefully to avoid knocking anyone with my bag, and found a teenager in a backward baseball cap—a Bruisers cap—grinning at me. "Sure am," I said after a beat.

"How's the shoulder?" the kid asked.

I laughed. "It's actually fine. I'll be at practice this weekend, if you're taking attendance."

"Autograph?" the kid asked, whipping off his hat to offer me the brim. There were a few scrawls on it already. This guy must be a superfan, because he'd already cornered a couple of my teammates.

"Sure." I patted my pockets, but came up empty. "Dude, I'm sorry. No pen."

His face fell. "I don't have one either."

"Here." I grabbed one of my cards out of my money clip. "Email this address and use the name Bess, okay? That's my sister. Her assistant answers my email. Tell Bess I wanted to send a puck to the guy I met in the subway."

He took the card, his face brightening. "Thanks, man! Can't wait to see you make it to the finals again this year! And it's, uh, your turn."

I whirled to find that it was indeed my turn to buy a new Metrocard, and that the growing line of people behind us was starting to get twitchy.

Right.

I tapped the screen and speedily bought a new card. Then I wished the teen luck and headed for the platform.

When I got home to Brooklyn's DUMBO neighborhood, the doorman greeted me with a shout of happiness. "Dude! Where you been? Good summer?" He grabbed my big duffel bag and put it on the luggage trolley, and I was happy to hand it over.

"Great summer," I said, high-fiving him. "What's happening here, Miguel?"

He made a face. "Same old nothing. You go anywhere interesting?"

"Vermont," I said. "Love it up there."

"Never been," he said. "No golf this summer?"

"No, thank God."

He laughed. "Got more luggage?"

I shook my head. "That's it."

"For seven weeks?" my doorman looked surprised.

"I travel light."

Miguel grinned. "A single guy like you? I guess you can get away with it. I'll send this up right away."

"Thanks, man."

Another elevator ride brought me to the carpeted hallway of my floor. I lived in a converted warehouse, with high ceilings and pre-war fixtures everywhere. When I turned my key and opened the door, I had to squint against all the sunlight. There were floor-to-ceiling windows, wooden floors, and exposed brick walls.

I loved this place. But it was awfully quiet and empty. I toed off my shoes and took a tour. The cleaning service had been here to dust and air things out earlier in the week. So my apartment was clean and fresh-smelling. When I peeked in the refrigerator, I found that it had been restocked. Eggs, fruit, and yogurt. The freezer held chicken and fish. The cabinet was full of protein bars and crackers.

Everything an athlete needed to feed his body. If not his soul.

My footsteps were audible in the silence as I paced into my bedroom. The bed was perfectly made. I pulled out my phone and sat on the edge of the bed. *Made it home,* I texted to Zara. *Doctor cleared me to play.*

There was no activity on her end. No message in progress. She was probably working. There was nowhere I needed to be until the day after tomorrow.

I texted Doulie next. *Bar burgers later, and baseball?*

No can do, he wrote back. *Taking Ari out to dinner before the madness begins.*

Right.

Cleared to play, BTW, I told him.

Awesome! See you on the ice.

I stood up and turned around, trying to picture Zara in my bed as I stripped off my shorts. Now there was a pleasant fantasy. I grabbed a pair of athletic shorts and pulled them on. It was time for a workout. I needed to beat some of the stupid out of me and focus on the season ahead.

My apartment had two bedrooms, but the second one was full of exercise equipment, also dust free thanks to my cleaning service. I opened a window blind to let in the August sunshine and then set up the leg press for a warmup.

I sat on the bench and began to press the iron in slow, rhythmic bursts. After the first set, I glanced around the room, taking in the amount of space. There was plenty of it. I could sell my gym equipment and give the room to Nicole. These weights weren't very useful to me in season, when I spent much of my day at the practice facility, anyway.

Christ. This building had a weight room, and I'd never set foot inside it. I didn't need this space all to myself.

As I began the second set, reality kicked in. It didn't matter if I had room for Zara and Nicole to join me in Brooklyn. Zara didn't like the city. And even if she did, I'd just bought her a house that was nicer than this space, with the backyard she'd said she wanted her child to have.

I tried to ignore the voice in my head, the one that said, *If she loved you, it wouldn't matter. She'd be here right now.*

No, wait. That was just my past talking.

Funny how I could never hear the difference before now. But my childhood had always been there—fucking up my expectations.

Telling me I was a loner for life, a guy that nobody would ever want.

Zara *did* love me. She was cagey as hell, but I could taste it whenever she kissed me—the same hunger I felt, too.

I was just going to have to wait her out. And play some damned fine hockey while I waited.

thirty-six
zara

October

AUDREY and I were hiding in the kitchen, scarfing down a plate of pumpkin mini-muffins that Audrey claimed were a little overdone. It was just an excuse to eat them ourselves, though. Now that Audrey's morning sickness was gone, her appetite was in overdrive. I was merely her enabler.

We weren't hiding because of the mini-muffins, though. We were hiding so that we could have a moment alone together to celebrate the big decision we'd made.

"He starts on Tuesday," Audrey whispered. "Seemed mean to start him on the weekend. I don't know why, though. He's going to be working weekends."

"Not every weekend," I pointed out. "We're still going to alternate Saturdays and Sundays."

Audrey patted her baby bump. "I know! And I don't care! I'm just so happy that he was okay with working the early shift four days a week."

Truly, it was an impossible luxury. Our first full-time employee—Roderick—was a single guy. He didn't even have a girlfriend. And he hadn't blinked when we'd told him the hours he'd be working. "I'm a *baker,*" he'd explained. "If I didn't want to get up early, I've made some terrible life choices."

He was going to be great. I could just tell. "How many days of training do you think he'll need?"

"It's really hard to say!" Audrey tossed another mini-muffin in her mouth and grinned. "He's my first full-time employee. I'm so proud."

"You're a goof is what you are." I eyed the muffins. Eating another one would really be overkill. "So... Who's going to tell Kieran? I'll flip you for it."

Audrey's eyes sparkled "You tell him. I'll watch."

"Tell me what?" Kieran's deep voice asked as he stuck his head into the kitchen.

I swear, we both jumped when we heard him. "Um..." Audrey hedged.

"We hired Roderick," I said, biting the bullet.

"What?" Kieran's face darkened. "He couldn't *possibly* be the best choice."

Audrey and I exchanged a glance. Roderick was an excellent choice. Impeccable resume. Great experience in the bakery at King Arthur in Norwich. And—not that we would say it out loud—hot as hell.

"Buddy," Audrey said slowly. "*Why* don't you like this guy?"

"He's a dick," Kieran said quickly.

"Based on what, though?" He'd been Mr. Charming as far as we'd seen. "How do you know him?"

"High school, right?" I guessed. Kieran was a little younger than I was, but I had a vague memory of teenaged Roderick.

"Yeah," Kieran said.

"So..." Audrey offered the plate of muffins to Kieran, who shook his head. "Is he still a dick? I mean, I don't want to hire a dick. But is he presently a dick or might he have outgrown it?"

Kieran made a face like he'd tasted something bad. "I dunno. I have to wipe down the machines and get going."

At that, he disappeared.

"What do you think?" I whispered. "Should we be worried?"

"I don't know what to think," Audrey replied in the same hushed tone. "Kieran has been surly for months. And he didn't give us much to go on, here."

He really hadn't. "We checked Roderick's references. They love him in Norwich. His baking blog has a big following."

"And we already hired him," Audrey said, brushing her hands of muffin crumbs. "It will either work or it won't. Let's not worry."

"Okay." This was why I loved Audrey. She didn't do drama. She was the sunshine that reminded me not to be gloomy. "I guess we'd better get back to it." I headed out of the kitchen. It was a quiet afternoon, and Audrey was due to go home.

"Now if I were you," Audrey said, following me. "I'd be looking for flights to New York in three weeks or so. There's a window of opportunity here—this baby will come in twenty weeks whether we're ready or not. So go visit your man while you still have the chance."

"Wow." I got a shiver just thinking about it. This was really the first moment when that had seemed possible.

"How's he doing, anyway?"

"Good," I said. I'd watched a livestream of one of his pre-season games last night. "He's in Philadelphia right now. Nicole and I will probably Skype with him on the weekend."

"Both of you? That's not the Skype call I'd be having with him." Audrey winked.

"Oh, stop." We'd had only G-rated Skype sessions. I'd shown him all the furniture I'd bought for the house. Purchases that had become easy the week after he'd left, when a check had come in the mail for me—more money than the coffee shop had earned in its first year. The memo line had said: Child Support Lump Sum Payment.

That stinker had managed to pay for my furniture, after all. And I'd put a down payment on a used car Alec found for me.

And, sure, I always called him when the baby was awake. I told myself that it was good for him to remember that we were a team—that I wasn't just an erotic fantasy of his. But it also kept us from having the big conversations. I don't think I'd realized before this moment that I'd been doing it on purpose.

"I'm still holding him at arm's length," I said slowly. "I am, right? Jesus."

"*Honey,*" Audrey said. "If you keep it up, he'll always *be* at an arm's length."

"I don't know how to stop," I said, realizing what she'd said was true.

"Buy a fricking plane ticket, go wrap yourself around him, and tell him how much you miss him. It really is that easy."

"You're probably right."

"I know I am." She grabbed her phone out of her pocket. "Jet Blue flies to JFK. Let's just see what the flight times are..."

thirty-seven
zara

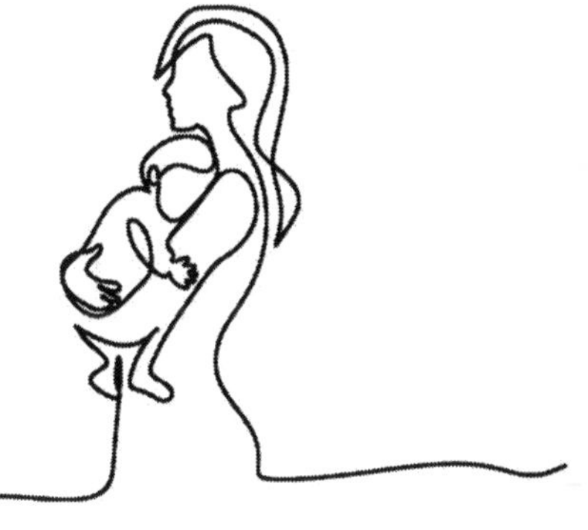

AS IT TURNED OUT, planning a trip to see Dave wasn't quite that easy. Dave's excitement over my visit was uninhibited. But when we sat down to find a time that worked for everyone, we hit snags.

His schedule was tight, and when we checked the flights, they didn't arrive and depart when we needed them to.

I'd offered to drive instead, but it would be five hours with Nicole alone and cranky in the backseat. Not the best option. I began to get discouraged as we looked at dates further and further out.

But then Dave called me back with a proposed solution—he had a couple of early season games in Florida, with a two-day gap between them. He could fly us to Miami for three nights—two with him at a resort hotel, and then one by ourselves when he rejoined the team for the Miami game. Nicole and I would have second-row seats.

"Book it," I said, tired of waiting. Now that I was all in, I wanted to tell him in person.

I did some panic shopping with Audrey. Now that our new guy Roderick had started, we were all breathing a little easier. Two days before I was due to depart, we hit the stores in Burlington for maternity clothes for her and a new bathing suit for me.

"Let's not forget lingerie," she said as we carried shopping bags down the outdoor Church Street mall.

Two black satin nightgowns were added to our stash—one for each of us.

It was a good day, and I let optimism bubble through my soul in a way that was rare for me.

Which was why, on the day of our trip, I was blindsided by the worst flight ever.

Earlier in the week, Nicole had come down with a bit of a cold. But toddlers were famous for having lots of colds as their little immune systems learned the ropes, and I didn't let it worry me. I was too excited to see Dave—at a luxury beach resort no less.

Nicole was a little weepy as we began our trip, but I assumed it was just the break in her routine. Then she was fussy during the flight and wouldn't eat or drink her milk. Still, not a big deal.

But as the plane started its descent, she began to whimper. And by the time I could see the lights of Miami, she was crying. The cries became howls. She buried the side of her face against my collarbone and cried like there was no tomorrow.

I couldn't soothe her with a trip up and down the aisle, because the Fasten Seatbelt light was on. She cried, and I shushed and patted her back as people began to stare.

"It's probably her ears," a flight attendant said, trying to help. "If she drinks something, it might relieve the pressure." She offered me a bottle of water, which I took.

But Nicole wasn't having it. She screamed when I tried to sit her up, and her crying took on that desperate, hiccup-y sound of the truly despondent.

The plane took four hours to land. Not really, but that's how it felt to me. And then came that interminable time before passengers were allowed off the plane. Everyone near me was tapping their fingers or toes, eager to flee from us.

I didn't blame them.

When I finally stood up and took a good look at her, one ear was bright red. She'd been rubbing it against me for almost an hour, so it could have been irritated, but I had a sinking suspicion that Nicole had a bigger problem—baby's first ear infection.

"I'm so sorry," I whispered in her good ear as she cried. "I didn't know."

Hell, I wasn't even sure I had baby Motrin in my suitcase.

By the time we were able to leave the plane and head for the baggage claim, I was a nervous wreck. And she still wouldn't stop crying.

Then I spotted a certain auburn head and a certain rugged smile. For a second I forgot to panic. There he was, waiting for me. Waiting for *us*.

God, I almost had to pinch myself.

Once he got a good look at us, his smile faded fast. "What's wrong?" he asked immediately.

"She won't stop crying. I think it could be an ear infection."

Dave reached for Nicole and took her from me like any good dad anywhere. He cradled her and whispered something to her.

"DADA..." she wailed.

I felt like crying, too.

Dave

The next couple of hours weren't easy.

To the irritation of the Uber driver, my child screamed all the way to the hotel, like we were trying to kill her. I called the team doctor in New York and asked him what I should do. He sent us to an overly bright urgent care facility, where a young physician's assistant diagnosed an ear infection and gave us a prescription.

"Give her a dose immediately," she said. "And a dose again in the night, if she wakes up. She should get some relief within twelve or twenty-four hours. And baby ibuprofen will help, too."

One pharmacy stop later, and we were on our way back in the hotel's courtesy car, with Zara looking shaken and bleary.

Still crying, Nicole relaxed into a fitful doze in her car seat. I reached across to Zara and took her hand. Her fingers laced into mine, but she looked out the window and bit her lip.

Then, finally, we'd made it back to the suite I'd booked. There was a crib waiting in the extra little bedroom and a bottle of champagne sweating in the bucket where I'd left it hours ago.

Ah, well. The best-laid plans.

Zara put the baby's medicine in a sort of eyedropper and squirted it into Nicole's sleepy mouth.

My baby girl was enraged. Unfortunately, Zara had to do it again with the pain reliever, and Nicole was inconsolable. She cried herself to sleep in my arms, and I didn't think I'd ever seen anyone look so bereft.

When I finally set her down in the crib and tiptoed out, I could hardly believe she was actually resting.

I walked quietly into the master bedroom, where Zara had sat down on the edge of the bed and then tipped her body back onto the comforter in defeat. "Wow," I whispered, trying to lighten the mood. "That was intense."

She sat up. "I'm so sorry. You went to all this trouble…" She glanced around the room, taking in the food, the wine bottle, the glasses. The chocolate I'd put on her pillow as a joke.

"Don't be sorry." I sat beside her. "Come here." I pulled her into a hug. "I know you're tired and stressed out. But she's going to be okay."

"I know," she whispered.

"And *we're* going to be okay. You have no idea how happy I am that you're here. I missed you terribly."

Her eyes leaked. "That's what I came all the way here to tell you. I missed you, too. So much."

"See?" I buried my face in her neck and found smooth skin to kiss. "It's us. In the same room. And that's all I really needed from you tonight."

Her arms came around my back, and I felt her body start to relax. Slim hands traced my spine, then my ribcage. "You feel so good."

"Come to bed with me," I whispered. "Let me hold you. You're probably exhausted." I could see it in her face.

Zara got up and wandered into the glamorous marble bathroom, murmuring her approval. She emerged a few minutes later wearing a black silk nightie I'd never seen before. "You like?" she asked when she caught me admiring it. "I bought it when I thought this was going to be a sex fest."

I cocked a finger and beckoned her. "Get in this bed, woman. We'll just have to see what transpires."

She gave me a tired smile, and I took my turn in the john.

When I returned, she was curled up on her side of the bed, looking anxious. "I hope she can sleep. And that the medicine works fast."

"If she doesn't sleep well"—I slipped into the bed beside her—"we'll take turns holding her. It'll be okay." I switched off the bedside lamp and rolled close to her. "How was your trip before the screaming started?"

"Fine? I can barely remember."

I curved my body around hers and put my hands on her shoulders. "Relax, baby."

She tried. I worked my thumbs into the tight muscles of her back and used my fingertips to ease her shoulders.

"That's…really awesome," she slurred.

"That's right," I whispered. "I believe it's the first thing I ever told you—that I'm great at stress relief. Pro level."

She laughed, but then her laughter died when I reached around and teased her nipple with my fingertips, tracing a circle around it until I felt it pebble under the silk. She arched her back, offering me her neck, and I began to drop kisses there.

"Mmm," she said with a sigh. "I thought I was too tired for this. But maybe not."

"I'm gonna do all the work," I promised, kissing my way down her arm.

She gave me a wise smile over her shoulder. "You must be desperate."

"I am." I rested my chin on her arm. "But not the way you mean. I'm a big boy, Z. I can go a couple of months without sex, if I know I'm going to see you again." Her expression softened. "Of course, now that you're here, I'm suddenly dying."

She grinned and I was happy to see that naughty sparkle return to her eyes. A defeated-looking Zara was more worrying than a screaming baby. "Where do you want me?"

"Stay right there," I said, putting a firm hand to her hip. "Don't you move unless I tell you to."

"Yes, sir." She said it cheekily, but her cheeks heated.

Just to make my point, I gently pushed her head against the pillow, facing away from me. "Close your eyes."

She snapped them shut.

"Good girl," I whispered as my fingertips began exploring her body. I dragged them down the front of her gown, sliding over silk and then skin when I reached her knee. Her lips parted in appreciation, and I felt her relax against me. "That's right," I coached, dragging my hand over her body again. I paid special attention to her breasts, which I was allowed to touch again. And suck. I worked the strap of her nightgown down and leaned over her body until I could get my mouth on her.

"Mmm," she sighed.

My hand worked its way beneath her gown, and I made a noise of appreciation when I found no panties in my way. "I do like this outfit. It's my favorite."

She smiled with her eyes closed. And when I ran a palm down her bare belly and between her legs, she shifted and spread her legs for me.

"That's my girl," I whispered in her ear. "Always ready to take my cock. You want it, don't you."

"Yeah," she gasped as I tucked my fingers into the slickness waiting for me.

My lips found the sensitive spot beneath her ear as I stroked her sweet pussy. She moaned and pressed against me everywhere.

It was all too easy to kick off my boxers, lift her leg, and slide inside her from behind. "Unhh," I exclaimed as her body welcomed me. We lay there a second, our breathing rapid, and I swear every cell in my body vibrated with expectation. "Now this is what I'm talking about." I flexed my hips and she rolled hers, too.

Heaven.

"You are perfect," I whispered over her shoulder.

She grabbed my hand and clutched it. "Pretty...great yourself."

"You make me feel lucky."

"Well, you're *getting* lucky," she pointed out.

"No." I chuckled in her ear. "I meant all of it." I lay down on my side and pulled her against me, even if it meant I couldn't keep up my good work for a second. But I needed her to feel this connection all the way down to her soul. I had a point to make, and now seemed as good a time as any. "I'd do it all again, Zara girl. With you. No regrets."

She went still in my arms.

"You're it for me. I don't care if there are gonna be earaches and lots of days missing you. I'll take it, because you're the best there is."

"I love you, too, honey," she whispered. "I think I always have."

My heart gave a big old kick. "Thanks for finally letting me know."

I felt her smile even if I couldn't see it. She pushed her ass back against me to remind me that we were in the middle of something important. That was Zara for you. She liked to keep the upper hand.

But so did I. So I rolled, taking her to her stomach, spreading myself out on top of her luscious body. I braced myself on my forearms and began to move, and she moaned her approval.

Skin kissed skin. I was against her. Above her. Beside her. *Inside* her. Everywhere I needed to be, all at once.

thirty-eight
dave

THE BABY WOKE AGAIN in the darkest part of the night. Zara got up to soothe her. She gave her another dose of medicine while I lay in bed listening, waiting to offer my services if we were in for a long night of passing a screaming child back and forth.

But Zara came back to bed fifteen minutes later, startling me out of a doze as she tucked a quiet Nicole in between us in the bed.

I reached down for my boxers on the floor and pulled them on, then lay down on my back, giving them some space.

We dozed. Then we slept. And nobody cried.

When I next awoke, there was sunlight on my eyelids and a little hand feathering its way through my hair. And when I opened my eyes I was startled to see Nicole a few inches from my face, looking right at me.

She was startled, too, blinking suddenly when our gazes met.

"Dada," she said, her voice small.

"Hi," I whispered, watching her. She looked surprisingly chipper given all the previous day's miseries. But, heck. I'd been young once. I knew exactly how different it felt to have the youthful resilience of childhood, instead of the muscle pain that greeted me each and every morning now.

I sat up carefully, checking in with my body the way a professional athlete in his second decade of play always did. I clocked all my minor aches and pains, then reached for my baby girl. "Come on," I whispered.

Nicole climbed into my lap, then looked over at Zara. "Mama," she said.

"Mama's sleepy," I whispered, because Zara was lying on her face, dead to the world. "Come with me." I grabbed some shorts and a polo shirt and carried her into the living room.

Funny how I could find the diaper bag and change a diaper before I was fully awake. Although I got stuck on the next bit. "Do you still drink milk in the morning?"

"Baba," Nicole said, which was her word for the sippy-bottle thing she drank from these days.

"Where do you suppose that is?"

Nicole walked over to the diaper bag, then began to root around in it. But I spotted the cup beside the hotel suite's little kitchen sink. "Here we go. Let's go fill this up," I said.

The point of staying in a luxury hotel wasn't the stylish furniture in the lobby or the elegant pool with the disappearing edge. The point was handing an empty sippy cup to the first concierge I could find, and watching that person scurry off to fill it up with milk.

"Baba," Nicole said with a frown, watching it disappear.

"They're going to hook you up," I promised. If I were a smarter man, I would have asked for coffee, too. "Let's look around while we wait." I spotted an aquarium across the way and carried her over to it.

As we looked through the glass, a grumpy-faced bass swam past us at a rapid rate, and Nicole gasped. "Fissy!" she exclaimed.

And, *wow*. It was so cool to hear new words coming out of her. She'd made a big leap forward since I'd seen her in Vermont, and I'd mostly missed it. Sure, I'd heard a few words on Skype, but that was nothing like holding her and hearing that little voice at close range.

Maybe it had taken me a little longer than it could have, but being

Nicole's father felt right to me now. *Your life has just changed for the better,* my sister had said on that first, terrifying morning after I'd come back to Vermont. *I hope you're not too stupid to figure that out.*

Well, sis. I got there. It just took a while.

"Excuse me, madame," a man's voice said behind me. "Is this yours?"

"Baba!"

I turned around to find a young guy holding Nicole's sippy cup, and it was full of milk. "Thank you," I said, flashing my key card. "Where do I sign?"

He handed me the bottle and a bill wallet, where I filled in my room number and a generous tip for Nicole's beverage of choice.

"Thank you, sir," he said, and was gone.

In order to let Zara sleep a bit longer, I carried Nicole out the sliding glass doors and across a patio. When the patio ended, the sand began. The beach was really wide here, so the hotel had made a shady enclosure with hammock-like chairs. Every one of them was empty now. I sat down carefully so the thing wouldn't swing sideways and dump us both onto the sand. Then I eased back and let Nicole make herself comfortable against my chest.

She lifted the sippy cup immediately and began to drink the milk. The poor kid was probably starving since she hadn't stopped crying long enough to consider food last night.

Kicking off my flip flops, I buried my toes in the cool sand. Somewhere in the distance, the ocean crashed against the beach in rhythmic waves. And seagulls chased each other on the horizon, their cries carried off by the wind.

"I gotta say, it's pretty nice right here," I told my daughter.

There was no answer, except for some slurping sounds. While I rocked us in the chair, she drank every drop, then handed me the empty bottle. I could almost hear her adding, *Listen, Dada, this bottle was too small.*

In a minute I'd get up and find out how to order some room service. After the night we had, I thought we were due for some serious chow.

But first… I dug out my phone. It was barely seven, but that meant my sister was up and showered and nearly ready to head for her office. I tapped on her ID in Skype so she could see Nicole.

She picked up immediately. "Heyyyyyy!" she squealed.

"Hey!" I repeated. "Look, Nicole, it's your crazy aunt Bess. Can you tell her hi?"

Nicole lifted her hand and waved at the screen, while Bess swooned. I let my sister chatter to the baby for a while, then I told her I needed to go see about breakfast.

"Wait," she said, remembering that I was alive. "Since you're here, it's time for my weekly nagging."

"I'm on vacation," I said quickly. We didn't need to talk about my contract extension *today*. Jesus.

"Look, I was talking to Hugh this week on another matter…" Hugh was my team's general manager. "He asked where you stood on the question of two years versus three, and of course I told him you just weren't ready to think about it. Eventful summer, blah blah blah…"

"Right. So?"

My sister bit her lip. "I wondered whether I should have asked him how he felt about a *one*-year extension."

"One year?" I didn't see how that really helped the discussion.

"Well, yeah." She gave me a cautious smile. "I thought maybe you were having trouble choosing because suddenly it was harder to think three years out." Her eyes flicked to Nicole. "A one-year would buy you some time to think things over."

"Huh." Then again, they could drop me after a year. "I'll think about it. Gotta go. Hotel pancakes are calling our name."

Nicole made a happy noise. I was pretty sure they were calling her name, too. I set her down in the sand to say goodbye to my sister, and Nicole plopped down on stubby knees to run her fingers through the sand.

"Come on, angel," I said, standing up slowly. "Let's go order some food."

She reached up to wrap her hand around my finger. And we

walked back inside together.

thirty-nine
zara

I WOKE UP ALONE. There have been times in my life when I woke up alone and felt sad about it. This wasn't one of those times.

When I rolled over on the thousand-thread-count sheets and heard…silence—beautiful silence—I knew Dave had gotten up with Nicole, and that she must be feeling better. I would have heard her if she needed me. And I trusted Dave not to wander the resort with a child in pain.

When I lingered on that idea, though, I realized something. I trusted Dave with Nicole. I really did. Why had I taken so long, then, to trust him with *me?*

That thought got me out of bed. I washed my face and brushed my teeth and put on one of the thick, fluffy robes hanging in the bathroom.

Then I paced the hotel suite for a few minutes, looking out of various windows, wondering when they were coming back—not because I was worried, but because I missed them.

It was probably only a few minutes later when the door clicked open and Dave appeared like a handsome vision in the doorway. Nicole was riding on his muscular arm, one hand casually resting on his shoulder. When she saw me, she smiled and said, "Mama!"

"You look so much better!" I cried, reaching for them both.

A group hug ensued until Dave stepped back to say, "Breakfast will be here in twenty minutes. I'm really hungry so I ordered one of everything."

"Oh!" That sounded amazing. "I need to find some milk for Nicole's—"

"She already drank one," he said, pulling her cup out of a pocket in his shorts. "But they're sending us some more for later."

"Wow. You took care of everything."

He smiled at me, and I got the same thrill I always did. "I spotted the p-o-o-l," he said. "It's a nice spot. We could head over there after breakfast? There's a kiddie area here somewhere, too."

"I can't wait."

Seriously, I was in love. Not only with the hot guy on the other end of the couch, but with this whole experience. I was still in my bathrobe while we drank a second cup of the coffee that room service had brought in a silver pot. I was full of eggs, bacon, and pancakes, too.

"Honey, a year ago, if someone had told me I'd be enjoying a family vacation with you and Nicole at a posh resort, I would have told them to get off the drugs."

Dave's smile was distant. I poked him with my toe. "Everything okay down there? Did you just hear what I said?"

"Um…" He looked up, chuckling. "Can you say it again?"

I gave him an affectionate eye-roll. "Is something on your mind? Or maybe we're all just overtired." Last night had gotten our adventure off to a rocky start.

"I tired you out last night?" Dave pulled my feet into his lap and squeezed my instep.

It felt great. "Seriously. Is something wrong?"

"Not a thing." He shook his head to clear it. "Bess asked me a question this morning. She had the strange idea that I should consider a one-year contract extension. But that's counterintuitive for a guy who's worried about job security."

Now here was a topic I had refused to weigh in on. I knew he was trying to choose between the two-year and three-year contracts. But I wasn't going to express an opinion, because I didn't ever want to sound like I was pressuring him to cut his career short.

"If I took a one-year contract, that's really a year and a half," he said. "Because my current one goes through June."

"Sure," I said, so he'd know I was listening. But Dave seemed to need to discuss this with himself.

His glance went to Nicole, who was sitting in front of the floor-to-ceiling windows, holding a teddy bear and watching palm trees move in the breeze. "She'd be three when a one-year contract ended."

"Right."

"I gotta say, I always had trouble with the idea of retiring." He worried the edge of his phone with his fingertips as he told me this.

"Who wouldn't?"

"Well, a guy with a *life*." He gave me a sad smile. "I mean—every athlete has trouble with the transition. That's just a given. But when I'd looked at my post-retirement years, I just saw… It was *blank*. I'd pictured myself standing in my Brooklyn apartment on that first morning, like, what the eff do I do now?"

I moved my body down the sofa, swinging my legs off his lap so I could get close to him. He wrapped an arm around me. "That sounds hard, honey. I can't even imagine."

"The thing is, I can now. I want to see what you've done with the place in Vermont, and I want to be there more than seven or eight weeks in the summer. There's someplace else I want to be now. If you'll have me."

"Any day of the week," I whispered, leaning against him, the coffee cup warming my hands. "That sounds wonderful. My house is your house. Literally." I sipped my coffee.

He snorted. "But I'm not joking. After I retire, I want to be with you and Nicole. I want to get married and the whole bit."

I choked on my coffee and then sputtered.

"Oh, hell," he said, taking the cup from my hands. "I told you I'm a rookie at this relationship thing."

That just made me laugh, on top of the coughing and gasping.

"Breathe, baby." His eyes twinkled. "Sorry."

"It's...okay." I coughed. "Just never expected you to say that."

"Me neither." He smiled and pulled me into his lap, setting my mug down and then whacking me on the back. "Bess is going to pee herself."

I laughed harder. There were tears leaking out of my eyes now, and it was anyone's guess whether they were tears of laughter or happy joy or a side effect of aspirating coffee. But I'd never felt so alive. And I finally understood something crucial—that Dave really did need me. It wasn't just chemistry. He'd dragons of his own to slay, and Nicole and I were part of slaying them.

He needed us as much as we needed him. And now he wasn't afraid to say so. Strong arms wrapped around me and I leaned back. He leaned down, whispering into my ear. "Thanks for putting up with an amateur like me."

"It's entirely my pleasure." It was my turn to be pensive, though. "If you do end up in Vermont..."

"Not *if*. When."

"*When* you end up in Vermont," I corrected, "What will you do to stay busy?"

"I don't know yet. But I don't need to know. You're there. My family needs me. I liked investing in that house next door. I could do a little more of that."

"Yeah, okay." I'd rented the colonial out to a young family with two little boys. The mom next door and I were already talking about sharing a nanny for a few hours a week.

"I'll give myself some time to think about it. There's always coaching. I could see if my teammates know anybody on staff at the University of Vermont."

"Interesting."

"I could open a bar and drive your uncle and Alec insane."

"You wouldn't!"

He laughed. "No. This family runs on coffee-shop hours." He

squeezed me. "But I might bring up the idea at Sunday luncheon just to see who blows first."

"You are evil."

"And you're a perfect angel from heaven."

I snorted. "There aren't any of those on this sofa."

"You're right," Dave agreed. "She's over there." He glanced at Nicole. "We'll take her outside in a few minutes? Go find your bathing suit. I'm going to call Bess."

Dave

"Is something wrong?" Bess asked when she answered the phone.

"I knew you'd lead with that." My sister lived to worry about me.

"You're on vacation, and I already got a call today. Pardon me if I wonder why I'm getting a second call."

"I've been thinking about your one-year option."

"Yeah?"

"Yeah." I hadn't been lying when I'd told Zara that I almost couldn't imagine retiring. It gave me the cold sweats. But lately I'd been listening to Zara describe the new house and the furniture she was buying. And the dishes in the hutch in the dining room. The omelet pan Audrey had given her for the kitchen.

I wanted to be there.

The future wasn't something I dreaded anymore. If they tossed my ass off the team tomorrow, I knew exactly where I'd go. I wouldn't even have to stop and think about it.

"Jesus," I swore as an idea began to take shape.

"What's the deal, big brother?"

"Maybe this isn't as tricky as I thought."

"The contract thing?"

"Yeah, the contract thing. If I take the one year, Nicole will be three at the end of it. I could spend eight weeks in Vermont next summer, and maybe see my family four or five other times before then. For forty-eight hours. Maybe."

"That's about right," my sister agreed.

I glanced at Nicole. She was toddling at top speed away from Zara, who wanted to put some kind of swim diaper on her. Nicole wasn't interested, though, and the chase was on.

Even if I only took the one-year contract extension, she wouldn't be a baby anymore when it ended.

Zara paused in the middle of the room, trying to guess the trajectory of our toddler. She stood there in shorts and a bikini top, hands on her hips, a slightly exasperated smile on her face.

I wanted to take her right to bed and untie that bikini top.

"*Ahem,*" Bess said into my ear. "I don't mind hanging up on other people to talk to you. But you have to actually talk."

"Right. Sorry. Okay—new plan. How about no contract extension?"

"Come again?"

"No years. I'll just quit while I'm ahead."

Only a gasping, choking sound came through the phone for a few seconds.

"Bess? You okay?"

"Jesus," she exhaled. "If you're even halfway serious, I need you sit with that idea for a few weeks. Play a few more games. Think about what it would be like to say goodbye in June."

"June, huh? I appreciate the vote of confidence, since that takes us deep into the playoffs again," I said with a chuckle. "But why do the women in my life keep telling me to go play hockey and think? I know my own mind. I have one more full season to play, and then I make a graceful exit right after Nicole turns two."

Zara had given up chasing Nicole and was standing stock still, a hand pressed over her mouth.

"Okay," Bess said slowly. "I think that's really brave and really amazing. And if that's what you want, I'll give it a few days and then let Hugh know."

"I'm not going to change my mind." I really wasn't. I loved hockey, but I loved my family just as much. Zara and Nicole deserved the same attention my hockey career had always gotten. And what's more, I was excited about giving it to them.

"Didn't say you would change your mind," Bess said. "It's me that needs a few days to get over it."

"Don't buy that yacht, little sis. I'm sorry I'm costing you a stick and a half at least."

"It's not about the money, dumbass. I just worry about you."

"I'm good, Bess. It's all good, or I wouldn't do it. Gotta run, now. I have a kiddie pool to find."

She signed off, and I hung up to meet Zara's startled eyes. "Did you really just do that?"

"I really just did." And it had felt pretty great to make a decision. "Let's go swim. Do you have sunblock? I don't think I remembered mine."

Zara blinked. "I really don't want to be the reason you give up your career."

I stood up and hugged her. The scent of coconut shampoo washed over me, and I took a deep breath. "The thing is, this kind of career comes to an end. Always. And this way I get to decide how that happens. I get to say when."

"You always were bossy like that," she joked, and her breath at my neck gave me goosebumps. The good kind.

"You better believe it." I gave her a quick kiss on the hairline because it was either that or a not-so-quick kiss. And we had places to go and things to do. "Hey, Nicole! I can't take you swimming unless you put on this special diaper. There's a fish on it and everything."

My baby girl turned around and squinted at me, considering. "Otay."

"Then get over here, angel."

She came willingly, and Zara gave me a glare that said, *I can't believe that just worked for you.*

Nicole exhausted herself at the kiddie pool. Then we went down to the beach, where I built a sand castle. Fine, a sand-blob. But Nicole liked it.

Eventually Zara talked her into wrapping up in a towel on a beach chair under an umbrella. And she took her nap right there as the Atlantic lapped at the sand a few yards away. Leaving her on one of our two chairs, Zara came and sat with me. I draped my legs over the sides to give her some room, and she leaned back against my chest.

"I could get used to this," she said.

"Next year we can plan a vacation without looking at the NHL calendar," I said. It was hard to wrap my head around. The game schedule had ruled my life since I was nineteen years old.

"Maybe we won't plan any big getaways for a while, though. We'll have to be a little careful with money until you figure out what you're going to do."

"Nah," I said. "We might as well travel before Nicole is in school. Besides, I have investments. And I think I can get three million for my Brooklyn place."

"Three million...*dollars?*" She turned around, looking hot as fuck in her sunglasses and bikini top. And the way she was sitting between my legs was doing things to me. I'd probably be carrying a towel in front of my body on the way back to our room.

"Give or take. I'll put it on the market in the spring."

"So..." She cleared her throat. "You don't even need to work, do you?"

"No. But I'll want to eventually." My phone buzzed in my pocket.

It was a text from Bess. *Okay. I'm over my shock. I get it.*

Good to know, I wrote back. *I feel good about this. I'm pumped.*

You should be. Now you can come work for me.

Say again?

Work. For. Me. How is that hard to understand? You can scout hockey players and lure them into my clutches.

Zara and I both laughed out loud.

We would kill each other, I pointed out. *Also, I can't do contracts. They make my eyes glaze over.*

Nobody is letting you near a legal document, my sister wrote back. *I'm the brains of this operation. You'll be the brawn.*

My head spun. *Can we talk about this later? Like, a year or two from now? Don't try to plan my life.*

But it's what I do!

I put the phone away. "Is it too early for a celebratory beer?"

"Never." She spun around and kissed me. Then she kissed me again, all heat and tongue and ambition.

I groaned my approval. "Stop, or I'll get carried away and then arrested for public indecency."

Zara sat back on her heels and laughed. "Maybe it's time to get out of the sun?"

I glanced at the sleeping baby. "Will she stay asleep if I carry her back to the room?"

"You can try," Zara said.

I gathered my sleeping child up and kissed her wispy hair. "Come on, angel. Let's go home."

And I realized *home* had a different meaning for me than it used to. It meant wherever my girls were.

I liked the sound of that. I really did.

THE
END

Made in the USA
Columbia, SC
09 August 2024

40256920R00198